Wind
Without
Rain

Wind Without Rain

Selwyn Dewdney

Introduction by John Stevens
General Editor: Malcolm Ross

New Canadian Library No. 103

McClelland and Stewart Limited

0-7710-9203-2

The Canadian Publishers
McClelland and Stewart Limited
25 Hollinger Road, Toronto

Printed and bound in Canada

Introduction

It was the fall of 1951 when I first read *Wind Without Rain*. The mathematics teacher whose humane job it was to ease the way for novices in that small rural high school sized me up at the end of my first week in the profession.

"You might like to read this over the week-end", he said, handing me his copy of Selwyn Dewdney's novel. "It paints a pretty bleak picture of teachers and teaching, but there's a lot of truth in it."

I told him that I would probably need to keep the book for a week or two, since most of my after-school hours were spent preparing for classes. But his was the better sense of timing. Once I had begun reading I had to go on to the end.

I returned the book to him Monday morning.

"You were right. It was bleak. If life is really like that in a small city, I'm glad I'm teaching in a village high school. Dewdney's West Kirby is as crude and materialistic as Sinclair Lewis's Zenith."

The math teacher smiled at the mention of Sinclair Lewis. In the early 1950's all recent university graduates in English had studied at least one of his satires on American life, probably *Babbitt*. He picked up my reference encouragingly.

"Yes, West Kirby is a little like Zenith, but I didn't think Dewdney was really much interested in the town except as a background for life at the school. Most of the characters—all the interesting ones, anyway—are teachers. Does John Westley strike you as being like Babbitt, then?"

"No, Westley is too young for that, and he's not even as bright as Babbitt was. He is like him in a way, though. He just drifted into teaching because he couldn't afford to go on for an M.A. in geology, the way Babbitt drifted into the real estate business."

The math teacher considered the comparison further.

"Some of Dewdney's characters are a little like the people in Lewis's novels."

"Especially J. C. Bilbeau," I said. "Thank God our principal isn't a hypocrite like him."

"No," said the math teacher, "but there are a few like him around."

"Oh, come on! He's incredible. In fact, Bilbeau and Westley are the main weaknesses in the novel. The other characters — Mary, Angus Macdonald, Dot Young, Donald Judd, even the caretakers, are real. I've met people like them already. But I can't believe that anyone as dumb as Westley could ever make it through university, let alone get himself hired as a teacher. And Bilbeau is entertaining as a sort of Uriah Heep caricature, but who on earth could believe that any school board would actually choose that bag of wind as a principal?"

The math teacher looked at me tolerantly.

"When we have our district meeting you may be in for a surprise."

He was right. At our district meeting one of the speakers was a Bilbeau in the flesh. As for John Westley's unbelievable stupidity, well, I did manage to avoid the impropriety of assigning his composition topic, "How I Spent My Summer Holidays," to my own grade nine class, but before the end of term I had duplicated most of his other new-teacher insanities, usually in the name of discipline, and, as with him, usually out of fear.

Recently, a second reading of *Wind Without Rain* held my interest as closely as that first one a generation ago. The novel was received at that time by both teachers and reviewers as a vivid portrayal of high-school teaching. The book could only have been written by a teacher, so rich is it in authentic details of school life as a teacher would experience them. Many readers were aware then that the author had taught for some dozen years in Western Ontario, the setting for his fictitious twin towns of Kirby and West Kirby. And many of us believed, wrongly, that a local scandal ignited by the book's publication had caused him to resign his teaching post to take up life as a commercial artist. The truth was somewhat different from the rumour. Although the novel had stirred up resentment and although Dewdney did leave teaching to work as an artist, he actually resigned in 1945, more than a year before the book appeared in print. Still, the rumour persisted, its plausibility fed by characterizations in the novel of such photographic vividness that one could easily imagine the real-life originals furiously identifying themselves and considering a suit for libel.

Those passions are long since spent, but at least one important theme developed in the novel is as timely now as it was then. Somewhat over-simplified it is this: A teacher must have a capacity for love in two fundamental ways. He must love and be a meticulous student of the art or science that he has marked off for himself as his "subject" to teach, and he must respect and try to understand the students he is introducing to that subject. Anyone attempting to teach with only one of those qualifications is at best half a teacher. Unhappily whole teachers are rare and some teachers lack even half the qualifications. Dot Young's derisive summing up of West Kirby's high-school staff might be interpreted as Dewdney's own generalization since, like him, she abandons a long career in teaching to risk life as a professional artist:

> I'm sick of teachers who lie awake nights wondering how to deal with chewing gum, the timid little tame rabbits who hop around doing what they're told, burying their noses in the dry leaves of books, afraid to look around them for fear of seeing something that would make them think.

However, Dot Young herself lacks wholeness. Cynicism sours her life, and in the end she returns to West Kirby from New York having found as many "tame rabbits" per hundred in the art colony there as in "the narrow little town" she despises. Even Donald Judd, the speech and art teacher whose easy cameraderie with the students John Westley envies, is little more than half a teacher, for his mind is all surface. His energetic choral speaking classes have a superficial gloss; his paintings are smooth, sophisticated landscapes which John, for all his technical ignorance of art, sees as lacking an essential element. They "seemed to convey no personal feelings: they were like the clothes he wore, a part of his outer costume." And his farewell speech at the staff picnic on his departure for the navy is cheerily vacuous. "I can't think of much to say... except that I've had a swell time, and it's been darn nice knowing you."

Only Angus Macdonald teaches with both qualifications. Despite his ironic disclaimers he enjoys his job. Sympathy and respect for his students and an ardent love of his subject have cleared his teaching of all fear and pretence, the qualities which bedevil his protegé, John Westley, who looks up to him at first as an infallible champion. Infallibility Angus lacks. Matched with a bland and emotionally immature wife, deprived by death of the son who might have made a bond between them, Angus faces life inwardly troubled that the universe may lack the order and meaning that man's reason attempts to impose on it. But courage is the bedrock underlying his nature, and it is this courage, as well as his humour and intelligence, which draws John to him. Except for those incidents which develop his close friendship with John and John's wife Mary, we usually see him as isolated from the other characters–at a party or at a staff meeting. Significantly, he has built his house on the island in West Kirby's bay, separated from the spiritually arid town by the water and the fresh winds that blow from the northern Canadian wilderness where he spends his summers on geological surveys. His house stands on an outcropping of the ancient Precambrian rock which he has made his life study. Toward the violent climax of the novel that rock, whose isolation has been endangered by housing development from the expanding town, is finally split and fragmented for the new home of J. C. Bilbeau, a far more successful teacher in the eyes of the businessmen who make up West Kirby's board of education. Soon afterward, the flaw in Angus's courage is also exposed. His stoicism cannot endure betrayal by the one he had counted on most.

In the thematic scheme of the novel Angus is associated with generosity, the life-giving natural elements, and the quest for knowledge. J. C. Bilbeau represents the opposite polarities of ruthless personal ambition, progress in its crudest commercial aspect, and the mere externals of education. In stature Angus is slight, unimpressive: Bilbeau is massive, imposing. Angus's voice is thin, tentative, Bilbeau's a fluent and resonant baritone. From the first meeting that J. C. conducts as head of the English department, John is fascinated by his confident efficiency. ("The meeting was over, and John wondered if a stop watch would have recorded a whole minute.") Possessing neither of the real qualifications for teaching, neither a substantial knowledge of his subject (his M.A. is from an unidentified American university) nor an ability to love, he substitutes for them an implacable pursuit of efficiency. His suavity and prosperous appearance impress the businessmen in the local Success Club (the real governing body of West Kirby) who invite him to address them at a luncheon session in the town's most imposing hotel. Here he sets forth his design for living and learning:

> Education, coming from the Latin *ducto*–to lead, is leadership . . . But what of education today, and tomorrow? . . . This is an age of transition. . . . The vast field of vocational guidance is unexplored. The situation calls for radical experiments. We must have educational engineers who will design newer and more efficient educational machinery . . .

The orotund banalities roll out in flood and his audience loves it all.

Once installed as principal through the influence of the Success Club, he manipulates his staff, especially John, by an astute blend of implied threats and rewards. After a year's leave of absence to tour American schools for "an extensive study of educational trends in the United States," Bilbeau launches his West Kirby Practical Education Project which is to implement his slogan of "Personality not Pedagogy." Under this philosophy of education literature "would no longer stress analysis and lengthy compositions or obscure rules in grammar, but would concentrate on public speaking, how to interview a prospective employer and similar real-life situations." Choral reading and dramatics are integrated in the curriculum, examinations are all but abolished and almost everyone is passed, mostly with honours. The staff is put to work writing objectives and outlines of attractive new courses that will decrease the drop-out rate, and extra-curricular activities are co-ordinated in what might nowadays be described as a systems approach.

By systematically organizing committees and delegating the donkey-work, Bilbeau manages to bring some of his staff close to nervous collapse while gathering to himself public credit for his showy reforms. His ultimate technological innovation, the Brunwald Improved Public Address and Intercommunications System, which allows him to listen in to classes and interrupt them at will for important announcements, precipitates a student rebellion, but Bilbeau turns even this uprising to his advantage, manipulating it to destroy Angus who had proved an annoying hindrance to his winds of change.

John Westley's painful vascillation between these two older men is the major conflict in *Wind Without Rain*. As might be expected in a realistic novel of social criticism, the plot developing this conflict is linear, all events being filtered through John's consciousness. Occasional flashbacks provide glimpses of his loveless childhood to suggest why he seems still in search of a father, but in the main the story tends steadily forward through time. Book I describes his first two years at West Kirby, including his first year of marriage to Mary. Book II traces his life through the next six years up to the rainy spring morning of 1943 when he reaches his agonized, redemptive decision.

Throughout the novel a wealth of detail accumulates to show what it was like to teach in a high school in the depression and early years of the Second World War. Through a series of vignettes the early chapters introduce us to John's callowness and insecurity and make clear how constricted was a teacher's life in those days: John before his bedroom mirror striking the pose that he hopes will impress the class. John vomiting up his breakfast on the first day of school. John on the school stage almost overcome with self-consciousness under the gaze of the students gathered for the opening day assembly. John meeting a college chum for a beer and recognizing guiltily that public expectations of teachers in 1934 rule out drinking in the local beer parlour. John marking his first set of examination papers, dismayed to find how long the first one takes (an hour and five minutes), delighted at a good answer in another ("Aren't you a smart little bugger!").

However, as the conflict between Angus and Bilbeau intensifies and John is gradually estranged from both Angus and Mary, becoming in effect Bilbeau's accomplice, the reader faces a problem of credibility. Dewdney never intends us to think of John as intellectually acute. He is at pains to make it clear that Mary is his mental and cultural superior. In the little home that they set up in West Kirby copies of Gorki and Dostoevski adorn the bookshelves, but it is Mary who reads them. When a social conversation with their friends Helen and Hal Rush rises to the level of wit John is confused; as the talk shifts playfully to art and music he ventures a hesitant remark "only to find that the conversation had slipped into another topic and left him behind." When he gives an account to Mary of Bilbeau's speech at the Success Club it is she who spots Bilbeau's false scholarship:

> "It all comes from the Latin *ducto*, I lead," said John.
> "*Ducto?*" said Mary. "I thought it was *duco*."
> "*Duco*—sure! What did I say?"
> "Skip it," said Mary. "What other weighty statements did he make?"

But even a man more obtuse than John might be expected to see Bilbeau for what he is. Evidences of his hollowness and duplicity mount and become ever plainer. Angus warns John; Elsie Braund, the brilliant young student actress who falls victim to Bilbeau's malice, warns him; Mary warns him; his own tense experiences in the principal's office warn him, but he remains incapable of facing reality. To the reader it is obvious that Bilbeau is a monstrous perversion of a teacher, a sterile wind without rain eroding John's confidence and warping his values. But not until one belated spring morning after a night of horror does John face the truth. That he sees it so suddenly and so late is hard to accept.

Wind Without Rain was published in 1946. Does the pother that Dewdney's J. C. Bilbeau brought into the lives of those fictitious characters in an imaginary Ontario town of more than thirty years ago seem hopelessly out of date and irrelevant today? After all, West Kirby Collegiate Institute had only six hundred students. A typical high school today has sixteen hundred and they are far less docile than the ones John Westley faced. Since that day in 1942 when the West Kirby student body was excluded from voting for its own president we have experienced student radicalism and the reduction of the age of majority to eighteen. Teachers, too, have become bolder and more critical. Does all the compliant committee activity in West Kirby's high school to put Bilbeau's reforms into effect seem unrelated to what could happen in the schools today? All those meetings to achieve co-ordination and integration, to rewrite old courses more attractively and increase student enrolment by preparing popular new offerings, to engineer educational activities and school governance for efficiency within a systems network–does all that seem like dried roses under glass today?

You will not think so, gentle reader, if you have been scanning your newspaper. During the past decade battalions of Canadian educational administrators have been touring American schools and directing northward the winds of change that they discovered there. Educational job opportunities for administrators have multiplied geometrically as the life of individual classroom teachers has become more busy and harassed. As I look up over the coffee cups to the morning paper I am reminded that the old Department of Education has undergone cellular proliferation into a Ministry of Education and a separate Ministry of Colleges and Universities, and that the latter organism has further subdivided into a Cultural Affairs Division whose Deputy Minister needs an Assistant Deputy Minister, advertised for thus in the August 21, 1973 issue of *The Globe and Mail*:

> This individual will have proven managerial ability to relate to a wide group of people involved in cultural activities; articulate in abstract thought, both verbally and in writing.

The syntax and choice of words in that passage might appeal to Bilbeau, but the ad's final sentence would draw him like an educational mating call: "This responsibility will be of interest to executives whose current salary is in the $30,000 range."

He would certainly be interested in the series of workshops

in "Leadership Analysis" conducted for school administrators this year by the Ministry of Education and the Ontario Institute for Studies in Education. One of the published behavioural objectives of the workshops was phrased this way: "to enable the leader to internalize the process of analyzing and becoming aware so that the process may be repeated in on the job situations as they arise."

Bilbeau would admire that locution's rising swell, but one can imagine Angus Macdonald cocking a quizzical eye at it and surmise the laughing comment on it that John's perceptive wife Mary might make.

"Why, that doesn't make any sense. How can anyone internalize the process of analyzing or becoming aware? They're already internal."

Both Angus and Mary would probably wonder, as perhaps the reader does, how the writer of such fuddled thought could pretend to lead anyone in anything. In the years since my first abrupt dismissal of Selwyn Dewdney's J. C. Bilbeau as an improbable exaggeration I have modified my view considerably.

John Stevens
College of Education
Toronto

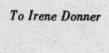

To Irene Donner

Whoso boasteth himself of a false gift is like clouds and wind without rain.

—The Book of Proverbs.

Book One

1

The train shrieked for a crossing. John looked out to watch a new Ford racing them along the broad highway that ran parallel to the tracks. The car slowed, stopped for the crossing, and flashed back out of sight.

The trainman came down the coach.

"West Kirby! This way out."

This was it.

John stood up, a tightening in his throat and chest, the veins tingling in his arms. His heart hammered a little. He tugged in nervous haste at the handle of the heavy suitcase on the luggage rack above. One strap buckle had caught on the edge of the rack. He got it down with a struggle, the physical effort easing his tension. Angus told me I'd like West Kirby, he reminded himself.

He smiled as he thought of those last hectic minutes at Mary's house: Mary's comical dismay when he had brought her the books to put in after she had the suitcase all packed, the way they had sat each on one end to get it closed, and kissed each other triumphantly—still sitting on the suit-case—when the two locks clicked shut. He lifted his father's old leather club bag from the floor and put it beside the grip on the seat opposite, glanced out the window across the aisle—there was the blue of Lake Huron again, but not a sign of West Kirby. Outside his own window the pastures, barns, cows, and fields of corn were still flying

3

swiftly past. Elms sailed majestically by in the middle distance, and distant woods and farms kept effortless pace with the speeding train. Down the coach a few were reaching for their luggage but no one seemed to be in a hurry. John sat down.

A corner of his pyjamas projecting from under the top of the suitcase at one end caught his eye. Mary had protested when he wanted to re-open the grip and tuck it in: "It wants to look out, John, so it can tell the others inside what's going on." He smiled again in spite of the peculiar panic that was building up inside him once more. It would be tough not seeing much of Mary before the Christmas holidays. But Angus would be there—waiting even now on the station platform, listening for this train.

The train shrieked again in a minor key that didn't help John's mood particularly. *Too-whoo-oo! Too-whoo-oo!* mournfully, as it swung sharply east, houses appearing suddenly on either side. As they rumbled over a subway John briefly glimpsed a new bridge—and the bay, smoky down at the far end, with a grain elevator, and boats. There was the hiss of escaping steam; the grinding of brakes. The quick ding-ding-ding of a crossing rang out and faded away. Houses multiplied, streets went by—more slowly now—with cars on them, and people.

John got up, grasped his bags. He paused to let a prosperous looking fellow-passenger by. The man paused in turn for John, smoothly flashing a salesman's smile. John matched his manners. The man's smile faded—with a curt nod of acknowledgment he walked briskly past. John blushed slightly, waited for a woman laden with parcels to go by, and followed, his heavy suitcase bumping his calves behind; through the narrow corridor, past the smoking

4

room, into the crowded lobby. The train was barely moving now—only the slow rumble of the wheels beneath revealed their motion. The rumble ceased; there was the brief illusion of a reverse movement. They had arrived.

John found himself at the top step in the blinding sunlight scanning the crowded platform for his friend. He stepped down to the platform still searching, made his way through the confusion, a bit worried. He had been so certain he would spot Angus at once. He put down his bags near the waiting-room door and again looked anxiously up and down the platform. The crowd was clearing, but there was no sign of Angus. He went around the end of the baggage room. There was a wide parking space extending to the street corner. Filled cars were driving off already: a taxi driver hailed John, who shook his head. Across the road was a large modern building: John read the name, 'King George Hotel'. This was certainly the spot to wait. He glanced at his watch; it was 12 : 08. He went back for his bags, returned, found a shady spot where he could lean against a platform wagon to watch for Angus's car.

It was annoying after the build-up—and it was so unlike Angus. He pulled out the letter, still in its envelope.

Mr. John Westley, B.A.
c/o Miss Mary Miller
126 Hartmond Street . . . .

John couldn't help that little glow of smugness over the B.A.—even now.

. . . . So we'll expect you on the noon train, Wednesday, Sept. 5th, at 12:05—to be precise. Don't worry about finding your way up—I'll be at the station; the principal, by the way, is expecting us over for lunch.

5

Perhaps he should phone.

No, John decided, I'll wait a few minutes first.

One year was a long time, but Angus would be the same. John smiled inwardly: *he* had certainly changed. Even if he went north with Angus again he could never repeat that summer's experience.

Green?

His smile went wry at the memory of that second morning of his summer with the geological survey.

"Daylight in the swamp!—Come and get it!" to the banging of the frying pan outside the tent in the grey dawn. John had huddled under his blankets, sick with fear. The others were all up: he could hear Hal whooping with ecstasy, splashing in the cold water of the lake.

Angus's crisp voice: "Where's Westley?"

Fragrant whiffs of bacon and coffee; the crackling of the fire.

Slim's answer, if you could call it that, "I guess Wes just don't care for the mornin' air."

Angus had looked in and taken one look at John's pale puffed face.

"Better stay in camp, Westley. Slim can take your traverse. I'd eat some breakfast if I were you—you'd feel better."

John warmed again to the sudden comfort of his chief's casual words that morning.

Later, when the others had gone, Angus had called him into his tent, and confided in him about his own first day in the bush.

"The only trouble with flies is the way they get under your skin"—his dark eyes had twinkled at the double play of the words. "I remember I went into pure panic at the thought of going through that torment even for another hour!"

It hadn't been Angus's sympathy, or his chief's casual acceptance of fear as a perfectly normal thing; nor even the common-sense advice that followed, and worked. The thing that made John love the man from that day on was something deeper, less easy to explain. It sounded silly to say it, even to himself, but it was as if his own weakness had created a kind of relationship between them that Angus had hungered for.

There had been a subtle bond between them after that. Not that Angus played favourites—the only outward sign was the way he pointedly avoided anything like it in John's case. For instance, the day they did the longest traverse of the summer. It was really Slim's job, but Angus had a weakness for taking on the tougher assignments. "Like to come along, Westley?"

Fourteen miles of spruce swamp, fire slash, alders, and muskeg. And on top of that they had to bump into one helluva big outcrop. Angus must have spent an hour and a half knocking off samples, and making notes while John paced off the distances: the man was a bear for punishment when it came to details. Dark came and they hadn't found the base line. Maybe they had crossed it in the dusk. No use having a compass if you thought camp was farther south and you had actually passed it! And John, toughened though he was by two months in the bush, had been ready to drop from weariness and hunger.

"Just as well the fly season is over," Angus had grinned to John as he began to gather dry brush. "There's nothing to do now but build a fire and keep warm till morning."

7

When dawn came, Angus found the line ten paces south of their fire. In half an hour they were home in camp eating hungrily at hot cakes doused with maple syrup, John's weariness replaced by the exhilarating thought that he and Angus had done the longest traverse of the season—together.

Good old Angus!

Opening some cans of beans for Old Bill one night before the others turned up he had told the veteran bush cook what a good guy he thought Angus was.

"Yeah," said Old Bill, punching down the bread dough. "The only trouble with these tough little sonsabitches like Macdonald is they never know when they're licked."

"What's wrong with that?" John had wanted to know.

"Sooner or later," observed Old Bill sagely, "they meet up with somethin' one size too big for 'em."

John came to with a start. He wasn't in the bush now, he was a green teacher, waiting for a colleague. He flexed his arm and looked at his watch—a quarter after. Better phone. He turned to go into the station.

A slightly-built, smallish man with a grey top coat and an old grey fedora came briskly around the corner, saw John, and strode eagerly to him, a quick warm grin of relief and recognition on his keen-looking face.

"Angus!"

Angus Macdonald said nothing, but the clasp of his sinewy hand spoke with greater intensity. The uncertainty and strangeness left John's soul as he drank deeply of the cup of welcome.

Good old Angus! "I knew you'd make it," he said aloud. Behind him came an older, taller man. Angus introduced them: "We've found our man! Mr. Nyes: Mr. Westley. This is your principal, John."

"Welcome, Mr. Westley," said Nyes. "I'm sorry we were late. I'm afraid I neglected to tell my daughter we would need the car when we did." He had a gaunt face with a deep vertical line in the hollow of each leathery cheek, but his eyes were friendly enough.

Nyes's apology having vindicated Angus, the three men were soon sedately on their way in Mr. Nyes's 1929 Packard, the two seniors in the front seat, the novice alone with his bags in the rear. Angus turned in his seat to include John in the conversation. John leaned forward to look out the door window, warm anticipation in his eyes as he watched the street. Everything had turned out all right so far.

"We'll go around by the city hall, Macdonald," said Nyes, "and show Mr. Westley a bit of the town."

They drove east, with a park on the left and residences on the right, small houses for the most part. "Park Street" —John noticed the sign and read it aloud.

"Getting acquainted,—that's right," said Nyes.

John mentioned the park.

"Well, it's nice enough," said Nyes, "but *the* park is over on the island. This street divides West Kirby from Old Kirby."

"Why Old Kirby? It's just Kirby on the maps, isn't it?" asked John.

"That's a sore point with Kirbians," explained Angus. "West Kirby is a sort of upstart town. The original Kirby was a fishing village at the mouth of the river. Then they built a mill at McAdams Falls and the boats began calling in for the flour. It's a good farming district hereabouts and

9

soon they had blacksmith shops, a tannery, general stores, and all the rest of it. When the wheat began to come through from the West they built elevators here, and the railway came in. Kirby boomed thirty years ago. The flour mill, foundry, docks, nail factory, a new large tannery, were all built soon after the turn of the century. When the valley was filled—it's pretty narrow—and the town got smoky, people began to live up here on the west side of the smoke."

"West Kirby is just an overgrown suburb of Kirby, then?" ventured John.

"My boy, if you want to live in West Kirby never make a statement like that in the hearing of any loyal—here's Third Avenue," he interrupted himself. "Victoria Street comes up the hill from Old Kirby and joins it a little farther along. This is your overgrown suburb. We are entering the thriving young city of West Kirby—at least it was thriving till the depression caught up with us."

The increased traffic bore them swiftly downtown past the usual assortment of houses, churches, trees, schools, and corner groceries one finds in any Ontario city. "There's the City Hall now, and this is Central Avenue." They turned right towards the lake.

"A nice wide street," commented John. "Reminds me a little of Portage Avenue in Winnipeg." No harm in letting Nyes know he had been around a bit. The banks and business buildings were all new-looking and substantial; there was room for angle-parking along the curb. Central Avenue dipped through a subway. Nyes pointed up. "That's where you came in."

"And here's the bridge," said Angus, "the pride of New Kirby and the chief reason why the new school was never finished."

The bridge was handsome but the view impressed John more. To the right and below, the bay lay blue and vibrating in the early September sun. Immediately ahead of them the island rose steeply from a rocky shore, but to the right it fell away, the narrow ledge of shore widening into a broad beach studded with orange and white entertainment booths. Beyond, at the end of the breakwater, the white-caps rolled in from the west.

The tires sang a new air as they left the concrete of the bridge and gripped the asphalt, driving the car up a winding climb to the left, past expensive houses standing among the trees of the steep hillside.

"The island!" announced Angus. "Where all the best people live." At the top of the hill they swung around a broad horseshoe curve to the right, into a quiet street; and stopped in front of a neat brick bungalow.

"Just leave your bags here; I'll drive you over to the school after lunch," said the principal, as they stepped out and ascended the few steps to the low, cool veranda. A young woman and a small boy were sitting there. "My daughter, Mrs. James—this is Mr. Westley our new maths and science teacher," introduced Mr. Nyes. "And Billy." He gave the six-year-old a playful poke in the stomach, to which he responded with a good thump on his grandad's backside. "Now would you like to wash up?"

John accepted with a gratitude just this side of indecency.

"There's a towel over there," Nyes pointed out, and left John alone in the spotless purity of a modern white-tiled bathroom. The toilet flushed more loudly than he had ever heard a toilet flush before. After washing he could not bring himself to touch the dainty guest linen and dried his hands on the corner of a bath towel. Looking in the mirror self-critically, John saw the same straight eyebrows and grey eyes, the same blunt nose, slightly sulky mouth, and unimpressive chin—a pleasant, somehow honest-looking face, but hardly to be distinguished from twenty thousand other Canadian faces. He smiled experimentally, watching his eyes anxiously to see if they would twinkle, his mouth to see if the corners curved winsomely. His hair went neatly back before the comb. He cleaned his nails. One more glance—if only he didn't look so damned young!

He had just rejoined Angus and Mr. Nyes in the living room when Mrs. Nyes stepped through the glass doors from the dining room, a tired little woman with hard brown eyes. She brightened up at the name. "John Wesley? Are you descended from the great John Wesley?"—the old familiar question, thought John. Patiently he explained.

"It's spelled W-E-S-T-L-E-Y. As a matter of fact the Wesleys' great-grandfather spelled it with a *t*, too—I looked it up once."

The spark of interest roused in Mrs. Nyes by the name died out. "Well, come to lunch." And they moved into the dining room and sat where they were told.

Mr. Nyes recited a brief grace. As they sipped their tomato juice he asked, "Are you a Methodist, Mr. Westley? I think your application only mentioned that you were Protestant."

"Well, I'm afraid I'm not much of anything. That is"— be careful Johnny! he warned himself—"I've not been able to settle down to one church. Back home we were Anglicans."

"And a good Church of Englander is careful not to go

12

to church too often"—Angus came to the rescue—"for fear people will think he's religious."

They all smiled at this, except Mrs. Nyes.

The conversation drifted on with the lunch. Finally coffee was served. As he drank his, John looked across at Angus while furtively feeling for cigarettes in his coat pocket. Did the Nyeses tolerate smoking?

Mrs. James, the daughter, noticed the gesture. "Is there time to show Mr. Westley your garden, Dad?" she asked.

"Why, of course," said Nyes. "This way." They followed him into the hall, through the den and out into a pleasant enough little garden. Angus offered a cigarette to John as Nyes pulled an old pipe out of his pocket. John did his best to enthuse over the flowers but gave himself away when he glimpsed an outcropping of grey rock over the fence next door.

"There's the Precambrian!" he exclaimed, looking to Angus for confirmation.

"That's it," said Angus with an understanding smile.

Nyes looked somewhat annoyed. "Never could see how anyone could get excited over a bit of rock, Precambrian or Postcambrian."

"But this is the only outcrop of Precambrian rock in a radius of four hundred miles!" John protested. "It's the rock you get up north, the Canadian Shield, it's the only thing we've got that nobody else has."

"We've got too much of it, if you ask me," said Nyes. "You can't grow anything on it. All it has is gold."

"And nickel, and cobalt, and silver, and copper, and molybdenum, and—why we haven't even scratched the surface yet!"

Nyes laughed. "I can see there's not much use talking

about flowers when we have two rock lovers present. You certainly have a convert, Macdonald."

"He didn't need much converting," Angus smiled reminiscently.

"Well, I suppose you are anxious to see the school and get settled," said Nyes. "Excuse me, I'll just see if there's anything Martha wants down town."

John and Angus strolled around the house to the car. "So one glimpse of Precambrian schist is worth all the flowers in your principal's garden!" said Angus. John grinned sheepishly.

"You should talk—I got the bug from you." They smiled together, intimately.

It's good to have a friend, thought John.

2

At the crest of the slope down to the bridge there was a break in the trees. Nyes stopped the car.

"Thought you'd like a real look at the two Kirbys," he said good-naturedly. "There's no better view than this."

Angus explained as John gazed across the water: "You're looking east. To the north down along the shore, where you see the elevator and factories, is Old Kirby; straight ahead, up on the hill, is West Kirby."

"West Kirby looks much bigger," said John.

"Actually there isn't a great difference," Angus told him. "West Kirby has a population of twenty thousand, Kirby a litttle under fifteen. But most of Old Kirby is out of sight in the valley back of the hill. You had a glimpse of it this morning looking down Victoria Street."

"The school," said Nyes, "is just to the left of the subway."

"Is that a public school beside it?" John asked. There appeared to be two schools: the nearer a modern two-storied red-brick building that looked more like a factory; beyond it was an old-fashioned structure with steep false roofs. They stood together facing north, on a grassy terrace that sloped gently up from the Lakeshore Road to the foot of the West Kirby hill.

Nyes released the brakes and they drove on down the hill and over the bridge.

"It gets a bit wearying," said Angus, "having to explain that the two schools are really one. From this angle you can't see the wing behind that connects them."

At the end of the bridge they turned left on the Lakeshore Road for a hundred yards, swung into the school driveway, passed the entrance of the newer building, and stopped before the other.

"Mr. Macdonald takes over from here," said Nyes, when they had taken John's baggage out of the car. "We'll see you in the morning at nine." He drove off, leaving the two friends alone.

John looked up at the building before him, a tall dirty grey brick box with a square central tower which projected slightly from the front wall. Dormer windows broke through the grey slate of the false roof; fancy iron spears and grillwork ran along the roof crests. Over to the right and in behind lay the L-shaped new building, squatty, with a sterile simplicity of line.

Angus smiled when John turned to him inquiringly: "The school architect from Toronto took one look at this and said, 'Nobody won that argument'!"

Looking over at the more modern building, John said, "At least, half the school is nice and new."

"Nice and new, is perfect!" John was surprised at Angus's reaction: he must have taken the words ironically. "You couldn't invent a phrase that more perfectly expresses the West Kirbian's idea of the ultimate in value. The word 'nice' has only one meaning in this town: inoffensive, prettily pleasing, agreeing with the standard taste. Of course, if it's nice, and new into the bargain, . . ." Angus turned to John, his eyes twinkling, as if the whole idea had been John's and finishing the sentence would have been pointless. John was flattered, and a little pleased by the unconscious wit he had displayed.

Angus explained as they ascended the steps that the building they were entering had been successively a girls' private boarding school, a real estate white elephant, a continuation school, and finally, when Angus first came to West Kirby, a high school. In the late twenties the Board decided to tear it down and put up a collegiate institute able to take care of the expanding needs of the city for a generation. The City Council balked, having the new bridge in mind. A plebiscite revealed that the citizens were more interested in being able to drive their cars over to the island beach on Sundays than in building a fancy new school for their children. So the old school stood, with half of the new attached.

"And they did build us a lovely bridge," Angus added dryly.

Inside, the central hall was dark, heavy with the odour

of old floors freshly oiled. On Angus's instruction John left his bags by the door and followed, feeling suddenly depressed.

Angus became the official guide.

"Two classrooms on that side of the hall, another on this side, and the library. Librarian, Miss Loretta Pettiker, a sweet little soul of uncertain age. Pictures on the walls donated by Daughters of the Empire."

At the end of the hall three stone composition steps went down to the right, a flight of worn wooden stairs up to the left. John followed Angus upstairs.

"Where do the other stairs take you?" asked John.

"Back through a short passageway to the rear wing of the new building. We'll go that way later."

They turned on a landing, climbed the second flight, and were on the second floor facing a corridor that ran to the front of the building.

"On the right two classrooms, lavatories, and stairs to the attic, used for storage. To the left, the men teachers' room, and two more classrooms."

Angus walked down the hall to the last door on the left, flung it open with a flourish, and announced:

"Your room, Mr. Westley!"

John entered and looked around slowly.

His room. Thirty-nine desks for students, and one large office desk for him. He sat down at the latter, opened the drawers. Empty. He looked over the empty desks. Tomorrow they would be filled, he thought, gulping.

Angus was looking out the window. "Look at your view," he called. John went over and stood beside him. The school lawn, the Lakeshore Road, a drop to the water, the bridge to the left, and across the narrow bay lay the island. "Like a miniature of the Sleeping Giant at Port Arthur—you've seen that, haven't you?" asked Angus.

"Only from the train, when it was getting dark," said John. He looked at the modest hump of grey rock towards the south end of the island. "Queer thing this one outcrop of Precambrian—my prof mentioned it in dynamic geology last year—he said it had them baffled."

"Well, there's some evidence of a fault, most of it under the lake. Isn't that a typical batholith, though?"

John looked at it, thinking of the endless ages that had passed before the ancient mountain core, shorn of the massive layers of rock above, lay exposed to the sun and air. He turned away. "What happens tomorrow?"

"The school assembles in the auditorium at nine—that's when you get your introduction. There we tell the youngsters what books they'll need, and after that they split up into Middle, Upper, and Lower Schools to hear their class lists read. Then they're free to go and buy books and the fun begins at Hatchett's and Boyle's downtown. We have a staff meeting; then we're through till Wednesday morning."

"It sounds simple," said John.

"Well, that's a thing I like about Nyes. He keeps organization down to a minimum. Things get a bit noisy now and then but at least there's a feeling of freedom—I think you'll like this school. By the way, you haven't met J. C. yet. You teach English don't you?"

"One class," said John.

"Well, you'll get to know him soon enough."

It was a bit puzzling, this sudden shift in the conversation. John felt uneasy.

He put it down to fear of the unknown life ahead, but

somehow too he tied it up with the smell of oil on the old floors, the atmosphere of stale age in the building. The view from the windows of his classroom and Angus's phrase 'feeling of freedom' had given him a lift until this casual mention of J. C. dropped him down again.

"Who in hell is J. C., Angus?" he asked with a sudden unaccountable irritability.

"Oh, he's James Campbell Bilbeau—spelled E-A-U— M.A., head of the English department. An impressive man. You'll like him—everybody likes J. C."

Was Angus being ironical?

"Is that a French name—Bilbeau?" John rolled it over mentally on his tongue: Bilbeau, Bilbeau, Bilbeau.

"The name may be, but there's nothing French about the man. However, you can ask him when you're introduced tomorrow morning. . . . . Now let's see the rest of the school."

As they descended the ancient wooden stairs John asked, "Don't you ever get tired of teaching?"

"That's a question I ask myself once every seven years —and still haven't found the answer. Teachers like me are sick to death of teaching and love it so much they'd die if they had to stop. There was poor old Gregg who died of a broken heart at sixty-six because they retired him at sixty-five. And I wouldn't be a bit surprised if old Pennington, who retires next June, goes the same way."

At the bottom of the stairs they turned into the rear passageway, emerged into a long corridor that led to the right.

"We call this the south corridor," Angus told John. "That door," he pointed left, "goes down to the furnace room and the formidable Willoughby—he's the school engineer. This rear wing contains the gymnasium"—he tried the door before them but it was locked—"and the assembly hall. The gymnasium is the biggest and therefore the best of its kind in Kirby County. There's a gallery over this corridor and over both ends of the gym. It was planned to go all around, but at the last minute the architect looked up the standard dimensions for a basketball court and he had to leave the south gallery out to get his dimensions in."

They walked down the south corridor past doors marked 'Gymnasium' and 'Stage'. They tried a third door, found it open, and looked in on the assembly hall. John was impressed by its size and plan. Generous aisles along the wall and up the centre gave easy access to the seats which were arranged on a sloping floor in ascending curves to face the wide deep stage.

Angus's attitude toward Bilbeau stuck in John's mind. They had stopped in front of the stage platform while John looked around.

"Angus, what's wrong with Bilbeau?"

Angus laughed. "Who told you anything was wrong with him? I suppose I'm biased: I have the little man's prejudice against physical bulk. But just between you and me, I have a strong suspicion that he's nothing but a big bag of wind. Maybe it's my Highland reaction to the Campbell in his name: you know there's a Gaelic proverb current since the massacre of Glencoe"—and he quoted it in the curiously soft gutturals of his ancestral tongue.

"What does it mean?" asked John.

"As long as there's a leaf on a tree, there'll be treachery in the heart of the Campbells!" Angus translated, smiling. "Outspoken people, those old Highlanders!"

They walked up the nearest aisle to the rear entrance; like all the other doors it opened into the same hallway.

"I think I'm going to like this school," John told Angus.

Going out, John found they were at the end of the south corridor and faced another hallway that led to the front entrance of the new building.

"Here's the physics room," said Angus, opening a door on the left, "where I hold forth daily, and you will bring your fourth year class for labs."

The equipment, furnishings, everything, looked new and efficient after the dinginess of the old building. Along one wall was a rock and mineral collection over which they paused. Angus had collected most of it personally and had a story for every piece of rock in the cases. Nickel ore from the Sudbury Bowl, gold from the Porcupine, copper pyrite from Flin Flon, lignite from Moose Factory, mica from the Cassiar mountains, talc from Quebec, granites, gneisses, porphyries, puddingstones, green malachite, and purple crystals of amethyst, rusty garnets, clear Iceland spar, red orthoclase—they spent an hour over the cases before they realized it.

Angus glanced up at the electric classroom clock. "Four already! I'd better take you over to Mrs. Gillespie's and give you a chance to get settled."

They left the physics lab, looked into the chemistry lab opposite, and came down the corridor to the front entrance of the new building. A sign projecting over a door on the left read 'Secretary's Office', one over a door to the right, 'Principal's Office'. They entered the former, while Angus scanned the pigeon-holes for possible mail.

"Where's the secretary?" asked John.

"Miss Jamieson? Oh, Ethel is probably out with her

lawyer. They've been going together for fifteen years, saving money! By the way, how's that little friend of yours in Toronto?"

"Oh, Mary's fine. I wrote you from there—remember? I hope to see her this week end or the next in Toronto. You know, if we thought this job would be permanent, we'd get married at Christmas, though I wouldn't be surprised if they bribed her to stay on another six months at Eaton's."

They were outside now, crossing the lawn to the entrance of the old building, where each picked up one of John's bags.

They took a short cut across the lawn to the sidewalk that bordered the Lakeshore Road along the front of the school grounds. Continuing for half a block, the concrete walk stopped abruptly, replaced by a broad dirt path. The hillside swept out from behind the school to loom above them. Here and there a horizontal ledge of limestone projected from the wood-grown slope. John stooped to pick up a piece of rock, glanced at it and tossed it out on the road. "That's some of your dolomite," remarked Angus. "It caps the crest of the Kirby escarpment—that's one thing they didn't tell you about in Toronto."

'No," said John, "never heard of it."

"It's a sort of miniature Niagara escarpment," he explained. "Comes out of the lake a few miles down the shore and disappears into it again in a low cliff called Lovers' View about half a mile north of Little Bend. You can see it best up at McAdams Falls. That's the only evidence I have for my fault theory—we've never taken any borings from the lake bottom, of course; it's deep offshore."

As they walked on, the cliff receded, leaving just space

enough for a large square house built in the same period as the old school, but less well preserved, which stood above the sidewalk on a little lawn. A waist-high stone wall buttressed the lawn against settling down into the contours of the hillside.

"Mrs. Gillespie's boarding-house," announced Angus. They climbed two flights of stairs to the veranda, where Angus pulled an iron knob beside the door, and a sharp clang within announced their arrival.

"I phoned Mrs. Gillespie this morning," explained Angus. "Told her you were only boarding a month or so till you got permanently located. That'll give you a chance to move if you don't care for it here. But it's handy to the school and you'll like it, I think."

The door opened cautiously and a grey head, obviously fresh from a beauty treatment, looked out suspiciously: deep furrows from nostril-wings to mouth-corners, small sharp eyes behind rimless glasses, cheeks that sagged below the jaw line in spite of high rouging. As though by sleight of hand, the sour mask vanished as she recognized Angus.

"Mr. Macdonald!" The smile and the welcome in her voice were genuine, heart-warming. "And this is the gentleman you were mentioning over the phone. Mr. Westley isn't it? I'm Mrs. Gillespie." She put a damp but firm little hand in his. "Come in, come in. Just set the bags by the stairs and come and have a cup of tea."

"Well, really—" Angus demurred.

"It's brewed already, sitting on the stove. Come into the dining room." She bustled ahead to get the tea while they followed and sat at the dining-table, covered with a not too white cloth.

They drank their tea, and Mrs. Gillespie showed them up to John's room, where Angus left him after inviting John to come over in the evening and telling him how to find the house.

Mrs. Gillespie was brief. "I hope you'll like it here; we have two or three high school teachers every year. Miss Purcell has been with me two years and Mr. Jarratt nearly four. The bathroom is right at the end of the hall; there are towels over there"—pointing to a towel rack on the back of the door. "Supper's at six," and she went out.

John Westley sat down, alone for the first time that day. Not a bad room, actually—big enough anyway. There were three chairs, two of them armchairs, rather shabby. The curtains were faded and hung without enthusiasm, the desk was old and battered. And yet it was homey, truly homey. There was a long mirror in the dresser and John stood before it, pleased to notice that it made his five feet ten inches look like six feet.

"Class, your attention, please!" He raised his chin, thrust one hand inside his vest, raised the other in a self-conscious gesture:

> *"Dearly beloved brethren, is it not a sin,*
> *That when we eat potatoes, we throw away the skin?*
> *The skin feeds the pigs, and the pigs feed you,*
> *Dearly beloved brethren, is (pause) it not (pause) tuh-roo?"*

He paused, vainly trying to suppress the smirk on his face.

"The class—will now—dismiss!"

There was a knock at the door, John hastily flung his club bag on the bed, opened it and began pulling things out as he answered, "Come in."

"Mrs. Gillespie told me I'd find you in. My name's Jarratt—call me Frank. I'm the P.T. man at W.K.C.I. Just thought I'd drop in and give you the low-down." He was tallish, well built, with a nervous edge to his heartiness. Nice enough face, thought John, seeing candid eyes beneath a brow made high by thinning hair. Between sentences he would bite his under lip, seeming to make the long monkey-like upper lip longer. They shook hands.

"John's my name," said John. "John Westley—no relation to the Methodist."

"Glad to know it—I had a Methodist uncle who got drunk every Saturday night and beat up auntie. She kinda liked it though. Howya getting on with the unpacking?"

In the hour that followed John got an outsider's angle on future associates, here and at school. There were five other boarders including the Miss Purcell whom Mrs. Gillespie had already mentioned, Frank informed him, and then proceeded to give the 'low-down' on the school. W.K.C.I. was all right. A swell bunch of kids and most of the staff members were pretty swell, too. Old Nyes was a stiff old guy, getting along in years. J. C.—that's what everybody called Bilbeau—would be the next principal. A smart man, J. C., just been there three years and had everybody eating out of his hand already—should have been a bank president or something big like that. Macdonald was all right, but didn't mix enough—not exactly stuck up, but, well—he didn't turn out to root for the team, that sort of thing! The kids liked him, though. And Jessie Willis—there was a real old meat-axe for you, but she knew her stuff. Pennington, classics, real Oxford graduate, was getting kind of doddery—this was his last year on the staff. There was a new history man, Klein. Jarratt had met him in the spring. Oh, they had some characters on the staff, all right. Dotty Young, for instance, painted screwy pictures—she had one at school last year and honestly, it looked like mama's last cow—what he meant was there wasn't anything to it—modern stuff, you know.

Frank mentioned them all, but the others failed to stick in John's mind. A gong sounded below.

"That's supper," announced Frank. "I'll wait for you if you want to wash up."

The meal was the usual boarding-house fare. Afterwards John sat in the living room with his fellow-boarders while they listened to the news, and *Amos 'n' Andy*.

He went upstairs feeling suddenly tired, turned and went down again, and found the phone. In a minute he was talking to Angus.

"Do you mind if I don't come over—I'm sort of tired."

"Don't blame you," said Angus. "What about tomorrow night? You can work on your lessons in the afternoon. . . . Fine, see you in the morning."

John went upstairs, overwhelmed by a sudden desire to sleep, went to the bathroom, brushed his teeth, came back to his room, changed to his pyjamas.

I promised to write Mary a line, he thought. Opening his other bag, he pulled out some paper and sat down at the desk.

"Dear Mary: For some reason I feel so sleepy I can't see straight, and it's only eight o'clock in the evening."

He sat for a moment trying to think of something to say about his first day in West Kirby. He heard feet on the stairs and looked out the door to see Frank coming up.

"Say, Frank, I'm so damn sleepy I can't keep my eyes open—what time's breakfast?"

"Around eight. I'll give you a call in the morning."

"Thanks a lot." He came back, shut the door, and rolled into bed.

For a few brief seconds he relived his disappointment at the station, the warm feeling of relief and security when Angus showed up, his pleasant impressions of West Kirby and the school.

This Bilbeau guy seems to be the only fly in an otherwise perfect ointment, thought John, and fell asleep.

3

Mr. John Westley, B.A., High School Assistant, Specialist in Science, age 25, recently appointed to the staff of West Kirby Collegiate Institute, awoke on September the sixth, 1934, in a bed upstairs at Mrs. Gillespie's boarding-house, fully conscious of who and where he was. Quite calmly he washed, shaved and dressed himself, with only a five-minute wait for a rather sour-looking Miss Purcell to slip out of the bathroom, hair tousled, in a blue silk dressing gown splashed over with gigantic orange poppies.

Downstairs, Googan, one of the boarders he had met the night before, was finishing his coffee alone at the table. "Mornin' professor!" he greeted John. "All set for the big day?"

Bacon and eggs, cold toast, soggy with melted butter, coffee. The others came down and ate, Googan left for work. No one talked much. John was finishing his coffee, conscious of a hard knot in his stomach. Suddenly excusing himself he rushed upstairs and vomited his breakfast into the toilet. White, and shaking a little, he went to his room and lay on the unmade bed.

Excitement, he diagnosed. Feeling better now his stomach was empty. He went back to the bathroom and gargled to sweeten his mouth. He lay down again, conscious only of a desire for sleep. Someone was coming upstairs, better get up. He went to the mirror, straightened his tie, inspected his neatly pressed blue serge suit. His colour was coming back; just that tight feeling in his throat and a great uneasiness in his bowels. His door was ajar and Frank looked in without knocking. "All set?" he asked. He carried a briefcase—must get one, thought John, looks more professional. John Westley picked up a small black loose-leaf note book, automatically felt in his back pocket for his wallet, went to get his hat and top coat.

"It's plenty warm, you won't need those," Frank advised. "I never wear a hat unless I have to. Healthier."

"Can a teacher get away with it?" asked the novice.

"Listen, take my advice and forget you're a teacher any time you're not inside the school door."

As they walked along the dirt path it was plain even to the psychically obtuse athlete that John was nervous.

"Got the first-day blues, huh?" he commented cheerfully. "Well, there's nothing to it today; just auditorium, read a list of names in the gym, staff meeting, and go home. Got your speech ready?"

"Speech?" Panic seized John Westley.

"Forget it—I was just kidding. Nyes is the only one that makes a speech. He'll mention you, and Klein—the other new teacher. You get up, the school gives you a hand, you sit down, and it's all over."

Ahead of them were three teen-age girls, looking back and giggling. One of them waved and Frank waved back.

"Second year kids," he explained. "The one that waved is Glenna What's-her-name. She's hot stuff."

"Do you use first names?" queried John.

"Sure, all but the older teachers. Sounds phony calling a girl Miss Smith, I always think. You're new to the racket."

"I took it for granted you knew I was," apologized John.

"Well, bluff it out. Make the kids think you know your way around even when you don't."

They were on the sidewalk now. Teen-age youngsters in groups of three and more walked laughing up to the new entrance, casually disappearing within. As they turned up the walk a car drove in, filled with students. John saw Angus at the wheel. His friend looked over as the car disgorged its laughing passengers, smiled, raised a hand in salute, then drove on to park beside the old school, where half a dozen cars stood already.

They entered the school and turned in at the secretary's office. A group of teachers stood inside the door, talking, laughing, shaking hands. John looked at them curiously.

They were all new to him.

"Mr. Pikestaff, Mr. Westley," introduced Mr. Jarratt. Mr. Pikestaff shook Mr. Westley's hand vigorously. "Glad to meet you, I hope you'll like it here," he said in a thin voice, with a thin smile. John caught himself staring at the exposed nostrils, at the openings of which black hairs curled like eyelashes.

Beside Pikestaff was Mr. Pennington, a charming old man with white hair. "It's a pleasure to greet a new face," he said, in an accent that was London rather than Oxford.

"When you've been teaching thirty-six years it's about the only pleasure left."

Just then an attractive blonde girl, with a business-like air that was somehow still feminine, came up.

"You're Mr. Westley, aren't you?" Then, before anyone had time for introductions, . . . "I'm Margaret Brewin. Mr. Bilbeau is having the English teachers together before things start and asked if I'd rush you along."

"Oh, sure," said John. "Excuse me"—to the others—and he followed her out.

Three teachers were sitting in pupils' seats near the teacher's desk, but young Westley hardly saw them for the fourth. Rising as John entered, he dominated the room effortlessly. It was not exactly his size, though he was a big man, well over the six foot mark, and bulky with his height. And it wasn't the striking bald head with its shaggy grey eyebrows, mobile mouth, thin feminine nose, and solid chin. It was the manner he had, a sort of casual acceptance of his inner power, that cast a spell on John.

Surprisingly, when they shook hands Bilbeau's was soft though the clasp was firm enough. His voice was rich, cultured, impressive.

"So you're Mr. Westley. I've been looking forward to meeting you. We *need* another man in the English department—the ladies have been having things all their own way." Efficient, the way he managed the introductions. "Miss Brewin, you've met. Miss Pettiker, first seat in the centre, Miss Garrell, behind her; and Miss Purcell—I believe you and she are fellow-boarders."

How am I going to remember all these names? wondered John.

"Now then, I shall not keep you more than one minute. I thought we might steal a march on the rest of the school and hold this little meeting to acquaint you with the English texts required for each of your classes. I have sheets here," (he handed out typewritten sheets, exactly five, one for each) "with the information each of you requires. You will note that the curriculum is outlined and an exact indication of relative time allotments for each phase of the work given. Will you just glance over these, so that I may answer any possible questions?"

He pronounced the *t* in my name thought John, glancing over the sheet, too dazed by Bilbeau's efficiency to read the words. This English will be a cinch, he gloated; why it's all mapped out here; all I have to do is teach it. Miss Pettiker timidly brought up a minor point and was answered. The meeting was over, and John wondered if a a stop watch would have recorded a whole minute.

Downstairs the hall was getting crowded, but not very noisy. Little first year children filtered silently through the crowd and into the assembly hall. But the rest stood in groups along the corridor, talking, laughing in a subdued sort of way, with an air of expectancy rather than celebration. As the six English teachers—J. C. a few steps behind —reached the bottom of the stairs, a general movement into the auditorium began. The teachers stood there, waiting for the hall to clear.

Some of those boys are a head taller than I, thought John. Why, they must even shave—observing a tall lad with blue, clean-shaven cheeks that might in another age have been covered with a black luxuriant beard. A slim-waisted girl wearing a yellow sweater that displayed her young breasts threw him into confusion with a smile meant for her companion. A little girl of twelve came by, clutching the string handles of a paper shopping bag. Curious glances in John's direction brought his hand unconsciously up to his tie. A sudden laugh beside him doubled his self-consciousness. The tight feeling in his stomach became almost a pain.

"Where do we go from here?" he asked his fellow-boarder, Miss Purcell. She smiled sympathetically.

"Oh, as soon as they're all in, we go up on the platform."

John pictured the staff in procession up the centre aisle, the students standing reverently, himself somehow pushed to the front, leading the rest, stopping confused before the platform not knowing how to get up on it. His pulse quickened, an acid taste gathered at the back of his mouth, his hands were cold and moist.

The remainder of the staff gathered nearby till the last sheep had strayed into the assembly hall; then moved off down the south corridor exchanging greetings, reminiscences, speculations. Angus came up with a Miss Young, a slim middle-aged woman with something unusual about her in spite of her plain face. She taught French and history.

"Aren't you the art teacher, too?" John asked her.

"No, Miss Garrell teaches art." Though she smiled, he wished he hadn't mentioned it. There was a bluntness about her that John found disturbing.

"Some people distinguish between artists and art teachers," Angus commented.

John was puzzled—wasn't she the "screwy painter" Frank had mentioned?

They passed the second entrance to the assembly hall,

entered the stage door which led through a little room cluttered with music stands to the stage wings. Out on the stage three rows of chairs awaited them. There was a dignified race to fill the back row. John sat beside Angus in the second row near the centre. The students were clapping, special outbursts as favourite staff characters appeared. The front row filled: J. C. sat at the extreme left, Mr. Nyes took his place in the centre, and for a minute staff and students sat facing each other, students frankly curious, the staff self-consciously pretending to be at ease.

John gazed at the mass of faces, suddenly aware that he was one of the ruling minority. How do so few control so many? he wondered. Here he was on the platform, belonging there. He recalled other platform appearances: that play he had taken a minor part in back in high school; going up to get his medal for marksmanship; the oratorical contest when he got stuck in the middle, said, "I'm sorry", and left the hall abruptly. He caught himself clearing his throat as if he had to speak. He uncrossed his knees, folded his arms, assumed an air of lordly indifference. Be casual, he told himself, so he put his hands in his coat pockets, leaned back, turned casually to say a casual word to Angus.

Mr. Nyes rose to his feet.

"Members of the staff," he turned briefly towards that group, "and students of West Kirby Collegiate."

Well, here we go, thought John, folding his arms again.

The speech lasted fifteen minutes at least, each succeeding minute lasting longer, as John's suspense increased. His absorption in himself blocked out all but a few phrases of the address: ". . . . the old familiar faces, and the new; . . . . to us who are getting along in years, the sight of so many fresh young faces (*laughter*); . . . . you can travel the width of this broad Dominion without finding a better school than West Kirby Collegiate Institute (*prolonged applause*); . . . . We're here to work (*some groans*) in the classroom, and play (*applause*) in the school grounds. Remember not to confuse the two (*scattered laughter*); . . . . There have been changes . . . . the new building has been repainted . . . . two new staff members"—John's heart pounded—"Mr. Klein, the new head of the history department," he turned to Klein, sitting over to his left; Klein rose and acknowledged the greeting of applause. A stocky man with a wide head and thick ears, he stood easily and grinned easily as though he were enjoying himself. John thought of a boxer after a victorious bout, clasping his gloves above his head, remarking, "Shucks, it was easy. Nuttin' to ut!"

"—and Mr. Westley, specialist in science."

John stood up and was sitting again before he had time to experience any sensation. He felt better. The applause had been quite adequate—he had half expected a boo or two, or worse—a titter. Anyone, he was sure, could see that he was a green teacher. He hadn't faced his audience, he had stood up with his hands on the chair ahead, raising his eyes to meet the crowd for a bare second, dropping them quickly, blushing a bit, sitting down quickly. Well, that was that.

The speech was over. A rustle of paper, the creaking of seats, and a subdued hum of conversation filled the hall as Nyes announced that heads of departments would announce the books each class was expected to buy.

"The department of science." That would be Angus. Angus Macdonald rose and was greeted with a good round of applause. John was disappointed in his voice—he hadn't

34

noticed before that it was not a strong one. In the large auditorium it sounded thin, with a curious hesitancy to it. John had a let-down feeling. He noticed students at the rear leaning forward with a strained expression, or turning to their neighbours to ask—he supposed—"What did he say?" He wanted to get up and tell them what a wonderful man Angus was—if they could only have known him as John had, up north. He wanted to tell Angus that he couldn't be heard very well at the back.

Angus sat down and John dropped a piece of paper on the floor that he had unconsciously twisted out of all recognition.

"The department of English," announced Nyes.

J. C. Bilbeau, M.A., rose impressively. The applause was polite but, to John's surprise, unenthusiastic. "Students of the first year are asked to bring a copy of *David Copperfield*, by Charles Dickens, edited by . . ." The voice was rich, musical, floating effortlessly to the back of the room, resonating from the walls. After the strain of Angus's delivery, it soothed John's soul to hear the thing done properly. Don't you see how easy it is? he pleaded mentally with Angus.

It was a pleasure to listen to J. C. And there wasn't any pretentiousness about him. He stood without posing as though he stood on his own hearth rug talking to friends. He had scarcely raised his voice at all. From where John sat Mr. Bilbeau appeared in profile against the royal purple of the stage curtain. There was something of the Roman senator about his head and figure; perhaps the dignity of the curtain behind suggested a toga, and the bald head— of course, that was it—and the slightly Roman nose. Even in profile there was something feminine in the curve above the nostril, the slight sharpness of the tip. But the solid chin, made more massive by the fullness beneath, the fierceness of the shaggy grey eyebrow with the reassuring mildness of the blue eye and suggestion of humour in the creases around it, drew the observer away from the nose, stating emphatically that its slightly feminine character, and the almost too-smoothly shaven cheek, were purely coincidental. Sweeping smoothly in a high arc above the shaggy brow, and over the curve of a capacious brain-pan, the outline of his head dropped to the base of the skull through a little forest of freshly-barbered hair to join a somewhat fleshy neck and disappear under the collar of his immaculate light-grey suit.

J. C. Bilbeau sat down.

There followed Miss Willis, a typical old battle-axe with pince-nez rimless spectacles, modern languages; Mr. Smith, mathematics; Mr. Klein again, history; and lastly Mr. Pennington, classics, who received an ovation that lasted fully half a minute. "The text book prescribed for use in the Lower School is Dunkel's *Latin Composition for Beginners*." He paused, while the older students tittered with expectancy. "The text book prescribed for Upper School use is Dunkel's *Latin Composition for Beginners*." The titters multiplied, reinforced by isolated and suppressed guffaws. Mr. Pennington paused as though having trouble with his memory. "All *other* students will be required to use Dunkel's *Latin Composition* . . . ." the remaining words were drowned in waves of laughter. Mr. Nyes rose and gestured for attention, while the student body struggled for self-control. The contagion spread to Nyes's furrowed face, and lingered there.

"Now that you *all* know——" and the laughter roared out

again, to subside more quickly "—what texts you will be required to buy, will the Upper School and fourth year students adjourn to the library, the third and second years to the gymnasium, and all first year students remain in here, to hear your class lists read by your Home Room teacher. After that you will be dismissed for the remainder of the day."

The applause died out in the clapping of folding seats against the chair backs as the school rose to file out, talking and laughing in high humour.

Having been told his home form would be a first year class, John remained as the others filed leisurely out, excepting Miss Purcell, Miss Garrell, Mr. Pikestaff, and Frank Jarratt. Mr. Pikestaff handed the class lists out. 1C was the heading on John's. Nervousness gripped him fiercely again.

Miss Garrell, a fat little creature in a black dress, read her list in a pert little voice—1A. Frank Jarratt read 1B with careless despatch. It was John's turn. He coughed to clear his throat, failed, and read anyway in a high husky voice.

"Donald Lunn, Bill—" he coughed again, successfully; "Bill McIvor, Mary McLean", and so on till he came to Zycinski. He had seen it coming, trying to seem nonchalant while flashing desperate glances at it. "John Zye-sinkski," he stammered. Nobody seemed to notice. He sat down.

Miss Purcell and Pikestaff read their lists; Pikestaff dismissed the youngsters and the five teachers followed their charges out of the emptied assembly hall.

"It's the staff meeting now, isn't it?" John found himself walking with Miss Garrell.

"That's right," she said brightly. "And what do you

think of our school? The first day in a new school is always so confusing isn't it? You're from Toronto, aren't you?"

"Well not exactly, you see—" He got no further.

"Is it true you know Mr. Macdonald? He's such a fine teacher. They say he's known all over Ontario." John would have interrupted to correct her, but her inflection made it clear that Ontario was Canada. "Wasn't it too bad about his son? A wonderful student—well, he wasn't brilliant in art—but in almost everything else—of course you're either born an artist or just not born." John was puzzled. Angus had never told him anything about having had a son. But Miss Garrell rattled on about what a *dear* Mr. Pennington was and how it was a shame he would be retiring next year, and on and on till they entered the library.

In the library the others were already seated, or standing in small groups. John looked for Angus, but he had found a place between Miss Young and Miss Pettiker. smiling rather absently at something the latter was saying. J. C. was talking to Klein, or rather listening intently with a look of keen intelligence. Three library tables had been pushed together end to end with Nyes at the head. Appropriately, John felt, J. C. took the dominating position at the opposite end.

"I'm not going to make a speech," said Nyes, his leathery face impassive, his eyes on the papers before him. The details of organization, classes, room changes, timetable and programme for the next morning were touched briefly. John tried to listen intently but heard little.

He was thinking, this is my first staff meeting. I'm not a student any more, not even a student teacher. This is a teaching staff and I am a part of it. How many? He counted: six, seven, eight opposite, as many more on either side of him, a total of eighteen or nineteen. He remembered a friend of his in college commenting on the faculty members at his graduation exercise: "There sit half a million dollars' worth of education!" How much would this bunch be worth? He went over his own education costs. The first three years, about $800 each—that's $2400; the next year $500, that's $2900, O.C.E. $400,—that's the year I really cut it fine, total, $3300. He multiplied. That'd be at least sixty thousand dollars. And that's not figuring on Angus —of course he's only a B.A., but the time he's spent on geology, if you added up the cost—after all, he's an F.R.S.C.

". . . . and Mr. Westley to supervise the west stairs."

John started at the sound of his name, like a pupil caught talking in class. Mr. Nyes removed his spectacles with bony thumb and fingers, and looked up. Yellow eyeballs protruded slightly between dark and careworn lids. "That is all for this morning, I think, unless there are any questions."

"In the matter of timetables, Mr. Nyes"—Bilbeau's voice broke the brief silence. "I wonder if you would explain—"

Mr. Nyes reddened slightly, and added, "Yes, I omitted to mention that on Mr. Bilbeau's suggestion I have allotted extra spare periods to the English staff on the basis of one spare for every two composition classes."

Mr. Bilbeau added, "I might explain that a number of my English teachers have complained of the heavy extra load entailed in marking English compositions."

"Aren't you afraid," Angus asked Nyes, "that we'll all

clamour for classes in English composition under such an arrangement?"

Nyes smiled. "We'll have to take a chance on that," he said.

Bilbeau was not amused.

There were no more questions. The meeting broke up like a class dismissed at four. "You'll be over tonight about eight?" asked Angus, coming up.

"Yes, I'll be there."

"Is there anyone here you haven't met?"

"Two or three I saw across the table. I guess they've gone——" he looked around the now almost empty room.

As they moved to the door a straight-looking man with black hair and blue eyes came over. Angus introduced him.

"Mr. Westley, Mr. Smith. Mr. Westley will be teaching maths in your department, I believe." Mr. Smith had that speculative look the head of a department assumes when confronted by a new teacher.

"I was looking for you," said John. "I suppose I should go over the course with you."

Smith opened and consulted his memorandum.

"Let me see. I teach 1B algebra—you have the other four first year classes." He spoke, as he stood, erectly, looking squarely at John, the light blue eyes expressionless as a bird's. He blinked too, like a bird, his mouth twitching leftward.

"Hmm, yes. Will you be over here this afternoon?"

"Why, yes. I could be. I didn't know whether——" he had intended to stick to his room getting up his first lessons.

"Then let's say in my room, 18, upstairs in the old building, at three. Is that convenient?"

"Oh, sure. Three o'clock, Room 18. I'll be there."

40

"Doesn't waste much time, does he?" said John, watching Smith walk briskly towards the stairs.

They walked out together, parting at the steps. Angus lived on the island and owned a car. He disappeared around the corner of the school to get it.

Of five hundred students and nineteen teachers not one was left in sight. John walked home alone.

4

John spent the early afternoon planning his lessons. After all, there couldn't be much teaching the first time he met each class. There would be seating plans to straighten out, and checking to see if they all had the necessary books; that would take half a period. So he decided he would fill in the remaining fifteen or twenty minutes of each period with a brief talk on the value of the subject. No, remembering his pedagogy, he corrected himself. Not a talk, but a discussion: "The class must deduce the answers under the guidance of carefully planned questions." What'll I ask them? Physics will be easy, I'll get a laugh out of that; right at the start someone will mention Epsom salts. Then we'll get into the meaning of physical, and so on. That's the first period. Then three algebras in a row. Well, ask them what good is algebra? Heck, they won't even know what algebra is. Tell 'em about the Arabs. Alchemy, al-gol—know any others? That kind of thing. What *is* algebra? *Al jebr*, the union of broken parts, and all that stuff. *X*, the little man with two legs, two arms, and no head—who is he? Sure—

I can fill in a period. Now, English literature, period 5. Well, what good is English? They can put in a period answering that. Next period's a spare. Next period 1C algebra—that's looked after. Period 8—English grammar and composition. Skip the grammar, give them a composition to do. Let's see, subject? Oh, ... he paused, looked out the window and caught a glimpse of the bay . . . . that's it: "How I spent my summer holidays."

He glanced at his alarm clock on the bedside table—ten to three. Better get over and see Smith.

Smith was waiting for him, busily transferring a pile of mathematical tables from the cupboard, where they had been locked away for the summer, to a more accessible shelf on the wall. He greeted Westley formally, drew up a chair and they both sat down. He reminded John a little of Miss Willis, only Smith was colder, more concentrated.

"Just out of curiosity, Mr. Westley, what *is* your mathematical background?"

"Well, I'm really a science man—I took honour geology right through. But I took pass astronomy in First Year as an option, and I got a bit of mathematics there in the lab exercises. Then in Second Year crystallography we went into plane geometry a bit. But nothing much, really."

"I see," said Smith, and proceeded to run over the term's work. "What do you propose to do tomorrow morning?"

John told him, hesitantly.

"That's one approach, of course." Smith obviously disapproved. "It's usually wise to get your class into working habits from the drop of the hat. If you cover the course early then there's time to drill, drill." John could see the dentist leaning over his face, one hand jamming the little mirror into his gums and holding the jaw down firmly, the other reaching for the dangling drill. *Z-z-z-z-z!* "No. You'd better start right in with Page One of the text," and he outlined the lesson for him. "These educational theories are all very well, creating interest and all that sort of thing, but it's no use creating interest, if you don't cover the course. Interest comes with proficiency and proficiency is the result of exercise. Work." The word threw a flood of light on Smith's character, philosophy, religion—a kind of ghostly black light that hung in the sky and threatened the dilly-dallier with daggers of blue lightning. John slunk out of Room 18 with an accusing conscience. This teaching was a more serious business than he had realized.

He went across to his own room, entered and crossed over to the window. The sky was a light grey monotone of high stratus clouds. Over the bay a shifting offshore wind flung down sudden gusty little squalls, the black patches of roughened water scudding over the surface of the bay, twisting, fading out, followed by more and more. Rain tomorrow.

He sat down at his desk to replan his lessons *à la* Smith. Halfway through he stopped in disgust. Who in hell was Smith anyway? He'd teach the way he wanted to. Well, not algebra of course, but the other subjects. J. C. had the right idea: give your teachers an account of what you want, printed in black and white, then leave them alone. He wondered what Angus's policy was in the science department. Probably he'd say it's your own business, he'd just let you sink or swim. The trouble with Angus was he didn't take things seriously enough. John remembered his rare references to teaching when they were up north—no particular words, but the general impression that teaching was a bit of a hoax, a kind of a conspiracy in which university graduates who were good for nothing else had invented a secure place for themselves in society, had hoodwinked the public into believing they were doing something for their children that was necessary and profitable.

John realized he had never paid much attention to Angus's views on teaching when they were together on the survey. To him then, so recently a high school student, the very fact that Angus was a high school science teacher had given him prestige enough. But now John, too, was a teacher, his equal in a sense; at least in a position to compare Angus with other teachers. Angus was more the university type; why had he never been appointed to a university? Of course he was only a B.A., but then there was his F.R.S.C.—he had even been quoted by his professor of dynamic geology, and with respect. I'll ask him some time, he decided, and rose to go.

Out on the Lakeshore Road the north-east wind flicked little tails of air here and there in the lee of the hill with playful zest. The clouds were lowering, thickening, moving faster to the eye, gathering definition as they moved. A sudden downdraught flung itself on him with fierce joy as he rounded the cliff and sighted Mrs. Gillespie's.

In the front hall he heard Mrs. Gillespie in the kitchen. "Who's there?"

"Just me." He went upstairs thinking he should have said, "Just I."

It was seven-thirty before he stepped out again, on his way to visit Angus.

44

Walking across the bridge gave him a new perspective. The threatening sky was making it grow dark already, clouds were driving swiftly from the east, dropping a sprinkle of fine rain occasionally. Down the bay a few lights showed faintly from Old Kirby. A lonely little launch chugged past the river mouth out into the dusk. Lights came on along the Lakeshore Road, and overhead, across the bridge.

John waited for a car to pass, then crossed the paved road and the radial tracks to the other side. It was his first good look at the near end of the bay.

Barely a quarter of a mile beyond, the main shore and the island were joined by a low curve of sand and mud that had originally made a peninsula of the island. But a channel had been cut through, giving access to the harbour for smaller boats from the south. Beyond, the lake was calm, darkening towards the west with the offshore wind.

Crossing the bridge John entered the shadow of the island and began the winding climb up Spruce Drive past the tree-secluded homes of the wealthy. At the bend near the top he turned back to repeat the view of the day before. The school stood small and unimpressively ugly against the dark mass of the West Kirby hill. Lights twinkled from city streets and homes beyond.

A little farther on he came to the left turn he had been told to watch for: a freshly painted sign on the telephone pole confirmed it. This was Mountain Crescent, lined with homes built in the rug brick period, smaller houses, mostly of the bungalow type, but eminently respectable. Somehow he couldn't imagine Angus living in one of these.

The pavement ended abruptly, the terrace between the cliff below and little mountain above narrowed. The crescent itself petered out in a dusty dirt road without sidewalks. In the gloom John made out Macdonald's garage. Zigzagging up behind was a concrete walk with frequent steps. As he climbed them it was too dark to see much of the house or grounds. He crossed the wide veranda and tapped the knocker. Almost immediately Angus was there, opened the door, shook hands, and drew him in.

The living room surprised him: it seemed to bear no relation to Angus's personality. Standard floor lamps and table lamps threw their light on standard chesterfield and chairs. A standard radio stood on the floor by the door. The drapes were standard, the wallpaper standard. The room might have been in any one of a million North American homes.

"Vera will be down in a minute. She has to go out tonight. I didn't realize it when you phoned last night, and when I did there wasn't anything we could do. You're taking the five train to Toronto tomorrow afternoon, aren't you?"

Angus excused himself, and John, left alone, speculated on Mrs. Macdonald's appearance. Angus had referred to her only rarely, but always correctly, leaving one to guess whether he was indifferent or merely avoiding sentimental display.

On the wall above the piano in a pair of oval frames and under convex glass were tinted photographic enlargements of a middle-aged couple. Somehow, John couldn't imagine their being related to Angus. On the piano were *Fingering Exercises from the Classics,* and a hymn book. Along the top of the piano was a little plaster bust of King George the Fifth, a larger one of Beethoven, and a flock of photographs—relatives, by the look of them—still no likeness to Angus in any of them. One undoubtedly was a recent photograph of the tinted woman who hung on the wall under convex glass. Over the chesterfield hung a large framed photographic print—John recognized it instantly —of Stratford-on-Avon. To one side was a little print of Gainsborough's *Blue Boy*, and balancing it on the other the figure of the Boy Jesus in the temple. A "real" oil painting hung just by the door, a lake with reeds in the foreground, mountains in the distance, and a white sail in the middle of the lake. Even to John's untutored eye it was not quite convincing.

Mrs. Macdonald came downstairs. She was nice—West Kirby 'nice'—surprisingly young-looking for middle age: her reddish hair showed no trace of grey, and her figure, though matronly, was not unpleasing. She must have been extremely attractive twenty-five years ago, thought John. She wore no glasses, had a pleasant rather ruddy face in keeping with the colour of her hair, and her cheeks dimpled when she smiled to reveal pearly dentures. Her perfume was not difficult to detect in the air—a standard perfume. She shook hands warmly with John, told him Angus had spoken of him, regretted that she was going out, hoped he would have a pleasant evening and come back again soon when she could be home. Yes, she was nice, and yet John felt relieved to see her go.

Walking into Angus's den from the living room was like passing into another world. There was a fireplace with a real fire in it, the mantel covered with rocks; bookshelves right up to the ceiling on either side. On the wall by the door two pictures hung, one a northern scene, the other a meaningless jumble of colour patches. The only remaining wall space was covered with photographs of northern scenes, a map of Kirby County, a geological map of Canada with coloured pins clustered in various spots, a pair of deer's antlers with part of the skull attached. There was a desk, flat-topped, very tidy, a movable typewriter stand, with slots for paper underneath. There were two big leather armchairs.

John and Angus sat between the flickering light of the fire and the steadier paler orange of the desk lamp. John felt as if he had come home.

Angus offered John a cigarette, then filled his pipe with English tobacco out of a small round green tin. John wished he had brought his own pipe though he rarely smoked it.

"Now then, tell us all about it!" Angus stretched out his legs, crossed them at the ankles, leaned back in the chair as though settled for the night, regarding John with amused affection through a cloud of smoke.

"Well, I *think* I'm going to like it."

"Not just what you expected?"

"I don't suppose anything ever is. West Kirby is quite different from anything I imagined. You know when you used to mention the island the picture I had in mind was Toronto Island where I visited an uncle one summer when I was about six. Of course you mentioned the rock but I pictured it as a little outcrop about six feet by three. To tell you the truth I had a theory you might have mistaken a big chunk of buried float for bed rock—you know, the conceited young graduate. You never were much for details, except when it came to things like classification or analysis, or map-making; then I used to think you were too fussy." Impulsively, John went on. "Angus, at the meeting this morning I couldn't help wondering why you never tried for a university job—I mean, it's none of my business, but where trained teachers are a dime a dozen, good geologists are rare as hen's teeth." John looked at Angus, and was sorry he had mentioned it.

"Can you imagine a house with a setting like this in Toronto, or Kingston, or London? You must come out in the daytime and see the lake from the west side of the house."

"Yes, I couldn't see much but a gap in the trees, but I figured there'd be a grand view." Does a man give up his proper life work for a house with a view? he asked himself.

"But a teacher's life is so narrow. Take Smith for instance, and Pikestaff—school teaching is their life; there just isn't anything else!"

"Oh, I don't know," Angus demurred, "Pikestaff is an expert performer on the electric guitar; and Smith is an elder in the First Baptist Church."

"Next thing I know you'll be telling me I should take saxophone lessons or join a church to broaden my life."

"Now there's a good idea—church, not the saxophone—there's no better way of establishing yourself as a solid citizen." Angus smiled.

"I guess I'll wait till I get married," John grinned. "Till then I can think of a better use for week ends. You know, I'm not sure it's a good idea to bring Mary to West Kirby —she has quite a crush on you."

"Maybe you're right. It would be better for her to keep any illusions she may have." He said it almost seriously.

"Do you know," said John, "I had something happen to me today that's never happened in my life before."

Angus raised his eyebrows interrogatively.

"J. C. pronounced the *t* in my name! The first man in the twenty-five years of my life to recognize the existence of that *t*. What do you think of J. C., really? It seems to me that he's like you, too big a man for teaching; he should be a—well, a bank president or something like that."

The pleasant friendliness of Angus's mouth changed subtly. He turned his head towards the desk lamp and its light suddenly threw his features into harsh relief against the shadows. As John watched, the inner humour of the man suddenly broke through.

"My boy," he said smiling, "if you take Bilbeau seriously, you become his enemy or his friend. I don't want to have any enemies, and I am choosy about my friends; so I sit on the fence, and find him at his present job an amusing spectacle. As a bank president he might not be quite so amusing."

John persisted. "But what is it that's so funny?"

Angus shrugged his shoulders. "You know what happens to a joke when you have to explain it. Keep your eye on the great Bilbeau and your mind open: the joke is there."

He got up. "I just remembered, I have some beer—will you have a bottle?"

"Sure, you know me," John laughed.

They went out to the kitchen where Angus dug out some very old cheese, a Spanish onion, butter and crackers. As they carried these and the beer back to the den, John thought: if it boils down to a choice, I'm going to be Bilbeau's friend.

J. C. was forgotten in the flood of reminiscences brought back as they recalled the last time they had had beer together in the hotel at Heron Bay a year and two months ago. Angus described his past summer, with a party of ten east of God's Lake in Manitoba. He pointed to the map on the wall. "Those pins outline the areas I've covered—on foot. And most of them before anyone thought of using planes." They pored over the map, seeing not paper, areas, and lines, but endless panoramas of bush and rocks and water stretching infinitely north and west, varying infinitely in sky and surface. Angus had been everywhere; from the sources of the Finlay in the Cassiar Mountains of British Columbia, to Eskimo Point on the west coast of Hudson Bay, and Lake Mistassini in the heart of Quebec province. And always one passion had driven him on, to unravel the riddles lying buried in the ancient Precambrian formation.

"That's a nice painting," exclaimed John. "Reminds me of that portage on the Missinaibi River just above the big falls—remember?"

"It is actually a print," corrected Angus, a bit didactically, "Tom Thomson's *Northern River*. It *has* caught the feeling of a last portage," he agreed: "the moment when you've decided there isn't any end to the portage, your neck is breaking from the portage strap, you're blinded with sweat and have just thrown your load off balance by brushing against a leaning deadfall. The flies are biting big chunks out of your neck and back of your ears, and you can't touch them because you've two paddles in one hand and the frying pan and tea pail in the other. Suddenly you feel the slightest breath of air cooling your brow, you hear a rustling of leaves, look up—and there's the silver gleam of water through the trees. What do you think of the painting over here?" he asked, smiling.

51

"Honestly I can't make head or tail of it," confessed John. "It just looks like a mess to me. Is that one of Miss Young's paintings?"

Angus looked surprised. "How did you know?"

"Well, Frank Jarratt—you know what he's like—he said he saw one of Miss Young's paintings and described it as 'screwy' so I guessed this is the kind of thing he meant. I don't know anything about art—Mary's the one for that; though I don't think she's fussy about the really modern things—I mean when you can't recognize anything at all in a picture, what is there to it?"

Angus laughed. "That's something we'll have to go into when we've got a clear evening ahead."

Sounds at the front door indicated Mrs. Macdonald's return. John, suddenly recalling that he was a school teacher now, felt his heart sink. Tomorrow he would face group after group of young savages, alone.

"Stay and have a cup of tea," urged Mrs. Macdonald.

"Or coffee if you prefer it," added Angus.

"Thanks, but I think I'd better get back—I'd like to get a good night's sleep to prepare me for the great ordeal." He laughed half-heartedly.

"Let him go," said Angus to his wife, "he'll be over again and you can feed him to the gills. Just a minute till I get my keys and I'll drive you home."

Fifteen minutes later John was tiptoeing up the dimly lit stairs of the boarding-house.

As he undressed a button came off his shirt. I'd better get out a clean one for tomorrow, anyway, he thought. But that means wearing the pin-stripe; and I wanted that for the week end. He went to the drawer of the desk, took out a spool of thread with a needle stuck in it, and sat down to sew on the button. As he did so he noticed the inside of the collar had begun to smudge.

I really should meet my first classes with a freshly-laundered shirt, he reflected, but dammit all, I can't afford to put on a fresh shirt every day of the week—they'll just have to get used to it.

He finished sewing, broke the thread, put the spool and needle away, and hung the shirt neatly on the back of the bedside chair ready for the morning.

5

A week later John Westley sat at the battered old desk in his room at Mrs. Gillespie's boarding house writing a letter to Mary.

"Darling, this teaching isn't going to be so bad after all. Today I had a really good day. My physics class is really nice—4A, all good students. I think I told you they put all the good students in each year in the 'A' classes. Angus claims he didn't have anything to do with it, so I guess I've Nyes to thank for giving them to me. Anyway we're proving just now that air has weight and it's a cinch to teach them. Every question I ask, three-quarters of the hands go up, and they seem to like me and think I know my stuff. There's one very sweet little dish that sits in a front seat and looks at me as though I were Einstein himself. But it's all right—she only makes me hungry for you; and besides she is in such awe of my *brain* that I doubt if she knows the colour of my hair. Honestly, it's a bit disturbing to have so many sweet young things around me—you'd better hurry up and marry me before the West Kirby Press headlines scream: 'Young Teacher Rapes School Girl in Corridor'.

"In between periods we're supposed to stand outside the doors of our room and supervise the halls. Nobody bothers much about it in our end of the school except Smith, and Miss Willis, of course, but I thought I'd better too for a while till I got to know my way around. Anyway I'm quite reconciled to it, watching the little girls go by.

"The second year physiog class isn't quite the way I'd like to have it, but I can handle them all right. I kept one boy in after four yesterday and gave him a good talking to—not bawling him out, just reasoning with him, and it worked. There *is* a bit of talking in some of my classes. I just clean it up in one corner and it begins in another—nothing much, just enough to bother me a bit. But most of the kids are pretty easy to handle."

John had two 'spares' a week. The one on Thursday afternoon he spent policing—the customary word was supervising—about fifty senior students in the library. He had forgotten to mention this in his letter—it was certainly different trying to make the big lads in Upper School bury their noses in their books. By dint of walking around and speaking quietly to each culprit he managed to keep the peace, but he was uneasily conscious of a lack of control. After all he was only five years older than some of them, and no bigger than the average. One lad particularly who persisted in talking greeted John's rebukes with a gentle —and infuriating—smile, and the words "Yes, Mr. Westley," so subtly insolent that John knew he would make a fool of himself if he took issue with him.

The other spare was the fourth period on Friday morning. John was sitting quietly at his desk, copying names into his register, when he was startled to see J. C. standing inside the door, observing his industry with a twinkle in his eye. John rose.

"Sit down, sit down!" said J. C. coming forward. "Just thought I'd drop in and ask you how things were coming along." He drew a chair up to one side of John's desk and sat down. In an instant, by some magic on his part, it was J. C.'s desk, and John was the visitor.

"I hear you're at Mrs. Gillespie's—all settled by now I suppose. Interesting character, Mrs. Gillespie, an interesting character."

"Yes, and some of her boarders are characters, too."

J. C. smiled. The J. C. smile was like his voice—everything a smile should be. It gave him a youthful air, seemed to take the object of the smile into his confidence. "I'm really a good fellow, just as human as you are," the smile said. "I like people. I make friends easily. I have a sense of humour." It would have been immodest of J. C. to put these facts into words, even to be conscious of them, so his smile performed the service unasked.

"And how do you like our school, John?" The Christian name slipped out as easily and naturally as if they had always known each other. Pronouncing the *t* had cracked the shell, the smile deftly pulled the parts away, and the Christian name tossed them into the air where they vanished. Westley felt pure affection well up within him for the man.

"I really like it here," he said with enthusiasm. "Of course, it's a bit strange at first but the staff is so friendly, and the students are friendly too."

"You are teaching in a first rate school—a first rate school," declared J. C. "Are you having any difficulties in English?"

"No, not yet, anyway. The way you've outlined the course, it seems to cover everything."

"It has been my experience," pronounced J. C., "that the more difficulties you anticipate and prepare for, the fewer you are going to encounter. Sometime I may let you look over my individual assignment sheets. To my mind far too much time is wasted on oral interrogation.

"By the way, Mr. Nyes informed me that you have had some dramatic experience."

"Well, I've been in a couple of plays at university. And I tried my hand once at directing one," confessed John.

"The Dramatic Club is organizing after four on Monday. Why not look in on it? We meet in the assembly hall."

"I'd like to," said John, and J. C. left it at that.

"You're a friend of Mr. Macdonald's I am told. A brilliant man. His scholarship is an ornament to the school." J. C.'s voice dropped a shade, becoming gravely sympathetic. "A great pity about his son. Of course, it happened before my time, but it must have been a great shock." He rose quickly, carefully placed the chair in its former position. "I suppose, had he lived, he would have been about your age." The gravity in his manner changed back to easy friendliness. "Well, let me know if there's any way I can help you," and he was gone.

Damn it all, thought John, he *likes* Angus, why can't Angus like him? Anyway you couldn't help taking J. C. seriously. You certainly couldn't call him pompous, and you had only to spend three minutes with the man to learn that he was tremendously efficient. And his personality was so pleasing too. Yes, he hated to admit it, but Angus was definitely prejudiced—why? He kicked the leg of his desk peevishly.

John's irritability cast a shadow over the rest of the day. He had intended to drop in on Angus at four and suggest a walk, but went home instead and fell in readily with Jarratt's suggestion that they take in a show that night.

On Saturday morning about ten o'clock the phone rang. "For you, Mr. Westley," his landlady informed him just as he was finishing his breakfast.

The voice on the other end was not too clear. "Hello, John? John Westley?" it seemed to say.

"Yes." He had hoped it would be Angus inviting him for a walk around the island, but the voice was unfamiliar.

"This is Ob—Magum—m—"

"Oh, yes," said John politely, hoping the next words would provide a clue. "How are you?"

"What the hell do you mean, how am I?" His mouth had evidently been away from the mouthpiece for the words came now clear as a bell. "I said, this is Tom McIntyre!"

"Tom! Tom McIntyre! Well for the love of Pete, how are you? When did you get into town?" Tom had been a fellow-roomer of his on College Street in Toronto, that last year, when he had really been a penny pincher. Tom had been a law student—a nice lad—fair, with a rather distinguished appearance.

Tom, he now learned, had been admitted to the bar and had put out his shingle over an office in Queen Street, Old Kirby, as the junior partner of his uncle.

"How'd you like to go fishing?" he asked.

"Sure, but where, and what about tackle?" John was doubtful. There was a staff party at Nyes's that evening, too. He mustn't miss that.

"All you have to bring is yourself and you'll be home before dark. Hop the two o'clock return trolley from the

Beach and drop off here. We're upstairs over the bank of Nova Scotia right on Queen Street. You can't miss it."

At two-thirty John was climbing the rather rickety stairs leading to rooms above the bank. Tom's office was tiny and unimpressive, but his uncle's rooms suggested without too much display that the firm of McIntyre and McIntyre was sound and solid.

"Come on out and have a beer," urged Tom. "No fishing for another hour." He glanced out the window as he threw his arms into his coat sleeves. "Think it'll rain?"

"No more than it has," predicted John.

"Come on, then." Tom clattered loosely down the stairs, his coat flapping, John behind.

Queen Street, Old Kirby, definitely could not vie with Central Avenue, West Kirby. There was an air of dinginess to the buildings due, no doubt, to the smoke, and Old Kirby's greater age. They turned into the beverage room of the Granville House.

Only then, Mr. John Westley remembered his profession. As the waiter wiped the beer slops from the little round marble-topped table, John glanced around half-furtively.

"You know," he smiled self-consciously to Tom, "I'm not sure I should do this any more."

"Do what?" Tom looked surprised.

"Consume alcoholic beverages in a public place. Think what the good, sober, tax-paying public would say."

"To hell with the public!" snorted the young lawyer. "Anyway they all do it—that is, the younger ones. It's very handy, actually. West Kirby teachers drink in Kirby. Kirby teachers in West Kirby. There's a road house out on the Lakeshore Road that's really something, and I mean something. You'd be surprised at the people you see out there. By the way, have you run into Aggie Purcell? You know her? Now *there's* a girl that really gets around. I've had her out myself—I ought to know."

"I suppose Frank Jarratt takes her out quite a bit."

"Frank? Oh, the coach. Why, Frank couldn't look a bottle-cork in the face. I met him just once, bowling, over at the 'Y'. Talks big and tough on Saturday, goes to church three times on Sunday, that's his type."

"Do you know anyone else on the staff?"

"Old Nyes—he's a dry old guff! That's all, except J. C. Bilbeau. Now there's a man who's going to count for something in these two towns. Addressed our Club last spring. That guy's got everything: humour, knows how to get along with the boys, the smoothest speaker I ever listened to. If I had what he's got I'd be a corporation lawyer pulling down fifteen thousand a year."

"I've wondered ever since I met him why he was just a high school teacher," said John.

"I guess he never had a chance to be anything but. He's a self-made man. Told us how he started off teaching public school—some little place in the sticks—couldn't afford college—worked up to be principal—took summer courses for his degree, then took a year off in the States, came back with the M.A. He's been here only a year, but I'll make a bet with you he'll be your next principal and that's just the beginning. That guy is going places." Tom gulped down some beer. "The guy's got ideas, too. He made us think about education—I mean think. He told us the new emphasis in education is on—let's see, how did he put it? —personality, not pedagogy. Lot of other good stuff too."

Tom drained his first glass, shook some salt into the second.

"You don't know Angus Macdonald, by any chance?" John inquired more casually than he felt.

"Never met him, but you hear the odd story. It's a wonder he's kept his job."

John's heart turned to lead and pressed hard on his stomach.

"How's that?" He despised himself for not revealing his intimacy with Angus.

"They say he's an atheist. I'm not much for church-going and all that, you know, and I know there's a lot of bunk attached to religion, but this atheistic stuff—you've got to draw the line somewhere—especially a teacher. Didn't want to have his son buried in a cemetery—they say he wouldn't go to his funeral. Yeah, there was quite a stink about that." He glanced at his wrist watch. "How's your beer coming? We're due down at the dock at four."

John drained his glass and they got up. He had eaten a light lunch and had developed a slight glow on the second glass; but McIntyre's views on Angus left cold ashes where the glow had been.

"Thanks for the drinks," he said. "Where do we go from here?"

"Down to the dock. McIntyre Senior is going out trawling for lake trout with old man Grossart. Told me to knock off and bring a friend along."

They walked back a block on Queen Street, then turned left towards the bay, through the railway yards and past some factories.

Down on the waterfront a little steam tug was puffing at her moorings. They scrambled on board to meet their hosts. Tom's uncle was leaner, more distinguished looking than his nephew. Grossart sat boorishly in his deck chair when John was introduced, reached up to shake hands and grunted out: "Teacher, huh?" Greedy little eyes took their measure of John, found him of no interest and turned away, suddenly tired. His clothes were disreputable.

The two youngsters looked in on the pilot, then went forward to the bow.

"Who is this Old Man Grossart?" asked John, "A harbour character?"

Tom slapped his knee, laughing loud and long. "A harbour character!" He laughed on until John felt annoyed.

"What's so funny?"

"That, my dear young fellow, is John G. Grossart. He's the harbour character"—he spluttered with mirth again—"who owns the Central Lakes Flour Milling Company, Kirby Iron Products, Lambert's Tannery, and half the city of Kirby. That uncouth harbour character happens to be one of the ten wealthiest men in Ontario."

"Oh," said John. It was his first millionaire and he needed time to adjust his sense of values. He thought of the careless clothes. If he, John Westley, had that much money maybe he wouldn't give a damn about what he wore either. If I had a million dollars! thought John, watching the grey jumble of oil tanks, warehouses, dredges, chimneys, and coal piles glide past as the boat headed out across the river mouth for the open lake.

The remainder of the outing John never cared to recall. As soon as they left the lee of the shore and began trawling in the deeper water, the motion of the boat, slight as it was, made him violently sick. Tom tried to persuade the Old Man to put in to the beach, but Grossart, who at the age of twenty-five was a moulder in the foundry he later would own, snorted with disgust. "We're going fishing," he grunted. "If he don't like the water why don't he stay on shore?"

So for two miserable hours John Westley sat shuddering in the bow, answering Tom's well-intentioned sallies with a sickly smile, or rising to puke briefly into the lake.

Eventually he reached home, damp, exhausted, without any fish. He asked Mrs. Gillespie to phone Mrs. Nyes, explain his condition, and excuse him.

Thus John missed what should have been his first staff party.

6

The alarm clock on the bedside table cut cruelly into Westley's sleep. Without stirring he opened one bleary eye to identify the intruder. It was still dark. He wrinkled his brow with drunken deliberation, closed the eye, rolled over, relaxed and fell asleep again. The clock, however, knew its duty.

"Brring—Brring—Brrring!"

He suddenly remembered. Saturday morning: six o'clock. Mary was coming! Mary was coming! Mary was coming!

He flung the bed-clothes back, leaped out of bed, fumbled for the switch, stood blinking in the sudden light. Pyjamas off! One, two! Underwear. Pants.

Mary is coming!

He sat down on the edge of the bed to pull on his socks. The socks had shrunk, he had trouble with the heels. Exhausted, he closed his eyes, sank back and lay on the bed, his whole body hungry for its warm comfort. The naked light shone directly on his face, glaring through the skin of his eyelids, flaming orange at him. Get up you damn fool, Mary is coming!

He got up slowly, finished dressing, washed and went downstairs. He had told Mrs. Gillespie he would break-fast downtown with Mary—not to bother. Half an orange lay on a plate at his place. He ate it leisurely—there was lots of time. It was getting light outside. Mrs. Gillespie put out her head, stuck all over with curlers; exposed a part of her white flannel night-gown. Her face had shrunk around the mouth and chin, in the absence of her dentures.

"Everything all right?" she whispered. To look at her one would have thought "everything" referred to some dark conspiracy.

"Yes, thanks," said John. "See you about 9 : 30."

Outside he shivered in the grey autumn dawn, hurried down the steps, along the road and over to the car stop. The east sky lightened. There was no wind and the sky was clear—a star or two still lingered in the west. Down toward the west channel a mist lay over the water, wisping upward along the island shore. Light caught the buildings on the beach, crept among the trees, glowed from the old grey rock of the mountain. The rails at John's feet began to quiver and hum, the red and silver trolley came swinging down as though it rather enjoyed being out on such a fine morning. It ground to a stop, picked him up, and gathered speed again. Two minutes later he got off at Central Ave-nue to change to the Victoria bus.

The bus droned up Central Avenue, turned north up Second, picking up men in overalls with lunch boxes, bound for factories down in Old Kirby. John got off at Second and Park Street, walked two short blocks to the station.

The railway station was a handsome building, bigger than the twin cities required, even for the summer tourist trade. John went into the waiting room, learned at the ticket window that the train was on time, sat down facing the clock. Six minutes more.

Poor Mary! Sleeping in the day coach from one a.m. to six! Lucky this was the end of the line. That should wake her up!

John tried to create the proper mood in himself. Mary is coming! But he failed to tear out the alluring picture of the flung-back sheets, the sweet memory of sleep. If only he could get a little more sleep. Just twenty winks, twenty blinks . . . blenty twinks . .

The train, which was a kind of combination steam tug and trolley, hurtled over water and land—"the ORRrr— i—ENNnnt—ex—PPPrr—ess!" shrieked the whistle. A big shaggy dog with the face of Mr. Grossart came bounding up the aisle, spied John, and jumped on him. John was terrified, but it only licked his nose.

He reached up to rub off the moisture. They were all laughing at him! He opened his eyes, stared sleepily at the girl in front of him. His nose was damp! She was laughing.

"Mary!" He jumped up and wrapped her in his arms. "I don't know how I fell asleep. Darling I just dreamed a big Newfoundland dog licked my nose, did you . . . ?" he laughed sheepishly.

"I am *not* flattered." Mary's eyes shone with happiness. "I had a scare when you weren't on the platform. Then I got mad. So I headed straight for the telephone booth and nearly tripped over you, sound asleep and looking as if you'd stayed up all night waiting for me, you poor thing —and I woke you up with a kiss on the end of your nose!" She laughed again, clasped his arm and hugged it close as he picked up her suitcase and they moved to the door.

"Right across the road is the King George Hotel, and in the hotel is a coffee shop, and in the coffee shop they have coffee—also toast, cheese, marshmallows, frogs' legs, chewing gum, and peanuts."

"Let's have some."

"How many?"

"Peanuts."

"Oh, don't be silly. Coffee, I mean." They went through the revolving door together, almost jamming it with the suitcase, the two of them giggling like a pair of John's first-year pupils. Emerging on the street, Mary took a deep breath and broke into a long yawn.

"Pawdon me," she said. John yawned in sympathy. They looked at each other and burst into laughter.

In the intimacy of a coffee booth for two at the back of the long narrow restaurant, they faced each other, waiting for their order.

Mary had the sweet oval face of an early Flemish madonna, and the same peculiar blend of the spiritual and earthy. She had taken off her fawn-coloured coat and sat before him fresh and desirable in a green dress with white polka dots. The long sleeves revealed only the hands; slim but practical fingers, neatly manicured.

A bracket lamp on the wall beside the booth cast its light softly on her face; warming the hazel eyes, flecking each iris with a subtly refracted gleam of transparent orange; caressing the smooth curves of forehead, cheek, chin, and throat; lingering richly on the quick warm lips, gleaming in the dark brown hair that swept back from the forehead almost to hide the little brown turban nestling on her head.

"I'm hungry!" said Mary.

"Me, too!" and he looked at her, hungrily. Her mouth curved merrily and the eyes smiled.

Grapefruit, cereal, milk and sugar, toast, marmalade, coffee.

"What are we going to do today, darling?"

John heaped another spoonful of flakes into his mouth, munched a minute, then held up his fingers and checked off each item. "First, see the town. That's easy—we'll walk home by way of Central Avenue. Second, see the school. Third, see the boarding-house—that's where we're having lunch. Then we're invited to Angus's place for the afternoon and a meal, after which we take in a show, and finally go to bed." He smiled, their eyes met and pulses quickened. "Mrs. Gillespie has thoughtfully provided a second bedroom on the same floor—Agnes Purcell's. She's gone home for the week end."

"Is it a nice bed?" Mary looked innocently curious.

"No you don't!" John chuckled. "You can't catch me!"

"I'll try," said Mary, dimpling.

"Maybe you have! Come on, let's get going."

Out on First Avenue they linked arms and swung exuberantly down the street, suitcase and all.

They passed a handsome new church.

"That, my love, is the First Baptist Church where the Reverend John Broughton holds forth, and Mr. Smith takes up the collection Sunday mornings."

"Let's go for a nice long walk tomorrow," said Mary.

"McAdams Falls, with a light lunch prepared and packed by the capable hands of Mrs. Gillespie!"

"Swell!" said Mary.

It was nearly nine as they reached Central Avenue. They paused at the corner while John pointed out the Bank of Commerce building, Simpson's, the Medical Arts building, and Ed's Cigar Store.

"Hello, Mr. Westley!" A boy went by on a bicycle, waving.

"Someone knows you, John," she blew a kiss gaily after him. "Bless his little heart, saying 'Hello Mr. Westley!' What's the matter?"

"If you do a thing like that again," John warned, every inch a school teacher, "I'll take you in my arms right here on Central Avenue and kiss the living daylights out of you!"

"Please, Mr. Westley, stop—you're squeezing my arm."

He squeezed it harder.

"Squeeze it again, John," she murmured.

Down through the shadows of the subway and out into the light.

"The bridge! The island! The bay! Oh, John, I never dreamed it would be so beautiful—why didn't you tell me? We could *live* in this town!"

"I'll build you a beautiful home in the island right under the mountain and we'll breed a sturdy race of islanders—or mountaineers, whichever you prefer. In the meantime we'll rent a house right beside the railway track and save our pennies for twenty-five years."

"It can't be so expensive to build on the island. Angus has a house there, hasn't he?"

"Yes, but he bought his property away back, when the only use most Kirbians made of that end of the island was for blueberry picking. They used to run a ferry from Old Kirby to the beach. Then they built the bridge and people got the idea it might be nice to live there. First the millionaires, now the well-to-do. It's not for mere teachers. Angus is the only teacher on the island."

"What about Mr. Nyes?"

"Mr. Nyes is a high school principal and that's the social equivalent of a doctor with an established practice, a bank manager, or the pastor of a big church. *Your* boy friend is just a teacher. A high school teacher gets about the same pay as a small grocer, a service station proprietor, a good bricklayer, a shop foreman, or a lake captain."

"Loafs all summer, quits work at four o'clock with Saturdays off, ten days at Christmas, and a week at Easter," commented Mary.

"Stays up till two every morning preparing lessons, marking exercises; spends his Christmas and Easter holidays marking papers, half his summers marking more papers, and the other half taking courses," countered John.

"Has nothing to do all day but lean back in his chair with his feet on his desk and ask nasty questions."

"Which his pupils are too dumb to answer so he has to keep them in till five o'clock and gets home late for supper."

"And a good thing, too, because he spends an hour and a half gorging himself at noon."

"All right, darling, you win—go marry a stock broker."

"But a stock broker has no time to spend on his wife."

"No time, lots of money." They laughed. "Look!" said

John. "There's what Angus calls 'the argument'." They were almost opposite the school.

"John, don't let it!"

"Don't let what what?"

"Don't you see, darling—the old school is frightened stiff—staring out at the lake, with all those glassy eyes, standing very still and pretending not to see."

"Not to see what?"

"The new school, of course. Can't you see the way it's crouching half around the poor old hen of an old school, just waiting to gobble it up?"

John laughed.

Mary's lips curved to the tribute. "Which of the glass eyes do you teach behind, darling?"

"Southwest corner, second floor, old school—see, the one with only one blind down. I'm the bane of Miss Hodges's life—always pulling the blinds up to let the light in. To Miss Hodges—she's the janitor's assistant—blinds are just for decoration. They must be pulled down exactly halfway all round the school, upstairs and downstairs."

"Well, if I were Miss Hodges I'd report you," said Mary. The cliff moved out to meet them. Mary looked up at the steep hillside. "Is that a piece of your pegmatite sticking out of the dirt up there?" she asked.

"Dolomite," corrected John and went into a learned dissertation which lasted up to the top step of Mrs. Gillespie's veranda.

John yanked the bell-pull lustily just to show Mary how it worked, flung both doors open, and bowed her in with a flourish.

Mrs. Gillespie came into the front hall, wiping flour off her hands. "So you're Miss Miller! We're real glad to see you. Why, you look fresh as a daisy, and on the train all night like that too! Here, I got a cup of tea ready for you thinking you'd be dead on your feet."

"I don't think—" John began.

"Why, I'd just love a cup of tea," said Mary.

"Well, Mr. Westley will show you your room. It's Miss Purcell's—she's away for the week end. It isn't just as nice as I'd—".

"I'm sure it will be lovely, Mrs. Gillespie."

Mrs. Gillespie hesitated as though wanting to say something confidential.

"Will you take the bag up, John?" asked Mary. John started up the stairs, while Mrs. Gillespie whispered in Mary's ear.

Upstairs John opened the door, showed Mary in, laid the suitcase on the bed, and took Mary in his arms. There was a long silence. She gently pushed him away, repented, and they kissed again.

"We'd better go down," she said with a kind of sighing breathlessness.

"What's this mystery between you and Mrs. Gillespie?" he demanded.

Mary giggled. She put her lips to his ear. "She told me where the bathroom was!" she whispered.

They came downstairs laughing, and into the dining room where Mrs. Gillespie had the table laid for a full course meal.

"Why, Mrs. Gillespie, this is wonderful! We ate at the station but after our long walk and all that crisp air I could eat a horse!"

They sat, ate, drank tea, and talked. Mary and John carried the dishes into the kitchen over Mrs. Gillespie's protests.

Upstairs again they went into John's room, carefully leaving the door open to observe the unwritten law of all boarding-houses. Mary looked doubtfully at the curtains, the iron bedstead, the shabby furniture, the pictures on the walls.

"It's not bad, for seven dollars a week, is it?" said John, almost with pride.

Shortly after lunch Angus phoned to say he would be over in an hour to pick them up, and did exactly that.

Since their one evening together a month ago, John had seen his friend only briefly on occasions at the school. He had been away every week end but this, and already the Dramatic Club had taken over all the time he could spare from lesson preparation. Besides there was that slight coolness between them over J. C.—all the more felt because the topic was avoided when they were together, consciously on John's part at least.

But now they were together again with the warmth of Mary between, the west wind scattering the fallen leaves gaily over the road, the sun shining warmly in the crisp autumn air, while clouds sailed overhead under a clean blue sky and the whole afternoon lay clear before them.

Mary and Angus liked each other at once, as John had felt they would. Angus had apologized for the ancient make of his car and Mary had agreed that he certainly should, proposing that they all get out, push the car down the embankment into the lake, and call a taxi. There's something so damned understanding about my girl, John told himself, reaching over to press her hand. There was some nonsense, too, about the gear shift and its proximity to Mary's knees that had them all laughing again before the car had gone a hundred yards.

Around the Crescent they rolled, Angus making his characteristic light sallies about the wealth of the islanders and their high respectability. Mary took back her first reaction to the car saying that she now felt sorry for it, it looked so self-conscious in this neighbourhood; and Angus gallantly responded that while he had noticed the self-consciousness, it was due to the fact that it was carrying a beautiful woman and feeling particularly high hat about it. So they came to the little weather-beaten garage at the end of the dirt road in high good humour.

"What a lovely place to live!" Mary paused at the top of the second steps in the zigzag climb to the house, and looked around. A tangle of birch, jack pine, poplar, and brush hid the lake to the west, but already they were on a level with the house roofs on the Crescent and could see the escarpment and buildings of West Kirby over the tree-tops to the east.

"You haven't seen anything yet," said Angus, coming up behind. "Instead of following the walk at the next turn, take the path there and I'll show you something worthwhile."

The path wound briefly through the bush, then out on a hog-backed ridge of outcrop, grey with lichen that crunched underfoot.

"The lake!" cried Mary, and they stood together, looking.

"Water, just water!" said Angus chuckling.

"But so much of it!"

72

There was a lot of water. It stretched to the horizon: west, and north, and south; darkening under cloud shadows and squalls, brightening again into a host of blues and greens, scattered over with the glitter of sunlight and the creamy white crests of the white-caps. A thousand miles of birch and balsam, spruce and muskeg, were in the sweet wild smell of the lusty north-west wind as it swept over Lake Huron, from the wide forests, myriad lakes and grey rocks north of Georgian Bay and Lake Superior, from the far reaches of Patricia and Northern Manitoba, from the west shores of Hudson Bay; as it tore white patches out of the silent clouds against the eternal blue, and whipped the clothes of the three little spectators about them.

Mary flung out her arms as if to embrace the wind, "I love you, I love you, I love you!" she cried.

"Just a minute," shouted John, "what about me?"

They all broke out laughing.

"I'll show you something else!" Angus looked flushed and boyish. "Come down this way, but watch your step." They followed another faint trail down the ledges, around a flat bit of swampy ground, over another outcrop, obliquely down towards the water through a little gully thickly overgrown with bushes and saplings. They could see the white spray and hear the roar before they emerged on a ledge twenty feet above the water. Out on the ledge the sun-spattered spray was dazzling white; the thunder of breaking waves was deafening.

John and Mary stood silent, unconsciously holding hands, Angus behind them. The roar of the waves surrounded them like a wall, made them feel that this primitive spectacle was a private performance held for their benefit. It was the fluid versus the solid, the irresistible force meeting the immovable object, the contradiction of life and death. The rock trembled, and was firm; the water smashed itself into a thousand drops and was whole again, drawing away in creamy green concave curves, to sweep in mightily again, and again, and again. The water was restless, changing, thrusting up, sucking down, eddying, surging blindly here and there, deep and liquid, shallow and vaporous, gurgling, roaring, pattering, fierce, gentle— everything opposite to that grim, black, sullen rock that crouched, waited motionless, silent, enduring forever, sinister, deep as earth itself, dark within, and pressing down, always down, with the weight of billions of tons: compact, hard, immovable.

The sun gave the savage scene the gaiety of a spectacle, the unreality of technicolor; warming the slicks of white foam and glistening black rock, rainbowing the spray.

They walked and climbed back to the first view, followed another path that led them to a side entrance of the house, and went in through Angus's den to the living room. Angus called his wife.

"Vera! They're here."

Mrs. Macdonald welcomed them warmly, and she led Mary off at once to comb her hair, which the wind had arranged in loose curls and tendrils.

Left alone, Angus said casually, "Feel like a glass of beer?"

"Sure," said John. "I think Mary would go for one, too."

Angus paused, reddened. "I hadn't thought of that," he said. "I don't make distinctions myself, but Vera would be scandalized. I'm sorry," he said awkwardly. "Vera's a bit conventional about smoking and drinking—she's lived in West Kirby all her life. You know the sort of thing; men may dissipate their lives away, but women must keep their ideals pure. We can be men, but Mary must be a lady. I should have mentioned it before."

"It's all right—I'll give Mary the N.D.S. sign. She doesn't mind me smoking where she can't, but we'd better forget the beer." They sat down, John in the chesterfield, one of those stiff-springed, tight-cushioned, undersized pieces, sold by the better furniture stores in the middle twenties.

"N.D.S." said Angus, thoughtfully. "Neuro-dynamic surgery?"

"No Drinking or Smoking," explained John. "By the way, what about teachers and N.D.S.?"

"Smoking is accepted—male teachers only of course, and preferably a pipe. Cigars are not taboo, but somehow they are one thing teachers never seem to smoke. Sipping cocktails is very high class—too high class for teachers. Hard liquor may be tasted if the situation leaves no alternative, but never, never tossed off with relish. Beer, of course, has somewhat unprofessional associations. Wine on the other hand is perfectly respectable if taken with cake at a wedding or funeral. And it just wouldn't do to be seen going into or coming out of the beer, liquor, or wine stores. In other words"—they heard Mary and Mrs. Macdonald on the stairs—"a good teacher leaves the stuff alone."

The two women entered the room. They were of the same height, and there was less difference apparent in their ages than in the case of the men. If Angus was obviously twenty years older than John, his wife might have been only six or eight years older than Mary. It was not merely that her complexion was ruddy and her red hair without a trace of grey; but there was something youthful, almost childish about her manner, the inflections of her voice, even in her figure.

They discussed the beautiful autumn weather, the cities of West Kirby and Old Kirby, the new bridge, the bay, and the island. John and Mary learned that in the days before the bridge it had been a struggle to keep contact with the mainland. Originally this had been a summer home only, and they had rented a house on the mainland; but year by year Angus improved the cottage and they found themselves staying later in the fall, coming out earlier in the spring, until they finally decided to try a winter.

"I'll bet it gets cold here in the winter," said John.

"Brrr!" laughed Mrs. Macdonald, "it makes me shiver just to think of it. It's not so bad now with the new bridge and the beach radial, and the roads and everything, but honestly there were times I thought I would go *crazy*. Do you know that one winter I didn't see Mom and Dad for five weeks?"

The big problem in winter had been getting to school. Angus would start off at seven in the morning on snow-shoes, breaking a new trail after every fresh fall of snow, down the south end of the island over the bar to the main-land, and along the then little-travelled Lakeshore Road. In the warm weather he used the ferry from the beach over to Old Kirby. When they dug the west channel he had trouble during the fall freeze-ups and spring thaws, solved by making himself a small flat-bottomed boat, which he would push over the ice into the open water, paddle across the channel, ram the bow up on the ice and pull to shore.

"And he was never once late in all those years!" boasted Mrs. Macdonald.

"No, I was never late till after they built the bridge and I bought a car. Went out at eight-thirty one morning and the radiator was frozen solid. I've always said that if you want to get somewhere for sure use your own two legs."

During the conversation John studied Angus with a newly critical eye. As they talked, Angus turned from one speaker to another giving a three-dimensional quality to John's impression.

It was a good head, no doubt about that—a neat compact skull, nicely balanced on the neck in a way that gave an Egyptian quality in his profile. There was a distinguished bearing to the head, in the thrust of the jawline rather than the chin, in the neatly turned curve of the back of the skull, neither too full nor too flat, in the parallel lines of forehead, nose, upper lip, and jaw, which gave a thrust to the whole face—keen, intelligent, without any trace of aggressiveness.

And yet there was a subtle air of indecision about the face, as though the intelligence analysed life so penetratingly that the will had no bias to give it force. The eyes were quick, keen, and dark, with a hint of temper in them, and a nervous habit of quick side-glances that John had never noticed before; not furtive, but evasive, certainly— as though certain thoughts went on behind that finely modelled forehead which were reserved to their owner; not for display even to friends. The grizzled, close-cut, grey hair swept back on either side of a widow's peak, as if to allow more light and air through to the quick brain beneath; the ears were small, lay close to the head with a faunish suggestion of pointedness to the upper angle. His smile was slow, twisted perhaps, but with ironical humour.

not cynicism. He spoke crisply with the diction of a teacher; when thoughtful the line deepened in the centre of his brow. No, thought John, he's a friend to be proud of—but just the same I don't know him nearly as well as I thought I did.

At five Mrs. Macdonald excused herself to get dinner. Mary wanted to help and was smilingly but firmly dissuaded. They spent the hour till dinner in Angus's den.

"What lovely colour!" Mary exclaimed as Dorothy Young's painting caught her eye. She looked around, then turned inquiringly to John. "This isn't the one you mentioned in your letter is it?"

Angus smiled wickedly. "So he couldn't resist a dig at it, eh? Well, few people can—that's one reason why I hung it."

John looked squelched. "I honestly can't see a thing in it," he said. "What's it called anyway?"

"A good question, and the answer is even better: 'Sunday morning'!"

John looked at the picture in bewilderment. "But it doesn't make sense. Where's Sunday? Where's the morning?"

"I think John will have to teach a few more years before he gets the point," said Mary.

Angus lifted his eyebrows in tribute. "Do you know," he told her, "I think you're rather bright."

Mary blushed with pleasure. John was getting surly: this was all over his head.

"Oh, John," she looked repentant—"we're being mean. It's just that you're looking for a scene or figures, and this is a mood in paint—like music. It's the way she *feels* on Sunday morning."

"Well, why doesn't somebody tell me these things?" John looked so boyishly plaintive that they all began laughing and harmony was restored.

They ate in the little dining room, remaining to talk over the table after they had eaten. The conversation swung around to the school, and inevitably to J. C. Bilbeau.

"Angus, what *is* this Bilbeau person like? John's letters are so funny—you've no idea the sales talks he's been giving me, almost as if he were trying to convince himself."

"Well," said Angus glancing quizzically at John, "in my opinion Bilbeau is the perfect example of the kind of man that gets ahead. I think even Vera would agree with that."

They turned to Mrs. Macdonald who flushed with annoyance. "Really, Angus," she said, "your sense of humour —" She forced a brief smile. "Mr. Bilbeau is the one topic on which we disagree. I think he's wonderful. He's been Superintendent of our Sunday School now for three years; and if you could see the way he has built it up—why, next to First Baptist, All Saints has the largest Sunday School in the city. Our membership is nearly four hundred: and the way church attendance has jumped—do you know, since he started giving prizes for going to church there are thirty-two scholars in the Junior Department alone with a perfect record?"

Angus smiled wryly. "You see, we really do agree."

"I'm not so sure Mrs. Macdonald isn't right," said John. "I certainly can't see anything funny about J. C."

Mary was hugging a smile to herself. Angus turned inquiringly to her. "You haven't met our hero?" he asked.

"No, but I feel as if I had. Only the picture I have of him is so confusing. He's as big as a house, he has a face like the angel Gabriel—only he's bald—he has a big

79

bag of wind instead of a tummy, and since John is sure he'll be the next principal, I'm sure he must have big flat feet! And—oh, yes! Whenever he opens his mouth he can pull out ribbons and ribbons of bee-yootiful sentences!"

Mary's air of bewilderment was so genuine they all began laughing, as Angus murmured, "You're positively psychic."

Mrs. Macdonald again refused to let Mary into the kitchen, declaring the dishes could wait; so the four made small talk in the living room until eight when John suggested they would be late for the show unless they left. Angus offered to drive them but they wanted to walk. He accompanied them around the Crescent, leaving them at the corner of Spruce Drive.

"I feel awfully sorry for Angus," said Mary.

"For Angus? Why?"

"He's so lonely!" said Mary.

"Yes, I suppose so. I never really thought of it before. You know it struck me as being queer that they never mentioned their boy—the one that died."

"Vera was talking to me upstairs. She said Angus has been different ever since their boy—they called him David —was drowned. Angus has never mentioned him since. But what really seems to bother her is that he doesn't go to church." She smiled mischievously. "Wouldn't it be lovely to see Angus in black cutaway, wing collar, and grey striped trousers, solemnly walking up the aisle with a collection plate? John, they're so different!

"There was a picture in Vera's room of David taken in his first long pants the day he started high school—such a cute little boy with curly hair."

"You'd think Angus would have had her put the picture away."

"Oh, they have separate bedrooms."

"You know," said John, "now I think of it, I can't imagine them sleeping together. It's not that she's not attractive or that he's not human. It's just that they don't seem to belong in the same room." His mind suddenly flashed back to the rooms. "Why, they have separate rooms downstairs, too. The living room is Mrs. Macdonald's and the den is Angus's!"

Mary was smiling.

"What's so funny?"

"Oh, men. Just men."

"What about just men?"

"They make such startling discoveries of something that's been staring them right in the face for weeks."

"Well, if you noticed it"—his voice was huffy—"why didn't you mention it?"

"Darling, it's so obvious."

"I haven't your woman's intuition. I've got to figure these things out."

"Oh, you poor old plodding mathematical scientist!" She hugged his arm. "Never mind darling, you're honest, and you are *much* cleverer than I at nearly everything— and I love you! Don't be cross at me, darling."

They were halfway down the deserted drive. It was dark and there was only the sighing of the wind in the pines around them. Mary looked up and the curve of her throat gleamed through the darkness. John crushed her fiercely to him, his heart pounding, knees trembling.

"Mary! Mary! Mary!"—he whispered passionately, thrusting his tense mouth against the warm-blooded willing lips. They parted a little and looked at each other, a mutual question in their eyes. John's body felt her warmth burning through his clothes.

"There isn't any key for my door," she whispered.

"I know." They embraced again till the distant clicking of leather heels on the sidewalk reminded them they were not alone.

Sunday morning was bright and clear; warmer and windless, though the chill of early October remained in the air where the shadows lurked.

Frank Jarratt shared the breakfast table with them, freshly shaved and looking very neat in a dark Oxford-grey suit. Oblivious to Mary's brown leather jacket and sport skirt and to John's plaid windbreaker, he inquired as to the church they planned to attend, and came out with, "Naughty, naughty, you won't go to heaven when you die," on learning they had other plans.

Mrs. Gillespie made up two lunches to eat at the falls. Gaily, they raced down the steps to the street and strode hand in hand northward along the path to the first car stop.

"Isn't everything perfect? The weather—and even the way the car came along just when we wanted it?" They bounced and swayed with the trolley, bound for Old Kirby. There were half a dozen other people in the car, obviously bound for church.

John scanned them with relief. No one he knew, and they weren't likely to meet anyone in Old Kirby. Jarratt's breakfast query bothered him more than he liked to admit. Can't a teacher live his own life outside of school? he asked himself angrily. Mary squeezed his hand, turning a face that said everything before the words came.

"I love you when you frown, John. You look almost intelligent!" His face relaxed. He breathed happily, and returned the pressure with such vigour she gave a little squeal and caused an elderly woman in black diagonally ahead to turn her head towards them coldly. The car jolted down King Street, picking up groups of two and three on the way, around the corner at Queen, eastward toward Victoria Street, where John and Mary jumped off, leaving the trolley to continue its climb up the hill toward Third Avenue and West Kirby.

It was simple enough getting to McAdams Falls. One simply kept the river in sight and zigzagged along the nearest roads. The erudite geologist John Westley aired his theories of erosion, made learned estimates of the valley's age as they wandered on. Occasionally they found that the road ended in a pasture or a farmhouse. They crossed fields and climbed fences to pick up the next one, arguing as to which way to turn. Finally they saw a big weather-beaten building through the trees, heard the sound of falling water, dipped down a little slope and were there.

The Falls were disappointing. The cliff was high enough —a full sixty feet—but the water came over in a thin sheet, and sprayed rather than fell down the face of the cliff. John was doubly disappointed for it was impossible without a rope to examine the rock strata exposed in the steep banks below.

"Let's walk around and see if we can get a look at it from downstream," he suggested.

They found a path on the other side that led them down by long easy slopes to the bed of the canyon. They passed through a gap in the trees out into the sunlight and stood at a point where they could see a part of the old mill around the talus slope of the cliff to the right. They picked their way over the boulders to the water, which was so low it gurgled between, as much as over, the rocks. Higher up they found a big bleached log of driftwood for a bridge and crossed to the wider ledge on the opposite side.

The Falls were more impressive now, but less so than the old mill, the foundation timbers of which reached almost to the base of the cliff.

"That mill is about ninety years old," declared John, guessing. "If old McAdam hadn't decided to locate on this stream, West Kirby might never have existed."

"And we should never have stood here looking at it!" said Mary solemnly. They laughed, holding hands.

"I'll race you back to the log," said Mary, suddenly turning and dancing from boulder to boulder, now this way, now that. John took up the challenge, overtook and passed her. At the log he turned triumphant. Mary was leaning weakly against a big rock, holding her arm. Her face was white. Back at her side, panicky, he asked her what was wrong. She couldn't answer. He looked at the elbow she was holding. "My elbow—I slipped—I feel sick."

"But it looks all right!" Relieved, he felt the bone. "You'll be okeh in a minute." He took her other arm, leading her carefully over the rocks, enjoying a little—even as he sympathized—the physical superiority of his sex. "It's all right, you must have hit the nerve. No bones broken!"

They had been so absorbed in the accident that they missed the approach of a slight middle-aged woman, a handkerchief turban-wise around her bobbed hair, a painting brush and rag in one hand and a matter-of-factness about her clothes and figure, that made even her unexpected appearance seem casual.

"Miss Young!" from John.

"That's right." She smiled.

"This is my—" John always hesitated at the stilted word —"my fiancée, Miss Miller."

"You're the artist, aren't you?" asked Mary, looking at her with approval.

"Whom I mistook in the hall at school for an art teacher —" added John, apologetically.

"Now that we've got everything important straight, how's the arm?" asked Miss Young.

"Better, thanks. I fell on the rock and hit a nerve or something in my elbow. Are you out sketching?"

"That's right."

"Could we see what you're doing?" asked John.

"Of course." She spoke directly, without any creative coyness, and led the way downstream to where a wooden box with the lid open stood on brass legs among the stones. A folding stool lay collapsed beside it.

"Your stool had a worse shock than I," exclaimed Mary, with her habit of reading emotions into inanimate things. She went around to look at the painting, followed by John. It was a little study of rocks and water—they saw the subject beyond, recognized the warm moss-greens, and reddish-brown of the weathered slimy wet rocks, the glints of blue from the sky, the transparent amber of the water flowing over the sunlit gravel bed. John saw a lot of other colours in the sketch that were missing in the subject. He wondered why anyone would pick this subject instead of the falls or the mill. Mary said, "Your colours are lovely. We saw a painting of yours over at Angus Macdonald's yesterday. We liked that too."

Honest John amended: "To be honest I didn't understand what you were driving at till Mary explained, and even then I didn't really get the point—about the title, I mean—till I met you here. Sunday morning for me used to mean being dragged to church to listen to dry sermons when I was a youngster, but I can see how those colours— maybe the lines too" (he hadn't thought of them till now) "say how you feel on a day like this."

Miss Young smiled warmly.

"It seems to me you are an unusually understanding couple. Did you happen to bring your lunch?"

They had, and soon they were munching sandwiches together with the relish of children at a picnic.

Dot, as she insisted they address her, talked about painting as though nothing else existed in the world, until Mary mentioned her part-time work at the Settlement in Toronto.

Dot had spent a few weeks of one summer teaching the children's art classes at the Grange, and had looked in occasionally at the Settlement.

"I couldn't have been there when you did—John will tell you my memory for people I meet casually is amazing," and she laughed at her own flattery. "Do you remember anyone who was there?"

"That was years ago," Dot remarked dryly. "But I do know Miss Mithers—you might have run across her there."

Mary's eyes lit with excitement at having found a common acquaintance. "You know her?" she asked incredulously, and added impulsively with a merry lilt to her voice, "Isn't she a scream? Or maybe—" she sobered as much as she could—"maybe you like her!"

Dot's slow smile almost gave John a picture of Miss Mithers.

"Miss Mithers dithers we used to say behind her back,"

Mary confessed, the irrepressible laughter in her eyes breaking out in girlish curves about her lips and cheeks, so it was all John could do to stop himself from kissing them before Dot's very eyes.

"Fat, fussy, and forty," said Dot, hastily adding, "I'm scarcely the one to mention her age—I'm in the fifties myself," and she smiled at John's unbelieving stare.

After they had eaten, Dot startled them by taking a worn metal cigarette case out of her coat pocket and offering them cigarettes.

"I know female teachers don't smoke!" she answered the question in John's eyes. Disconcerted, he began to protest. Dot anticipated him. "I've found that an artist gets away with a good deal that's not forgiven in a normal person. It's really very handy, being thought queer!" she smiled.

"But *why* can't a teacher be human?" protested John.

"Why can't a minister, or a politician? It's the nature of the beast. But let's steer clear of shop. One reason I paint is to get somewhere where I'm surrounded by *real* things and have a chance to forget about unreal people and the artificial situations they create."

A little later she excused herself—there was another subject nearby she had been saving for just such an afternoon as this, and the sun was good for little better than an hour.

They looked up through the trees to the west. A bank of cirrus clouds was wisping up into the sky. The treetops swayed a little.

"You're right," said John, not missing the chance to display his store of knowledge. "That's a low pressure area coming up, looks like the beginnings of an east wind too."

They parted, promising to see more of each other.

On the way home John and Mary were quiet, remembering their week end together and how soon it would be over.

Back to Mrs. Gillespie's, and early supper, a taxi to the train. A brief discreet kiss at the station, the Hshsh—Hshsh—Sh—Sh—of the train gathering speed, hooting its lonely call into the evening, shrinking into the distance and out of sight.

7

John Westley was beginning to have a little trouble with discipline. The serene confidence of the first two weeks had been more and more dissipated by the conspiracy of events thereafter.

First there was that smart-aleck in the library with his infuriating smile and "Yes, Mr. Westley." Their relationship had now reached the stage where John ignored him—as far as possible—but wherever he went in the room that maddening smile seemed to follow him. It spread too, or seemed to. Now whenever *anyone* smiled, John read the same mockery into the smile; and spoke sharply at the smiler, which brought about more smiles. With the smiles, the conversation became more general, less furtive. It was a frustrating experience to squelch unruliness here, only to have it break out around and behind. The library period was becoming a nightmare—and was producing nightmares in John's sleeping-hours. He would wake up at night after ineffectually trying to pound that smiling head against the wall or floor; always his pounding was weak, his arms nerveless. Or he would be punching at a smiling face, and pulling the punch in spite of himself, so that a blow begun with all the strength of his body behind it became a feeble push.

And his second year class was really worse, at least where noise was concerned. He found himself saying, "Please shut that door!" in an unnecessarily harsh voice whenever a student left it open, fearful that the noise would pass into the hall and invite a visit from the principal passing on his rounds. Every night after four his room would be half filled with detainees, who weren't much better then than during class.

He had them write 'I must not talk in class' five hundred times, he had them copying whole pages from the dictionary, he made them sit with folded hands for half an hour. He lectured them in brotherly fashion, in fatherly fashion; or earnestly implored them to be better, threatened them with double detentions, triple detentions, a week's detention; appealed to their better natures, made insulting references to their home environments; spoke sarcastically, angrily, in soft ominous words; bellowed like a bull. Everything new that he tried seemed to be a solution, but quickly lost its effectiveness.

To make matters worse he had agreed to spend two afternoons with the Dramatic Club after four and that promised to develop into a daily affair. The club wanted to put on a play, they wanted Mr. Westley to find one for them, they wanted Mr. Westley to direct the play, they came to ask Mr. Westley about stage properties, whether they couldn't have make-up this next time, and so on.

John skimmed through all the classics and made six half-hour selections drawn from as many periods of drama; a miracle play, Shakespeare, Molière, Goldsmith, Goethe, Eugene O'Neill. The club decided to put on two plays before Christmas and four after.

He found himself dismissing detained students early so as to find time for tryouts, rehearsals. He gave them punishment exercises to do at home, hand in before nine in the morning; and forgot to check the next day.

Even the first year classes were getting restless. 1C, his own form, in particular. In algebra he could keep them busy, but English was different.

"The Daffodils." The Goddamned daffodils.

"I wandered lonely as a cloud."

Teacher: "How can a cloud be lonely?"

Answer: "If it's the only one in the sky it's lonely." (Laughter—especially one or two lingering 'haw, haws' that get under John's skin.)

Teacher: "Why does the poet shift from the word 'crowd' to the word 'host'?"

No answer. One hand rises. A little girl gets up, shy, confused.

"Well?" encouragingly, reassuringly, nursing the one little answer.

Silence. The girl is blushing, looking at her feet.

"Come on!" a hint of impatience in spite of himself.

"I forget what I was going to say." Roars of laughter. He smiles to placate the class, and boils with anger at their callousness.

With reading now, it wasn't so bad. They liked reading. And they listened, till John picked a weak reader. Then the talking began. He would look for someone who was inattentive, and ask him to read. The student wouldn't be able to find the place.

"Detention!"

"Come in at four!"

"See me here at four o'clock!"

"I'd like to have a talk with you after four!"

"If you can't do your work in class you'll have to do it after four!"

"Detention! Stay in! You'll have to stay in! I'm sorry you'll have to come in after four!"

And there was the seat-shifting solution.

Bill and Ed were cronies. Put one at the front, the other at the back. Fine—for two periods. Then Bill in the front is resentful, goes out of his way to make trouble. Ed is too far back—develops new cronies. The infection spreads.

There was, of course, the balm of 4A. They were all good students, or at worst a fair average; all had good working habits. And John liked physics. He would console himself with, next period I have my physics class, or, never mind, tomorrow I have 4A again.

But John's relations with the students were happiest in the Dramatic Club.

He had been quite impressed by the first meeting. For a group of adolescents it seemed to him they conducted things with a sophistication many older groups could well have copied. It was not merely that the minutes, nominations for a new executive, and other routine, were handled smoothly; but when the president threw the meeting open for a discussion of the year's programme there were a dozen students up on their feet to make suggestions and discuss them.

The president, Grace Morley, spoke logically, briefly, and always to good purpose. A slender dark youth, Jerry Dorland, who rose frequently from the floor to make or attack a point, also attracted John's eye. He seemed to be popular, even with the sprinkling of boys present.

It was annoying to find three girls to every boy, though John, on reflection, knew why. Acting was a bit sissy. Every red-blooded boy in the school was out to make the school rugby team, Junior or Senior. To be rehearsing for a play when he might have been practising for a football game would have been an act of treason for any able-bodied W.K.C.I. boy.

A week later the new executive got together and invited John to sit in. J. C. had dropped in quietly at noon one day to ask him whether he would take over the Dramatic Club. So at the executive meeting it was Mr. Westley this and Mr. Westley that, and Sir the other thing. John had suggested his historical sequence of dramatic selections, which they accepted enthusiastically.

The Literary Society met on alternate weeks in the assembly hall for a programme that lasted from three to four-thirty. Musical solos, orchestra and Glee Club, recitations of poetry, and reading of a bi-weekly edition of the school magazine, plus a fifteen minute skit, had comprised the usual programme; occasionally varied by cutting down on the poetry and music to produce a half-hour play. The cream of the fall term programme was skimmed to be served in one large pitcher of rich nourishment called 'The Christmas Concert'. In March a three-act play was produced which ran for three nights. 'Commencement' came in May.

So with his Nativity play chosen, and a Falstaff scene selected from King Henry IV, John turned to casting. He decided to discover at once the best dramatic material available in the Club and proceeded to try out everyone in it for general ability. His tests occupied one long meeting of the Club: everyone had to walk up on the stage, strike a pose of his own composition to interpret the idea of despair, repeat the words "Darling, darling, you are asking the impossible!" with appropriate feeling, and make a graceful exit. The Club loved it, rocking with laughter at one little first year girl who stood centre stage, raised both hands in a formal attitude of surrender to indicate despair, repeating the words in a low monotone, and scuttling offstage like a thin little rabbit; and at the slim dark lad, Jerry Dorland, who caricatured the whole thing with abandon.

Rehearsals were happy affairs. There was of course the irritating business of players who got detentions and didn't show up, but on such occasions John stepped into the breach and would read as many as three different parts to keep things going, even affecting a soprano voice to fill a female part, which delighted his students hugely. At university he had never played more than a few minor parts, but here he was the Director. Normally rather quiet and self-conscious in the presence of adults, he found release among these adolescents. Rehearsals were fun.

There was the excitement, too, of discovery.

A week after the original tryouts a country student in third year, a rather plain looking girl with a broad face and sullen mouth had come to him and asked to be in a play. Skeptically, he had told her to turn up with some other late applicants for her tryout. The minute she stepped on the stage to try John's standard test he knew she was a find. The idea of despair cried out of every line of her body as she stood there, hands limp, eyes stony, head and shoulders turned slightly aside—as though there had been one little hope after all the others had gone, which the body had moved slowly towards, only to have the mind, already dismayed, reject it. Her inflections were almost a repetition of the first year girl's monotone, but it was an effortless melancholy quietness that rang bells in Westley's brain.

"What is your name again?" He had forgotten it.

"Elsie Braund. I'm afraid I'm not much good."

"Not good?" John was about to burst into protest, but saw something in her eyes that humbled him. "Don't worry," he said, "you're good enough for a start."

Later he learned that none of the staff had been impressed with her academic worth. He mentioned her to J. C. who had said: "A peculiar girl. Her spelling is atrocious. I can't understand how these continuation schools encourage such students to go on." When John mentioned her casually to Starling, the stocky little chemistry teacher, the reaction was startling. "In all my twenty years of teaching I've never taught anyone so—" he groped in his dusty bin of unpleasant adjectives, coming up with the worst—"so *darn* irritating. Just *sits* there with that darned sour face looking out the window as if I didn't exist. And stubborn? I can't do a thing with her—can't do a thing."

But can't you see?—John had wanted to say. Only there was no one to listen. Not even Mary. For she wrote back: "Darling, I have a feeling that little hussy in the Dramatic Club, for all your talk about her homely face, will bear watching." But it was exciting. He would put her on the stage and show them all.

By the end of October John's daily routine was established. On an average day he got up at a quarter to eight, finished breakfast about eight-thirty and walked to school, usually with Frank Jarratt, arriving at twenty to nine. Like most of the staff John visited the office to check his mail box before going to his room. Nyes's office door was invariably open to reveal a side glimpse of him working at his desk. Miss Jamieson, the secretary, sat at her typewriter tapping a pencil absent-mindedly, as though impatient for nine o'clock to come so the office would empty and she could get down to work. She always smiled at him as though he reminded her of a little lost brother of hers who had been run over by a car. So convinced had he become of this that one morning he asked impulsively: "Did you have any brothers?"

"No, why?" The question was as unexpected to her as the answer to him.

"Oh," he blushed. "There's something about your face that reminds me of—" he improvised desperately "—a boy —a young fellow called Jamieson I met at college. Thought there was just a chance he might be your brother —you know—a small world and all that sort of thing!"

"No, my folks decided one like me was enough," she dismissed him with a busy smile.

From the office he would walk down past Angus's lab— where he sometimes paused for a word—and on to climb the creaky old stairs of the old school and turn left into the men teacher's room; thence to unlock his own door, let the waiting students enter, and go in himself. Then it was a matter of writing homework exercises on the blackboard, interviewing students about this and that, or dashing out to see Mr. Smith, or Angus, or J. C. about some departmental detail.

At eight fifty-five a warning bell rang, the room quickly filled up. At nine the second bell rang. Then John called the class to order, checked the attendance from his seating plan, filled in the attendance slips, and led the class in a recitation of the Lord's Prayer, unless there was to be an assembly.

The afternoon was like the morning except that at two minutes to four his home form returned for a final check on attendance, and was dismissed at four. Then came detentions, rehearsals or meetings of one sort or another, so that it was usually five, often closer to six, before he got home.

Supper at six; the news over the radio at six-thirty followed by *Amos 'n' Andy*, a programme John could not have missed without isolating himself culturally from his fellow-boarders. Actually he enjoyed it.

Seven-thirty to ten he spent as a rule preparing lessons, checking exercises, occasionally reading. After that there was social activity under the Gillespie roof; visiting with, or being visited by, Frank. Occasionally Agnes Purcell would drop in, often with Margaret Brewin, the girls' P.T. Instructor. Once or twice a week Mrs. Gillespie lured them down for a cup of tea and some of her jaw-breaking cookies.

Some time between eleven and twelve, John would go to bed.

At seven o'clock in the evening of the second Monday in November John was called to the phone.

"Hello!"

"Mr. Westley?" It was a woman's voice with a vaguely English accent.

"Yes."

"This is Mrs. Bilbeau speaking. We are having a bridge party next Friday for the members of the stahff (queer sort of accent, thought John). I wonder if you could come?"

"Why I'd be glad to," said John. "At about what time?"

"A quarter after eight?"

"Why, yes. To tell you the truth, Mrs. Bilbeau, I'm not much of a bridge player."

"Oh that's perfectly all right, you will have plenty of company in that respect. You will come then, at eight-fifteen?"

"I'll be there. And thank you!"

John consulted Angus concerning dress.

"It's like most other West Kirby social rules," said Angus, his eyes amused. "The ladies dress, the men do as they please, dark suits of course preferred. How's your bridge—have you learned anything since that game on the train?"

"Not a thing," confessed John.

"God help you. Bridge is standard recreation for teachers. It's the only game that provides tension enough to take their minds off teaching. And watch your bidding. Two no trumps is a reckless bid with this crowd. Have you been over to J. C.'s yet?"

"No."

"Well, you'll have an interesting evening, even though you can't play their game. Maybe you and Dot can sit it out together."

"Can't she play either?"

"Loathes the game—she'll probably find an excuse to miss it. She never gets invited elsewhere to a bridge. But naturally the J. C.'s invite everyone. The J. C.'s don't play favourites." Again that vague anti-Bilbeauism.

John, Frank, and Agnes shared a taxi, Agnes in a lovely gown of blue silk and lace with a black seal wrap, long black gloves and a blue kerchief over her hair. John was in party mood as he sat beside her in the rear seat of the car, very conscious of her perfume and reputation for "high stepping." It was hard to believe the taxi held three teachers heading for a bridge party.

It was easier to believe as they entered the door.

J. C. was there indefatigably waving the ladies upstairs, whipping out coat hangers for the men, slipping their coats deftly into the hall closet, smiling pleasantly and shaking hands with each new arrival.

"Glad to see you, Mr. Westley!" John never knew which name to expect from J. C. When he came to think of it, it was only when they were alone that J. C. called him John.

The living room was large, longish, with a fireplace in the centre of the one long wall. Already a dozen were in the room. John looked around. There was no sign of Angus, but he spied Dot Young in a rather smart brown dress, and moved towards her. Smith and his wife moved between, and he escaped from them only to encounter Miss Willis, thin and majestic in her black crepe silk dress which took unnecessary precautions with its high neckline.

"Mr. Westley! I've seen so little of you since you began teaching across the hall. You must come in for a short chat some time after four. But then I hear you are always so busy then."

"Been hearing about my detentions, eh?" John grinned self-consciously.

"No, no! Your dramatic work. Mr. Bilbeau was saying just a minute ago how well you were doing."

"Well it's nice to hear that." John was genuinely pleased. J. C. didn't go around slobbering over people—if he said John was all right the chances were that he was.

Miss Willis had turned away and John reached Miss Young.

"Hiya?" grinned John sinking into the empty chair beside her. "Angus told me you can't play bridge any better than I can, and believe me, that's an insult."

"It depends on *why* you can't play bridge, doesn't it?"

"I can't play bridge because I never got around to playing much bridge I suppose. I never could understand why Angus likes it."

"Probably because it's the best defence in the world against an evening of banal conversation."

"Yes, but he doesn't *have* to accept invitations."

"You're not married, and haven't been single long enough to have observed the complications of marriage. Have you met Mrs. Macdonald?"

"Yes," said John noting that like him she used the formal name and not the informal. "But I don't get the point."

Dot Young looked down the room. "Here's Mrs. Bilbeau," she said.

Mrs. Bilbeau came up, or strode up, to be more accurate, looking decidedly incongruous in a purplish affair of an evening gown, when obviously she should have been wearing a tweed suit and brogues. She spoke nasally and with one of those accents common to eastern Canadians of "good family": she would say "bawths" and "I cawn't" in one breath, relapse into common Canadianese the next.

"How do you do, Mr. Westley!" she acknowledged the introduction. "And have you met my daughter Catherine?"

"How do you do, Miss Bilbeau." He found himself left alone with Catherine, and not unpleased. Though she was taller than he there was something so unaffected and direct about her that he was attracted at once. And he liked the healthy colour, the regular features and pleasant grey eyes. They chatted about West Kirby, Old Kirby, the school, and the people they knew in common, until the room had filled and she excused herself.

Then followed the exciting business of matching tally cards to discover partners for the first table. There were seven tables; three in the living room, two in the dining room and two squeezed into the sunroom. A few of the older women, including Mrs. Nyes, sat apart to spend the evening comparing recipes and operations, and exchanging accounts of engagements, weddings, births, illnesses and deaths.

John discovered his partner to be Miss Pettiker, the Librarian. He had glimpsed her often enough at school, performing her duties inconspicuously. Here she was a frail timid little soul in a frail timid little costume, smiling nervously whenever addressed.

John took her arm and led her to Table Six in the sunroom and she even giggled a little when she had to squeeze past Mr. Starling to reach her place. Mrs. Smith, a dowdy little woman with plump hands and a face like a pie, dealt the cards with the slickness of long hours of practice. Starling passed, Miss Pettiker passed, Mrs. Smith bid a heart, John, holding nothing but the king and jack, bid one spade.

Miss Pettiker bit her lips nervously, drew upon an unsuspected reservoir of courage and twittered: "Two spades." They all passed, and Miss Pettiker laid down her cards: four timid little spades, the two, three, seven and nine! Fortunately the rest of her hand was fairly strong and they were down only two.

John never got out of the sunroom, though he did move to the next table after Catherine Bilbeau played opposite him and they won handsomely.

It was John's first real contact with some of the staff members and his first meeting with most of the men's wives.

Edward Starling, the shortest man on the staff, looked taller when he sat. With his sharp aggressive nose and horn-rimmed glasses he was a formidable man to face in a bridge game. He kept his mouth compactly shut, to open it sharply and decisively when he made his bid, and cocked his head a little to one side when bidding, like a bird doubtfully eyeing a mouldy kernel of wheat. Starling kept the score, and handled Mrs. Smith, who was inclined to raise a technical point now and then, with tactful skill. He would be a good teacher, decided John.

Harold Klein and Agnes Purcell were the next couple. Agnes was an expert player, but John misunderstood her bidding, overbid, was doubled by the alert Klein, and they went down. Klein and Agnes Purcell were succeeded by Mr. Pennington and Miss Willis. Miss Willis played with ferocious efficiency; Pennington like an English gentleman, apologetically just making his bid. Catherine Bilbeau arrived with Henry Pikestaff, a nice contrast in characters. Catherine robust, Pikestaff pale and thin; she making her bids and playing her cards decisively, but with a casual air; he hesitating, with a thin frown of worry, fearfully placing his card on the table as if it were a stick of dynamite.

Two by two most of the others came to his table, including Frank, who was having the time of his life and was the life of the party; Mrs. Klein, who played efficiently but without enthusiasm; and finally J. C. By this time John's bidding was completely reckless. After the first round Bilbeau elevated his shaggy eyebrows slightly, thrust out an aggressive underlip, doubled, redoubled, squeezed, finessed. John was hopelessly at sea.

"I guess I should learn how to play bridge," he remarked ruefully and unnecessarily, looking at his score.

J. C.'s eyes twinkled good-humouredly, but he made no comment.

The last rubber concluded, sandwiches were served and the buzz of conversation rose. John found Dot again and squatted on the footstool beside her.

"Where have you been all evening?" he asked.

"Two tables—in here all night. I didn't see you moving around."

"Two tables, in the sunroom, all night!" said John, and they both laughed. "You know the game wouldn't be so bad, but they all take it so seriously. By the way Angus never turned up. Doesn't he take in these parties?"

"I expect something happened to Mrs. Macdonald. Her health is rather delicate, you know."

"*Her* health, delicate?"

"It's true. I know she doesn't look it. But she gets attacks of some kind. Angus doesn't talk about it, and nobody seems to know. General opinion puts it down to a weak heart and lets it go at that."

John would have liked to go into the matter further, but he didn't feel he knew Dot Young well enough to pursue the subject. It was strange how complicated things were getting. J. C. and Angus. Why this unaccountable dislike of Angus for J. C. when J. C. had nothing but good to say of Angus? And both of them were obviously too big for a high school job, yet both were apparently content to remain. Is teaching a rut? Once you're in are you stuck there for life? Would John Westley never be anything but a high school teacher?

That night in bed, while bread and butter, lobster paste, peanut butter, olives, salad dressing, pimiento, cheese, shortbread, French pastry, jam tarts, angel cake, ice cream, and coffee churned around within his stomach, his brain wrestled with the problem. Why does a teacher teach?

He went back over his own short career. High school at home, and his mother's death, the summer after that in Muskoka, when he had discovered his passion for rocks; the interview with his dad, the busy doctor who never had quite enough time for his son.

"Of course you're going to college. If you like rocks, take geology. Get a job with a good outfit and you're set for life. Besides, you'll see the country."

First year at university. Second year . . . . his father's first attacks of arthritis. There were visits home . . . . everything the same, except that little Bill was growing up, and John got along better with his stepmother.

At the end of his third year he had it out with his father, who by this time was getting badly crippled. John learned that he had put all his savings into a government annuity and had decided to move to Montreal where he could take treatments for his back and where his second wife's relatives lived. He talked things over with his stepmother.

Finally it was decided. A straight eight hundred dollars to finish his education, after that he would be on his own. He went north with the geological survey—Angus's party. Angus had advised him—teach. There's no other job will give you two months in the summer that are your own. To get anywhere in geology you need your M.A., and even then jobs are scarce. Finish your Fourth Year and get your degree, go to the College of Education for another year, then teach. If there's an opening at West Kirby I'll see that you get it. If not there are always good openings for a science specialist. Teach.

That is how he had come here. He remembered what his palaeontology prof had said. "Teaching high school? A good idea. I taught for ten years in St. Catharines, after I graduated, took my M.A. and Ph.D. extra-murally. It's hard work but there's nothing like it for drilling yourself in fundamentals. A lot of people teach before they find their life work. It's a good stepping stone."

Teaching!

"Please, Mr. Westley, I don't understand."

"Sir, why do you have to study algebra?"

"I don't like English and I can't do it."

"What's the use of memorizing a lot of stuff you can't remember five minutes after the exam?"

"I was *not* chewing gum, it was just a piece of paper."

"Please, I don't know."

"I can't remember."

While you're worrying, John told himself, why don't you worry about your discipline?

But he was too tired, and fell asleep.

104

8

By the
middle of November two coming events were dominating
school life: the Christmas concert. And examinations.

It was a trying time for John Westley: all his efforts
were bent on making the Christmas play a great success,
and at the same time his classes must make a creditable
showing when they wrote their exams.

And discipline was still a problem.

It had got no worse, except that John had a feeling that
conditions would soon become chronic. He needed no reminder that he was on probation for his first year. And the
inspector might turn up before Christmas.

They explained to John that the inspector's visit de-
pended on the weather. If the December snowfall were
heavy and the country roads impassable in Kirby County,
the inspector would come before Christmas, leaving the
country schools until the January thaw or even till spring.
Otherwise he turned up right after the holidays.

So John's discipline *must* improve soon. And, inspector
or no inspector, he couldn't teach his best without discipline. If his teaching suffered it would show in examination results. The physics class was safe enough, but there
were a dozen physiography students who weren't working,
and his first year algebra and English classes were getting
behind. 1C particularly, seemed to be full of problem
students.

There was Roy Ritchie, detained one afternoon for talking and laughing too freely. After four he came up to
John's desk defiantly.

"Where do you want me to sit?"

John contained his temper and politely indicated a seat. Later he talked to him.

"I suppose you know why you are here?"

"Because you told me to come."

"And *why* did I detain you?"

"I dunno."

"Well, I'll tell you why, since your memory is so bad. You were guilty of insolence."

"I don't know what those big words mean."

"You were cheeky."

"Well, I'm sorry. Can I go?"

"How do I know you're sorry?"

"I said I was didn't I?"

"I mean really sorry."

"I said I was sorry."

John gave him a hundred lines to write out, feeling frustrated. It was like trying to cut hay with a rubber scythe.

Two days later Roy Ritchie was chewing gum. John told him to put it in the basket and come in after four. Roy slammed the desk noisily, clumped heavily to and from the waste basket, throwing the pellet of gum into the basket so that it made a loud 'ping'. John doubled the detention.

The second interview was even less satisfactory than the first.

"This is your second detention. Do you know why I detained you this time?"

"No."

John boiled over. "Say 'sir' when you answer!" he shouted.

"Yes, sir."

"Why did I detain you?"

"I guess you ought to know." There were snickers of laughter from surrounding detainees.

"I guess I *do* know!" John shouted. "You've been insolent and defiant and you're no better now. If your mother had any manners she'd have taught you a few by this time!"

Roy shouted too, "You can't say that about my mother and get away with it!"

"I'm only telling you the impression you are giving me of your mother. If you display bad manners in front of people they can't help thinking your mother doesn't know any better."

Roy got up, "You say anything more about my mother and I'll walk out!"

"All right then. Get out!" John yelled, shaking with rage and pointing to the door.

It was all so stupid.

Another of John's problem cases was Donald Lunn, big, fat, and lazy; but with such an infectious quality to his grin whenever John scolded him, that the whole class would burst out laughing. John felt the infection himself, and found it all the more annoying to feel the corners of his own mouth twitching upward in an involuntary response. That of course was a signal for the whole class to get out of hand. Then John would suddenly lose control of himself, shout futilely for silence, and finally detain the class.

Invariably this class detention would back-fire.

Miss Willis came over to John's room at four-fifteen one day. 1C was serving a class detention. Two boys had previous after-four engagements with her. John flippantly offered to saw each boy in half, and asked her whether she preferred having them cut lengthwise or laterally.

Miss Willis smiled coldly. "I'm afraid that would not be a solution," she told him.

John shrugged his shoulders and gave her the boys, feeling at the same time that he had weakened his authority.

One of the bigger girls held up her hand after Miss Willis had carried off her victims.

"What is it?" asked John.

"I have a detention with Miss Brewin—"

"You'll sit there till I dismiss the class!" roared John with sudden ferocity.

The next morning he discovered his first clue to the secret of inspiring fear.

There was one first year girl who was an adept at getting under his skin. Whatever he said to her she sat there with a silly smirk. She gave him no cause for complaint in any other respect though her answers in class were scatter-brained enough. It seemed that whenever he asked her a question she simply said the first thing that popped into her head—always with that silly smirk. Fortunately the answers were never the type that brought a roar of laughter from the class—she was actually much less disturbing than the Lunn boy, but he *liked* the Lunn boy, and loathed her silly smirk and the pin-headed personality behind it.

On this particular morning the feeling came to a head. He was going over an equation at the blackboard. Peggy was leaning forward talking to the girl in front of her. John marched to her seat and stood glaring down at her, speechless with pent-up resentment. Just as he found his voice he noticed a peculiar twitching in the side of her neck. The smirk had never left her face, but there was this twitching. She's nervous he thought—no, it's the artery in her neck, her pulse, her heart is hammering away—he could almost hear it as he watched the quivering pulsations. She's afraid! She's horribly afraid of me!

His staggering discovery cut off the anger at its source He turned away without a word, went back to the equation. Strangely enough the class was very subdued for the rest of the period.

At this stage John Westley was becoming so obsessed with his discipline problems that even walking to or from school was a worry. If a group of students was walking behind him, every time they laughed he was quite certain the laughter was directed at him. He would imagine remarks like: Didn't we put it over on old Westley in English today? (*laughter*) Did you see old Westley's face when Ed told him that old gag about losing the book he'd done his homework in? (*laughter*) Wasn't it a *scream* the way old Westley blew up in physiog this morning? (*screams of laughter*) He imagined them poking fun at his clothes, his youthful appearance, mimicking his voice and the way he walked. Then he would call himself a fool and throw it off, until another tinkle of girlish laughter, or the coarse haw-haw of an adolescent boy, coming from behind, would start it all over again.

He had achieved a kind of control. By dint of constant supervision, threats, detentions, and keeping his classes busy, he had attained a kind of noisy industry. But always there was the feeling that at any moment a crisis would arise that would bring a complete collapse of his control. And the price he paid in nervous expense was heavy.

Mondays he would go back to school prepared for the worst and discover that things weren't as bad as he remembered them. On Tuesdays, the week-end lethargy had lifted from his students, and he began to feel the strain. Wednesday morning was the hardest. Once noon had passed he would tell himself the week was half gone: just two more days and that blessed Friday night would come. So the weeks passed.

The inspector failed to show up and exams drew near, as did the Christmas concert.

The selection from a nativity play had gone over so well at a Friday 'Lit' that he decided to put on the whole play for the Christmas concert. There were hundreds of details: peasants' smocks for the shepherds, a dummy sheep for 'Mak' to steal, the angel's costume, music for the chorus of angels back stage, a manger and other stable props, and all the minutiae of the actual rehearsals.

Miss Garrell was very much interested, and promised that her students would look after the stable and all the properties thereof. A week before the play she had produced one little cardboard cow. Desperately John approached Dot Young, and together with a couple of students from the Dramatic Club they worked a solid Saturday at the school to produce a life size cow and a donkey cut out in beaver-board, a dais for the Virgin Mary, and a manger.

The dress rehearsal for the concert found John as excited as any of the children, but a good deal more worried. The confusion was staggering.

Thursday afternoon a notice had gone around the class-rooms to the effect that the dress rehearsal would begin sharp at seven and all participating were expected to be in the assembly hall promptly at that hour.

John had a copy of the programme and found that his play came in the second half, two numbers from the end. He spent the supper hour doing last minute jobs: touching up the cow's nose which had been badly damaged by careless handling, dashing over to Central Avenue for forgotten cold cream, up on a ladder rewiring a valance which hung too low, phoning one of his shepherds who had a cold at the last rehearsal and stayed away from school that day, phoning home to ask Agnes Purcell not to forget the Virgin Mary's costume, checking the make-up kit, and generally fussing over all the things that remained to be done.

Promptly at seven he was in the auditorium, had located his brood, counted heads, and sat down to wait.

The hall was half filled with excited students. The orchestra members were seated in the pit, blowing, sawing and hammering away at their instruments in a horrible cacophony, having the time of their lives under the pretext of warming up. Girls ran around from group to group jabbering . . . . "Isn't it *exciting?*" Boys sat back with their feet up on the seats ahead, enjoying the rare luxury of feeling at home in school. Every minute the curtains would part and someone would dash out and down into the auditorium, or a teacher would rush up on the stage, fumble for the curtain opening, and disappear back-stage, where the lights were continually flashing on and off in all the colours of the rainbow. At ten after seven Mr. Gray, the choirmaster from St. Andrew's who conducted the orchestra, had still not arrived. Mr. Nyes came out, was greeted with cheers and hand clapping, which made no impression on him and died away before his upraised hand.

111

"Since the orchestra is not ready"—he spoke sharply—"we'll proceed with the next number, a recitation by Ernest Moore." Ernest Moore obliged with a juvenile rendering of a juvenile poem about a juvenile. The clapping was hilarious. There followed a dance. Eight charming girls in the full bloom of maidenhood—except that two were rather fleshy and one completely fleshless—executed a Kerry dance with graceless ease. The voice of Margaret Brewin floated out from the wing.

"Girls you'll have to do that all over again and put some pep in it!"

Mr. Smith bawled down from somewhere behind and above. "How are those lights?"

Miss Brewin came out on stage and looked up. "Could we have more red?" The lights went out. Silence and darkness. They went on again—completely red.

"That's too much—just a little."

They went out and came on in the original colour.

"That's better."

The lights flickered and turned yellow. Miss Brewin gazed up, opened her mouth, thought better of it, retired to the wing and the girls began again:

"O for the pipes of a Kerry dancer!"

It was exactly the same as before.

"Next number!" shouted Mr. Nyes before the audience had time to clap. John gathered up his flock to depart backstage just as Mr. Gray rushed up, got out his baton, and the orchestra swung into the march from *Tannhauser*, while on the stage the curtains opened to reveal the legs of Mr. Smith on top of a ladder which two boys were holding.

"Close that curtain!" exploded Mr. Smith in the clouds, over the strains of *Tannhauser*, which suddenly wailed into silence as Mr. Nyes came up on the stage, shouting. "What's the matter? I asked for the next number. Mr. Gray will you kindly hold that orchestra number." He stuck his head between the curtains, said something acidly backstage then turned, his face a magnificent crimson, and said "All right, Mr. Gray your second number please. We'll have the first later."

"You mean you want the second first?" Mr. Gray was confused.

There John left them for the dressing rooms and for the next hour he and Dot Young and Grace Morley were busy covering fresh young complexions (with two or three pimply exceptions) with cold cream, grease paint, eyebrow shadow, lip-stick, and, in the case of the shepherds, Mak, and Joseph, crepe-hair beards.

By this time Mr. Smith was at the limit of his endurance, striding across the stage with an armful of lighting fixtures glaring at two frightened little dancers in pink who stood there as if the whole thing were a nightmare. Miss Brewin, Mr. Nyes, and Mr. Gray were in nervous conference, pointing now at the stage, now at the curtains, now at the lights; and a boy in the orchestra was taking advantage of the lull to practise over and over again a difficult bar in his saxophone solo.

John went timidly up to the three teachers to learn when, or if, the play was to go on.

"But Mr. Gray, the girls just aren't used to that tempo. We've been practising with the piano and—"

"Miss Brewin, I *know* they're not used to it. They'll have to *get* used to it. That's why we're rehearsing."

"But there isn't *time!*"

Mr. Nyes looked from one to the other, opened his mouth and closed it again, his face red with frustration. John caught his eye.

"Mr. Nyes, I was wondering if the play—"

"The play will go on, when we're ready for the play, and not one minute sooner, Mr. Westley!" All the frustration found outlet in John's direction. "If people were ready with their numbers when their numbers were called for, all this confusion and delay would be obviated." He was again the man of action.

"Miss Brewin, the dancers will have to stay after the rehearsal and get their numbers right if it takes all night. Now let's get on with the next number." He glanced at the sheet. "Glee Club!"

Mr. Pikestaff came up. "We gave our third number two numbers back, because the—"

"I don't care how many times you gave it. This is the place in the programme for it and I want it now! And the programme goes on from here ready or not! Now then, Glee Club, PLEASE!"

They all sat down, the Glee Club assembled, and sang in unison, with considerable enthusiasm. That done there was a creditable violin solo, followed by a gymnastic display directed with alacrity by Frank Jarratt. A reading from *A Christmas Carol* came next and John rushed back stage as the orchestra tuned up for the number preceding the play.

The wings were jammed with girls from the dances, boy gymnasts, soloists, stage hands and a sprinkling of teachers. John stared in dismay, then leaped into action with the shepherds, putting up background flats, piling up gym mats for the hillside, covering them with a grass mat and strategically placing sandbags as stones for the shepherds to sit on. They worked feverishly behind the curtain while the orchestra blared away in front. Dripping with nervous sweat John paused, looked the set over, moved a stone two inches to the right, beckoned to the First Shepherd to take his place, whispered hoarsely up to Mr. Smith "Turn those lights down more, please," gave the curtain signal, and raced the opening curtains to the wing, almost knocking over Grace Morley who was prompting.

The lighting was good, and the set adequate: for the audience, accustomed to brightly lit social farces, the effect was breathtaking, and John sighed with relief as the First Shepherd, rubbing his hands slowly and stiffly, drawled out the words in a heavy voice:

"Lord! what, these weathers are cold, and I am ill happed. . . ."

The curtains close. Joseph and the shepherd race silently off with the mats, rocks and grass, as a flute solo, "Nowell", rises with thin uncertainty from the orchestra pit. On with the wing flats—John lashes them desperately together— the bed, the bench. The soloist stops, begins to repeat, wavers uncertainly. "Blink those lights! We're ready!"— John's shouted whisper aloft. The flute breaks off—John swears silently—waves for the curtain—well, it's only a dress rehearsal!

The comic scene in Mak's house, where the shepherds discover their stolen sheep in bed with Gill, disguised as a babe. Curtain.

A trumpet solo intervenes: "O Little Town of Bethlehem", while John and his crew switch the scene sweatily back to the hillside. The Second Shepherd rips his cotton smock on a nail. "O Little Town" wails to a conclusion, the lights change. Curtain again.

The shepherds back on the hill, sleepy. The lights come up. Dawn, Enter Angel. Sings:

> "Good fo-olk fear not, but le-et it show
> Right joyous your be-haa-viour. . . . ."

Get ready for the chorus.

John stands tensely, anxiously, beside his octette. They watch him. "I'll beat three!" he whispers. "One! Two! . . . ." On the third beat John bellows lustily to supplement the choir.

"NOW U-UNTO GOD . . ." in full fortissimo.

The silent chorus looks scared, then starts in at the beginning just after John, realizing the magnitude of his mistake, turns his voice off as quickly as he had turned it on. In the auditorium the audience titters audibly, their amusement piercing Director Westley's soul.

The last scene: Mary, Joseph and the manger; the shepherds bringing their gifts. The chorus again as the curtains close.

It was over. John, soaked with perspiration, wrung the hands of the shepherds, of Mary and Joseph, of the prompt, tried to laugh as they patted his back and said it was only the dress rehearsal. They went to get their make-up off and John missed the remainder of the show. When he looked in an hour later the orchestra and dancers were practising. Mr. Gray and Miss Brewin shouting at them and at each other. Mr. Nyes sat resignedly in the front row, waiting for it all to end.

9

It was all over. The weary weeks of teaching, the strangeness of new surroundings and a thousand new faces, the frustrations, the laughs behind his back, the long straining hours, the tenseness, the stink of stale sweat, the nightmare of, what classes do I have tomorrow? the threat of inspection, the steady grind and drill of preparing for the judgment day of examinations.

All over.

And the play was over too. John felt the satisfaction of having done a good job—the final performance had made a hit with teachers and parents and trustees. Against the gloomy background of inadequate discipline and teaching, he saw the play, bright and luminous.

"Too-whoooo! Too-whoooo! Too-whoooo!" shrieked the train in wild abandon, and wheels clicked gaily on the rail joints.

I'm making good and I'm going to Mary's for Christmas . . . . jingle bells, jingle bells . . . . thought John Westley; and the train hooted through the blackness outside with John seated securely in its lighted bowels gazing exultantly out through the transparent scales of glass.

His spirits sobered as he turned to the battered briefcase beside him. Exam papers. Marking.

No, he thought, holidays aren't what they used to be. I've got papers to mark, papers to mark, papers to mark.

Mary met him at the West Toronto station driving her father's shabby old Chrysler. They drove out Bloor Street,

117

turning north just short of High Park and five minutes later stopped before a small, neatly trimmed, white brick house. The snow, fallen overnight, had still not been dirtied in the side streets; the air was full of Christmas sparkle, the stars shone wishfully for the bright warm home beneath. John and Mary pushed open the door, already hung with a Christmas wreath. The whole family was there. Mary's mother embarrassed John—and gently touched a deeply buried wound—with a warm hug and kiss. Dad Miller held out his hand, and John winced under the carpenter's strong clasp.

The two younger girls clamoured to stay up and watch John eat, which they all did, talking two and three at a time about Christmas, what did he bring them, guess what *we're* giving *you*, you still don't look like a teacher, and other similar sweet personal trivia. John soaked up the family's affection like a tired swimmer basking in the summer sun.

The girls were shooed off to bed, the parents lingered over their coffee a little longer before they, too, tactfully withdrew, leaving John and Mary together on the chesterfield.

"It's so *good* to be here!" John said when they had kissed long and silently. "So good."

In the morning John started in on his papers—eight sets. Systematically he piled them on Dad Miller's desk: four algebra sets, two sets of English—literature and composition, a set each of physiography and physics.

First the physics. No, that's the cream—leave it to the last. What's hardest? The English—get that out of the way.

He opened the first paper, looked at his marking sheet. Question one: "Quote twelve lines beginning:

'*I wandered lonely as a cloud*—'" Those damned daffodils! Well here goes!

J. C. had provided two sheets, a detailed typewritten marking scheme, and a sheet headed: 'General Instructions for Marking English Papers'. Both where signed 'J. C. Bilbeau': below was typewritten: 'Head English Department'. A marvelous man for details, thought John gratefully. Opposite 'Memory Work' on the second sheet he read: 'In marking memory work attention will be paid to essential punctuation, to spelling, and to versification. A mistake in any one of these constitutes a MAJOR ERROR, for which deduct one mark. Other minor aberrations will be considered MINOR ERRORS, for every three of which one mark is to be subtracted from the total.'

"*I wandered lonely as a*—da
Da-da da-da da-da da-da
Da-da . . . one mark off for spelling . . .
Da-da da-da da-da da-da . . . one minor error . . ."
And so on, to the end.

John looked up at the clock—five minutes gone on one question.

Little Donna came into the room and looked over his shoulder.

"Watcha doing?"

"Marking papers—go 'way!"

"Donna, can't you see he's busy marking papers?" her mother bustled past with a mop. "Don't bother him."

Question two. "Name three characteristics of the early English ballad that are common to (a) Helen of Kirconnell (b) the Twa Corbies (c) Binnorie."

John marked the question, looked up at the clock. Fifteen minutes more had passed.

And so on down the paper. At the end of an hour and five minutes he had marked one paper. It was a failure: thirty-six marks out of a possible eighty. Not so good.

He calculated how long the one set would take: one hour and five minutes multiplied by thirty-seven papers—forty hours and five minutes! Oh! No! he protested. What about my holidays? He looked over the papers, dividing likely passes from failures. Ten likely failures—Louise should have passed. Damn you, Louise, why didn't you pass? he muttered.

He marked another paper, watching the clock. Forty-eight minutes. That was better. But this was a bright lad, who always had a ready answer in class—and he too had failed, with only thirty-one marks.

"*Damn* his little hide!" quoth Mr. John Westley, B.A., High School Assistant.

Time out for lunch with Mom Miller and the three girls; Mr. Miller and Mary ate their lunch at work. The telephone rang once. Mrs. Miller answered it—"Yes, I'll tell him,"—and came away from the phone beaming. "Another job right after Christmas," she told John. "Three weeks' work. If this keeps up we'll be able to give Clara another year at high school!"

The Millers had been through their share of depression hardships. The first time John had visited the Millers, two years ago, the easy optimism of the family had told him nothing of their scanty means. Mary was in her first year at University College; and John assumed, even though she referred to her father as a carpenter, that he was a contractor and doing fairly well. It was not until the following spring, when Mary told him with a brave effort at cheerfulness, that she would have to get a job to help out the family, that John realized how hard the Millers had been hit. Mary had only turned sixteen when she entered college with a scholarship; but even when she won a second—in psychology—at the end of her first year, it only amounted to tuition fees; and Dad Miller had sadly remarked, "You can't eat scholarships."

Her work was pleasant enough—clerking in Eaton's book department, and she had been promoted twice in her year and a half there. If only, thought John, Clara wouldn't take Mary's sacrifice so much for granted. She wasn't nearly as bright as Mary and was talking already as if it were settled that her father and older sister would see her through university.

Back at it in the afternoon. As the answers became more and more boring with repetition, the game became more and more fascinating.

Race the clock, watch for failures: that was the game.

Each paper was marked a little faster, with occasional set-backs when a long answer or a difficult decision (five marks for this, or six?) frustrated him and caused him to groan aloud, attaching nasty little epithets to the name of the examinee. Occasionally a girl would get full marks for a question, provoking, "Why, you sweet little honeybunch!" or a boy get his memory work perfect, "Aren't *you* a smart little bugger!" This of course all *sotto voce*, lest he sour the sweetness and darken the light of the Miller household. More often it was a grunt or an expletive as his black marking pencil viciously circled a goose-egg in the margin or jabbed a heavy line at a misspelled word. When little Donna came near again he growled at her so ferociously that she shrieked equally in fright and delight, and stayed away. By five he had marked half the set and had his time down to twenty minutes per paper. Eight had failed already, but most of the remainder he considered safe.

He eyed the remaining seven and a half sets with dismay. More calculations: another two days for the English, four days for the Algebra, two days for the rest—"Oh Lord!" he groaned aloud.

Mary came home, her cheeks appled from the cold, blowing her nose with a white handkerchief. Dad Miller came home, stamping his feet on the threshold; stepped inside to grumble cheerfully about the weather.

They had supper.

Lingering over the supper table Mrs. Miller said:

"What do you young ones plan to do tonight?"

"Marking papers for me!" muttered John glumly, not looking at Mary.

"John!" Mary was hurt, and the hurt went right around the faces at the table back to John.

"I'm a stinker—to heck with the papers—let's take in a show."

"Yes, let's!" Simultaneous cries of enthusiasm from the two youngest. Clara smiled knowingly.

"Fat chance!" she cried.

During the dishes Mr. Miller buried himself in the paper, John listened to the late news on the radio, suddenly thought of his exams and idled through another paper. Halfway through he found himself into his little game again. Absorbed, he was startled to feel a warm hand on his cheek, stealing around under his chin. It was Mary. She sat on his lap, snuggled her hands under his coat, pressed her face against the buttons of his vest, brushed his lips with her hair; then looked up, mischievous love in her eyes.

"Hello, school teacher."

"Hello! Are you the little girl I told to come in after four?"

"Mm, mmh!"

More of the same till Clara came over and looked at them, disgust and envy mixed in her gaze.

"Nuts!" she said.

They laughed.

"Now then," said Mary, with determination. "I'm going to help you. Where do I start?"

"But . . . . I thought we were going to take in a show."

"Come on, Mr. Westley—I said, where do I start?"

Mary marked the memory work in the remaining questions, caught the contagion of the race with time, and the fascinating problem of wrestling for marks with each paper. It was only ten-thirty when the last paper was refolded, its mark recorded, the set snapped up in a rubber band.

"You're wonderful!" said John and punctuated the sentence with a kiss.

Christmas was due on Tuesday, and Mary had Monday off. Saturday evening, and part of Sunday and all day Monday they toiled at the papers, performing the miracle of cleaning up all the composition, one science, and most of the four algebra sets.

It was a Christmas to remember for John, after the almost affectionless festivals in his own home the past six years. He missed his young half-brother in retrospect, but relations between him and his father were always better when they were apart, and while he had overcome most of his original prejudice towards his stepmother, he never could feel at home with her. The Millers deluged him with presents, filled him with turkey, and made him unforgettably one of themselves. It was a day when he could forget teaching: the only reminder was a warm one; Mary's gift to him of a handsome brown leather briefcase.

With Mary back at work again he went on with the papers, grimly setting his marking pencil to the paper and fixing his eye on the clock. At last there was nothing left but half a set of physics, and he let that go until his return to West Kirby.

Saturday afternoon he and Mary went skiing, returning to find everyone out. They went upstairs to change: it had begun to thaw and their ski clothes were damp with melted snow.

John was using Mary's room: she had moved in with her sisters for the visit.

"John!" He paused, unlacing his shoe.

"Hello."

"I left some undies in the bottom drawer of my dresser. Could I come in? Are you decent?"

"I'm decent."

Mary came in, naked as God had made her.

John stood up, trembling. "Oh God!" he said, "Oh God!" and caressed the lovely shoulders, touched her gentle breasts reverently.

The storm door opened down at the front of the house and Mary was gone.

10

January: handing back examinations, tabulating results, filling in reports . . . . and the inspector!

Freed from the pressure of the Christmas play—though he carried on with the bi-weekly dramatic bits—John could turn his energies toward fighting the bugbear of discipline. They had won the first round; the second would be his!

He sat down one evening to figure the thing out, going over and over in his mind the incidents of the fall term that had bothered him most. That dream. The one where he had—he couldn't remember the student's name—anyway he had him on the floor, he held him by the throat and was banging his head on the floor, only his head wouldn't bang hard. The head was hard and the floor was hard—it would have been so *satisfying* to bang and bang that head into unconsciousness! But something made him weak, something held him back, kept him from using his strength. The feeling of frustration welled up sickeningly again.

Fear.

Fear was the answer.

He was afraid of them; so they weren't afraid of him. They knew he was afraid. Somehow they knew.

What was there to be afraid of? They couldn't hurt him. He was stronger than any one of them; probably could handle any two. Why was he afraid?

Afraid of his job. Afraid the principal would see. Afraid the other teachers would see. Afraid the pupils would see his fear.

I'm just a damned coward, thought John.

A deep anger rose within him. I'm not a coward. I'm afraid, but I'm not a coward. If it's got to be a fight, by God it will be a fight. Fight fire with fire. They've given me a taste of fear: let them see how it feels!

The next morning he strode into his first class with fire in his eyes. It was 1B algebra. He went to his desk; barked out an order. The class responded amazingly. They were docile as sheep. The lesson went off smoothly.

Period two. 1C algebra: I'll show the little bastards. 1C buckled down to work like a new class. John relaxed. This was easy. We can be friends, he thought. No need to fight them, just show them who is boss and it's all over.

A pupil asked him a question and he went down to his desk to help him out.

Zing!

Something hit the back of his neck just above the collar, stingingly. He half turned, rubbing his neck and finding a ball of wet paper in his hand. He looked at it—astonishment, fear, and anger mixed plainly on his face.

"Who threw that?" he shouted, looking toward the back corner of the room. He strode down the aisle pointing at each boy in turn, bellowing "Did you?" receiving a negative shake of the head from each. All the boys.

He gave the class a lecture which was received with smiles. He shouted and the smiles grew. One innocent lad was smiling with the rest. He was one of those good students who irritated John because he was always good, perhaps a little too conscious of his goodness. Blindly, John chose him, grabbed him out of his seat, shook him till his head was a blur. No one was smiling now. John's panic grew. Hatred filled the room; there was open disgust on two or three girls' faces.

The bell rang. The class filed out. John watched them savagely. A big boy turned back to another, saying something with a sarcastic smile. John rushed him. "So you don't like it! Then how do you like this?" and grabbing the back of his collar and seat of his pants he started to push him out the door. The boy flung his head back and struck John full on the mouth. Pin-points of light floated before his eyes as he staggered back, his hand to his face. He could taste the blood. One of his teeth felt as though it were loose. He went back to his desk and sat down, trembling, feeling sick.

Later that day J. C. stopped him in the hall.

"I wonder if you could come over to my room some time?"

"Certainly," said John, puzzled by his manner.

"Are you free by 4.30?"

"Yes."

"Fine. Could you come over to my room then?"

"Yes. Surely."

J. C. smiled kindly, turned and went on his way.

Now I wonder what that's about, John asked himself, with a feeling that something was wrong.

He had seen very little of either J. C. or Angus since Christmas. Both had congratulated him on the play. Angus had said, "That's the most competent job I've ever seen on our school stage." J. C. told him, "Their diction was excellent, the acting first rate. Congratulations. We have made a real find in you." He had felt hurt because some of the staff had made no comment whatever on the performance, and these words made him whole again. J. C.'s opinion he valued more particularly because that was more in J. C.'s field. After all, geologists are not authorities on drama.

But now J. C. wanted to see him about something.

At four he felt so low that he dismissed the half dozen detained students, went to the teachers' room, put on his outdoor clothes and started home. The feeling of depression he put down to the incident of the morning. Suddenly he remembered his appointment, turned and ran back to school past grinning students. A few bolder spirits made remarks: "Forget something? What's the rush?"—good-naturedly. John hung up his hat and coat again and arrived breathless in J. C.'s room at 4.25. J. C. was interviewing a student in a cool impersonal way.

"Did you not read the instructions on the sheet?"

"I didn't see that about 'before nine o'clock'."

"You see it now?"

"Yes, sir."

"You are sure you can see it?"

"Yes, sir."

"That's all, Borden." J. C. dismissed him, followed him to the door, shut it after him, and returned.

"Sit down, John," said J. C.

"Thanks." John sat down, looked at J. C. inquiringly. Mr. Bilbeau's face had a peculiar sort of quality to it that John couldn't decide whether to label sexless or womanish. It was the skin. He must shave at noon, thought John.

"I thought I'd have a word with you about your English results—oh, nothing to worry about," as John's eyes dilated involuntarily in alarm. "It's just a routine of mine

128

about this time of year. Your English marks were a little low—" he consulted a sheet lying on his desk—"let me see, average for the class 61 as compared with a general average of 64—ten failures. No doubt you have an explanation."

John sat there stupefied.

"But you never said anything before . . . ." he found himself stammering.

"Now, don't worry," said J. C. "I don't suppose the principal has noticed it—he seldom does unless I bring such matters to his attention. I am sure you are doing excellent work, certainly your dramatic efforts have been of the highest calibre, and I'm sure your class work is equally conscientious."

John, shaken by the events of the day and this sudden blow, wilted before J. C.'s magnanimity.

"We'll say no more about it," said J. C. kindly. "I want you to know that I consider teachers of your ability an asset to the school. You understand that in a position like mine it is necessary to take precautions. But only as routine, only as routine."

John was silent, inwardly fighting to keep back unbidden tears.

"You know John," said J. C. confidentially, "the head of a department is in a peculiarly difficult position. There is the principal above him, expecting a certain standard— there are of course the inspectors as well, and then he has a responsibility to teachers in his department. If you only knew the petty little problems I'm annoyed with every day. That is why I find it necessary to protect myself.

"As a matter of fact"—he warmed to his subject—"it is even necessary to protect oneself against one's students.

That was the origin of my assignment system. Give the student a printed sheet with detailed instructions, and you save yourself an endless amount of trouble. When a student comes to you in difficulties you merely point to the sheet and say, 'Did you read that?' "

J. C. looked at John as though John were the student. He almost felt impelled to answer timidly, "No sir!"

"It looks like a good idea," was all he said.

"By the way, John"—there was something very heart-warming in the intimacy of the name, though it was more like the intimacy of parent with child than one between equals—"have you attached yourself definitely to any one church since your arrival in West Kirby?"

"Well . . . . no," said John.

"Of course, you have been sampling. You are an Anglican, I believe."

"Oh yes," said John, "but—"

"I don't believe I have seen you at All Saints yet—of course St. John's would have your sentimental preference and I suppose, boarding at Mrs. Gillespie's, it is really the closest—the rector is a splendid man, a scholarly preacher. But we of All Saints feel that we have built up an organization that appeals particularly to young people. You are fond of children."

Was it a question? John answered, "Oh, yes, I like children."

"I knew it," said Bilbeau. "Otherwise, one couldn't do the splendid work in dramatics you have accomplished. I have been wondering whether we couldn't interest you in young people's work at All Saints. We have a *very* live Sunday School"—J. C.'s eyes twinkled—"if I weren't a modest man I'd take a good deal of the credit myself."

"Mrs. Macdonald was telling me about it a couple of weeks ago."

"Oh, yes—Mrs. Macdonald." There was a shade of coolness in his voice which quickly passed. "A most devoted worker in our Junior Department. I have often thought what a great pity it was that Mr. Macdonald didn't interest himself more in the work of the church—a great pity. With his splendid abilities he could do so much. But now, what about yourself?"

John hesitated. "What kind of young people's work were you thinking of?" he asked.

"Well, we particularly need young men for our boys' classes. I know—it is in some ways an imposition to ask a teacher to give up an hour on Sunday afternoon or morning to teach Sunday School, but the rewards are great— the rewards are great."

"I'm afraid I couldn't teach regularly," said John, "You see I go down to Toronto some week ends—my fiancée lives there—"

"Of course, of course," Mr. Bilbeau smiled understandingly. "We are all young only once. What I had in mind was an occasional substitution, just to get acquainted with the organization—I know that you will like it at All Saints. But it won't be necessary to commit yourself: when is your next free Sunday?"

John cudgelled his brains anxiously—hadn't he made plans for next Sunday? No, he wasn't going to Toronto before the end of the month. There was something else— if only he could remember! "As far as I know I'll be free next Sunday," said John.

"Splendid!" J. C. rose to end the interview. "We'll expect you at All Saints next Sunday at a quarter to three."

"But I've never taught Sunday School before!" Panic seized him. "I don't know anything about it!"

Bilbeau laid a reassuring hand on John's shoulder as they walked to the door. "Don't worry about that. Tomorrow morning I'll let you have a copy of *The Young Christian Quarterly* with complete lesson outlines for three months. Ten minutes with your Bible on Saturday night is all a man of your intelligence needs to spend in preparation. It's all in the outline—a child could teach it. Now, I won't keep you, John. I know you are busy."

John left Bilbeau's room completely dazed. He had known his English marks were a little low, but surely they didn't expect him, a green teacher in a new school, to teach as well as the others in his first term. Of course J. C. had done it for John's own good and he had been very friendly actually, he had even confided in him. And he wouldn't have asked him to teach in All Saints Sunday School unless he had a good opinion of him.

John made a face as the thought of teaching, even for one Sunday. He could imagine Mary's mirth when she heard of it. Oh John, she would say, All Saints! and explode in that sudden little guffaw of hers, so unexpectedly like a masculine laugh, and yet so femininely characteristic of Mary. She would laugh till the tears came, and he would join in finally, and then she would look at him through her tears, her smile curving irresistibly in preface to another outburst. John, which one of the saints are you —a Latter Day Saint?

Well, he didn't have to tell her about it. Except that—

he recalled the day when he had failed to turn up at her cousin's wedding. Mary had been furious till he finally confessed that his one and only good shirt had not come back from the laundry.

"John"—she had looked right into him with those clear warm eyes—"if our love is going to last a lifetime, it must be based on faith in each other, and if we start hiding things or dodging facts, that faith just can't last." Tears had filled her eyes, and she had said with a kind of desperate earnestness, "John, we mustn't keep *anything* from each other, not even the little things!"

No. He would teach a class for J. C. Bilbeau—but he would tell Mary, and let her laugh, and he'd laugh with her.

Immediately after dinner on Sunday afternoon John borrowed a Bible from Mrs. Gillespie, facetiously dusting it off after she had handed it to him; immediately regretting the gesture when she assured him indignantly that she read a chapter every night before retiring. There was an embroidered silk marker in it with a verse worked into the design—

> Holy Bible, Book Divine
> Precious Treasure, Thou art Mine.

On the fly leaf was written: "To my darling Fanny, on her twenty-fourth birthday, from Thomas."

He had already gone over the outline provided him by Mr. Bilbeau but thought it advisable to read the passage on which the lesson was based, the first fifteen verses of Chapter Six, in St. Matthew's Gospel.

John was a bit puzzled as to how to treat the passage, which dealt with hypocrisy and worship.

Take heed that ye do not your alms before men . . . .
When thou prayest, thou shalt not be as the hypocrites . . . .
Moreover, when ye fast, be not, as the hypocrites . . . .

The whole idea obviously was that religion should be a private personal sort of thing with as little external display as possible; and John, having very little external *or* internal religion, heartily agreed. But that, he told himself, was why he never had believed much in church going, or public religion of any kind; and here he was expected to teach this kind of lesson in a church where apparently they put a tremendous emphasis on externals. Well, the Lord's Prayer was included in the passage—he would concentrate on that.

"Our Father. . . . ." John thought of his own father, bedridden now, married to a woman who thought of nothing but clothes and making a good impression. He would talk about fathers and sons—maybe he could show these kids (Bilbeau had told him he would have a class of eight-year-old boys) how important fathers were and how easy it was for the first little separations to grow into a chasm. But *had* it been his fault? It was his dad who had been too busy, or too tired, to bother with him. Not at first. His heart ached when he thought of the time his dad had driven him out in the country over the snow in a cutter one winter to visit a patient. They had really been pals that day. It was later that they grew apart, especially after his mother died. After that he had been a complete orphan actually. If only he had been adopted by someone like Angus, or even—

Angus!

John suddenly jumped out of his chair and rushed down to the phone. He kicked himself savagely all the way downstairs—he *knew* he had forgotten something.

"Angus?—it's John . . . . I'm terribly sorry—I forgot our date completely . . . . I know I could, but I promised J. C. I'd take a class for him at All Saints this afternoon."

There was a little silence at the other end of the phone; John couldn't tell whether Angus was angry or amused.

"I'm terribly sorry Angus—I'd much rather go for a tramp, but I promised—well, it isn't so much that, but they're expecting me . . . . and—" he clutched at the excuse—"it's too late to let them know now."

Angus's voice came back. "Oh, well—" yes, he was disappointed—"there will be more Sundays—you're not going to make teaching Sunday School a habit?"

"Oh, heck, no! I only agreed to substitute once, and when J. C. asked me if this Sunday were free I—I got mixed, and thought it was next Sunday you and I were going for a tramp."

All Saints Church was right on Central Avenue, two blocks east of the city hall, on the south side of the street. John learned later that the original building had been a little country church, the first in the district and seventy years old before they pulled it down in the twenties to make way for the modern structure.

When he reached the church he almost rubbed his eyes in disbelief. Like the school it was only half built, yet even more awkward to the eye. Evidently the parish had had more ambition than money. The basement was built on a generous scale, but only the chancel and transepts had been erected above it, so that one ascended the impressive stone steps at the front, walked across a concrete expanse where the body of the church should have been, and entered to find oneself between the two transepts in front of the choir.

Inside, John stood looking about him in the gloom, impressed by the size and colour of the east window. "To the Glory of God, and in Loving Memory of Gladys Matilda Grossart", he read, "born 1849, departed this life the year of Our Lord 1908".

There were voices over the south transept. John started, hearing Bilbeau's resonant baritone beside him.

"A magnificent window," he said, "contributed by Mr. Grossart to his mother's memory when this church was erected in the late twenties."

"I met Mr. Grossart," said John, with some complacency. "I was out on a fishing trip with him and the McIntyres."

"Indeed!" Mr. Bilbeau was impressed. "I didn't know you were acquainted with anyone outside of the Macdonalds."

"Oh, I roomed with Tom McIntyre at college." John tried to make it all seem offhand—millionaires were routine social contacts as far as he was concerned. He couldn't resist adding: "Mr. Grossart never impressed me as a church enthusiast."

Bilbeau agreed. "No, formal religion has very little appeal for him, I fear. He is one of nature's noblemen. But this city owes a great deal to Mr. Grossart, a great deal."

They moved over to meet the other teachers who seemed to have just finished some kind of a conference. There were only two other men: the remainder, with a few exceptions, all young women, two or three of them surprisingly young and good-looking. Vera Macdonald was there, and greeted John enthusiastically.

"It's *so* nice to see you here. I wish," she said wistfully, "you could persuade Angus to come with you some Sunday."

They descended stairs to the basement where they were met with a roar of young voices and an indescribable confusion of chairs and children. "Nearly four hundred"—at least three of the teachers to whom he had been introduced had mentioned the number. As he looked around he could believe it: children were crowded like ants into the long low basement room.

John was shown to his group, a ring of chairs packed with fifteen or twenty young boys all displaying their best clothes and worst behaviour. He had barely seated himself when a loud bell clanged. Miraculously chairs were pulled into line, everyone sat down, and silence reigned as Bilbeau appeared on the platform.

The ceiling was so low he almost touched it with his bald head. "Hymn Number 721," he announced, "the 721st hymn." There was a rustling of hymn books, the opening bars sounded on the piano, everyone stood up and burst into song, Bilbeau beating time with a stick, coming in a little ahead of the school on each line with a voice which didn't seem to be quite in tune, but was penetrating enough.

There was something just a bit comical about such a big man conducting with so much earnestness such little people who had so much noise in them and so little music. John did his best to sing, but felt embarrassed.

"Then awake!" (J. C. beating his stick now on the edge of the platform.)

"Then awake!"

"Happy song!" (Come on now, let's *have* it!)

"Happy song!"

"Shout for joy!" (At least the kids love it, thought John.)

"Shout for joy!

"As we glad-lee mar-cha-long!

"We are MAR-ching on with shield and banner bright
We will WORK for God and battle for the right
We will PRAISE His Name, rejoicing in His might
And we'll work till JEE-su-us calls!"

Mr. Springett, the rector, appeared out of nowhere, and read swiftly but with suitable intonations the prayers and responses. John sat down for the prayers and squatted forward with one hand over his eyes, until, looking through his fingers, he noticed that all the others had knelt facing their chairs. Self-consciously he swung around and knelt before his, resting his elbows on the chair and his head on his hands.

The actual lesson went very swiftly. By the time John had heard fifteen boys repeat with frequent prompting their memory texts from the previous Sunday, half his time had gone, and he was just getting nicely into his explanation of what a hypocrite was, when another loud clang of the bell announced that lessons were over.

Mr. Bilbeau rose again—John was sure this time that his polished dome would strike the ceiling.

"I can't give away any secrets—" he paused suggestively, beaming with suppressed good news while every head in the Sunday School cocked its ears—"but I think Harry has some good news for us in this Sunday's announcement."

Harry appeared, a thin pale young man with horn-rimmed glasses. He greeted the applause with a serious smile.

"Last week's collection," he read, "twenty-five dollars and three cents. This week's"—nearly eight hundred eyes strained politely forward—"twenty-six dollars and sixty cents."

There was a little outburst of applause which subsided as Harry's mouth opened again.

"Last Sunday's church attendance from the Sunday School—one hundred and fifteen. This Sunday, one hundred and sixteen."

Again there was some clapping, but evidently a more significant figure was on its way.

"Last Sunday's total Sunday School attendance, three hundred and eighty-three." There was an electric tension in the air and even John knew what was coming. "This Sunday our total attendance was—" Harry stopped to enjoy the suspense, then shouted enthusiastically, "Four hundred and eight!"

The Sunday School went wild—for a Sunday School. There were even some quickly suppressed whistles from the boys' classes.

J. C. Bilbeau stilled the storm. "It is highly gratifying to have achieved our goal," he said, still beaming, "but I am going to set a still higher goal before you. There is a Sunday School in this city"—a little boy in John's class leaned forward, his dark eyes snapping, and whispered excitedly—"First Baptist!"—"which has a record attendance of five hundred and ten students!"

Harry sprang to his feet. "Whaddayasay, All Saints, can we do it?" Mr. Springett squirmed in his chair on the platform.

The applause was almost indecorous.

The final hymn was sung, and the school dismissed.

Mr. Bilbeau overtook John on his way out. As Vera passed he nodded to her coolly, and turned back to John.
"Well," he beamed, "you have been with us on a notable
occasion—a notable occasion. We have been aiming at this
objective for three years," and he smiled again with the
triumph of achievement.

"It was quite a small Sunday School when you took
over, wasn't it?" asked John.

"Very small. If I remember correctly the average attendance barely reached the century-mark. And how did you
get along, John?"

"Oh, I'm afraid I was just nicely started when the bell
rang," John began—

"No matter—no matter. Did you notice their enthusiasm, the spirit of the school?"

John had, and acknowledged it. Just then Mr. Bilbeau
looked behind him, where one of the good-looking teachers
was waiting. "Excuse me," he said, turning to her, and
John escaped, a little resentful that he hadn't a chance to
see more of the girl but thankful that he hadn't been asked
to come again.

John left the Sunday School confused. This Sunday Bilbeau didn't quite belong to the smooth, efficient, dominating Bilbeau of the school. Not that he had shown any lack
of these qualities. But it was all so trivial.

Beating time for the children as they sang, the way he
put a friendly arm around his female teachers—somehow
these things lowered Bilbeau in his eyes.

Why?

Was J. C. insincere?

John shrugged his shoulders impatiently. Damn it all, he asked himself, why did I come in the first place? I'm no Sunday School teacher.

11

John's battle with his classes went on. Round two was not the easy victory he had visualized—he was no more than holding his own: giving more blows, but receiving just as many. More than once he thought of sending problem cases to the principal, but pride—and a touch of fear—always intervened.

The inspector came and went. After haunting the school for three days he observed a work lesson in algebra for half a period, came in to see him at the end of his physics period, and was gone. John was almost disappointed by the weakness of the climax after so much suspense.

As the winter term wore on, remembering the one girl who had unconsciously revealed fear of him, he watched all his classes closely. Gradually he discovered that others, mostly girls, feared his sudden barks and hostile stares. But the great discovery lay ahead.

His physiography class had settled down and was doing good work—for them. But he felt they were lazy, capable of more industry, and attention. Passing down the hall one day he had heard Miss Willis's voice raised in anger and saw her through the door window vigorously laying down the law. It might be worth concentrating on, he thought. A few days later in the middle of physiography class the idea came back to him, as he was drawing at the blackboard, and heard the restlessness behind his back.

Deliberately, Mr. Westley stopped in the middle of a line, put the chalk on the ledge, turned and walked calmly to his desk.

Quietly he said, "There is not enough attention," and paused.

"AND THERE'S TOO MUCH NOISE!" he shouted.

The effect was stunning. The class sat there frozen to their seats, not moving a muscle, every eye staring at John with *fear* in it. John swung around to the blackboard his face twitching with scarcely-controlled mirth. At the blackboard he picked up the chalk, even tossed it once in his hand as if to say "See what I can do when I feel like it!" then continued the line where he had left off, a broad smile on his face.

The first real victory.

He tried it on the next class and the next and the next. It worked. Every time. He smiled grimly as he went about the school, head high. I showed the little bastards. Who's afraid of who now, he thought, recalling his grammar only to toss it loftily aside.

It was so simple, after you found out.

Someone's got to be afraid. The one that's afraid first, loses the battle. If you're afraid, they're not: if you're not, they are. When you have yourself under control, the other person is afraid of you. So simple, he said to himself again, amazed at the beauty of its simplicity.

The Big Play came and went, competently directed by J. C. John helped with the make-up. He was disappointed in the type of play, though he laughed as much as anyone when Aunt Harriet was discovered under the bed eaves-dropping, got out and stood up, with her bloomers showing. But it was deflating to hear everyone praising it up to the skies merely because it had amused them. They hadn't made such a fuss over *his* play! Even the students he had coached so thoroughly for the Christmas concert, now that they had parts in the Big Play, treated John with some condescension. They were in the 'big time' now. He was secretly glad Elsie Braund had not been cast for a part though she had seemed as anxious to be as anyone. Wait till they see her in that Molière thing, he thought.

He had culled the opening scene from a translation of *Le Médecin malgré lui* where Sganarelle and his wife quarrel. He could find no one to take the part of Sganarelle adequately, but by dint of much private coaching he had succeeded in building up Bill Atkins, a large, awkward, but sensitive Upper School lad, into a fair semblance of the character. Elsie seemed to take as much to comedy as she did to its opposite; and the selection was a big success. John felt refreshing waves of pure pleasure sweep over him as he watched her, every line of her body expressive, but especially her hands. "Look at Master Clever"—scorn in every finger of one outthrust hand. "I have got four poor children on my hands"—and there they were! "I laugh at your threats"—knuckles on hips, the fingers pointing contemptuously down and back. And even as she cowered under his blows, her arms defensively over her head, the hands went on talking: "Wretch! Villain! deceiver! cur! scoundrel! gallows-bird! churl! rogue! scamp! thief!"

But the reaction of the staff! Of course they had seen her in nothing but this one performance, but even then couldn't they see there was drama in her very finger tips?

No. They couldn't. "Lazy . . . . Doesn't seem to be interested in anything . . . . Reads excellently, but her spelling! . . . . As a student she's hopeless . . . . I'll admit she can act, but in the classroom?—arsenic's too good for her."

Angus was really the only one who made any kind of a satisfactory comment. "That girl is an extraordinary actress, but she's a misfit here. She'll probably end up as waitress in a restaurant."

"But why?" protested John.

"I'm no psychologist."

"But shouldn't we all be psychologists? Shouldn't we take a kid like Elsie and find out what's wrong with her?"

"Maybe we should be taking society and finding out what's wrong with *it*." It was one of those perverse moods of Angus's in which he seemed to get a kind of pleasure out of baiting John.

Supervising in the library one Thursday, John fell to day-dreaming. He would build Elsie up. Next year, in the Christmas play, he'd build it around Elsie, *force* the public to recognize her worth. He'd organize a drama league in the city, put on a three-act play, make Elsie the talk of the town, persuade the Rotary Club to sponsor a trip to New York or Hollywood. He pictured the local paper: a cut of Elsie, her arms full of flowers a radiant smile on her face, holding his arm—taken in New York in her dressing-room back stage after a record-smashing first night.

The reporters crowding around, the flash of camera bulbs.

"How do you account for your brilliant success, Miss Braund?"

Elsie turns to the ordinary-looking school teacher from a small Canadian city. "I learned more from Mr. Westley rehearsing for one play than I have picked up in all my years in New York and Hollywood."

Contracts. "Mr. Westley, if you sign this, in one year you'll be the biggest producer on Broadway."

He caught himself stroking his chin, calmly weighing the offer—and broke into a sheepish grin. Two boys happened to be watching him. One nudged the other, indicated John with a wave of the eyes, then moved a finger to point significantly at his own head, grinning. John's eye, roving the room to make sure he had been unobserved, caught him in the act, froze the grin into a ghastly imitation of a thoughtful frown, and inspired the finger to scratch the head meditatively. The other boy's eyes dropped furtively to his book. There was a time, thought John, complacently, when they would have gone on grinning at me to my face.

Until the middle of the winter term John had scarcely been conscious of the larger school world around him, absorbed as he was in the problems of his own classes and in his dramatic work. He had not even seen a rugby game, between W.K.C.I. and K.C.V.S.—Kirby Collegiate and Vocational School.

The two Kirbys were keen rivals in hockey as well, but Old Kirby had the edge; not only because it had the longer hockey tradition, but there was the natural advantage of having the frozen river for rinks all through the cold weather.

This rivalry in sports affected school life in various ways. Above all it stimulated, and was stimulated by, cheer practices: special sessions in the assembly hall before a

Big Game, when teachers and students assembled to work up the spirit of victory demanded of the occasion.

As a boy, and even in his early college days, John had taken a normal interest in sports. But his own high school had never had the pretensions of a 'city' school; it had never made any serious attempt to imitate the American system of organizing sports into a gigantic community enterprise whose activities commanded national attention.

So John was unprepared for the almost religious nature of these cheer practices.

The practice before the hockey finals was as good a sample as any John had seen. It began with the school song led by Bud Rawley the cheer leader, a lad with the lungs of a horse and no inhibitions.

> *"West Kirby stalwarts gird yourselves*
> *And march forth to the fray:*
> *Shout one and all in unison*
> *To keep our foes at bay.*
> *Our banners streaming in the wind,*
> *We hold our honour high;*
> *And never will we cease to fight*
> *For W! K! C! I!"*

Bud retired to get his blood pressure down to normal, while Frank Jarratt led the team up on the platform and introduced each member:

". . . . Then there's Percy Evans. That's Perc blushing away third from the end. Step up, Perc!"

Perc stood forward, red with embarrassment, a nervous grin on his face, his hands behind his back, his eyes on his toes or shifting sheepishly to his team mates and quickly back again.

"Perc may be scared to death on the platform. But out there on the field he's as stout a halfback as you'll find in the twin cities!" And so on.

The team filed down, Bud reappeared, to announce in picturesque sports jargon the imminent clash. The light of battle filled every loyal West Kirbian eye.

"Are you READY?" bellowed Bud.

"*YEAH!*" the school roared back.

"WHO'S ready?"

"*WE ARE!*"

"THEN WHAT ARE WE WAITING FOR?"

Two assistant cheer leaders raced up to stand on either side of Bud, and the three, swaying from side to side, their arms and bodies beating: "A-one—a-two—a-THREE!"

On the third beat the school burst into its chant:

> *West Kirby, West Kirby,*
> *W.-K.-C.-I.*
> *Boomalaka, Boomalaka,*
> *Do or die!*
> *Bust 'em in the middle!*
> *Sock 'em in the eye!*
> *Double-u, Double-u,*
> *K.   C.   I.!*

The organized rhythmic roar was awe-inspiring. In spite of himself, John felt a wave of emotion as the school rose on the last two lines, and every loyal West Kirbian did his best to rupture his larynx.

At the door afterward John spoke to Angus. "I never realized there could be so much noise in one room."

"That's because you've never heard a real Hitlerian 'Sieg Heil'."

Angus had a habit of making such cryptic remarks. The German words meant nothing to John, although he had studied scientific German at college. And it was curious that Angus should mention Hitler—there really wasn't any connection he could see. Hitler was a funny-looking lunatic that the local paper was still ridiculing, though the Toronto papers seemed to be taking him more seriously now. John hadn't paid much attention: the man was a clown and the editorials making fun of him were wasted, he thought.

Early in March the Senior Dance was the big event for the students. It was John's first contact with his students on the same social plane—the informal Rugby Scrimmage in the fall was just a kid party after all. But the Senior Dance was *formal!*

John was amazed by the transformation in some of the girls he taught. Their long graceful evening gowns matured them overnight; while their young complexions and budding figures gave them a contrasting freshness that was irresistible. He found himself feeling shy and gauche talking to a girl from his physics class whom the day before he had embarrassed in front of the class by exposing her ignorance of the fundamental laws of light. John went home that night wishing that he had Mary with him, to show these sophisticated young things that he too was a bit of a gay blade.

Easter examinations came and went. A new time-table whereby the exams were split into two sections ten days apart gave John time for marking: two half days completely free, and the evenings clear of lesson preparation. He went to Toronto for a week at Mary's with only two sets left to mark. The educational association of the province met that same week, but John was too absorbed in Mary to give it more than a passing thought. The wedding had been fixed for the end of June and they spent their time looking at furniture and fixtures, arguing over the number of children they would have, and deciding how much they could save monthly on John's salary.

12

John's social activities through the winter, limited by the necessity for keeping his nose to the school grindstone, had largely been confined to a few evenings and afternoons with Angus.

Angus had been amused by John's account of his Sunday School experience, and lightly caustic on the subject of Bilbeau's organizing ability. He had been even more amused when John asked him how he would go about teaching religion to children, then pretended to take the question seriously.

"First of all," he had said, with a mischievous twinkle in his eye, "I would put through legislation making it illegal for any child to read the Bible." John's mouth fell open. "Then I would see to it that every copy of the Bible had printed plainly on the cover, the words, 'For Adults Only'. Then I would prohibit all parents and teachers from giving religious instruction to children."

"But that's—that would mean that a whole generation would grow up in complete religious ignorance!" John protested, a little shocked even though he realized Angus wasn't in earnest.

"Would it?" asked Angus, smiling. "What about prohibition? Was drinking alcoholic beverages eliminated by prohibiting their sale? It seems to me that your generation grew up with the idea that it was smart and grown-up to sneak a drink of bootleg liquor."

"Well, yes," said John, "but what's the connection?"

"The point is," said Angus, who was serious now, "that religion has always been purest when it was an underground movement, or at least a protestant movement. What Bilbeau is doing at All Saints is the one thing best calculated to kill religion. His children learn to identify religion with progress and success. Progress means expansion, and success is reached when All Saints Sunday School is the biggest in the city. Tie up religion with a successful institution and it dies."

Remembering Tom McIntyre's reference to Angus's alleged atheism, John wondered just what Angus really thought about the "things that mattered". But there was something about his friend that discouraged John from asking. Only once did Angus raise a little the blind to the window of his private life.

It was a Friday evening early in February. Angus's wife was over at her mother's for the day—a not infrequent practice of hers. The staff meeting to discuss the inspector's report had lasted until after six, and John had invited Angus to have supper with him at Mrs. Gillespie's.

About seven o'clock they drove over to the island, put the car in the garage and walked up the ash-strewn walk to the house—there had been a thaw and the path was icy.

It was one of those still, clear winter nights when the stars are intimate, prying closely into earthy affairs, the unnatural brightness of curiosity in their cold eyes.

John remarked that on a night like this one could almost reach up and pick himself a basketful of stars.

Angus replied that picking up stars, provided there were a creature gigantic enough to indulge in the practice, would be like picking up hot potatoes.

Looking back as they entered the house they saw Orion rising in the east.

Seated comfortably in one of Angus's big leather chairs, sipping Angus's version of a Martini, John continued on the subject of stars.

"Do you know, there's the one argument for the existence of God that no one can get around."

"You think not." Angus was stating rather than asking.

"Well, as far as that goes, I'm an agnostic. You can't prove there *is* a God, you can't prove there *isn't*. It's all a matter of opinion."

"Yes, and your opinions are largely at the mercy of your emotional outlook."

"Oh, I wouldn't go that far—I'd like to believe there's a heaven for instance, but I'm pretty skeptical about its existence, as an actual place, that is. But the thing that's impressed me about science is the marvelous way everything works into a plan. A scientist is *forced* to believe there's design in the universe."

"Or complete chaos." Angus looked smaller and older. There had never been such an air of indecision about him. His eyes were hard, focused in the air.

"Take the dark nebulae. Barnard catalogues a hundred and eighty-two of them. What are they? Chaotic masses of inert matter, probably fine dust. What's their function, origin, significance? Take the stars themselves, and their so-called majestic movements. *We* are doing most of the moving. Binaries, novas, clusters, nebulae, giant stars, dwarf stars—a thousand years ago the most learned men distinguished one star from another only by its brightness. Now there are a hundred *kinds* of stars, and scarcely two of a kind are of the same brightness. Nature is chaos, infinite variety. It's the mind of man that invents order for his own convenience."

"But what's science, then, and truth?"

Angus smiled. "I'm talking nonsense of course," he reassured John. "But sometimes I get the feeling that science is like fishing. You make a net with a specific mesh, cast it in the lake, haul in your fish and—presto! All the fish are of a size."

"I don't get it," said John.

"Well, take your stars. There's an infinite variety of them in the heavens. So we classify them—"

"The net!" interrupted John.

"Exactly! Or rather, a hundred nets. And each time we think there may be a fish that doesn't fit one of the hundred, we make ourselves another net."

"But the spectroscope!" protested John. "They're all made of the same stuff!"

"What stuff? Atoms. What are atoms? Miniature solar systems, electrons dancing around a nucleus. And the nucleus is energy—a concentration of nothing in a highly active state."

"But it works! It's useful!"

John thought, there's something wrong with his reasoning but I can't get hold of it.

152

"Of course it works. I'm not disparaging science as a useful tool. It's the claim of science to be able to establish truth as an absolute that is absurd."

John's mind, never far away from his job, shifted to education.

"Do you tell your classes things like this?"

Angus smiled. "My business is to teach facts, not theories. I'm happy if incidentally they learn to think for themselves, and I certainly don't want to ruin that possibility by telling them what to think."

Again it was not what Angus *said* that bothered him. It was something back of what he said. John saw, through a glass, darkly, vague dark shapes in Angus's soul, disturbing shapes—something like the terrifying meaningless chaos Angus talked about. Damn it all, there's something wrong with Angus's thinking: life isn't chaos!

There were other times with Angus that he remembered. They had gone out one Saturday on snowshoes, from Angus's back door, down the south bank of the island and out along the shore ice six miles to where the Kirby escarpment emerged from the lake under a blanket of snow and ice. They scraped the snow from a flat rock, made a fire, fried some bacon and eggs, boiled coffee, and ate their lunch in the open, toasting their toes gently at the fire.

"Not much for a geologist to see right now," remarked John, sipping hot coffee from a tin cup.

"Now that's where you're wrong, dead wrong! Here you sit, surrounded by the most active, versatile, and essential mineral in the world, and you ask, where's the rock?"

John looked around, startled. "Oh!" he laughed—"you mean water."

Angus went into a long dissertation. Beginning with the character of the surface—the hard rhythmic ridges of the wind-swept snow, the gentler contours of the fresh snow in the lee of wind-breaks, the clusters of hoar-frost over the ice in the hollows along the shore where water had soaked through the snow above—he deduced what had happened, was happening, would happen underneath; to the snow and ice itself, to the sand, and gravel, weeds, driftwood, dirt below; until under his deft touches, the snowy stillness moved and breathed, was swung into the ceaseless current of change, a part of the eternal flux of things. As he talked —with his old fur cap askew on his head, in his shabby mackinaw, and pants tucked under bush socks, squatting on a snow-crusted rock, his moccasins flat on the trampled snow, one hand relaxed across his knees, the other pointing, sweeping the horizon, gesturing—John could not help thinking, what a grand-looking prophet he would make with the keen nose and eyes thrusting out of a bushy beard!

One Sunday afternoon they went over to Dot Young's studio, a bare room over a run-down corner grocery out on 21st Street North, not far from Old Kirby Park.

It was John's first glimpse of an artist's studio and he was disappointed. No glamorous divan, or soft glowing lights: just a bare shabby room with sketch boards and canvasses stacked haphazardly along the wall, even piled flat on the floor. There was an easel and a small table where the paint box and palette lay; the former open, revealing a chaos of paint tubes, old and new, full and squeezed dry.

Dot had been working on an abstract canvas based on a little snow sketch in water colours.

Angus and John looked at it.

"This is the one you were telling me about last week," said Angus. "I think I'm going to like it."

"You know," remarked John, feeling he should say something intelligent, "if you were to hang the two together it would help. I mean, when I see the little one it helps me to understand the big one. About how long would it take to paint a picture?"

"That's like asking, how long is a piece of string?" smiled Dot. "I might dash off a sketch in half an hour, or potter about with a canvas for six weeks."

After they had poked around among the sketches against the wall for a while the tea was ready. There were only two chairs; a wooden grocery box supplied the third seat. Dot noticed John's wondering eyes.

"I suppose I could fix this place up a bit; but it's nice and homey this way. It's a good room to work in."

"Work?" John was puzzled. "I thought this was a kind of a hobby—I mean a way of filling in your spare time."

"Yes, that's the trouble, most people do."

"Well, it's pleasant work, isn't it?" John persisted.

"Yes and no. It's absorbing, but terribly wearying too, when things don't go right and you can't discover why."

John thought that over.

"Watch out!" Angus warned Dot. "When he gets that meditative look it means he's working on one of his embarrassing questions."

John grinned self-consciously. "It's rather a silly question I suppose, but which would you say was more important: your painting, or your teaching?"

"To me, my painting; to the public my teaching. I think that's my answer." Dot frowned thoughtfully. "Except that if I didn't paint I couldn't teach, but if I didn't teach I could paint a whole lot better."

"No, but which do you think is more basic; more important in every sense of the word?"

"Well, if you want my honest opinion the world could get along better minus all the teachers than it could minus art—mind you, I'm using the word art in its big sense, including music, sculpture, dancing and literature, as well as drawing and painting. A teacher is merely an interpreter —he takes the knowledge and experience of the past and feeds it in small doses to the present. An artist, if he really is one, creates."

"But a teacher creates too. He takes an ignorant child and makes him into an educated one."

"Just the way a cereal factory takes a kernel of corn and makes it into a corn flake," supplemented Angus.

"That's processing," declared Dot, "not creation. You take a normal intelligent child at the age of six, coop him up in a room ten months of the year for ten or fifteen years, and feed him doses of arithmetic, geography, spelling, algebra, French, woodwork and zoology, giving him enough exercise and entertainment to keep him healthy and happy. What do you create? A perfect factory or office employee, with habits of industry, punctuality and docility. That's not creation. If anything, it's a sort of paring-off process; at the end of fifteen years you have *less* than you started with. You begin with a potential man and end up with a sort of mechanized mouse."

It occurred to John about this time that he was getting into rather queer company. Angus and Dot were not normal people. He admired them both tremendously; in fact the company of other teachers had become tedious, much as he liked most of them. But Angus with his next-to-atheism, and Dot with her radical views on art and education, both went a little too far. They lacked balance—no, not balance; in a way they were quite balanced. But they were impractical, that was it.

It was all very well to criticize, but a man had to be practical to get along. Here was Angus with all his ability, stuck in a high school apparently for the rest of his life. Why? Because he was impractical. Of course he had worked out a good kind of life for himself in a way, but look at his salary. J. C. mightn't be *quite* as intelligent, he was a bit narrow-minded when you came to think of it; but there wasn't any doubt that he would get ahead. J. C. was headed for bigger things.

And J. C. was practical: he got results.

John's English results at Easter were a big improvement over Christmas. It was really quite a simple matter—John had merely marked them less stiffly, and the results were gratifying. J. C. had noticed, and congratulated him. Of course, the marks had nothing to do with better teaching, and J. C. was bright enough to know it. Probably Nyes expected a certain standard in marks, and naturally Bilbeau had to protect himself. He certainly couldn't tell John outright to mark more easily—he just mentioned the marks, hinted that Nyes might notice, and left it up to John. J. C. had been practical about the whole thing. Mr. Bilbeau had brought up the matter of Sunday School again, but John had managed to slide out of it and hadn't been asked since.

It was difficult to get to know J. C. intimately. In the first place John felt that as a new and younger teacher it was not in his place to make the advances. Besides, J. C. obviously was too fair-minded to play favourites, and did not allow himself an intimacy with one member of his department that he would not adopt with another. So John admired him from a little distance, observing his manner of doing things, unconsciously imitating him in some things, consciously in others. For instance he found himself one day in class, announcing the content of the course which would be subject to examination at Easter ending with:

"—and from now till the end of the term you may expect nothing but hard work. Hard work." The quiet repetition of the last words was so typical of Bilbeau that John caught himself wondering if he had become Bilbeau, by some miracle. It was a rather comfortable feeling, one of poise, self-confidence, almost of loftiness.

April and Easter, followed by May, and before he knew it the final exams were upon him. Outside, the trees were bursting with fresh green leaves, the clouds were racing under the blue sky, white-caps curled over the green-blue waves on the bay. But within, the electric clock clicked and the minute hand leaped at two minute intervals, to the steady whisper of pens on paper, as young heads bowed before the great god Examination, rising at intervals to stare meditatively into space, to bow again while the pens moved on. John paced the floor, or sat at a desk at the back, or leaned against a window sill, watching, interminably watching, while the students wrote.

More marking, more reports. Finally there came the last pay cheque, the last staff meeting—at which Mr. Pennington was presented with a handsome leather-bound edition of *Shakespeare* as a parting gift—the last meal at Mrs. Gillespie's, the last trip to the station.

As John looked out the window of the rapidly accelerating train, heading south, he reflected to himself, this is the last time I'll be seeing the new bridge before I get married.

13

John and Mary Westley spent their honeymoon in a Muskoka cottage, visited John's family in Montreal for a week; and came at the end of August to West Kirby, where they boarded at Mrs. Gillespie's and began looking for an apartment.

On the second day they found what they were looking for on the corner of Second Avenue and Fifth Street, one of the three new apartments over Pearcey's Drug Store.

"It's all so new and clean," Mary complained, "I won't have any work to do!" When they learned they could move in on September the first, they decided then and there to take it.

They celebrated with a rapturous embrace behind the landlord's back, bought a brick of ice-cream and two big bottles of Canada Dry on their way back to the boarding-house, and completed their celebration by treating themselves and Mrs. Gillespie to generous draughts of home-made ice-cream sodas.

In the morning they went over again. Mary measured the windows for curtains while John drew plans of the rooms, inspected the stove, banged the refrigerator door, and flushed the toilet to see that all were working smoothly; then signed—feeling himself to be quite the business man—a one-year lease on the apartment.

The apartment was somewhat far from the school: about twenty minutes' brisk walk if one took the short cut over the tracks, half an hour by way of Central Avenue. But Klein, who had a car, and lived only four blocks over, on Eighth Street, offered to drive John to and from school daily.

The big advantage was that it was so close to downtown; a fifteen-minute walk took you to the show, or to the dentist, or to pay your light bill. Slaght's Marketeria was only a block down the street, and the drug store was under the same roof.

It was all very convenient.

And, as Frank Jarratt had pointed out to them on their last day at the boarding-house, the Sixth Street United Church was only a block away.

"Isn't that a pity," Mary had responded with a sigh.

Frank had looked at her in a puzzled sort of way.

"We won't be able to go," she explained gravely. "We're Anglicans!"

They had moved in the Saturday before school opened and by Monday night had things pretty well organized, even to the hanging of the curtains.

At 8:30 Tuesday morning Klein drove up in his sedan. John exchanged greetings, accepted congratulations on his marriage, and climbed in beside his fellow teacher.

"Not quite the same as last year, eh?" remarked Klein.

John assented, thinking of the contrast. Last year, walking to school from a dingy boarding-house: this year driving, and leaving behind to wait for him a tidy little apartment and a sweet little wife. Quite slushy this morning, aren't you, he told himself.

This first morning was very different.

They parked in what some of the teachers liked to call "the quadrangle"—at any rate there would be one there some day, when the school was finished. Walking over to the new school entrance, ascending the steps with dignity, casually nodding to or smiling at a familiar student face, John felt above his quickening pulse the calm self-possession of the veteran. A year ago it had been *a* school; now it was *his* school.

In Miss Jamieson's office there was the usual group of teachers. They came forward to shake John's hand warmly, congratulating him on his marriage; Miss Willis, Mr. Starling, Margaret Brewin—and Dot Young. He was glad to see them all, exchanged witticisms, asked what kind of summer they had had. Mr. Starling had taken a teachers' summer course, Miss Willis had been marking departmental examinations in Toronto, Margaret Brewin had been to Europe—Paris no less, and Sweden.

"And what kind of a summer did you have?" asked John of Dot Young as they strolled down the corridor.

"Rotten, thanks," said Dot. "I took Mother down to Detroit for a change—we have relatives there—and she was ill the whole time. So when she improved a bit we came home."

They saw Angus in his lab and went in. Angus had been over to the apartment briefly on Sunday evening.

"Oh!—Oh!" said John. "I just remembered J. C. is having his English meeting now. I've got to dash."

He left unceremoniously and ran up the stairs two at a time, arriving breathless at J. C.'s room.

More handshaking, congratulations. "I'm sure we'll all be very happy to meet Mrs. Westley," said Mr. Bilbeau warmly. He referred briefly to Agnes Purcell's sudden summer marriage; which was news to John.

Another surprise: Dot Young came in. John looked so astonished he induced a thin smile on her face.

In short order the meeting was under way.

Seated on the platform later John looked over the assembled staff. Nyes was there of course, with J. C. beside him. Miss Garrell, Smith, Klein, Margaret Brewin, Starling, Pikestaff: all were familiar faces now. Angus was over on the right, with Miss Willis, Miss Pettiker, and a new man. There's a typical teacher, thought John. He was tall, thin, and rather stiff-looking: wearing horn-rimmed glasses behind which small eyes looked straight through the thick lenses in a fixed stare into space. His profile was a straight line from which a thin gristly nose and a full lower lip projected. The latter was pressed resolutely up from a sharp bony chin against the upper lip. That's the new classics man to take Pennington's place, he concluded. He leaned over to Dot. "What's the new man's name?"

"Audubon, I think."

"Who is taking Agnes Purcell's place?"

"A Miss Collier. She's just behind us."

John leaned back casually, turned and exchanged greetings with Frank Jarratt, who sat beside her. He had just time to glimpse a small dark girl with a big nose, little chin and large brown eyes before Nyes rose to his feet, silenced the students and began the proceedings.

Announcement of texts, reading class lists, staff meeting, followed each other as of old. In the library John met Nita Collier formally. She spoke in a quick shy voice, and smiled as if she wished she could really smile but under the circumstances hoped one would understand. John joked about his own first day—told her how frightened he had been a year ago—and was rewarded with a grateful smile.

"You'll like it here," said John.

He meant what he said. One year ago he had been a university student suddenly thrust into the society of adult teachers. Now he was an equal among equals. These were his friends. It was true some of them were a bit stodgy and desiccated; but here, back-stage, there was a group feeling that rode above their differences. Twenty High School Assistants, the only ones of their kind in the city, a small minority ruling over thirty times their number. John imagined there must exist the same solidarity among a group of Anglo-Indians in an outpost on the Afghan border. Over the line lay the black hordes of the ignorant and the superstitious; a handful of white officers with their semi-educated native regiment defended the world of enlightenment. Well, it was something like that.

Nyes looked older this fall. Nothing could age those tough cheeks nor could the grooves, running like drain pipes from the eavestroughs under his eyes, have deepened. But the eyes had no light in them and the voice was tired. Even the hair lay wearily on his head.

Everyone else looked just the same.

Klein's car was filled going home: three of the women were in the back seat, going uptown. They chatted about their summer wanderings, remarked that everything and everyone were just the same—except Mr. Nyes. They had all noticed the change in him.

Dropped off at his own corner John raced up the stairs to the apartment, the fragrance of steak and onions floating down to meet him. He burst through the door, down the little corridor and into the kitchen, flung his arms around Mary, lifted her up, sat her on the edge of the sink and kissed her a dozen times.

"Darling, you're wonderful, the dinner is wonderful"—he·dropped her on the floor, and lifted up the lid of the frying pan, sniffing ecstatically—"and teaching is wonderful, now I'm married to you." He kissed her again, while Mary fought his caresses with elbows and hands, laughingly. He picked her up, carried her into the bedroom, threw her on the bed, shut the door, pulled his hair over his eyes and made a horrible face, advancing with ape-like gesture, menacingly. "And now, my dear little dumpling, I have you in my power," he laughed in his best Frankenstein-monster bass, "and I'm going to EAT YOU UP." The tussle ended by their tumbling on the floor. Mary jumped up. "Oh, John, you've mussed the bed and—" a look of horror came over her and she dashed out of the room—"the steak, the steak! My poor little juicy steak and onions."

They saved the steak and ate it.

Angus dropped in that afternoon. Impulsively Mary greeted him with a hug. Angus reddened behind a smile that showed he loved it. They had a bookshelf in the living room which Angus quickly located.

"Dostoevski, Gorki. Which of you is the Russian?" He turned and looked from one to the other, squatting on his heels.

"Not me," said John. "Mary's the little Rooshan."

"I *love* Rooshans," Mary confessed. "They're so—" she frowned a little, pensively—"so Rooshan!" and they smiled.

"Now that you're here for more than the flying visit you paid us Sunday—I hope," she added "will you please instruct me in my duties as the wife of a high school teacher. John's been telling me all sorts of things but he's really just a baby teacher yet."

When John's reaction had subsided, Angus put on his best pedagogical face and made his reply:

"The wife of a teacher in West Kirby Collegiate Institute will observe the following rules:

"(a) She will neither smoke nor drink."

"What about swearing?" asked Mary.

"Unthinkable!" said Angus. "Please don't interrupt."

"(b) She will appear at all staff functions to which she is invited."

"Fully clothed!" added John.

"(c)," continued Angus, "She must know how to play bridge and how to entertain, at the same time remaining inconspicuous and respectable."

John protested. "It's impossible for my wife to be inconspicuous."

"And very difficult for me to be respectable," added Mary.

"(d) Her place is definitely in the home."

"But what is home without a mother?" asked John.

They went into the possibilities of a family till Mary warned John with her eyes and steered the conversation elsewhere.

When John came upstairs after seeing Angus to the door he found Mary subdued, staring out the window.

"What's wrong?"

"John, we shouldn't have mentioned babies."

"Why not? After all Angus knows the facts of life."

"It's not funny," said Mary.

"But damn it all, if we can't be ourselves with Angus . . . . for all you know losing his son doesn't necessarily make him begrudge babies to his friends."

"I know, but let's be careful. Angus has been hurt enough."

"I think you exaggerate the whole thing, Mary. After all, even though he's lost his boy, and hasn't much in common with his wife, he *is* living the kind of life he likes. You don't know how much a man's work means to him. I don't mean his teaching, though I think he really enjoys that, even when he pretends to be cynical about it. But he has his rocks. Did you know he was writing a book on the Precambrian?"

"But John, that only proves that his normal life is starved; his writing a book is only a kind of substitute for real things like—like love and children."

"I suppose my interest in rocks is the result of an empty love life."

Mary dimpled: "I haven't noticed such a terrific urge in you to go looking at rocks, the last six months."

John laughed and hugged her.

School was very different this year.

John was determined at the outset to establish a firm hand over his classes. He was surprised to notice that his first year students looked smaller than last year's crop of newcomers, until he remembered his own reaction as a senior student in high school, "They get smaller every year."

While he checked the seating plan John eyed his class with the intensity of a small child watching his mother reach into the cookie jar. Halfway through the period a dark-complexioned boy who looked as if he already shaved leaned forward to whisper to the boy in front. John consulted his seating plan. "Bob Wheatley!" The lad started as if struck, blushed crimson.

"Aren't you satisfied with that seat?"

"Yes, sir!" He sat tensely, as did the class.

"Then attend to business!" said Mr. Westley, impressively, and went on with the lesson.

He told Mary about it at noon.

"When I think of the torture I went through last year just because I didn't have the sense to jump on them right from the first!" he said. "Do you know there isn't *one* cf those first year kids that isn't afraid of me? Except maybe the repeaters, and are they surprised?"

"Is that good?" asked Mary.

"Well, maybe afraid is too strong a word. But they certainly respect me."

"So do I, darling," said Mary mischievously. "You're such a big strong man!"

"You can laugh all you like, but you just try taking my job for a week. It's the law of the jungle: I eat them or they eat me. I've *got* to have their respect, Mary." John put down his fork and glared at Mary, as though she were an insubordinate student.

"Yes, John dear," she said in a meek little voice, dimpling.

A month sped by.

Enjoy teaching as John might, Sunday morning was the highlight of the week. At nine o'clock he would roll lazily out of bed, pull on his pyjama bottoms, and turn on the radio to get the news and a negro spiritual programme that followed. The news was Mary's signal to get up. They breakfasted in their dressing gowns to *Listen to the Lambs* or *L'il David Play on Your Harp* or *Nobody Knows the Trouble I've Seen*. Then came a string quartet for half an hour. If it rained they read; usually they read anyway, or washed the dishes from the night before. On fine afternoons they went out for a walk, sometimes to McAdams Falls, at others down along the south shore, or over to the island to visit Angus, never tiring of his view.

Mary's first introduction to the staff came early in October: the annual invitation from the Nyes's—a bridge party, inevitably.

John had not played a hand since the Bilbeau party but Mary was with him, he knew everybody, and was in high spirits.

"Just watch me bid!" he told Mary as they separated to take their places.

With the recklessness of his mood he bid high, destroying wherever he sat the atmosphere of cautious bidding—at some tables the scores were phenomenal.

The reactions were various. Miss Pettiker giggled, it was what she would have liked to do; Pikestaff endured it patiently, wearing a weak smile. Angus was there, and tolerated John's frivolity but gave him the worst trimming of the evening. Mrs. Macdonald was just a bit sharp in a nice way. But Mrs. Smith was furious, particularly at losing to such an obvious ignoramus. "I didn't realize," she stated nastily, "that I'd be asked to play bridge with . . . ." The blank was worse than any word she could have used. John's spirits sank, till he looked over, saw Mary in the beautiful black velvet that made her skin startlingly alive, her arms and neck ravishingly young. She was talking, laughing, in that alert, charming way she had: a sort of sophisticated naiveté—or was it naive sophistication? Seeing her so, his heart burst with pride and his spirits soared again.

He spied her later talking to J. C.—J. C. at his best: witty, deferential, dominating with a deprecatory air, smiling with that rare but devastating smile.

Even as J. C. smiled, he took Mary's arm in a casual way and led her over to be introduced to another staff member. She smiled back at Angus, who returned her smile stiffly.

Just then J. C. turned, spied John. "Mr. Westley! Your wife and I have been looking for you." Though he raised his voice only a hairbreadth above normal, it had the quality of attracting ears. John suddenly found everyone looking and hastily closed the gap between him and Mary.

"Mrs. Westley has just been educating me on the subject of painting. She tells me this is an original."

"This" was an old-fashioned oil painting in greens and browns, a landscape involving a lake, some mountains, trees on either side, and grass; almost identical with the picture in the Macdonalds' living room. It was in an elaborate gilt frame with a special light overhead, obviously highly valued by the Nyes. "Now I know nothing about oil painting—what do you think of it?"

John mumbled something, then thought of and mentioned Dot Young.

"Of course! Miss Young, the versatile member of our English staff. I believe she's here?"

By a curious coincidence Dot had just joined Angus. For

a third time he was deserted. But Dot's face was pale and she was not smiling.

By this time tea-cups were suspended half-way to chins all over the room. Mrs. Nyes was sitting on a straight chair beside Miss Willis and Miss Garrell at the end of the room, and all three were looking. Miss Pettiker's sparrow face was pert with curiosity. Even Frank Jarratt, gallantly passing sandwiches, sensed the tension and looked over.

For some reason John's mind skipped back to a vivid sermon he had heard as a boy: the Sadducees and Pharisees crowded about Jesus showing him a coin.

Dot looked at the picture and faced up to J. C. whose smile was just a shade crooked.

"Mr. Westley here was suggesting that we consult an expert," he said smoothly, deferentially.

Dot's voice was even and quiet. "For its time and place, a good sincere copy," she stated.

"Copy?" Mr. Bilbeau's shaggy brows rose skeptically towards his bald crown.

"Miss Nyes never did, or pretended to do, anything else," said Dot. "I knew her as a girl. She gave me my first painting lesson."

The conversation started again. Tea-cups continued their restless trips from saucers to lips and back again. Frank passed more sandwiches.

Klein drove them home and they talked trivialities.

Upstairs in the apartment Mary went to the bathroom without a word, came out, went into the bedroom and closed the door.

John stood in the hallway with a silly little defensive smile on his face.

"Mary!"

No answer.

"What's the matter?"

No answer.

John had had two other sessions like this with Mary, each time over something he had considered trivial.

He tried the door, opened it, saw Mary, as he expected, with her head buried in the pillow.

"Mary."

She never stirred.

"Was it about Dot—I mean mentioning her name?"

No answer.

"Mary, it came out before I thought. Mary don't *be* like this!" He shook her a little, gently, knelt down by the bed and snuggled his head up to hers like a repentant puppy.

An hour passed before Mary would really talk. She sat up, looking tired, her eyes bloodshot.

"I have never, ever, seen such a piece of tactlessness in my whole life. Putting Dot Young on the spot before all those stuffed shirts. You and your J. C.! Why don't you go and live with him?"

"But he only asked—"

"As if it wasn't as plain as the nose on your face that he was baiting her. Honestly, men are so stupid!"

"Well," John feebly protested, "it was your fault, too: if you hadn't gone over to that picture with him."

"What did you expect me to do—tell him I didn't feel like looking at pictures?"

"And what was *I* expected to do, thumb my nose at him when he said, 'Here, come and get your wife'?"

"You didn't have to drag Dot in."

"I *know* I didn't, but I did and I'm sorry. I'm a stupid,

tactless fool, and I'm not worth a hair of your head but you needn't rub it in!" John was almost weeping.

Mary melted, and the incident was over. Or so John thought.

The next day over their coffee at the supper table Mary brought up the subject again.

"John, what do you see in J. C. Bilbeau that makes you admire him so much?"

John hesitated—"I suppose, what everybody else sees. Everybody likes J. C. Why do you ask?"

It was Mary's turn to hesitate. "Oh, perhaps I'm just being silly—maybe it's just a hangover from last night, but John, I have a feeling it's important. Of course we don't have to be carbon copies of each other; we're two different people with different tastes. But your J. C. is a kind of type, he stands for something that makes me squirm inside, and it worries me that you don't see it too—Angus sees it, and so does Dot Young."

"Darling, you're just worked up over last night. There really wasn't anything to it. I don't think J. C. meant any harm—he's just out of his element with pictures and said the first thing that popped into his head. It was just a first impression, anyway."

"John, it wasn't the incident alone—I knew what he was like before that happened. When he took my arm—" a grimace of distaste tensed her nostrils for a brief second. "John, he's false *inside*. He's nothing but a front"—her smile suddenly broke through—"with no behind!"

John put down his coffee with an irritable gesture. "Mary, how can you say a thing like that when you hardly know the man? I've known him for a whole year, and I think he's damned intelligent, and practical—and he's been swell to me right from the first. You've just been prejudiced by Angus!"

"Angus has known him for three years," Mary reminded him, "and he's older than you, and he's been around a bit more."

"All Angus has ever done is teach in a little high school. Why is he stuck in a little place like this?"

"I don't see the connection," said Mary, "but I can give you the answer. It's Vera."

"Vera? What in hell has Vera got to do with it?" John's irritation turned into sulkiness.

"I only asked what Vera had to do with Angus being stuck here."

"Haven't you noticed, John, how Vera is a little girl who never grew up? The way she depends on her parents; her ideas, all borrowed from her parents or her friends, not one little idea worked out by herself? Can't you see Angus falling for her pretty young face—and she was pretty—I saw their wedding picture in her bedroom—she was beautiful when Angus married her."

"But I still can't see—"

"John, what would a girl like that do if Angus were offered a university job?"

"I'd say she'd jump at it."

"And leave her mother and father and West Kirby? Do you know she almost boasted when she told me the farthest she had ever been from home was down to London to get her wedding materials—she must be in her middle forties and she's never in her life been farther than sixty miles from home!"

"Well, it's a pretty far-fetched theory if you ask me.

And if Angus made such a mistake marrying her," John added triumphantly, "he could easily be wrong about Bilbeau. I think Bilbeau is all right, and I'll go on thinking so till I see real evidence—not any fancy imaginary evidence—that he's otherwise." John clenched his jaw and thrust out his chin to show he meant what he said.

Mary shrugged her shoulders; then suddenly smiled, came over and kissed his head.

"Now what?" said John, but the irritability was gone. He looked up at her appealingly. "Let's not quarrel any more." They went into the living room and sat together on the chesterfield, John laying his head against her breast. "What were you smiling at?" he asked her.

Mary smiled again. "When you get that determined look in your jaw you're just like a little boy trying to look grown-up. It gets the mother in me, I guess," said Mary.

During the evening of the Nyes's party, Mr. Nyes had excused himself, looking quite ill. The following Monday he failed to show up and as the week wore on the report went around that he had had a slight stroke. On Wednesday a notice went up on the bulletin board announcing a staff meeting for that afternoon.

After four John went into the men's room to wash his hands. Starling, Klein and Pikestaff were there talking.

"There's no question about it," said Starling. "Nyes is finished."

"That puts J. C. in the saddle, I suppose," said Klein.

At the meeting J. C. was in the saddle, looking grave and responsible. Margaret Brewin and Frank Jarratt were missing. Nyes always started his meetings on the dot, full attendance or not. But J. C. spoke to Pikestaff who sat beside him.

"Mr. Pikestaff, I wonder if you would look up Miss Brewin and Mr. Jarratt."

"Certainly," and Pikestaff whipped out of the room.

The staff waited at the table, talking in low voices now and then. J. C. stroked his chin meditatively looking down the corridor of teachers' heads and shoulders to the empty chair at the end.

The missing teachers arrived and quickly found seats. J. C. glanced down at a paper in his hand, which John was startled to observe was shaking slightly. J. C. noticed it too and placed the paper firmly on the table.

"I believe you all know why this meeting was called," said J. C. "Mr. Nyes is ill, not seriously, we hope, but he has been advised by his physician to take at least a month off, possibly more. I am sure it is the desire of the staff that we extend our sincerest wishes for a speedy recovery. I have asked Miss Jamieson to send to his home a suitable expression of our sentiments." J. C. paused. There were a few feeble "Hear, hears!"

"The Board of Education has appointed me acting principal during Mr. Nyes's illness. I appreciate the impossibility of taking his place adequately and I know you will all afford me the fullest co-operation in my temporary stewardship. Miss Blodwin of the supply staff has consented to take over most of my classes for the month ahead.

"I do not propose to make any changes in the organization of the school. My aim is to carry on with the customary routine. However, in view of the fact that the inspector's visit may occur before Mr. Nyes returns, and since I shall be held accountable to the Board of Education for the impression he gets of the school, I propose to visit each classroom and each teacher briefly. Please do not get a mistaken impression: I am merely protecting myself against unforeseen contingencies. The visits will be strictly routine and not in any sense of the word critical."

Mr. Bilbeau's eyes roved the ranks of teachers, coming to rest on Mr. Starling, who had taken off his glasses and looked suddenly ineffectual.

"A question, Mr. Starling?"

"I was wondering," he said gently, "whether any of the other teachers have noticed an increasing tendency towards gum-chewing in the school. It seems to me something ought to be done about it."

Of all the trivial details to bring up, thought John, looking across and down the table.

"I think Mr. Starling is right!" Miss Willis spoke up. "There's too much gum-chewing going on. Why, only this morning I had to detain three pupils in one class. It seems to me some of the students are taking advantage of Mr. Nyes's absence. I think something should be done about it."

The subject changed to whistling in the halls, and then to the manner of collecting attendance slips.

Mr. Smith outlined at length a device he had been using for some time in connection with attendance slip collection. Frequently a draught would blow the slip from the blackboard ledge by the door, and when the monitor came in to collect it, it was gone. Mr. Smith informed the meeting that a chalk brush laid on the slip would keep it in place.

"Wouldn't it be difficult to see the slip?" objected Miss Willis.

Mr. Smith explained that one left the slip projecting sufficiently to be seen and seized.

The meeting was getting out of hand. Mr. Bilbeau firmly took up the reins:

"There seems to be a general feeling that the situation might become too lax. I suggest that each staff member see to it that these points are checked before they go too far. Mr. Starling, I wonder if you would act as convenor of a committee to look into these matters—with power to add of course—and report back at our next staff meeting? Now, if there is no further business I declare the meeting adjourned."

14

One evening in the middle of November Mary answered the phone, while John in the little room which he used for a study stopped marking exercises to listen. It was always fascinating to guess from what Mary said who was talking and what it was about.

"Yes?"

"Oh, Catherine! How are you?"

Catherine, Catherine who? wondered John.

"Why no. I'd love to come. . . . ."

"Thursday at eight? . . . ."

"Oh, that doesn't matter, he just buries himself in a book."

"Who buries himself in books?" John called out.

Mary hung up and came in. "You're going to stay in next Thursday night. I'm invited out, and you, Mr. Westley, are not."

John learned that Mary had already been invited to join a women's discussion club by Catherine Bilbeau, and this was the confirmation.

"What are you going to discuss, babies and the price of eggs?"

"None of your heavy sarcasm, Mr. Westley. We're going to study politics and economics; all the things that matter."

John remembered then that Klein had said something about his wife having organized such a club the previous winter and that Catherine Bilbeau was the secretary.

"Well," he remarked, "I hope it does some good."

"It may not change world history," said Mary, "but it should make *me* a little smarter."

Through Mary's contacts in the discussion club, and through the Kleins they began to build up a circle of friends and acquaintances. In John's first year he had given practically all his time to teaching. But this year, with Mary, he began to get into the stream of West Kirby society.

The particular stratum in which they found themselves might have been called the younger intelligentsia, if it could be said that any intelligentsia existed. In any case this was the only group, drawn from the professional and semi-professional classes, which seriously discussed national and international issues. Of the two the latter aroused much more interest. There was a tendency to disparage Canadian affairs as mere pawns in the larger game. This not only satisfied their craving for the dramatic, but increased their complacency: a confused smugness, which alternately criticized and accepted the Canadian political set-up. In one breath they would pour scorn on Canadian democracy as a blind tool of the vested interests; in the next point out that Mussolini, Stalin, and even Hitler were bound to fall because, unlike Canadians, they had no democratic traditions.

In Mary's group were two social workers: Catherine Bilbeau, who had charge of rents in the relief department, and Peggy Collins, a school nurse. There were four others: a middle-aged librarian, a doctor's wife, the wife of a public school principal and Helen Rush, formerly a music teacher, married to the assistant manager of Kirby Lithographers.

The Rushes were their favourite married couple. Hal was short, dark, and swarthy, given to making serious statements flippantly, and pretending his flippancy was profound. On their first visit—the Rushes lived in a small stucco house near Old Kirby Park—John had been confused by this habit. In the midst of discussing a current book and its social significance Hal had dropped the remark that one book of Horatio Alger had more social significance than any other half-dozen books he had read with the possible exception of *Pilgrim's Progress* and *Moll Flanders*.

Mary had caught on immediately and felt that *Anne of Green Gables* was more profound than anything Alger ever wrote; but Hal maintained that Alger first brought to the masses the great American myth of the poor and honest orphan who worked his way up the ladder of success to become a millionaire, and in so doing, had done more than Washington, Lincoln, or Calvin Coolidge to lay the foundations of modern American culture.

That had brought up the subject of West Kirby culture.

"There ain't no such animal," asserted Hal.

Helen disagreed. "Of course there is," she contradicted.

The Westleys exchanged glances and sat back to enjoy the battle.

"Okeh," said Hal, "what *is* culture?"

Culture they agreed, involved a definite standard of values, which found original expression in the arts.

"All right, where is your original self-expression in West Kirby music?" asked Hal.

Helen smiled in slow triumph: "The drummer in the Orange day parade."

Hal grinned suddenly and conceded the point. They asked the Westleys if they had seen the spectacle, and described the drummer, an ancient town character now on relief, a veteran of the Boer War, who had beaten the drum behind King Billy's horse every year since 1905 with a tenacity and independence of conventional rhythm that won him a storm of cheers whenever he passed.

The argument went on. Helen scored another point with the town band concerts in Island Park Saturday evenings. Her arguments weakened when they turned to paintings: the only illustration she could think of was the art exhibit at the West Kirby Fair which, John and Mary gathered, consisted of copies in oil and lead pencil of calendar scenes, cute puppies, and Their Majesties the King and Queen. Desperately Helen brought up Dot Young; but Hal would not allow her as a legitimate West Kirby artist: after all, her work had been rejected by the Fair committee.

Hal had to concede that the obituary notices and correspondence column in the *West Kirby Times* were true expressions of West Kirby culture. They told the Westleys about Miss Mildred Smythe-Perkins, a well preserved spinster-about-town and self-styled newspaper columnist whose claim that she wrote for the papers was not without foundation, for a letter of hers appeared at least once a week in the correspondence column on every imaginable topic from total abstinence to the menace of Catholicism. So that in a literary sense at least Hal admitted that West Kirby culture overflowed abundantly in all directions.

By the time they came to the art of building, John and Mary had entered into the spirit of the thing, and John distinguished himself by citing the ultimate in West Kirby architecture, All Saints Church. The new bridge was dismissed in a sentence by Hal.

"Nuts!" he said, "The new bridge was built by the International Steel and Iron Construction Company, and it still isn't paid for. It's like the syndicated features in the newspaper, and advertising art—imported from an alien culture."

John asked about the theatres.

"Hollywood, strictly Hollywood," said Hal.

The Rushes were musical of course; but Helen had seldom played the piano since her marriage.

"Every time I sit down to play," she told them, "it's like sitting between two mirrors: on either side of me are rows and rows of pianos and sitting at each is one of my old pupils. I'd rather listen to the phonograph."

They had a modest library of records, and, when they had added to the collection between visits, would play their latest acquisition for the Westleys. One night it was Wagner's *Siegfried Idyll*.

"I don't know why you had to buy that," Hal told his wife. "All the Wagner I like you could put in your eye."

"I rather like Wagner!" John stated rashly. He had never really listened to music before he met Mary; and

181

only since then as a sort of concession to her—and out of a vague curiosity as to why people did it.

Mary's eyes looked their astonishment. "Why, John, you've hardly ever heard—"

But Hal had already begun. "Wagner is a manic-depressive if there ever was one: bloody thunder one minute and the caress of a feather on a baby's bottom the next. Give me Bach or Gershwin, you can skip practically everything in between."

Mary and Helen laughed together. "That," said Helen, "is why I have to apologize for him wherever we go."

John began to say, "But seriously, don't you think Wagner—" only to find that the conversation had slipped into another topic and left him behind.

It had soon become apparent that Klein's political thinking was not quite orthodox. John had the usual Canadian apathy towards politics. "They're all the same," he would say, referring to the political parties, "Out for what they can get."

Klein disagreed. He was full of the disturbing new ideas of the Co-operative Commonwealth Federation.

"The Liberal and Conservative Parties are just tools in the hands of the big corporations. Canada has reached the stage of monopoly capitalism. Production is out of gear with distribution."

John didn't quite understand.

At the College of Education the students had been addressed by a representative of the Teachers' Federation. There had been much discussion of maximum and minimum wages. To John, who had just completed a school year, including tuition fees, on four hundred dollars, the idea of a minimum salary of $2000 per annum was staggering. And that the teachers of the province, ostensibly in the profession for altruistic reasons, should organize to protect their well-oiled hides, smacked of an unholy greed which revolted him. Why, it was just like a trade union!

Klein seemed to have a different idea about trade unions. There was a strike on down at the King George Hotel and Klein had asked John if he would like to make a contribution to the strike fund. John asked what the strike was about and was told that waitresses were making only nine dollars a week. John explained that he and Mary were having a lot of extra expenses in setting up married life; perhaps later they could spare something.

John sounded out Klein on education.

"I'm not sure that I know all the answers," he told John. "It is certainly high time our children learned to think for themselves, and not believe everything they read in the capitalist press. But we've got to teach them the basic facts and skills too, and that's such a big job there isn't much time left over to teach them to think."

"Well, suppose things were fixed so that our children never got more than one hour a week of schooling. What would you give them?"

"I guess I'd give them an hour a week on the Bible," said Klein.

"But they don't open the Bible in high school from one end of the year to the other."

"Which is one reason why we have capitalism, and wars."

Klein was a stout Baptist. He taught a Bible class on Sundays, which was largely attended by young people who respected his honest convictions. Several other staff members with cars drove fellow teachers to and from school on the understanding that they contribute to expenses; but Klein steadily refused any recompense from John.

"It's foolish," he declared. "I have to drive past your house anyway; it costs me no more in time or expense."

John's salary of $2000 per annum no longer seemed quite so magnificent. In the first place the Board of Education had craftily manoeuvred the local teachers into a voluntary rebate of fifteen per cent of their salaries as their contribution to reducing the hardships of city taxation during the depression. Besides this another two per cent or so went into his pension fund. In his first year John had saved nearly $900, but all of that had gone on furniture and summer expenses. Now that he was married he found that his monthly pay cheque of $168.43 didn't allow very much leeway over current expenses and there were the two payless summer months to provide for.

The only member of the Board that John had seen so far was Mr. Parker, the real estate man, who had appeared at the previous Easter to present the annual Board prize of ten dollars to the student with the most nearly perfect attendance record over five consecutive years.

Mr. Parker was handicapped by a tendency to overweight, but magnificently unaware of any handicaps. He had the maritime bloom on his full cheeks, which gave him the appearance of perfect health. Black beady eyes, full of earnestness, peered through the thick spectacles: his nose was a small curved beak. He was a little man, and for all the weight around his waist he gave John the impression that if he rocked up on his toes just once more he would naturally levitate, ascending rapidly to disappear through the ceiling, completely dematerialized.

A fine man, Mr. Parker.

About the middle of November Nyes began coming to school again half days, looking ten years older. The school was tense with rumours of an early inspection. But John was absorbed in whipping his play into shape: a dramatized version of *A Christmas Carol*, rewritten from Martha Cratchit's point of view by an obscure English schoolteacher. Martha Cratchit was a beautiful part for a stage virtuoso—the writer had taken advantage of the Dickens sentimentality to put Martha through the whole gamut of human emotions in half an hour. John was depending on Elsie Braund's economy of expression, her utter sincerity, to avoid the bathos.

The inspector came.

John was daydreaming at his desk when Fred Hubble the janitor came in to look at his thermostat.

"He's here!" John's tilted chair came down with a sharp thud.

"No!"

Fred came up to the front of the room, looking back for a moment. He spoke in a low voice, his usually pleasant round face looking **sour**.

"This guy is really tough."

"No! What's his name?"

"Berryhill. He came into the gym this morning just after I had dry-mopped it. You know, Mr. Westley, that's all we can do till 7:30 the next morning." Fred went through an elaborate imitation of the inspector, leaning over, rubbing one finger on the floor, turning it up for John's inspection. "Mr. Hubble"—he mimicked the inspector's voice—"would you want your daughter to sit on a floor like that?"

John laughed sympathetically.

"Mr. Westley," said Fred Hubble indignantly, "I have been caretaker of this school for twelve years and that's the first time any inspector ever told me my floors were dirty!" He looked back over his shoulder, moved towards the door. "Well, I'd better be going."

Between periods John had got into the habit lately of chatting with Miss Willis in the corridor: the old girl could be quite human at times even to the point of smiling sourly at a risqué reference.

Today they were discussing the inspector. Miss Willis had been down to the office where she had a glimpse of him.

John said it was the suspense more than the actual visit that made him nervous.

Miss Willis let her hair down. "Even now," she confessed, "I'm still nervous when the inspector comes around. And there's no reason for it—it isn't like it used to be."

"How did it used to be?" asked John.

Miss Willis tightened her lips in retrospect. "When I began teaching we were all frightened to death of the inspector, naturally. They wanted you to be frightened so you would do better work. And you were frightened of the principal and frightened of the Board."

"And the youngsters were frightened of you!"

"Of course. They had to be."

A pair of boys went by holding hands as adolescents often do. Miss Willis's eyes flashed.

"That will be ENOUGH of THAT SORT OF THING!" The boys parted hands, blushing; two or three around them smiled.

"Looks as if they're still afraid of you," John grinned tactlessly.

Miss Willis smiled grimly, completely her teacher-self again.

John was duly inspected: only one visit. Mr. Berryhill had a large owlish face on a long scrawny neck; a complete contrast from the quiet business-like inspector of a year ago. After shaking hands with John he sat through a complete English lesson in silence. At the end of the period one of the boys left a book behind. Mr. Berryhill picked it up and stood by the door, as the class filed past him, and casually gave it to the right boy when he came along. That old monkey doesn't miss a thing, marvelled John.

The Christmas concert came and went. Mary and Dot Young helped with the make-up for John's play. J. C. appeared in the make-up room while they were busy giving the cast a final powdering. He paused to watch Mary at work. "I think," said he, "we're very lucky to have the Westleys on our staff," and as she looked up briefly, he smiled.

After the concert—Elsie as Martha Cratchit had been everything John had hoped for—there was a brief session in the library with tea and sandwiches for the staff. Three or four prominent citizens and their wives were present including two members of the Board. Mary and John were introduced to both. "A very fine little play," said Mr. K. L. Mullins. He was tall, thin, blond and bald, his scalp and nose vying with each other in fiery redness. "Congratulations on your fine work," offered Mr. J. K. Leathorne, a shabby looking man for a lawyer. John explained to them that he hoped to enter the play in the regional Drama Festival at London in February. "A fine idea," said Mr. Mullins with no visible enthusiasm. But somehow J. C. had overheard.

"A thoroughly *splendid* idea!" he declared in a ringing voice, impressing the two lawyers from the Board at once. "When you have a good thing," said J. C. earnestly, "it's an act of selfishness to hide it. And," it seemed to John his eyes twinkled mischievously, "it will not do our school any harm to get a little extra advertisement."

Mary said, "It would be a high school group against adults; but it would be fun trying anyway."

Mr. Mullins, Mr. Leathorne, Mr. Bilbeau—and Mr. Westley—agreed. And Mr. Bilbeau smiled again to Mary.

"Didn't I tell you," said John to Mary that night as he helped to pull her slip over her head, "J. C. isn't such a bad egg?"

"Well," said Mary, "he would have to be awfully dumb not to see that he had a good thing in you and Elsie Braund. Honestly, I was amazed at her acting."

"Well, I put in a lot of time coaching her," said John complacently. "But just between you and me"—his honesty getting the better of him—"there was hardly a thing I showed her that she didn't think of a better way of doing."

Mary turned the light out and rolled over on her side after a goodnight kiss.

"Mary."

"Mmn?"

"Mary I'm really not such a whiz as a director. I've just had a couple of lucky breaks, actually."

Mary turned towards him, felt for his face in the dark and stroked his cheek. "Darling," she said, "When you talk like that, and I know you mean it, I really love you."

John snuggled close, without speaking. It was good, being married to Mary.

January came. 1936.

John and Mary spent Christmas in Toronto, returning for their first New Year's together. Alone in their apartment on New Year's Eve, for Mary had a bad cold and neither of them felt like a noisy celebration, they watched the last minute tick by, heard the hysterical shrieks and hullabaloo over the radio that announced the old year was gone.

"It's been a nice year," said Mary.

"This one will be nicer," and they kissed long and solemnly.

The school had settled back into its customary routine with Mr. Nyes at the helm again, more like his old self. Only in a nervous twitching of his fingers at odd moments was there any indication that he had been seriously ill.

Angus was over a few days later. The conversation swung round to school affairs and for once Angus did not steer it away.

"I'm glad Nyes is back," he said.

"I'm not so sure," objected John, "I have a feeling J. C. would be a better principal in lots of ways"—thinking to himself, Nyes never got excited over my plays—"It seems to me he's more progressive."

Angus smiled tolerantly.

"Listen, Angus!" John leaned forward with the impetus of a fresh idea. "Remember the first staff meeting we had with J. C., when he threw the meeting open and people like Starling and Smith started talking about chewing gum and attendance slips. Maybe it *was* dictatorship to pass the buck to Starling and adjourn the meeting; but who is going to sit and listen to a lot of yaps making mountains out of molehills? If that's democracy give me a good old-fashioned dictatorship; or more accurately," he amended, "a modern enlightened dictatorship."

"John, that sounds like fascism!" Mary was shocked.

"What's in a name!" John was scornful. "Let's take *any* form of government—whatever the name—that's going to get us out of this depression mess and give us a future. Anyway the Nyes have educated one generation and produced a depression: let's give the J. C.'s a chance and see if they can do any better. They can't do much worse."

"It seems to me," said Angus, "that there's some confusion here. In the first place we are assuming that J. C. is what you call progressive. Two questions occur to me, first, what do you mean by progressive? and second, is J. C. progressive in that sense?"

"Yes," said Mary, a little surprised that such a simple question hadn't occurred to her. "What do you mean, 'progressive'?"

"Well, in education, it means awareness of what other people are doing in education. It means—" the memory of Tom McIntyre's talk sprang to his aid—"I remember something he said once. It means putting personality in the place of pedagogy."

"Good words!" approved Angus, smiling. "What do they mean?"

"What do they mean? Why they mean—well—you put your *self* into your lessons, not the dry old stuff you are supposed to teach. Well, not exactly that—you have to teach the dry stuff anyway—but you make them see through your eyes; you don't just depend on a stuffy old technique drilled into you at college, the inductive method, the deductive method and all that."

"John uses the *se*ductive method," Mary explained, her eyes sparkling.

Angus took the unconscious hint and went home.

15

Early in the New Year John met Mr. Bilbeau in the south corridor.

"Just the man I was looking for," said J. C.

John looked up inquiringly.

"The Success Club is having a luncheon next Monday at noon," he informed John, "in the King George Hotel. I wonder if you would care to be my guest."

John blushed with the flattery of the invitation. "Sure—yes, I'd like to very much—" Why on earth would he ask me? he wondered.

"It appears," Bilbeau told him, "that each year the Success Club devotes one of its luncheon sessions to education. Mr. Nyes has felt unable to carry on his duties in the Club and I have been honoured as his successor. I was informed, when asked to give the educational address, that it has been Mr. Nyes's custom to introduce one of the younger teachers on the school staff at each of these annual meetings, and since you are the newest, and youngest, and one of our most promising"—Mr. Bilbeau broke off, as if, on impulse, he had said more than he meant to.

"I'd certainly like to go," said John gratefully.

"We may be a little bit late for the afternoon session at school"—Bilbeau's eyes twinkled, and seemed to make John his accomplice in truancy—"But I'll speak to Mr. Nyes, and we'll see that your class is supervised."

In the interval between invitation and event John made inquiries about the Success Club.

"It's a purely local sort of super-service club," Hal told him, when the Rushes were over that week end. "It's something like the Rotary Club, only there's no hard and fast rule about membership: just the general idea that no one but the best in his field will be invited to join, and they don't exclude members of other service clubs. Once you're in the Success Club you're really in. If you ask me, it's the real government of West Kirby."

"I thought Grossart really runs the town. Is he a member?"

"Grossart is an anti-social cuss—I suspect actually he has an inferiority complex about his education. But of course, if he cracks the whip the members of the Success Club dance as briskly as the next guy. Well, you'll get good food anyway."

Angus seemed to be amused by John's invitation. "If you can pick up an extra cigar when they pass them around, bring it home for me," he said, "and I'll put it away for Christmas. I went to a Success Club luncheon about eight years ago: bored them to death talking about the Precambrian—that was after the F.R.S.C. business—but they gave me the best cigar I ever smoked in my life."

But Pikestaff was impressed. "Mr. Bilbeau has certainly taken a shine to you. I went as Mr. Nyes's guest when I first came here, and it certainly was a privilege. Only—the cigar smoke!" Pikestaff coughed thinly in retrospect.

Mary failed to get excited, though she ironed John's best shirt for the occasion. When John went to school Monday morning he was so perfectly groomed that the boys raised their eyebrows, the girls opened their eyes, and significant smiles spread through the room.

On the way to the hotel John sat self-consciously beside Bilbeau in the latter's new Buick, too impressed with the importance of the occasion to wonder how his patron could afford such a car on his salary as head of the English department.

He had never seen J. C. in such mellow humour. "I've been finding out things about the Success Club since you invited me," he said. "It's quite an honour to be nominated for membership."

"Quite an honour," J. C. repeated his words. "An honour I had been looking forward to ever since I came to West Kirby." He drove easily, leaning back, with his hands resting firmly on the steering wheel; a powerful man in full control of a powerful machine. A smile played over his mouth, his chin was raised in an attitude that gave him a sudden startling resemblance to Mussolini.

All the members of the club wore buttons on which were printed their given names or nicknames in bold type, their surnames underneath in inconspicuous letters. John got the impression that here familiarity was a sign of distinction: to be addressed as "Mr. Westley" somehow implied an inferior social status.

He found himself seated at the table between "Joe" and "Spike", both of them fleshy business men, who made a polite remark or two, then politely ignored him. The tables were arranged in a T, with J. C., as the main speaker, in a prominent position. John thought, he looks far more at home here than he does at a staff meeting, and a second later was startled by a combination of belly laughs and guffaws to which J. C. contributed his share with a curious rasping noise on each intake of breath.

The luncheon proceeded, until finally coffee and cigars were served. John looked at Bilbeau, uncertain about smoking, then thought, heck it's not often I can get a good cigar, accepted, nibbled off the end timidly, and lit up with the others, feeling that somehow he and the cigar didn't belong together.

The chairman rose—"Ed" was the name on his button— and introduced "Jimmy" Bilbeau as a good fellow and an up-and-coming man in the educational world. That the club approved of their new member to a man was amply evident in the warmth of their applause. John noticed it and thought of the student applause in assembly. It's just that the students don't realize what an unusual man he is, he thought.

"Mr. Chairman—or should I say, Ed?—and gentlemen." The resonant baritone boomed gently through the room, and as he spoke Bilbeau smiled, as if to say, I know you are my friends; this is where I belong.

After the conventional joke (J. C. on looking around was reminded of the man who—) and the subsequent roar of laughter had died away, Bilbeau got down to business.

"It is my great privilege, and even greater responsibility," he told them, "to be head of the English department in the largest school in Kirby County. I say privilege because," he paused gravely, "there is no greater privilege than the guidance of young minds along the path of truth; responsibility," and he paused again as if to summon the strength to bear it, "because there is no heavier responsibility than to undertake such guidance."

A silence weighted with privilege and responsibility fell over the room.

"Education, coming from the Latin *ducto*—to lead, is leadership. If I may, not irreverently, use the expression, an educator is a kind of shepherd leading his flock by the still waters of truth: mental truth, and moral truth. And the teacher of English has the added responsibility of passing on to the next generation that great heritage of British culture on which is founded the unsurpassed greatness of Britain and her Empire, of which we are so proudly a part.

"The poet Wordsworth, at a period in British history when all England's glory seemed to be past, expressed the value of our literary heritage:

> *"Milton thou shouldst be living at this hour—*
> *England hath need of thee . . . .*

"In his own small way each teacher of English is a Milton, recalling to the world the priceless heritage of the English tongue.

"But what of education today, and tomorrow?

"We live in stirring times. This is an age of transition. There are voices urging us forward into greater feats of enterprise. There are other voices, coming from far countries where flags and hands are red, but heard even in this great land of ours, urging a return of barbarism, threatening the overthrow of all that makes life worth living.

"We must go forward or backward, we cannot stagnate: forward to freedom, or backward to barbarism.

"Gentlemen, if you were to ask me what one word best sums up for me what I look forward to in education that word would be progress. And if you were to ask me what kind of progress, I would add the word practical. Practical progress. To progress each generation must be further ahead than the last. And to achieve progress we must aim at practical results.

"You will all, as practical and successful men, agree with me, I think, when I say that our schools have in the past put far too much emphasis on theory."

"Hear! Hear!" came several voices, and there was some handclapping.

"Of what use to a salesman is the ability to write and speak perfect English prose, if he cannot talk a prospect into buying his product?"

John noticed that everyone was listening intently now.

"Of what use to a factory worker is ability in higher mathematics, if he has not learned to balance his budget and keep his expenditures within his means?"

There was a strong outburst of applause at this point.

"Of what use to a stenographer is a knowledge of physics or mechanics, if a repair man has to be called in every time two keys jam together?"

There was laughter.

"Gentlemen, there is no one in the country who believes more firmly in higher education than myself. We cannot have too many university graduates.

"But how many high school students ever get to university? And why should the taxpayers' money be wasted teaching ancient history and French and trigonometry to children who, when they find their place in society, will be store clerks, delivery men, typists, bread salesmen, and factory help?"

A vast enthusiasm lit every eye in the room. It was plain to John that Bilbeau was their man.

"Gentlemen, we cannot afford to be sentimental. There are those who will ask, how can you know which five per cent of the students entering a high school will go on to a higher education? To that I reply, if we want to know, there are ways of finding out. The vast field of vocational guidance is unexplored. The situation calls for radical experiments. We must have educational engineers who will design newer and more efficient educational machinery. We must, because if we do not, there is danger ahead. We are all aware of subversive elements in our midst, introducing ideas incompatible with the traditions of democracy and free enterprise. Who are the victims of this propaganda? Gentlemen, the victims are the waste products of our present educational system: the youngsters with a half-baked education; an education that makes them discontented with their present lot and encourages them to think along lines that lead to chaos and anarchy.

"No," concluded Mr. Bilbeau, "we cannot afford to allow this process to go on. I am for progress in education —practical progress. To quote from the catechism of the grand old Church of England, we must so teach our children that they will grow up to maturity content in that station in life unto which it shall please God to call them."

Round after round of applause greeted Bilbeau's final

words. "Spike", who, John learned later, was no less a person than R. J. Baldwin, owner of the King George Hotel and past mayor of West Kirby, turned to John with enthusiasm and said, "Isn't he a dandy, your principal?"

"Well, he isn't the principal—" said John hesitantly.

Baldwin waved a hand impatiently. "He will be," he said, and it was as if he had added—"We'll see to that!"

At home John gave an enthusiastic account of the luncheon, quoting bits that he had remembered.

"It all comes from the Latin 'ducto', I lead", said John.

"Ducto?" said Mary, "I thought it was duco."

"Duco—sure! What did I say?"

"Skip it," said Mary. "What other weighty statements did he make?"

"Well, he quoted Milton and all that stuff, and then he really got down to brass tacks, pointed out that education has been too theoretical—what we want is practical progress. He laid a lot of stress on that."

"What other kind of progress is there?" asked Mary.

"Well, the idea is, that if someone is going to be a waitress, there's no point in teaching her French and algebra. I mean, what good is it?"

"What are you going to teach her—how to improve her looks and figure so she'll get more tips?"

"If you're going to be funny there's no point in talking about it."

"But John you haven't told me one thing Bilbeau said that means anything. What did he say?"

"He said a lot—he said enough to keep those men listening with both ears; and he got a lot of applause too!"

"John, just name one point he got across, why did he get the applause?"

John tried desperately to think of something—Mary would laugh if he quoted that bit about the catechism. "You know I never can remember what people say, but the point is, Bilbeau is a really progressive educationist, and knows how to talk to business men. He's going to get ahead, Mary."

The telephone rang in the nick of time. "I'll answer it," said John, noticing irritably that Mary was smiling, as though he had said something childish, but cute.

16

John was just racing up the stairs to his room after four one day late in January when he passed Miss Garrell. He greeted her without stopping, but near the top of the stairs something he had seen in her eyes made him glance back. She was standing there, looking up with her mouth open.

"What's that?" He leaned over the railing impatiently.

"Mr. Nyes passed away this afternoon at four."

How appropriate, at four o'clock, was John's first irreverent thought. "No!" he said aloud in shocked surprise, hoping he had put everything in it expected of him.

"Yes!" said Miss Garrell, triumphantly. "He went home at three-thirty, feeling ill; and sharp at four o'clock he died. I was right in the office when Mrs. Nyes phoned."

John went back to his rehearsal, outwardly sober, inwardly seething with excitement. Things will really move around here from now on, he thought.

He announced the principal's death to the cast. After

mumbles of sympathy and some show of shock they wanted to know when the funeral would be, and whether the play would be called off now.

Telling Mary about it at supper he was depressed.

"After all, darling," Mary pointed out, "you weren't particularly close to him."

"It isn't that. It's the way the kids reacted—myself too. A man dies and all we can think of is how it will affect our little lives."

"Well, if you ask me, it's a healthy way to react, when it isn't a personal loss."

"I suppose your first reaction if I died would be, where can I get a job?"

"Very likely. Eat your macaroni, silly, before it gets cold."

John gulped down his macaroni with a good appetite.

The funeral was held in the First Baptist Church, the clerical member of the Board, Rev. Gerald Eby, officiating, Nyes's own pastor assisting.

It was a proper funeral. The whole Board of Education was there, except Mr. Mullins, whose absence occasioned some disgust among the student body. "Drunk as usual", was their verdict, which contradicted the more intimate knowledge of adult gossips, who claimed that he could drink any man or woman in Kirby County under the table.

Nyes's immediate family was there, Mrs. Nyes looking a little less tired than usual.

Six senior boys acted as pall-bearers, and the whole Upper School, at their own request, were seated in specially reserved pews behind the chief mourners.

The Reverend Mr. Eby outlined Principal Nyes's career;

characterized his devotion to the academic life as an example to the community which it would long profit by and cherish; spoke of the "literally thousands" of young people who had been influenced by his teaching and guidance —some of them now outstanding leaders in the community —and ended with a personal tribute to the man who, in Mr. Eby's earlier years, had exercised a profound influence on Mr. Eby's life, and who, in their latter associations, as between a member of the Board, and principal of one of the Province's outstanding schools, had never failed in his duty nor enjoyed anything less than the fullest measure of confidence.

Back at school, as everyone had expected, James Campbell Bilbeau, M.A., was in charge. Technically he remained acting-principal until the end of the school year, when the Board would automatically confirm him in the full principalship.

His first staff meeting was almost a monologue and broke all records for brevity. He would, J. C. explained, expect the same measure of co-operation from the staff as had been afforded Mr. Nyes, and proposed to make no radical changes in organization or policy. In view of the fact, however, that some teachers had mentioned a prevalent laxness in school discipline, due no doubt to Mr. Nyes's inability to remain as full-time principal in the fall, a laxness which the inspector had not overlooked in his report, he felt that they must all, to protect themselves, put forth an extra effort to remedy the situation.

Above all, something must be done immediately about hall supervision. There was an understanding that teachers were on hall duty from the quarter till the hour, but a good deal of laxness had developed. Hereafter, any teacher not found on duty in the halls would be warned; and if he persisted in neglecting his duty would be asked to make an explanation to the Board.

Teachers exchanged glances in dismay.

"Mr. Bilbeau," Angus was smiling wryly as he spoke, "do you not think that this sudden emphasis on police duty may arouse a resentment in staff and students alike which will defeat the purpose you had in mind in proposing it?"

Bilbeau turned white. For a second he was unable to speak. When he did, it was with an intensity of resentment and spitefulness that startled the staff.

"Mr. Macdonald, I have long been aware of your personal hostility. It is now perfectly obvious to the whole staff." His colour and self-control returned. "I have made a perfectly reasonable request for co-operation and can, I believe, expect as reasonable a response. Is there anyone else on the staff who sees eye to eye with Mr. Macdonald on this issue?" He thrust out his underlip belligerently, and looked up and down the two facing rows of teachers. There was a tense silence. Klein's chair scraped a little on the floor and every head turned nervously to where his big square hand gripped the table just across from John.

"Then if there is no further discussion the meeting is adjourned."

Everyone except Klein rose hurriedly, urged by a common fear of further unpleasantness. Klein rose heavily and went out without speaking to anyone. John looked around for Angus but he had disappeared.

Later that week John noticed that the girl who collected his attendance slips had changed her ways. Formerly if he had neglected to fill in the slip she had smiled, and said she would collect the others on the floor and come back later for his. Now she stood quietly inside the door and waited for him to make it out.

A notice came around one day.

In view of the fact that the janitorial staff has complained frequently of finding gum stuck to the floor, or adhering to the underside of desks, school will be dismissed at a quarter to four today in order that the home form of each room may have time to remove all the gum.

> J. C. BILBEAU
> *Acting Principal.*

Hall supervisors were appointed: two teachers for each floor of the new school and old. The hall supervisors were delegated to inform the other teachers in their areas that they would be expected to be outside their doors assisting in hall supervision except when actually teaching.

The next day John walked past the science room looking for Angus. Angus, as usual, was inside, and alone.

Angus's smile was sour. "How do you like the new regime?" he asked.

"Oh, it's not so bad. You have to admit that ten days has made a big difference. Say,"—he wondered why he hadn't thought of it before—"how about a real tramp down the south shore before the snow goes? Mary would love it, if we can find her some snowshoes."

Angus was enthusiastic.

Saturday morning found them out in front of the Macdonald eyrie helping Mary get her snowshoes on; Mary watching with interest, one furry blue mitt on the shoulder of each as they crouched over her feet.

Out on the lake the weather was changing, low grey snowladen clouds blotting out the cold winter blue. John pointed them out. Angus laughed. "We'll weather any blizzard," he told them. Knowing his experience they were content to follow.

The shore ice had buckled and broken in December winds, and in the lee of its peaks, plateaus, and pinnacles were high drifts gouged deep wherever breaks in the ridge had allowed the wind to sweep through. Now the three would trudge through fresh layers of powdery snow, snowshoes like velvet slippers; now on an old drift, wind-frozen to the hardness of concrete, their snowshoes clattering, their moccasined feet feeling the hard gut of the web.

An hour after they had left the island, the sun was shining dimly through a kind of haze that was neither cloud nor mist. It began to snow gently: it was quite calm.

Angus paused, looking for something, casting a casual glance or two at the weather. Then he went on.

Suddenly the wind came, and with it a wall of snow. Angus disappeared from sight, John held Mary's hand and walked beside her. The tracks ahead filled in as fast as they found them. Mary looked anxiously at John, a ghostly snowman with white eyelashes and ruddy face.

The snow stung their faces; the drifts were in flux; the distinction between earth and air disappeared as each element reached into and was absorbed by the other.

"Where's Angus?" shouted Mary. John let go of her hand to protect his eyes from the driving pellets. She disappeared in a swirl of snow. Panic-stricken he lunged after her, stepped on air and found himself floundering in a tangle of arms, legs, and snowshoes.

It was a drift in the lee of a huge upturned ice cake that Angus had sighted before the blizzard struck them full force. He had already scooped out a hollow and now the three of them working with their snowshoes for shovels soon had a roomy little cave dug out.

Warmed by their efforts and out of the wind they squatted in their snowy haven watching the grey wilderness sweep by the opening they had come in by, little back eddies sprinkling them with snow-dust. Mary's face was rosy from the cold, glistening with melted snow; Angus looked younger, more relaxed than John had ever seen him before. All three were smiling; smiling at the way they had cheated the storm, at the storm itself, huffing and puffing outside their door, at their isolation from the world.

"Do you think the storm will last all day?" asked Mary. There was so much hope in her voice that they all smiled again.

Mary got some sandwiches out of John's pack and they ate hungrily.

"You know," said John between munchings, "I never realized before how much we miss by not being Eskimos."

"Too bad we haven't a chunk or two of frozen fish for you to chew to complete the illusion," said Angus.

"Have *you* ever had any?" asked Mary.

No, Angus hadn't, but there were many things he had done in the numerous summers and one winter he had spent up north. He told them of a seal hunt on the west shore of Hudson Bay, of the eider duck culture of the Belcher Island Eskimo, of the time his plane had been forced down in the swamp-riddled wilderness of Northern Manitoba: things he had seen or heard. He had stories about hungry wolves, and lost trappers, fires, and sudden death; of the prospector who lost partner, canoe, and grubstake in a rapids on the Wenisk River, had fought hunger, flies, and despair in a six-hundred-mile tramp overland to the nearest Hudson's Bay post, and had died of measles a month later in North Bay.

The snowdrift at the mouth of their refuge grew as they watched, until the opening was a half-moon window. They began to feel the chill of the snow.

Some driftwood projected out of the cavern floor. They broke it off, whittled slivers, and started a fire, Angus remarking as he helped that they should know better. In five minutes they were outside, thigh deep in the new snow, their eyes streaming with smoke-tears.

The wind was stronger, still from the west, but there was less snow. As they watched, the blizzard thinned, and they could see the shore line for a hundred yards either way. The sun came out, dazzling them with its reflections from the snow. The sky was miraculously blue again.

It was nearly March. On the tenth John was to take his cast down to London to compete in the Drama Festival. He had already consulted J. C. on a number of details, but had neglected to mention costumes. So on a Wednesday morning he knocked at the open office door, and walked in. J. C. raised his eyebrows inquiringly.

"It's about costumes, Mr. Bilbeau, for the play. At the Christmas concert we just used anything we could get; but in a case like this—" he explained what he needed. J. C. demurred a little on the cost but finally consented.

"By the way," said J. C. "Will you write out a list of

those who will be going to London with you? There's no hurry, but I should like to have it for reference."

John made out the list then and there. J. C. glanced over it. "Yes," he said, "I think all these students are in good standing. Except—" he pushed out his under lip: "I see you have Elsie Braund down here."

"Well, naturally," John was vaguely alarmed. "The play would be a complete fizzle without her."

"Don't you exaggerate her importance? After all she is a weak student. A teacher complained to me about her only yesterday."

"I know her school work isn't good," defended John, "but she can act rings around anyone else—she has a future in acting. You wouldn't refuse her permission to go, would you?"

"Personally, no," explained Bilbeau gently, "but if any teachers objected to her going I should be in a very difficult position."

"But what about *her* position?" John was thoroughly worked up over it now. "After all, we've been rehearsing for weeks. She has been working like a slave with the one thought in mind of playing the lead in this play at the Drama Festival."

"I'm afraid that any ideas you have put in her head are your problem, Mr. Westley."

"But what about *her*. This is the only thing in school that means anything to her, It's her future."

"Mr. Westley, you are thinking in terms of Elsie Braund and her future; my responsibility is to the school and the school's future. If we make a practice of giving special privileges to students who do not co-operate in the classroom, we are going to discourage the co-operative students."

"But making an exception doesn't establish a practice."

"I'm afraid I can't see eye to eye with you there," said J. C.

There was a finality in his manner which not only ended the argument but made John feel that he was merely a wilful adolescent trying to impress his whims on a calm intelligent parent: a parent who listened tolerantly but had long ago fixed on the wiser policy. He left the office, ill with frustration. How could he tell Elsie?

Passing Angus's room he looked in, but Angus was busy with a class.

On the way upstairs he fought the thing out in himself. Without Elsie the play would flop. How could he tell her? *What* could he tell her? No. He would see J. C. tomorrow and tell him: Elsie goes with us, or no play. He breathed deeply, bracing himself for this act of defiance. I won't make a scene, I'll just tell him the truth; that we're not justified in putting this play on in London without the key actress. He's a reasonable man. Yes, that's what I'll do. He just doesn't realize how important Elsie is to the success of the play.

John felt better. He had made his decision and would abide by it. He entered his room and turned up the side aisle. There was a knock on the door behind him. He turned back; a student with a note from the office which read: "Sorry to bother you, could you come over again for a minute?"

In the office again, J. C. said, "John I've been going over the matter we were discussing, and there's one item that escaped my mind which has a bearing on the situation."

"Yes?" John's heart leapt with anticipation. Good old J. C.! He had thought it over, decided he had been hasty.

"It just occurred to me that if we were to make an exception in the case of Elsie Braund and allow her to go there would still be the possibility of illness or accident occurring at the last moment."

"Oh," said John, "in that case we'd simply have to use her stand-in. But she won't . . . ."

"Then you *have* a substitute for her!"

"Sure, if worst came to worst we could put Betty Armitage in, but—"

"In that case," J. C. sounded as if John had made a complex thing out of a simple one, "there is no real problem. I think in fairness to Miss Braund you should let her know as soon as possible."

John found himself three seconds later standing stupidly outside the office door.

Well, that was that. "In fairness to Miss Braund" he should tell her "as soon as possible". Otherwise he would not be fair to Elsie. He must be fair. It was only fair to be fair after all. Be fair, John—we must all try to be fair.

Between periods in the corridor John spied Elsie and asked her to see him at four. She smiled, then looked disturbed, reading his face too well.

She came in promptly at four and went directly to the point. "He's been talking about my marks."

"Yes, Elsie. I told him it was no use putting on the play without you, but—"

"In fairness to those who co-operate in the classroom"— Elsie was a marvellous mimic, it was J. C. right to the

E-A-U, in Bilbeau—"we cannot extend special privileges to the few who fail to co-operate."

"Well, he said how much he regretted—"

John was silent. "I did my best, Elsie. I just wasn't good enough."

"You don't need to feel bad," said Elsie, regressing into her country English. "He taught me for two years and he had it in for me from the first."

"I don't think there's anything personal in it, Elsie."

"Oh no, nothing personal. Listen, Mr. Westley, when Mr. Bilbeau is impersonal like a fish that's when he's really poisonous. You teachers don't know him like we do."

Klein dropped in at that moment to see if John were ready to drive home with him.

"I'll see you again, Elsie."

John talked it over with Mary, told her the whole story. But he said nothing about the clash between Angus and J. C. at the staff meeting. Bilbeau's sudden outburst was something John had tried to forget. There was no doubt about it now: J. C. hated Angus. But at least he had made a strong, and till then successful, effort to hide his feelings. Everyone made mistakes. Mary would have said, there you are— there's a glimpse of what's behind the face of Gabriel. Now it was certainly too late to mention Bilbeau's spitefulness with Angus. Mary would have jumped to the conclusion right away that it was spite in Elsie's case, too. But the cases were entirely different. J. C. might hold a grudge against Angus: it was understandable enough in a way how Angus could get under a person's skin. Discrimination against a mere kid was another matter. No, Bilbeau just wasn't like that.

210

As it was, Mary was indignant. "So he won't let her star in a play after all the rehearsing she's put in. Why did he let her rehearse if he's so interested in her studies?"

"Well, I felt that way about it, too," said John. "Only, going down to London she would have to miss classes for two days, and anyway I suppose he's had enough to think of without checking on who's in the play and who isn't."

"Well, John, if you want her in that play, stand up to Bilbeau and fight for her. After all you don't have to put on these plays. You're not paid for it."

He looked across the table at Mary. "What else can I do?" he asked her helplessly.

Mary was looking at him strangely. John had the momentary feeling she was another person, an older woman, strong and wise, as she faced him squarely with steady grey eyes, the dark brown locks of her hair on either side of her calm oval face, accidentally symmetrical. She was young and mature at once: the warm blood of youth in her cheeks, a sibylline wisdom in her eyes. When she spoke she was suddenly Mary again, the warm-hearted girl he loved.

"John, darling, I'm worried, not just over this—I'm worried because I can't see where we're going—where you're going, really, because wherever you go I'll go too. I can't laugh any more at Bilbeau. He's getting too strong a hold on you. John, you're trying to sit on the fence and you can't: you can't give in to a man like him without becoming a Bilbeau yourself—and, John, I never saw it before, but if you get like him I can't go along with you—I can't, I know I can't."

John opened his mouth to say, You know you're talking nonsense Mary, but closed it again.

"There's Angus too," Mary pleaded. "His life is built on so little, and he depends on you—in a way he needs you more than I do."

John knew what she was talking about; and didn't know. "Maybe you're exaggerating, darling," was all he could think of to say.

A quick anguish pinched Mary's mouth and cheeks. She looked pathetically over at John.

"Darling, maybe I am. I'm so confused. I wish I could see clearly—when I was talking a minute ago I thought I could. But, I can't!"

"Let's go to a show," suggested John, getting up.

Mary's smile suddenly made her whole again. "That's probably the only sensible thing we've said since supper. Let's!"

John pulled her down to him. "You're a sweet kid," he said; and they forgot about school.

The next day John hit on what he hoped would be a solution of the Elsie problem. He asked Elsie to turn out for a last rehearsal, which Elsie did. In as impersonal a tone as he could muster, John told the cast that he had a difference of opinion with the principal, but the latter had insisted on the policy of low marks, no privileges. He then told Elsie that he would not blame her if she walked out on them. If she would consent to be assistant director, and especially, coach Betty Armitage, they might still put the play over. Otherwise it would be hopeless.

Elsie stayed, and John felt he had joined a student conspiracy to foil J. C.

Ten days later John's company, with Mary, but minus Elsie, took the Wednesday evening train for London, via

Stratford. Sleeping arrangements had been made at the Y.W.C.A. and Y.M.C.A. Their play won honourable mention in the district semi-finals. In commenting on the West Kirby group the British adjudicator made some deprecatory remarks about the diction. He could not understand how a director as capable as theirs had shown himself to be, should have shown such regrettable ignorance of the English tradition "in regard to his ahhs!" And, with some insight, he wished particularly to commend the restraint with which the part of Martha Cratchit had been played: unfortunately, he said, that restraint seemed to have been imposed from without instead of having developed from within.

This crumb of comfort went to Elsie. John came home conscious of his debt to her, unconsciously very pleased with himself. J. C. seemed to be happy about the whole thing, giving it special mention both at the next assembly and at the first staff meeting thereafter.

17

Early in April John came home for dinner at noon after a routine morning to find Mary mysteriously changed. A kind of mischievous excitement lurked in her eyes and round the corners of her mouth, but she gave John no time for questions. Usually she left meal preparations to the last minute, but today she frisked him into the kitchen, plopped a big spoonful of creamed potato on his plate, followed it with two sizzling pork chops, a pile of green California peas, and half a dozen pickled beets. A bottle of ginger ale and a glass stood by—"I'd have made it beer, darling, but for the damn old school," said Mary, ignoring his amazement and eager questions. "Just eat your dinner," and a roguish smile, were all the satisfaction he got till his plate was clean, and she handed him half a brick of ice-cream in a cereal dish.

"What in the name of God is going on here?" he finally demanded, lifting his empty plate to make way for the ice-cream.

Underneath the plate was a letter.

The envelope had been opened, but the letter was inside. It was postmarked Hamilton, Ontario; otherwise the envelope gave nothing away.

John drew the letter out, unfolded it. The ice-cream lay melting in its dish, unheeded.

The stationery was that of a Hamilton school. The letter was from the principal.

DEAR MR. WESTLEY:

I happened to attend the recent Drama Festival in London on the insistence of my daughter who has a passion for things theatrical. May I congratulate you on the excellent standard of performance shown by your group from West Kirby Collegiate. That a high school group should be capable of competition on an equal basis with adults in the field of dramatics, is, I feel, a high tribute to the skill and artistry of your direction.

Should you happen to visit Hamilton before the middle of May I should be very happy to meet you personally. We have a keen dramatic group in our school here and have recently been looking for guidance in this field.

If you are interested in visiting us, might I suggest the week-end of the 9th as a convenient time?

Sincerely yours—

John looked at the unfamiliar signature. "Never heard of him," he said loftily, tossing the letter on the floor, and drawing up the dish of ice-cream to let its velvety coolness slide down his throat.

"John Westley!" Mary stood up in mock indignation. "That's no way to treat a nice letter."

"Huh!" with supreme indifference. "Get fan mail like that every day at school."

"You dumbhead! Don't you know an offer of a job when you see one?"

"Uh?" John hastily retrieved the letter and reread it. "Nothing here about a job."

"Of course not! Do you think he'd offer you one before he's seen you and sized you up? But don't think he hasn't asked the inspectors all about you!"

The air John rode on to school that afternoon was not all in Klein's tires. He could scarcely keep from flourishing the letter before Klein's eyes. He kept diving his left hand into his inside breast pocket to see if it was still there.

At school he rushed straight to Angus's room.

"Take a look at this." He opened the letter and thrust it under Angus's eyes.

Angus read it without displaying any great emotion.

"A nice letter," he commented.

"A nice letter! That's what I thought, till Mary said it's as good as an offer of a job."

"I suppose it does amount to that. What are you going to do?"

"That's why I came to you. What should I do?"

Angus stroked his chin evasively.

"Go and see him, I suppose."

"But Angus, don't you think it's as good as an offer?

Don't you *want* me to better myself? I mean—well, you're being a sort of wet blanket."

"Do you think I want to see you, and Mary, leave here?" Angus smiled with a touch of bitterness. "I'm not over-staffed in the matter of friends, you know."

"Oh. Well—yes. I hadn't thought of that. But seriously what should I do, forget about it?"

Angus considered the problem objectively.

"First of all, you'll have to decide where you want to live—Hamilton, or West Kirby. Then there are little matters like salary and working conditions." He paused, giving the matter more thought. "First of all, I think I would interview the principal and find out all you can about him, the job, and the school. Get him to make an offer. Then come back here, show this letter to Bilbeau and ask his advice. When you get that you'll be in a position to decide."

"Do you think J. C.'s advice is important?"

"If J. C. hears about it, the Board will be informed. Undoubtedly Hamilton will offer you more money. If they want to keep you here they'll have to raise your salary. If you decide to stay here and they don't know about the offer this letter might just as well not have been written."

John made his appointment, had his best suit pressed, packed away his best shirt that Mary had ironed in her best manner, and took the train for Hamilton. He met the principal, saw the school, looked up another member of the staff whom he had known in college, and came back considerably impressed.

Mary and he sat up late Sunday night discussing the pros and cons.

Finally John got out a sheet of paper and listed the points in pedagogical style. Mary looked them over.

"John, do you know what we've done?"

"No," said John. "What?"

"All but one of these pros we've tagged with an objection. John, we don't *want* to move!"

"No," said John. "I don't think we do. I'll show that letter to J. C. in the morning and see what he says."

At twenty minutes to nine the next morning John marched through the door labelled 'Principal's Office'.

J. C. looked up from his desk.

"Mr. Bilbeau," said Mr. Westley, "I have a letter here I thought I should show you."

"Sit down," said J. C., "while I read it."

John sat down while J. C. read his letter.

"I suppose," he said eyeing John thoughtfully, "you interviewed the sender of this letter."

"Yes," said John. "He offered me $300 more than I'm getting here."

"Well," sighed J. C., "you know how difficult it is for small cities to compete with places like Hamilton. You are accepting?"

"I haven't decided yet. I thought I'd like to have your advice."

J. C. looked over approvingly. " I can't say anything on such short notice, of course, but I think you have done the right thing. Will you leave this letter with me until four?"

John did so, and went about his day's work.

At four precisely a message came over from the office: Mr. Bilbeau would like to see Mr. Westley right away.

In J. C.'s office were seated Messrs. Parker and Mullins.

They rose, shook hands with John, reseated themselves as J. C. drew up a chair for John and retired to seat himself behind his desk.

Mr. Mullins, as chairman of the Board, was spokesman.

"Mr. Westley, there are two things we would like you to know. First, that we appreciate the work you are doing in West Kirby, second, we don't want to see you go. Unfortunately, there is not much that we can do. Only last year the Board made a ruling that all salary increases should be uniform, based on either the acquisition of higher qualifications or on length of service. It was felt that unscrupulous teachers could use a situation such as yours to play off one Board against another."

"You mean," said John, "that I might use any offer you might make of an increase, to jack up the offer Hamilton has made me?"

"Exactly." Mullins smiled pleasantly. "So we cannot offer you an increase," he paused significantly, "officially."

"Does that mean," John asked tactlessly, "that there might be an *un*official," he hesitated, then fell into the mood of the thing "—adjustment, *after* I made the decision to stay?"

"I can only repeat," said Mullins, "we are not in a position to offer you anything. We would like you to stay. Mr. Bilbeau speaks most highly of your work here."

Mr. Parker spoke up. "Young man," he said with nasal impressiveness, "West Kirby is an up and coming city, where a person with ambition and know-how can go a long ways. We're in the tail-end of a little depression now, but we've weathered them before and come bigger and better every time. I'd think twice before leaving this little beauty spot. I know," he waved his hand defensively, "Hamilton has a mountain too. But—" and he leaned forward with the real estate man's glitter in his eyes—"how far away can you see Hamilton mountain? Why everybody knows it isn't a real mountain anyway!"

Anything after the mountain would have been anti-climax and the meeting broke up, John promising to inform them of his decision within the week.

Walking home he spied Dot Young half a block ahead and quickened his pace to overtake her. It took ten minutes to get within respectable hailing distance, for Dot was a determined pedestrian.

They walked up Central Avenue together, John full of his problem.

"My advice is, take it," said Dot. "I've lived and taught in West Kirby all my life: I know the town and I know teaching. West Kirby is full of big ideas, little men and old women. The big ideas are floated by little men like Parker to line their own pockets. The old women are the school principals, church elders, bank managers, and city council."

"But wouldn't I find the same thing in Hamilton?"

"I don't know. Maybe it's universal. But personally, if I had the chance I'd leave tomorrow. I'm so sick of this narrow little town with its stupid moral and social fixations. I'm sick of teachers who lie awake nights wondering how to deal with chewing gum, the timid little tame rabbits who hop around doing what they're told, burying their noses in the dry leaves of books, afraid to look around them for fear of seeing something that would make them think. No, don't ask me for advice. If you asked me whether you should live here or in central Greenland I'd say go to Greenland: at least you'd have some space around you."

The whole thing turned over and over in John's mind as he walked up Second Avenue. $300 raise . . . . the sun setting over Lake Huron . . . . Angus . . . . the Hamilton principal saying, "This is our chemistry lab. As a science teacher you'll be interested in the monel-metal table tops, the very latest thing!" . . . . the day with Mary at McAdams Falls . . . . J. C.—"an excellent piece of work, Mr. Westley" . . . . Elsie, bitter, imitating him . . . . Angus—that glimpse of him standing alone at Nyes's party.

"We're staying," John announced simply to Mary as he stepped in the door.

"That's nice!" said Mary. "I knew it all along of course."

"As a matter of fact, now I come to think of it, so did I."

Under J. C.'s organizing genius the school was running smoothly now, more smoothly than it had in Nyes's time. After the first epidemic of rules and regulations and what had seemed to many a tendency to high and mightiness, the new routine had become habitual.

John noticed the difference now as soon as he entered the front door. The halls were silent. Students came and went, but with a purpose, going somewhere, not aimlessly wandering to put in time until the bell rang.

Nyes's theory, if he was ever conscious of a theory, had been that as long as a pupil got into the classroom ready for the day's work it was no one's business how he spent his time before then. Bilbeau worked on the theory, completely conscious, that a pupil should be under control from the moment he entered the school. Students arriving early and those who stayed for lunch were herded into the assembly hall, gymnasium, or library, where they were gently but firmly supervised. Fifteen minutes before the hour, morning and afternoon, teachers were expected to have their doors open and students required to go straight to their rooms from their lockers. Loitering for any purpose was rigorously discouraged.

The old hit-and-miss assemblies, often called on short notice, were replaced by definite assembly periods, twenty minutes every Monday and Thursday morning. Where students once chose any seat they pleased there was now a definite seating plan for the whole auditorium.

Mr. Smith was assigned a spare period each morning to check attendance and 'lates'.

Six new bulletin boards suddenly appeared at strategic intervals through the school and were soon covered with mimeographed sheets of rules and regulations.

The staff squirmed a little under this tightening process, but was not really upset until the week when notes initialled by Smith began to appear in their letter boxes:

There have been omissions lately in your attendance records. In fairness to the office would you kindly give the matter your full attention hereafter.

John walked into an indignation meeting in the men teachers' room.

Audubon, the new classics man, was talking. "—two periods last week, one of them I had permission to leave early to go to the dentist and Miss Pettiker marked my class, the other the class didn't come to me at all—I had exchanged classes with Starling so that he could have mine an extra period to complete an experiment."

Starling chipped in. "Yes, I'll verify that. I'm all for tightening up, but this is carrying things too far."

"Well," remarked Klein, "we all know who is back of this."

Pikestaff interrupted. "That's what *I* thought. But I went to Mr. Bilbeau and asked him. He said that he asked the Secretary to make out the notice on Mr. Smith's request and was sorry there had been any resentment."

"Did you tell him you resented it?" It was John's turn.

"Oh, no, of course not, but I think he inferred from what I said that some members of the staff were not very happy about the thing."

"In that case," said Klein, "it's Smith's responsibility. What are we going to do about it?"

"Why not go to Smith and tell him?" asked John, naively.

Pikestaff and Starling gaped.

"We couldn't do that!" they spoke simultaneously.

"Why not?" asked Klein.

"Well," said Starling, "that would be like laying a complaint behind Mr. Bilbeau's back."

After four the same day John was initiated into membership in the Boiler Club.

"Doing anything?" Ken asked him as they met on the stairs.

"Not for fifteen minutes, why?"

"Come on down to the boiler room and have a smoke."

They descended into a huge room filled with two huge boiler-furnaces; the ceiling an intricate pattern of pipes great and small, the walls at intervals punctuated by valves, levers and gauges; the floor frequently wet from hosing. In this dream of the world of tomorrow, paying not the slightest heed to the steady click of meters, the sudden alarming clack-clack-clack coming from the metallic bowels of one of his monsters; calm in a world which seemed capable of exploding at any minute and blowing up with it the entire school with its contents, sat Bert Willoughby the engineer.

Bert visited the boiler room from seven till ten in the morning and again from four till seven in the afternoon. John had seen him only once since he had come to W.K.C.I. and the one glimpse had frightened him away from the furnace room till Audubon's invitation.

So John made his debut into the most select club of all, consisting of Bert Willoughby, Fred Hubble the janitor, Ken Audubon, and himself. Bert had built up such a potent fear of his personality and so vast a respect for his engineering skill that no principal, acting or otherwise, dared to set foot upon his usually-damp-from-hosing pavement. And Bert never went upstairs except for an emergency; a phone connected him with the office. All the staff members knew him as Bert, even though some knew him only by reputation.

The men's room was not, like the boiler room, calculated to inspire respect for the men who occupied it, either by size or contents. There were two pipes running up one corner next to the lonely window, which looked out on the windowless exterior of the gymnasium wing of the new building, but there the resemblance ceased. It was just a room where one hung one's hat and coat, where one lingered only when the conversation was of more than passing interest.

Audubon and Pikestaff were evidently absorbed in such a conversation one day late in May when John came in to hang up his dripping raincoat, for they looked up suddenly and guiltily when he entered.

Audubon was flushed. "What's your candid opinion on the matter?" he asked John.

"What's the topic?" asked John lightly as he came over.

"Bilbeau and Macdonald," said Audubon bluntly. "I've been trying to tell Pikestaff here that I'd have picked Macdonald for principal any day."

The idea was new to John. "Of course," he said, "there's nothing wrong with Angus, but J. C. is obviously the type —I mean, Angus—" he repeated the first name with self-conscious pride in his intimacy—"wouldn't even want the job."

"And Bilbeau does, that's pretty obvious too," said Audubon, his eyes looking small and detached behind the thick spectacle lenses.

"Everyone respects Mr. Bilbeau," declared Pikestaff. "After all, he's a member of the Success Club, and he's superintendent of the second largest Sunday School in the city."

"I suppose," retorted Audubon, "there isn't the same respect for Macdonald."

"Well," said Pikestaff, "I know for a fact that he doesn't go to church. And a lot of people are wondering why he never took a university job. I've nothing against him personally, but I think Mr. Bilbeau is a finer type of man."

"What did Bilbeau do before he came here?" asked Audubon.

224

"He taught in Windsor." Pikestaff thought. "Before that he got his M.A. in the States."

"Yes," said John, "he worked his way up from the bottom. He began as a public school teacher in some village or other, got his B.A. extramurally and was principal of the same school—I think—before he went to the States. And I know for a fact he got his M.A.—A.M., they call it down there—in one year. So he must have been pretty smart."

"Or picked it up at a third-rate college. Where *did* he get it?"

Neither John nor Pikestaff knew.

"Well," said Audubon, "Macdonald is a first rate teacher: I know that from the way the kids talk about him. Looking over the scholarships the other day, over the past ten years, I notice half of them are science. I haven't noticed any English scholarships since Bilbeau took over—he's been here nearly four years, hasn't he?"

"Three," corrected Pikestaff.

"It's hardly fair, though," said John, "to judge by scholarships. I heard J. C. talk to the Success Club, and he seems to be more interested in the students who aren't of university calibre."

Audubon was unconvinced. "It's a good story," he said. "In any case, I don't like the way Bilbeau has his knife into Macdonald. If I hadn't been new on the staff I'd have said my say about policing the halls, too."

"As to that," said Pikestaff, "I was as surprised as anyone when Mr. Bilbeau said what he did. But I think he was just trying to show that he was in control of the situation. It certainly wasn't very tactful of Mr. Macdonald to speak up like that at the first staff meeting."

Audubon looked over at John with his eyebrows raised, and evident disgust in the set of his mouth. As he did so the bell rang, and the three filed out of the room to take up their police duty.

John's last class had been dismissed. He had only one student working out a neglected homework exercise in algebra on the blackboard. He suddenly tired of waiting.

"If you get stuck with any of those problems, leave it and go on to the next. I'll be back in fifteen minutes."

I shouldn't do this, John told himself on the way down to the boiler room but she won't get raped while I'm gone. Probably do her good if she were. *I* can't stir her up.

Down in the boiler room there was no one but Bert Willoughby. Bert sat there as usual, smoking his pipe, and staring sourly at the nearest boiler. Why he sat in a rocking chair, which he never rocked, no one had ever found out. A broad stubby nose and deep lines where the heavy cheeks sagged made him look like a bulldog.

John had learned to greet Bert with a casual "Hi", to pull up a chair, light a cigarette, and smoke in silence till Bert chose to speak.

After a while Bert spoke. "Why aren't you home?"

"Oh, I've got a kid up in the room," John explained, "doing homework."

"Uh," grunted Bert.

"Heard you cutting grass this morning. Is that all you've got to do these days?"

"Uh," Bert puffed a moment, then jerked his head towards the boiler. "Gotta get them boilers cleaned out soon."

"Why don't you ask the principal to give you a hand?" Bert was unusually talkative. "Damn near did!"

226

"Yeah?" John always found it impossible to avoid imitating Bert's brevity.

"Sonovabitch came down here this mornin'!"

"No. Did he?"

"Uh."

"What happened?"

"Just come down to have a look, he told me." A ghost of a smile twinkled in Bert's eye.

"What did you say?"

"Just told the bugger to git the hell outa here. I'm workin' for the Board I told him an' if he has any complaints to bloody well take them there."

"My God!" said John, "you didn't!"

"Uh."

"And what did he say?"

"Didn't say a thing. Just turned white as that wall over there and went back where he come from." Bert told it in the matter of fact way one would describe what one had for breakfast that morning.

"He'll report you," said John.

"No fear of that."

"What makes you so sure?"

"Because when a man's as scared as that man was he keeps his mouth shut."

"J. C. Bilbeau scared!" John was incredulous.

Fred Hubble came in. "You got a kid up in your room?"

John jumped. "I clean forgot!" He butted his cigarette and dashed upstairs to dismiss her.

Fred Hubble confirmed Bert's incredible little story that same week. "Sure he's scared of Bert," he told John. "I saw him comin' upstairs right after Bert told him off, and his face was yellow. But don't ask me what happened."

18

Ever since John had informed the principal that he had turned down the Hamilton offer, J. C. had gone out of his way to be nice to him. On two occasions after the roads had cleared he had offered to take the Westleys out for a drive; but Mary had answered the phone both times and found an excuse— one valid enough, the other invented. John had protested but Mary said firmly, "The less I see of that man the better I'll like him."

The week of the Twenty-fourth of May, John and Mary were discussing what they would do on the holiday.

John was all for buying a bunch of firecrackers and rockets and going over to Angus's place to shoot them off over the lake. Mary agreed enthusiastically.

John said, "Or better still, let's go out to a beach and go in swimming. After all, it's a national custom to go in swimming on the Twenty-fourth. The Fathers of Confederation certainly knew what they were doing—"

Mary smiled. John suddenly saw the point. "You know ever since I was a kid I got July the First mixed up with the Twenty-fourth of May. I never could see why we go on celebrating Queen Victoria's birthday on the Twenty-fourth after she's been dead and buried for a generation. But somehow it's a more Canadian kind of holiday than the First."

The phone rang. John answered.

"Oh, hello, Catherine! No, we haven't made any definite plans. . . . . Sure that'd be kinda nice—wait till I ask Mary." He turned from the phone. "It's Catherine Bilbeau

—she says the family is driving down to Bayfield on the afternoon of the Twenty-fourth, and how'd we like to come along for a picnic supper?"

Mary's face fell. "John, we were going to invite Angus and Vera."

"I know, but after all, J. C. has phoned twice before—it wouldn't look right—"

"I know. Okeh."

It was a perfect day for the Twenty-fourth, and J. C. was in high good humour. John sat in the front with him, the three women in the back.

Mrs. Bilbeau, they learned, had a friend in the country, one of *the* Horners—whoever the Horners were—who had invited her to go riding with her that afternoon. So they turned into a private driveway a few miles out of town and stopped before a substantial brick house, where Mrs. Bilbeau stepped out. John carried jodhpurs and riding-boots for her up to the veranda where a maid answered the door, took the riding clothes from John, and disappeared after Mrs. Bilbeau.

In the car again more than the physical weight of Mrs. Bilbeau had been lifted. John's spirits rose as he heard a lively chatter of conversation from the back seat. Catherine really was a peach.

It was not long before John and J. C. were talking shop: Mr. Nyes's regrettable passing, the problems of teaching, and John's plans for dramatics next year.

"If I were you," advised J. C., "I'd talk your plans over with Mr. Smith.

"Mr. Smith?" John was nonplussed. What had Smith to do with plans for next year?

"I'm afraid I am not at liberty to say more," Bilbeau smiled apologetically with the same high good humour he had displayed all along. "I expect the Board will issue a statement in due course. In the meantime, will you treat my little slip as strictly confidential?"

John promised—completely baffled by the incident. Was Smith going to take over dramatics in the school? Why would the Board announce that? He mulled it over and over in his mind. Had Bilbeau resigned? But that was impossible—unless, of course, he had been offered a better job elsewhere. Somehow he couldn't imagine Bilbeau leaving.

At Bayfield they drove down to the fishing wharf, and bought some fresh lake herring. They ate their picnic lunch at an outdoor table in the park. No one mentioned swimming—with J. C. along it didn't seem quite the thing. John smoked two cigarettes in the park. He knew Catherine took the odd cigarette, but neither she nor Mary joined him.

Driving homeward John found himself in the back seat with Catherine, Mary beside Bilbeau. He was relieved to see that under the pressure of J. C.'s charm and good humour, she seemed quite reconciled to his company. I knew, he thought to himself, that she'd like him if she just saw him at his best. And Catherine was a lot of fun: they argued all the way home about everything from women's hats to the best day of the week to eat fish, till Mary would look back mischievously and ask, "Do you two find those open windows a bit draughty?"

"Where are we?" asked John, debating whether or not he would light a cigarette.

"Just coming to where the 'Horsers' live," said Catherine.

J. C. looked swiftly back at her in disapproval, but said nothing as they turned into the driveway again. It was getting dusk. The night was cool, and sweet with the fragrance of bursting buds.

"Catherine, I wonder if you'll run in and see if Mother is ready?"

Catherine went to the door, knocked, and disappeared within.

They sat waiting for five minutes.

J. C. explained that Mrs. Horner had gone to Havergal with his wife and that the two together were incorrigible conversationalists.

Another five minutes passed.

"By the way," said Bilbeau, "while we're alone together, I should mention that the Board has decided to raise John's salary an extra hundred." He smiled benevolently. "There was some discussion, but fortunately I was there."

"That's pretty decent of you!" said John. "We weren't really expecting it, but we certainly could use another ten dollars a month."

There was still no sign of mother and daughter.

"John, I wonder if you would mind running in to break up the conversation. I'm afraid if I went I'd only get involved myself." J. C. chuckled lightly.

"I'll go," said Mary suddenly, but John was already out of the car, had crossed the lawn and was feeling for the steps in the dark.

He knocked twice before anyone came. Catherine opened the door. "Come on in," she said, "we've just been sneaking a smoke before we go home."

"Your Dad's getting impatient—but I'd certainly like a couple of drags."

John went in to find himself in a large old-fashioned living room with a polar bear rug on the floor and a deer's head mounted on the wall above the fireplace.

"Mother and Mrs. Horner the Horser are out looking at a new litter of coach dogs. I had them just on the point of going, when Mrs. Horner remembered them. I saw them last week so I stayed here to smoke in solitude."

"Does your mother smoke?" asked John.

Catherine laughed. "Mother is a trial and tribulation to Dad; she was brought up in a family that pioneered in women's vices: the more recent vices of course. But I will say she doesn't smoke at home."

They heard loud women's voices approaching from the rear of the house. Mrs. Horner was a complete explanation of Catherine's phrase "where the Horsers live". She had an accent cut from the same cloth as Mrs. Bilbeau's; it was plain that the two belonged together. John was introduced, and they all moved to the door.

Mrs. Horner came out to the car, met Mary and greeted J. C., who was surprisingly cordial.

It wasn't till they were on the final lap of their home journey that John suddenly realized he was now in the front seat again, and Mary behind. He couldn't remember how it happened. Wasn't Mary still sitting with J. C. when they came out? No, come to think of it, she was standing outside when she met Mrs. Horner—she must have got out when she saw them coming.

J. C. said practically nothing all the way home and the conversation was desultory behind. Everyone was tired after a long outing.

Outside their own home at last John thanked the Bilbeaus for the trip and picnic. Mary had run into the house with a brief goodnight. John followed her, vaguely disturbed. It was so unlike Mary to be ungracious. He was relieved to find her in the living room turning on the radio. She turned as he came in and smiled.

The smile was not quite like her usual smile.

"Anything wrong?" he asked.

"Oh, no," said Mary, and the smile deepened. Only the lamp by the chesterfield was turned on, and in the half light the smile was enigmatic, the eyes dark and mysterious between the half-closed lids. "Actually I've been highly complimented."

John looked at her, his heart beating audibly. "Mary, what's all the mystery about?"

Mary waved a hand airily and turned to the radio dial. A 'hot' trumpet performed erotic gambols somewhere behind the loud speaker. "After all," she said, "it isn't every day that a Sunday School superintendent makes passes at a girl."

John was impatient. "For the love of Pete what *are* you talking about?"

Mary picked up a cushion, caressed it, looked lovingly into its eyes and languidly wrapping her arms about it, began dancing to the radio music.

John strode over, turned off the radio, pulled the cushion away from Mary and took her wrists. Mary drew herself up to her full height.

"Sir, the hand that has touched the hand of the angel Gabriel shall never—" She sat down suddenly, her shoulders shaking with waves of laughter. Finally she looked up, tears in her eyes. "Oh, John, thank goodness I've got my sense of humour back. To think that J. C. Bilbeau fancies himself as a Casanova—" and she was helpless in another paroxysm.

John smiled, feeling the corners of his mouth rigid with the muscular effort.

"Are you trying to tell me that J. C. made a pass at you when you were alone with him out in the car?"

Mary suddenly sobered. "Darling, what do you think I've been trying to tell you?"

"Mary, are you making this up? Because if you are it isn't funny."

Mary stood up suddenly. "Maybe it isn't funny. Maybe it proves what I've been trying to tell you all along, that your precious J. C. Bilbeau with the bald head and hairless paws is a big joke and a plain ordinary common garden variety of masher into the bargain. When I think of the gall of the man! Here he is with one arm around my shoulder, patting my hand with his, and telling me that it really was wiser for a teacher's wife not to smoke, and what a charming girl I was and what a pity I should ruin my health and looks—" she burst into her little feminine guffaws again. "Honestly, John, you should have seen his face—such moral concern all mixed up with such an unholy desire to mash." She wrinkled her nose in disgust. "It isn't as if he had the sex hormones to make a real pass. What I should have done was throw my arms around his neck, put my big brown eyes three inches from his little piggy ones, and say in a voice broken with passion 'Oh, Mr. Bilbeau—Jimmy! I'm so unhappy! Take me away with you—far away, to a place where we can build a little nest'"—she broke into half-hysterical laughter again—

234

"Oh, John, I can just see him grab for the door, fall out of the car, pick himself up and run screaming up on the veranda yelling bloody murder!"

She sobered again. "Now I'm tired, and I'm going to bed. You'd better stay up for a while and get your hero fitted into his latest role."

Alone, John sat speechlessly, silently, his mind racing backward and forward over the day's events. If only they had phoned Angus an hour sooner! How on earth could Bilbeau have done a thing like that?

Then he remembered J. C. in Sunday School. The one day he had taught there, going out he had glanced back and seen J. C.'s hand casually resting around the girl's waist in a fatherly gesture. But that was all, just a fatherly gesture. So he put his arm around Mary—what was wrong with that? Mary had kissed Hal, and Angus too, before this. It was so typical of the feminine mind, making a mountain out of a molehill.

Imagination, the whole thing.

John Westley's bank book on June 5th, 1936, showed a credit balance of fifty-five dollars and twenty-six cents. In his pocket and in Mary's purse were an additional thirty-eight dollars and some small change.

"Better count that too," said John.

John and Mary were snuggled together on the chesterfield, an atlas on their knees to support the paper on which they were doing their figuring. They added the amount of the June pay cheque, a hundred and eighty-two dollars.

"The next pay day will be September thirtieth or thereabouts. That leaves roughly, ninety-three dollars a month. Now how are we going to get around that?"

"Well, we could go home to mama," said Mary.

"Rent," said John, "at thirty-two a month for three months. We've got to pay rent whether we live here or not."

"We could sublet it," said Mary hopefully.

"Who would want to live this far from the lake in the summer? Then," he went on inexorably, "there's travel. Toronto and Montreal: there's another fifty down the drain —with the rent that makes practically a hundred and fifty. Balance, a hundred and twenty-five. Food, hydro, water, telephone for September, forty dollars. That leaves forty-two dollars a month for food and clothing. Then we wanted to spend a month in Muskoka, as well as two weeks with your family at the cottage. We just can't make it. If we want to have a decent summer we'll need to borrow at least a hundred dollars."

"What about your Dad?" asked Mary.

"You know how I feel about that. I still owe him nearly two hundred dollars."

"Darling, what's happened to all our money?"

"Now **listen Mary, you** can be flippant if you like but the fact is we need at least a hundred in cold cash. We can't get through the summer without it."

"Couldn't we get an advance on next year's salary from the Board?"

"Ha! ha! That's a laugh. Listen. I was talking to Smith about salaries; we were discussing ten pay cheques a year versus twelve. Do you know what he said?" John's face was so ridiculously serious Mary smiled. "Mary, this isn't a joke. He said, anyone who can't save enough in the ten months of teaching to tide him over the two summer months shouldn't be a teacher."

"He didn't!" Mary was still amused.

John allowed himself a brief smile. "Mary, I'm going down to the finance company tomorrow and borrow a hundred dollars."

The finance company had offices on the third floor of West Kirby's only skyscraper, the Medical Arts Building, which soared some eight stories up from Central Avenue into the blue vault of heaven.

The girl at the desk smiled discreetly on being informed of John's mission. "Just a minute please." She opened a door and called, "Mr. Browning!"

Mr. Browning was a curious little man, dressed neatly in dark grey, with a grave little face. He came up to John and shook his hand, with a delicate suggestion of reserved sympathy that made him feel that this was an undertaking parlour and that he had just lost his nearest and dearest.

"Come this way, please." Mr. Browning led the way into one of three enclosures, each just large enough to contain a table, two chairs and a steel filing cabinet. "Will you sit down here?"

"I just want to borrow a hundred dollars," said John, irritated by the ritual. "I teach at West Kirby Collegiate—here's my teacher's membership card."

"You are married?" asked Mr. Browning hopefully.

"Yes," said John.

"Why, then there will be no difficulty at all. For what period did you wish our service?"

"I need a hundred dollars to see us through the summer," said John. "I could pay it back by Christmas."

"I see, I see. Excuse me *just* a minute, please."

He returned with a handful of forms.

"Now then, your name please?"

237

"Westley, John Westley—there's a *t* in the Westley."

"I see, how do you spell it?"

"W-E-S-T-L-E-Y."

"And your first name?"

"John."

"Your age?"

"Twenty-eight."

The questions droned on. John's name, age, height and weight, occupation, religion, education, financial obligations including instalments on radio, car, refrigerator, furniture, etc.; name of wife, her age, occupation, religion and so on, number of children living, any children over sixteen ——

John pointed out facetiously that he would scarcely have been a father at the age of twelve.

Mr. Browning was severely silent.

"Now then," when it was all over, "we'll need your wife's signature, Mr. Westley."

"I thought your advertisement specified 'No co-signers'."

"Just a precautionary measure. We have to protect ourselves."

"When do I get the hundred dollars?"

"The moment we get your wife's signature."

John phoned Mary to meet him there in half an hour and went over to the hotel for a hair-cut.

The town hall clock struck twelve as they walked out of the Medical Arts Building with ten crisp ten dollar bills in John's pocket.

The spring term drew swiftly to its close. Examinations loomed large, driving teachers and students into a last frenzy of preparation. But underneath the routine tension of June was a question that strung staff nerves still more tightly. What would next year bring?

It went without saying that J. C. would be at the helm; he had been there for nearly five months already. But J. C. was not an easy man to know, and the acting principal was not necessarily a preview of the real thing. His staff was sniffing cautiously at this new wind. They knew where it came from but what kind of weather it would bring with it was another matter.

Only one thing was certain: the weather was due to change.

Book Two

19

It was
a lazy Saturday afternoon on Wasaga beach, one year later.
John lay sprawled on his belly, a towel over his head to
keep the fierce sun from burning into his brain. His sun-
browned legs were buried in sand, which Mary was lazily
pushing up over him with her feet. The lake breeze was playing a little game with her luxuriant hair, tossing it around
her face whenever she would turn her head to look over
anxiously towards the road through the trees.

"John." There was a muffled grunt under the towel.

"Why didn't Dad come this morning?"

John rolled over. The towel fell off his head, the sand
trickled away from his legs. He lay on his back, one arm
flung defensively over his eyes.

"Blow-out on some lonely road maybe; or in the jug, on
a charge of reckless driving."

"Oh, don't be silly."

The conversation had exhausted John. He lay limp as a
log.

"John."

He grunted.

"Oh, you're just like a pig. I talk to you, and you just
grunt."

John grunted again—a good pig-grunt.

"John, do you think Dad will remember to get the
Pablum?"

"Uh-huh," said John, turning, and half-rising on one elbow.

She jumped to her feet, showering him with sand. "There he is!" and raced up the beach, her legs femininely boyish as she ran.

John watched her, thinking, she shouldn't run like that just two months after having the baby. He would have followed her, but couldn't work up the energy, and rolled over on his back again, shading his eyes with one wrist, as he squinted up into the vibrating blue.

He smiled, thinking of that day in the hospital when they showed him the tiny wrinkled face, tomato-red, looking like a little old man; screwed-up tiny fists rubbing the cheeks in a pathetically helpless way.

His son.

He remembered Mary wearily content in the high white hospital bed, gesturing with a faint smile towards her flat abdomen.

It had been incredible last winter that the skin could have stretched another quarter-inch, but her body went on swelling till John would watch her anxiously every time she moved. Then, at last, after weeks of intolerable suspense—

"The General Hospital—and make it snappy!" he had said, hoping the taxi driver was impressed.

It had lasted nearly a day. John phoned from the school: "Mrs. Westley, is she—feeling all right?" He smiled, thinking of the student nurse's answer. "Oh sure! She's just loving it!"

'To Mr. and Mrs. John Westley, an eight-pound boy— Charles.'

A cute little fellow: he should be, too, they had paid plenty for him. It had been a strain, paying back the loan company and financing the baby too. But they had managed. The hundred dollar raise had helped—after the first pay cheque in the fall they would be over the hump.

It had made John feel a bit silly and self-conscious, being a father. And his nose was still out of joint; since baby Charles had come there was precious little mothering left over for John.

He sat up, rubbing the sand out of the hairy side of his shins. He picked up a pebble and tossed it into the water. *Plop!*

In a way it had been nice last year, in spite of complications at school. They had certainly seen more of Angus.

Those Sunday evenings had been pleasant—dutiful Vera's night with her parents—when he had come over alone, and chatted about this and that. It was nice thinking of the copy of his book that stood in the Westley shelves, for all its black scholastic binding, and the dry title *Precambrian Classifications Reviewed and Revised.*

There was the night Angus had scoffed at the popular notion of scientists as cold, calculating creatures. "Actually," he had said, "they're not so far removed from the old alchemist sitting in front of his glass retort, watching a mixture of ground-up dried toad-skin boil away in a saltpetre solution, adding seven drops of distilled snake's blood to see what would happen." He was gloomy over the future, the day when organized research and abstract mathematics would take the groping out of science.

And then Mary had said—she had the craziest imagination: "I can just see poor old Angus at ninety-five; superannuated from teaching, his family, his friends all gone, his island home long since fallen in ruins—nothing to live

245

for but his science—and now he reads in his journal that scientific guesswork has finally been eliminated. He stares out the window. Tears trickle down his cheeks and rain pours down outside. There is nothing more to live for. He goes to the gas jet, turns it on full—"

Her voice had been so doleful John and Angus burst out laughing.

John stared over the blue waves beyond the beach.

Angus was really a good egg. For instance, the way that kid warmed up to him the time Angus and John went down to the boat-house with Mary last fall to rent a canoe.

George—that was the name—had come up, grinning, and Angus had introduced him to John and Mary. "This is George—" passing off the lapse of memory with, "Now, how could I forget the last name of the most promising science student I ever had?" George's grin had widened phenomenally. And then, Angus's affectation of utter scorn when George showed him the paddles leaning together in the corner—and George's alacrity in fetching the best in the boat-house.

When they had paddled out into the lake beyond the west channel they looked back—the magical effect of steep rocks and trees along the shore blotting out every trace of civilized life so that Angus could say, "If you look closely to the left of that clump of jack pine you'll see the mast of my radio aerial." He had smiled whimsically. "I must cut it down, it spoils the effect!"

But the real glimpse of the bond between Angus and his students had come with the student revolt. John recalled the three young revolutionaries in Angus's lab, standing in the doorway, Ralph Borden the team captain, red-haired and defiant. "They weren't afraid of Angus," he told Mary later, "and he talked to them straight from the shoulder, too—no soft-soap or anything—but in five minutes he had them eating out of his hand."

"If they had been afraid of him," Mary had said, "they'd have bitten his hand and run away."

What was that comment Angus had made? Something like: "Rebels usually have more decent instincts than any other class of people. What else makes them rebels? Young Borden has been spunky all right, and fair-minded too." And then added: "His father is lucky to have a boy like that."

That time they drove to Bayfield with the Bilbeaus and J. C. let that reference to Smith slip out, he had known then that something was in the air. But he hadn't dreamed that Smith would be acting-principal: that had been a much bigger surprise than the announcement of J. C.'s projected trip to the States. Bilbeau should be back in West Kirby by now. John looked forward to his return—there would be exciting changes. And even Angus would be glad to see the principal again—after Smith!

In a way he felt sorry for Smith. He would never forget that staff meeting—just a week after the revolt. That rapid blinking habit under the blackness of his straight eyebrows —the way his pale blue eyes struggled to avert themselves as the stern will fixed them on his staff—the dozens of nervous lines around his mouth and eyes and nose—you could see what he had been through. There was a kind of icy strength about the way he sat erect and faced them all.

Dot of course had never admitted his strength. "Haven't you noticed most of the strong characters are shot through with fear, like the man who has never touched a drop of liquor because he's frightened to death he'll like the stuff and won't be able to leave it alone? That's the Smith type," she had said.

That day in assembly had been the pay-off—the way the students had come into the hall, banging the folding seats down as they sat, an ugly undertone of defiance in the angry hum of conversation.

Smith, coming out alone on the empty stage.

There had been an ugly silence. Smith had opened his mouth to speak and then—

"Boo!" a lonely male voice set off the explosion.

"BOOO!" roared the student body, and "BOO!" again, and again and again.

Smith had started to speak, but no one heard him. He got red in the face, shouted, screamed, shook his fists, then stopped abruptly, his face still purple with rage, turned and left the hall.

Well, thanks to Angus's cool head and popularity, nothing more had happened.

Smith had been too rigid to bend, so he had broken. It was pitiful, seeing him stand in the gym the night of the Formal, managing a ghastly smile to staff wives, watching the Big Apple, powerless to do anything but stand there stiffly, his eyes glassy with suffering. He had stuck it out until June, but it really had been pathetic seeing him around those last weeks.

Anyway, Smith was gone now.

And Bilbeau would be back.

John got up on his feet, brushed the sand off, and began walking back to the cottage.

He looked forward to seeing Donald Judd again.

"Call me Donald," the new art teacher had said, "That's my name, and I like it. If my name were Don that's what I'd want to be called."

He knew a lot about dramatics, especially stage settings, and he and John made a perfect team. Donald was about John's height, but slim and graceful in his movements, with a handsome dark head, and an extraordinarily charming smile.

The students had taken to him quickly, referring to him as "Donald Duck", and accepting him as one of themselves, with a freedom that John envied and at the same time felt was unwise. He seemed to be quite fearless.

Husson had been another newcomer, English and history, a quiet young fellow with dark curly hair, glasses, and a little, gently pouting, mouth.

As John turned into the avenue of cottages where the Millers were staying he recalled Judd's comment at the end of his second day in the school.

Pikestaff had posted a newspaper clipping on the bulletin board before the Christmas holidays, and it was still up: an article from the West Kirby Times announcing the Success Club's sponsorship of Bilbeau's projected tour of American schools on a year's leave of absence, and predicting great things for West Kirby as a result of Bilbeau's educational survey.

Judd had been hired by telephone during the holidays and had never met J. C. Pikestaff pointed to the clipping and told Donald what an able man the principal was.

Donald had looked oddly over at John, and commented: "I don't know what this guy Bilbeau has got. But after the build-up, it had better be good!"

20

There was no doubt about it: 1937 was a big year for the Kirbys. Let Hitler shriek over the radio for *lebensraum*; give the Japanese a free hand to restore order in bandit-ridden China; let German and Italian militarists play away with their new weapons of air power in Spain. North America and the two Kirbys were separated from all this by two oceans. Now that munitions factories were going full blast in Europe, trade—of a kind—was reviving. No matter how bad the political situation, no one would be so stupid as to start another world war. Here in West Kirby the relief rolls were dwindling. Things were picking up in the Kirbys.

Situated exactly at the corner around which prosperity had been waiting so long was the handsome new home of a handsome new paper. Readers of the *West Kirby Times* and *Kirby Sentinel*, after long weeks of breathless suspense, finally picked up from their doorsteps the first issue of the *Twin City News*—the result of the long-expected merger of the two rival papers.

A chain grocery on Central Avenue shortly afterwards built a new 'modern' store. The current fashion in glass store-fronts hit West Kirby with refreshing gusto: by the end of the year half the buildings on Central Avenue had their faces lifted. Government building loans further stimulated construction. Prospects of increased tax money moved the city council to think in terms of spending rather than saving. The Board of Trade, the service clubs, the Retail Merchants' Association, were seized with a mild recurrence of the old boom fever.

Men of vision looked forward to a magnificent future. The mayor of West Kirby foresaw the day when the two cities would be merged into one Greater Kirby, the metropolis of the north, growing by leaps and bounds to become the leading city of Western Ontario. The Board of Trade sprang into activity, inviting industries to locate in the twin cities, where labour was cheap, taxes were low, and power abundant.

And Bilbeau was back.

The new spirit abroad in the two Kirbys had found a focus and new energy in the person of James Campbell Bilbeau, M.A., Principal, West Kirby Collegiate Institute, recently returned from an extensive study of educational trends in the United States.

Change was in the air and J. C. was for change.

And the Westleys were back.

"What the hell!" John had exclaimed as he opened the door and put the three suitcases down.

Mary, weary though she was from carrying Charles, began to laugh. "John, I knew all summer we'd forgotten something."

Strewn over the floor were dozens of back issues of the *West Kirby Times.*

John picked up one that seemed thicker than the others, unfolding it. "Well what do you know!" He showed it to Mary, excitedly. "We've got ourselves a new paper—the *Twin City News.*"

The apartment was hot and stuffy. They opened the doors, pulled up the blinds, and pushed the window-sashes as high as they would go. While Mary fixed up the crib and tucked Charles away John relaxed in a chair to look over the mail.

"Guess what!" he called through the door. "Catherine's relief job folded up and she's working down in Toronto!" Looks as if things are really picking up, he decided, turning again to look at the *Twin City News*.

There wasn't much of interest. He opened a second paper.

Splashed out on the front page was a magnificent cut of J. C. Bilbeau, bald head and all! Avidly, John read the copy underneath.

LEADING EDUCATIONIST RETURNS
Collegiate Principal Given Civic Welcome

The noon train today was met by the Mayor of the city, officials of the Success Club, and other prominent citizens of West Kirby, to welcome home J. C. Bilbeau, M.A., eminent educationist and principal of the West Kirby Collegiate Institute.

For nearly eight months Mr. Bilbeau has been on extended leave of absence, engaged in a study of educational trends in the United States. In his welcoming address at a special luncheon of the Success Club, the Mayor expressed his confidence that the trip, sponsored by the Success Club, would result in "sweeping changes in the local school system that will raise the present standards of education, high as they are, even higher."

John read on to learn that Mr. Bilbeau had visited "literally hundreds of educational institutions, including high schools, colleges, and universities" during his absence, taking in points as far apart as New York, Los Angeles, and Oklahoma City. J. C. had "gleaned a wealth of information that will be of incalculable benefit to education, not only in West Kirby, but, he hoped, throughout the province," although he made it clear that the general impression he derived from his survey was that "in most respects, Ontario schools lead the world."

On an inside page was another cut showing Bilbeau, the Mayor, Parker, Mullins, Rose—president of the Success Club—and other notables, at lunch. John was just recalling his own lunch with the Success Club when Mary called:

"John, will you put the stuff away from our bags while I get lunch?"

"Darling," he protested, "I'm just reading about Bilbeau—you should see the write-up!"

Mary came in, carrying a quart sealer of preserved cherries. "John, can you open this?"

John gave her the paper, grasped the jar firmly with one hand, strained at the top with the other till it gave.

Mary was chuckling.

"What's the joke?"

"I can just see them all at a banquet in heaven fifty years from now," she said. "Bilbeau with wings, a gold halo hanging over his shiny dome, and a halo of fat under his chin—and Mullins tossing off one glass of nectar after another, trying to get drunk."

John smiled. "What would Parker be doing?"

"Oh," said Mary, her eyes sparkling, "there would be an angel leaning over to give him another helping of ambrosia, and Parker would have his earnest little rosy face next to the angel's ear, whispering confidentially that he knows of a nice little lot on the island that can be picked up for a song."

She turned to Bilbeau's portrait on the front page. "He's getting fat, isn't he?"

J. C. was putting on weight, John decided, when he went over to the school the next day, and discovered Mr. Bilbeau busy in the office. It was the same man, the same bald head and tufted eyebrows, thin nose and solid chin; but fleshier, and radiating a good humour and self-confidence that, while they attracted, made John feel awkward and insubstantial by contrast. They shook hands.

"How are you, John?"—his voice was just the same too perhaps a shade mellower. "Sit down." He waved John to a chair, and sat down as though he had the rest of the day to spend with John.

"We certainly missed you, Mr. Bilbeau," said John.

Bilbeau smiled complacently. "Well," he waved his hand deprecatingly, "a lot of people have said that to me in the last few days; but it's a pleasure to hear it from the member of my staff on whom I am counting as much as anyone to put this school of ours out in front. Well out in front." He smiled again, holding his head up a little in a gesture that made John think of Franklin D. Roosevelt.

"Were you in Washington?" John's question slipped out impulsively.

—"and met the President." Bilbeau answered the unspoken question, dropping his head slightly. "A great man, the American President. Of course, we merely shook hands —I am only the principal of a little Ontario high school after all—but I was lucky enough to be lunching with a group of distinguished educationists at Columbia and we were driven over to Hyde Park—a lovely place! But enough of myself—" and J. C. congratulated John on the birth of his son, asked after Mary, and even went out of his way to mention Angus's book and what an asset Mr. Macdonald was to the school. As he showed John to the door he added:

"By the way, I want to discuss with you certain plans I have in mind in connection with extracurricular activities.

You can expect to be called into the office in a day or so."

John went out, warm whisperings of things to come in the air about his head. J. C. was back, and was expecting John to share in his plans for building up the school. And that antagonism between him and Angus was dead and buried. How else could he have spoken so approvingly of him? It was the beginning of a new life!

You can eat your cake and have it too, thought John, apropos of nothing at all.

School opening under the new Bilbeau was breathlessly brief.

J. C., his mellow baritone resonating musically through the hall, welcomed "my friends" the staff and students to the beginning of what he hoped would prove "an epochal year in the history of the school", referred modestly to "my eight months as a travelling student", and stated that in no school on the North American continent was there a group of students as intelligent, loyal, and co-operative, as that which he now addressed.

There would be no need for heads of departments to announce text-books, neither would it be necessary for class lists to be read and for students to re-assemble in the classrooms. Class lists were posted on the bulletin boards; and as they filed out of the assembly hall students would receive instructions and time-tables for the morrow, as well as lists of the books and supplies they would need for every subject in each grade.

Mr. Green, middle-aged and plump, was introduced as the new English head. Mr. Miles, who would be the first music teacher the school had ever had, was identified—he was fair, young, and wore horn-rimmed glasses.

"I should like at this point," proceeded the principal, "to make a third, somewhat unique, introduction."

The school leaned forward.

"We are all conscious of the high calibre of the ladies and gentlemen seated on the platform at this moment."

The rows of upturned faces stirred; John tried not to look smug.

"Typical of this high standard is a gentleman on our staff who has found time even while teaching—and he is an outstanding teacher—to indulge in geographical research that has been recognized by the most eminent scientists of the nation."

Everyone was looking at Angus. Angus was looking uneasily down at the floor. John was expecting J. C. to correct the word "geographical".

"Not content with such recognition, this teacher has written and published a book—" here J. C. picked up a copy of the book in question, holding it high for all to see, then read the title—*Precambrian Classifications Revised and Reviewed* (there was a little laughter) "by Angus W. Macdonald."

On the platform the teachers clapped their hands politely but the student body burst into a spontaneous tribute to Angus that swept the hall. Mr. Bilbeau turned graciously to Angus, smiling benevolently, motioning to him to rise and accept the tribute.

Angus looked small and ill at ease. He rose, hesitantly, and waited for the fresh burst of applause to die away.

"Thank you!" was all he said, and sat down.

There was more applause, but it fell a trifle flat.

Three minutes later the students were streaming out of the school on their way downtown to buy books. History had been made already. The ceremony of school opening, that hitherto had lasted at least an hour and a half, was all over in less than fifteen minutes.

That Bilbeau meant business was soon apparent.

The next day Angus, Audubon, Miss Pettiker, Donald Judd, and Mr. Green (the new English head), were called to the office. John first heard about it at the next meeting of the Boiler Club.

"It's like this," said Ken Audubon. "West Kirby is a school that's little known outside of Kirby County. Now that we're staging a Twin City revival it is time the school acquainted the world with the fact of its existence. A certain amount of publicity has been achieved through our dramatic activities—"

"A bow, please!" demanded Donald. John smirked.

"But," and here Audubon wagged a long finger in a manner more reminiscent of Nyes than of Bilbeau, "we have a school paper which has long lain in a state of neglect."

"That's true enough," said John. "In the old days they used to read choice selections at the Lits, but now the Lits are gone they print an issue four or five times a year of a thing that costs ten cents, isn't worth half a cent, and nobody reads. What was J. C.'s idea?"

"A bigger and better school magazine, published in the fall at the height of the season. He thinks we can sell three thousand copies at one crack. Tells us the circulation of half a dozen American school magazines and passes samples around. Waves half a dozen prize-winners and wants to know if we can do better. Then he asks Macdonald point blank if he will take the editorship."

"Angus looked dazed," said Donald. "'What makes you think I can do it?' he wanted to know. J. C. mentioned Angus's book, his reputation, poured on the oil in big dollops."

"What did Angus say?"

"He asked who was to write the magazine, staff or students. J. C. was very surprised: students of course. Mr. Macdonald would be expected to act only in an advisory capacity, naturally. Mr. Green and Miss Pettiker would be kind enough to criticize the articles from a literary point of view; Mr. Judd would take care of the cover and illustrations."

"What about you, Ken?" asked John.

"Sales promotion, circulation, finance!" said Audubon smartly. "As a classics teacher presumably living in the dead past, I was honestly pleased to be asked to handle the money end of it. As a matter of fact J. C. knew that I had done that sort of thing in university. I mentioned it in my application for this job."

"Oh," said John. "Well, I wish you luck!"

"While you're doing that you might find us a little write-up on the Dramatic Club, past, present, and future."

"Ouch!" said John. "I'm not much of a hand at writing."

"Who asked you to write it?" said Audubon. "A kid does the writing: you do the re-writing."

He even poked fun at Angus the next day: "Going literary on us now, eh?"

Angus smiled wryly. "I suppose I'm one of those people who can't say no—I may even have been flattered by the invitation; it probably takes as much skill to edit a good magazine as it takes to write any kind of a book. Anyway, it should prove interesting: I haven't the slightest idea of

258

how to go about it. May I come in tonight and talk it over with you and Mary?"

It was a treat to watch Angus tackle the problem. He had brought a dozen issues of other school magazines with him. They set up the card table and sat in conference around it. Angus took off his coat, folded it neatly over the back of the chesterfield, put on his rarely used glasses, got out his automatic pencil and scratch pad.

"Problems," he said: "(a), to analyse the contents of twelve school magazines. (b), to plan a new magazine. Now then, the analysis." He divided the magazines between John and Mary, listed them by number on his scratch pad. "All right," he said briskly, "give me the contents of each magazine, whoever is ready first."

In an hour Angus knew what a standard school magazine should contain: in two hours they had drafted the first number of the new magazine. At the end of the third hour Angus had a list of stories and articles opposite the names of the teachers most likely to get them from the students.

"I had no idea Angus would take to that kind of thing so easily," said John.

The school magazine launched successfully, J. C. turned to the Christmas concert.

John, Donald Judd, Gerald Miles, Frank Jarratt, Dot Young, and Margaret Brewin were called in.

J. C. sat at his desk, the others in a semi-circle around.

"I have called you in," he said, "because you are the teachers who have been chiefly responsible for the success of the Christmas concert. First of all I wish to congratulate you on the success of previous concerts."

Nevertheless, he went on to tell them, with more co-operation—and he cited instances gleaned from his travels—a higher standard could be reached. Hereafter they would consider themselves a committee: it might be as well to start planning early. Mr. Miles would look after the music, especially the orchestra: Mr. Jarratt, the boys' athletic contribution, Miss Brewin, the dances; Donald Judd, the staging and lighting; Miss Young, the costumes and properties. John would look after the play. The principal suggested that they meet in his office at four a week later, with ideas for a complete programme.

The school assemblies came next. Would Messrs. Westley, Miles, Judd, and Miss Pettiker, kindly consider themselves a committee to act with him in the matter? Mr. Miles for the music; Mr. Westley, dramatics, Mr. Judd, the stage end of things; and Miss Pettiker for student contributions. He himself would look after the matter of outside speakers. He suggested an immediate survey of the entire student body to discover talent.

The remainder of the staff looked on half in envy at being left out of the current, half in fear of being swept into it. Their fear was realized: J. C. had more ideas. There were the students. The students must be made to feel at home—they loved parties, why not humour them?

So a committee was formed to organize a First Year Party, a Junior Party, and the traditional Rugby Scrimmage.

There was a noon-hour supervision committee and a hall supervision committee, and a committee on examinations, all under Starling's leadership.

At staff meetings it was no longer a case of mere teachers discussing school problems in piecemeal fashion. Now they were directors of a great organization, executives, determining the policies that would shape the lives of thousands of students. There was no long harangue from the principal, there were no wearying minutiae from the teachers. A meeting consisted of reports from committees, recommendations, brief discussions, votes; and would have been over by five o'clock but for a tendency on J. C.'s part to reminisce. The reminiscences were brief and colourful at first, and generally to the point. It was well on into the term before the principal ran out of the colourful incidents of his year's leave of absence, and the staff noticed a tendency to longer stories with less point, and interlarded with "When I was lunching with the President of Princeton", or "The Superintendent of Education for Los Angeles and I", which continued to impress but began to weary, his audience.

Donald Judd had long since become a faithful member of the Boiler Room Club; even going to the length of spending the odd spare period down there. John was busier than ever under the new regime, but he still found time on rehearsal nights to slip down after four for a brief smoke before the group collected in his room. Six weeks after school started he went down one night to find Donald there alone.

"I keep forgetting," said John, "that this is your first year with J. C. How do you like him?"

Donald laughed. "That big bag of wind?"

John was startled: it was exactly the same phrase that Angus had once used. But for once he curbed his impulse to protest.

"He does talk a bit about his trip in the States, but heck, so would you, if you were in his shoes."

"I'm not thinking about that," said Donald, "I don't mind how much he talks about himself if he's got something to talk about. But when a man spends a year studying education you expect to get some ideas on education out of him. We know all about the big shots he's met, and the big schools he's been to, but where are his *ideas*?"

John was disturbed. "Why, the way he's organized things, all the committees, and school parties——"

"Did he have to go to the States to learn that? And what's it got to do with education?"

"Well——" John groped a second for an answer "——it certainly helps with teaching."

"Sure it helps, but it's not education. I haven't any doubt the boy has a few tricks up his sleeve he's picked up in the States; but I'll bet my bottom dollar he pulls them out one by one, so he'll get every ounce of publicity out of them they're worth. No, Mr. Bilbeau is a smart man when it comes to looking out for Number One and putting on a good show, but as far as education is concerned he's bluff from the word 'go'."

"I certainly don't know where you get that idea of him," said John, thinking to himself, it's a pity Donald is so damned conceited. The talk had made him uneasy and he closed the discussion. "Well, you may be right. Anyway, as you say, time will tell."

The Clarionet, as the school magazine had always been called, came out in mid-November. Angus spent the last week before it went to press sweating over the make-up, handing back articles to teachers to return them to students for corrections, then chasing teachers to chase students to have them back again in time. Audubon put on a spectacular sales campaign. Donald Judd's Poster Club made nearly a hundred posters which were plastered all over the school. John wrote two publicity skits to put on at assemblies, and a competition was launched with prizes for the highest individual sales. A specially trained corps of girls sold copies at football games, to every store in town, in restaurants, and from door to door. The total sales amounted to 3100 copies.

"And we can do better next year," declared Audubon.

There was a foreword by the principal.

It has been my recent privilege to observe a great many schools in action and to discuss the problems of secondary education with leading American educationists. Basically, I believe, there are no finer boys and girls, or a more loyal and co-operative staff, than are to be found in W.K.C.I. In these dark days, when war threatens in Europe, it is a great privilege to be a leader of young people. In youth is our faith and our hope: faith that whatever may betide, our young men and women will have the strength and vision to see it through; hope that in the new world of tomorrow they may build a noble structure on the foundation we have laid so unworthily.

To the editors and to the contributors to this magazine, I extend my heartiest congratulations on the inauguration under such happy auspices of this new venture.

J. C. BILBEAU
Principal

The Christmas Concert, everyone agreed, was the best yet. Miles sweated over the orchestra for three months and got results. The play was well received. The dances were fairly successful—though Margaret Brewin maintained that West Kirby girls were all born with wooden hips, and the gymnastic display—got up by Jarratt in the last week —a bit ragged, but passable. For the first time they used a master of ceremonies, coached by Donald, and tied the programme together. Donald Judd was a magician at quick changes. With half a dozen boys trained to jump at the flick of an eyelash he whipped props off and on miraculously. And Dot, whose nerves were well insulated, had everything ready when it was needed: forgot nothing.

So it went with the activities of every other committee: the school parties, hall and cafeteria supervision, assemblies, and the rest.

Mary was not so impressed with the value of all these things. She found that she had to set the supper hour at six-thirty, and even then John was late occasionally. Not infrequently he would take his lunch to school. And in the evenings it was work, work, work: preparing lessons; reading plays, revising, cutting, culling, adapting them to high school use; working out stage movements and "business"; phoning about props and costumes.

The baby of course absorbed a good deal of his parents' interest and time. Fortunately little Charles, named after John's father, slept a good deal, even when they had people in. As a teacher John had more time at home than the average man and found himself playing nursemaid more often than he cared to admit to casual acquaintances. In their first two married years he had been the independent male, only helping with the dishes on special occasions and with lordly condescension. Now he discovered there were less congenial tasks, and that offering to do the dishes was a very useful dodge for avoiding disagreeable diaper duties. Little Charles was a pleasant plaything if he was fresh and sweet from the bathtub or dressed for visitors, but being unable to do anything more intelligent than grab at buttons and coo with reasonable competence, there really wasn't much a man could do with him.

John worried a good deal, and his greatest worry was the Big Play. He worried over choosing it, he worried about the cast, and above all he worried over the final performance. It was all right if he didn't think about it—while teaching, for example. But when he woke in the morning and thought of the play his stomach contracted in a knot; going to and from school he worried again. Only rehearsals gave him release: John poured all the pent-up energy of his adrenal secretions into directing. Halfway back in the assembly hall watching a scene, he would suddenly see something amiss, stride down the aisle, vault to the platform, shove the dazed performer to one side:

"Like *this!* Put some *life* in it! You're not wood, you're made of bone and muscle. . . . . *Move!*"

"*No, no, no!* Don't move when you speak, don't speak when you move, I *know*, I told you to in the last scene but that's an exception—the lines weren't important. Don't forget, the audience is stupid—it's a big dumb animal that can only do one thing at a time. If you move, it doesn't hear what you say, if you speak, it misses what you do. Divide them. Separate them. Like this!"

He yelled at his cast, pushed them around, or pleaded in a voice dripping with sarcasm. And they loved it; or if they sulked it was only a prelude to something better at the next rehearsal.

The real reward was in the performance. Not that John was ever satisfied. But his youngsters would come through on the final night; always they exceeded his expectations, adding something of their own he had never thought of, or improvising in a desperate situation. For instance, in that play where Bill McGee was the burglar and Ken Holden the householder. Ken was threatening Bill with a gun. It was a tense moment. A door was supposed to slam behind Ken, diverting his attention so that Bill could grab the gun. The door didn't slam. Bill calmly lit a cigarette, held out the match for Ken to blow out. While Ken blew, Bill gently lifted the gun. The whole operation was so smooth, swift, and unexpected, Ken's reflex so natural, and the dazed expression on his face so utterly unrehearsed, that the audience spontaneously burst into a little round of applause.

So John was always sincere when someone congratulated him afterwards, and he said, "Don't bring the bouquets to *me*: it's the cast that earned them."

21

On a Sunday afternoon late in March Mary and John were sitting in the living room; Mary knitting a jersey for Charles, John reading in a desultory way. Outside it was grey, drizzling.

John put down his book, turned on the radio to get the symphony. There was too much static. He turned it off, went over and looked out the window. Rain. Grey sky. He came back and sat down.

"Mary, what's happened to that little dream of mine?"

"Which one was that?" asked Mary.

"Getting out of teaching. Remember the idea I used to have—teach for two or three years, save up a little nest-egg, then go back to Varsity, get my M.A. in geology?"

"Mmmmmm," said Mary.

"When's it going to happen?" he asked. "Am I going to teach all my life?"

"I don't know," said Mary, counting her stitches.

"Oh you don't even listen. Mary, we haven't saved one cent, and we've been married nearly three years. Oh, I know, we have a washing machine, some nice furniture, books, and a baby—we haven't wasted any money—but when am I going to get even a year off to study? Mary, are we going to be stuck here all our lives? Sure, it's a nice place and we've lots of friends here and I'm in a good school; but I don't want to be a teacher, I never wanted to be a teacher. I want to be a geologist."

"But John, we've got a baby now."

"I know, but we have everything we need for a while. If we really saved for two years I could take enough time off to get my M.A. Mary, I can't go on like this."

Mary stopped knitting and looked at him, her eyes calm but reflecting his trouble. "I know," said Mary. "You're working too hard."

"Oh I can stand the work, but I'm just not getting anywhere. Every day I say to myself, next year we can start saving. Is it going to go on like this the rest of our lives? Is that how Angus got stuck here?"

She looked at John, alarm in her eyes. "Darling you don't think that I—"

"It's not you Mary, or me. I wanted you, I want Charles, I want everything we've got. But I don't want to teach. I don't want to get like the others—even Angus. There's something wrong with teachers, I don't know what. Maybe it's the artificial life cooped up with thirty or forty brats in a room six hours a day. Maybe it's the way people look

267

at us, talk to us. Maybe it's just simple little things like sneaking smokes in the boiler room, or listening to kids 'Sir' and 'Mr.' us all day. I don't know. But I *do* know that before long I'm going to be like all the others, like Jessie Willis, Starling, Pikestaff—a teacher!" John put his forehead down between his hands. "I don't know. There's something wrong."

"Well," said Mary, "you've been working too hard."

Charles began crying.

They both went into the tiny nursery that had been John's study. Chubby Charles Westley stood on his fat little bowlegs with his napkin dangling from one hip, sobbing pitifully.

"Oh John," said Mary, "you didn't pin him up properly."

During the past year and a half there had been a noticeable cooling off on Dot Young's part, or at least John had felt it so. Perhaps there lingered in himself a resentment against her over the incident at Nyes's when he had, so to speak, handed her over to J. C. for public exposure. Having been in the wrong, resenting his own conduct, he had transferred the resentment to her. She in turn sensed this and withdrew a little. Or perhaps it was just that, as a spinster, she didn't go for babies and Charles's arrival had frightened her off. But early in May he and Mary received a notice of an exhibition by the newly-formed art group, Dot, surprisingly, among them; and they went to the opening night.

The exhibition was in the basement of the public library: there were, perhaps, fifty paintings. Nearly all of them were landscapes or still life; only two were portraits, and they were surprised to learn that one of the portraits was by Dot. The catalogue was not enlightening: it merely said "Head, N.F.S." They took Dot over to the portrait and demanded an explanation. Who was it? Why had she been holding out on them? Wasn't it the first portrait she had done? What was in her mind when she did it?

It was a painting that stimulated questions. It was a woman's head, looking directly out of the canvas in bold colour which had a curiously dry feeling—a far cry from the juicy yellows, oranges, reds, blues and greens of her earlier abstract work. Dot wasn't very anxious to talk about it. No, it wasn't anyone in particular, and if it said anything she couldn't put it into words—that was probably why she had painted it, she thought. As a matter of fact she hadn't intended to exhibit it, it wasn't really a serious painting, but the more she had worked on it the more it had interested her. They went around with her, looking at the other pictures, enjoying her quick dry criticisms. The three left early. Dot had invited them over to the studio: she wanted them to see another head she was working on.

They stumbled up the dark stairs behind her, saw the light go on above, entered the studio, blinking. Dot was putting water on for coffee. Her smock hung over a canvas on the easel. She strode over and jerked the smock off.

"I've got some more work to do on it yet."

It was the first picture John had ever seen that gave him a direct emotional experience.

"My God!" he said.

Mary gaped.

There was no mistaking the shaggy eyebrows and bald dome. Hitler's cowlick and square moustache were no more typical of Hitler than these were of J. C.

It was horribly like and horribly unlike the man.

The nose was thin and twisted, sinister. The mouth was broadened, the lips parted, in a caricature of J. C.'s smile that made of it a rapacious leer. The jowls were fat and smug. The ears had been lengthened, with voluptuous lobes.

But the terrifying quality about the face was not in any of these features. It stared out of dark empty eye sockets.

"Why did you leave out the eyes?" asked Mary, as if she hadn't heard Dot say the painting was unfinished.

Dot smiled nervously, a disquieting smile; it was so unlike her. She picked up a brush from the floor, dusted some dry colour out of it with her thumb.

"I just can't seem to paint them," she said. "Whenever I do I just get the sickening feeling that they shouldn't be there."

"Is *that* what you think of J. C.?" asked Mary.

Dot didn't answer directly. She stood looking at the portrait as though it were a window through which she was looking.

"I'm leaving in June," she said, her lips colourless from the tenseness of her mouth.

The coffee began to boil.

"Sit down and I'll tell you about it."

They sipped the scalding coffee.

"You know," said John, "I'm not as surprised as I should have been."

"There are things about J. C. I can't put into words," said Dot. "Some of them I got into that——" she gestured toward the canvas. "I've tried to explain to myself why I loathe J. C. and I can't—at least I can't explain why I feel it so strongly, the sick feeling I get when I think of him. He's so essentially false!" They had never seen Dot let her-

270

self go in this way before. "J. C. is a kind of symbol of all that I hate about teaching, and people. I suppose I'm just being psychotic, but I do hate people—all the small people, the little people who can't think for themselves, can't see for themselves, go groping around for a J. C. to lead them, a J. C. to worship, a J. C. who twiddles them around on his little finger until he is ready to use them."

"But damn it all, Dot," protested John, "you are doing the man an injustice. I think," the idea came to him with sudden force, "there are people like you and Angus—and Donald Judd, I think he's another—who are too strong to be dominated by him, and you *have* to hate him, maybe loathe him, to stand out against his influence."

"Anyway," said Dot, "I have made up my mind."

"What are you going to do?" asked Mary.

Dot smiled. "I'm going to do the craziest thing I can think of: here I am fifty-nine years old, due for my pension in three more years, and I'm going to New York to learn how to paint." She sat there, her eyes steady above the coffee she was drinking. "I don't know why," she said, "but you two are the first I've told."

John stared at her, unbelievingly. She certainly didn't look that old. But even had she been ten years younger, for a woman with a mother to support, established in a community that tolerated her eccentricity and gave her security, to throw it all up, and start at the bottom again!

"I know, you think I'm brave." Dot's eyes were hard with suppressed emotion. "Actually I'm not. It's just that I can't live with fear any more: fear that I'll die without painting one canvas I like, fear of what teaching has done to me—will do. Fear of the Bilbeaus and their big clumsy fingers messing up my life by squeezing out a little more efficiency. No, I'm running away—running for my life from all the little people I'm afraid of and can't hit back at."

Mary said, "We've often wondered why you hadn't done something like this long ago."

"I'll tell you why," said Dot. "It was another kind of fear: fear of the unknown, the unfamiliar, fear that I couldn't make my own way. But now this fear is greater."

Dot asked them to keep her secret till she had sent in her resignation at the end of May. She would tell Angus herself.

All through the winter John had been sharing an entirely different kind of secret with his classroom neighbour, Donald Judd.

A ventilator connected their two rooms so that when one teacher or class was noisy those in the other room could hear things plainly. And once a week, beginning late in the fall term the sound effects from Room 16, where Judd taught English and art, became more and more interesting. At first it was merely reading aloud in unison, but as time went on this changed. One could distinguish girls reading together, then boys. Later the girls' reading would be interrupted by roars from the boys, or the boys' by shrieks from the girls; roars and shrieks under complete control. Other sound effects came through: hisses, the rhythmic stamping of feet, ululating noises, hysterical laughter; sometimes with stunning suddenness, at others building up into loud crescendos, or dying away into whispers.

After a few weeks John wanted to know what was happening. Donald was blandly innocent. "Oh, just reading exercises. Are we bothering you?"

"You certainly are," said John, "but if it gets too bad I can always cover up the ventilator."

As a matter of fact it was quite easy to give his class a work lesson in that particular period each week, and both John and his class looked forward to the period as a break in the deadly routine of the day.

By the middle of the winter term the sound effects became so interesting that John wanted to see Donald's class in action.

"Wait another month, till your play is over," said Donald. "I want to try it out in the assembly hall. You can hear them then."

He kept his word.

When John came into the auditorium Donald was arranging his students on the stage. He glanced back, waved to John, then stood in the pit directly in front of his expectant class, his willowy figure in a light grey suit poised like an orchestra conductor.

He turned, nodded to the boys, dropped his right hand, and the reading began.

In glancing through his teachers' periodicals John had noticed references to the new interest progressive schools had been taking in choral reading. But this was the first he had heard; and coming from a first year class whose limitations in reading he knew only too well, it astonished him.

The poem was Gibson's *The Ice-Cart*:

> *"Perched on my city office-stool"*

a boy's voice began, rather high and nasal, not strong enough for the assembly hall.

> *"I watched with envy while a cool*
> *And lucky carter handled ice"*

Judd's right hand dropped, his left hand beckoned, and the girl's voice continued dreamily:

> *"And I was wandering in a trice,*
> *Far from the grey and grimy heat*
> *Of that intolerable street."*

The girl's voice came through clear and sweet; behind it a background of subdued sound from the boys that hit exactly the greyness and grime of the intolerable street, along with a hissing effect from the girls that made John see the shimmering heat waves rise from the pavement.

The reading went on in measured rhythm, exciting, alive. It was all there, "the big white bears" chasing the "shining seals", the seals escaping, secure on the ice-floes . . . . falling asleep . . . .

> *"The carter cracked a sudden whip!"*

The boys cracked the whip with a vigour that startled John; the poem returned to the mood of the opening lines, and was over. The youngsters relaxed, laughing, pleased with themselves, looking to John as he walked up and Donald turned smiling.

"Marvellous!" said John. "If anyone had told me a first year class could do anything half as good, I'd have said he was crazy."

"Oh, they can do better," said Donald, "but they're scared to death up here. Do you think we could try them out in assembly?"

J. C. heard them a day later, beamed his approval and when they appeared at the next assembly, though they didn't do as well, they brought the house down.

"Oh I know it's nothing to speak of as a work of art,"

said Donald later. "But look at the life they get into it compared with solo reading. And imagine what a mess the same bunch would make of singing. Now if I had a really good bunch, hand-picked, I could go places."

22

Easter exams.
Presiding, morning and afternoon. Every day, all day.

Interminably pacing the aisles, or sitting at the back of the room, staring at the backs of twenty industrious heads, leaning against the window ledge twirling the blind cord, and more interminable walking back and forth, to the periodic click of the electric clock, and the weary scratching of pens. Students, with their papers folded, yawning, or doodling on their test paper, letting a blob of ink ooze blackly into the absorbent blotter, digging holes in their erasers.

The fall and winter terms had never fled by so quickly for John. The machinery of school routine, established in the fall, ran smoothly as a Ford V-8. Even the inspector had been impressed and said so to the assembled school.

But John had been a little disappointed. J. C.'s return had promised so much. What had happened to the educational revolution West Kirby looked for?

The holidays passed.
Then early in May it happened. Starling brought around a note from the office that had the staff tongues wagging five minutes after it appeared.

School will be dismissed at three p.m. this afternoon to make possible a staff meeting of unusual importance. Teachers are asked to see that the halls are cleared, and to be in the cafeteria, by three-ten sharp.

J. C. BILBEAU
Principal

Between periods John looked across the hall to Miss Willis, and found her looking over at him, for once unconcerned with hall discipline. She came across, her eyes bulging behind their glasses, her bosom heaving with excitement.

"This looks like the thing we've been waiting for!" she gloated.

"What does?" He couldn't resist the temptation.

"Didn't you read the notice?" It was incredible, her manner said, that he could have read it, and still not have known what she was talking about.

John's own excitement was scarcely less than hers.

As John entered the basement cafeteria a little after the others he had the feeling that they were all taking part in an underground conspiracy. Such talking as there was seemed furtive, subdued: expectancy filled the room.

"What in heck are we meeting down here for?" Audubon wanted to know.

Pikestaff was actually whispering, to Miss Willis.

Angus and Judd sat together, the latter smiling sardonically.

It was nearly 3:15 and no Bilbeau. Another minute passed, and another. The mystery thickened: the principal prided himself on promptness.

276

At last came the sound of footsteps, and voices—more than one person was coming!

Bilbeau reached the doorway, paused at one side, and ushered in two men. The short one was Mr. Parker, chairman of the Board, and the other John had seen beside Mr. Bilbeau at the Success Club luncheon.

The chairs had been arranged in a semi-circle about a table at which only one chair had been placed. J. C. signalled with his eyes: John and Pikestaff caught the signal, and brought forward two extra chairs.

"Ladies and gentlemen of the West Kirby staff," said Mr. Bilbeau, remaining on his feet. "I have brought two —" he paused modestly—"friends"—the two friends smiled recognition of his friendship for them—"here this afternoon for a special purpose, a purpose connected with a plan to whose execution I have long looked forward. Without speaking any further I'll ask Mr. Parker, who needs no introduction here, to introduce our guest."

Mr. Parker grasped himself, and "this opportunity to address a private gathering of the staff", referred to the stirring progress that was being made in the community at large, the "sterling qualities of your principal", and made a few other generalities. Finally, after he had begun rocking on his toes, almost to a point of aerial suspension, he introduced, "a man who more perhaps than any other had his finger on the very pulse of West Kirby life, a man whose work kept him in close contact with that dynamic industrial figure who so generously supported every worthy movement in the community, and so modestly remained in the background, a man whom the members of the Success Club have recently elected to their presidency, Mr. Rose."

Mr. Rose was an anti-climax. After sugaring his audience briefly, he informed them of how the membership of the Success Club had long felt high school education was missing the point. In an address to the Club over a year ago Mr. Bilbeau had shown that he shared with them a common vision of what ought to be done. "Therefore," he concluded, "in partnership with the Board of Education and your principal, we have agreed to sponsor what might be called —but for the unfortunate association of the phrase—a New Deal in education for West Kirby. I regret that pressure of business makes a longer stay with you impossible. Mr. Bilbeau will explain the plan to you in detail. Rest assured, this plan has the heartiest support of your community."

He was gone before there was any time for applause. Mr. Parker followed him half-way out, paused and looked back in comical uncertainty, then whipped out of the room after him.

J. C. rose for the final revelation.

The plan was comprehensive. It was to be known as "The West Kirby Practical Education Project", and was divided into two parts, Preparation for the Professions, and Preparation for Business and Industry.

Training for university would continue on the present basis, except for certain "cultural credits", to be explained later. But only a small minority were expected to concern themselves with university preparation. The remainder of the students would be registered in the Junior Industrial Course, and the Senior, the latter to be introduced at the end of two years. There would be graduation certificates for both courses.

The immediate concern was therefore the Junior Course.

Subjects taken would correspond roughly with those already on the curriculum but would be re-planned to lay the emphasis entirely on the practical use of the subject. For instance, history would no longer be a dry recital of dates, and reigns, and campaigns, but a study of the life of the community in its relation to the past and present. Literature would no longer stress analysis and lengthy compositions, or obscure rules in grammar, but would concentrate on public speaking, how to interview a prospective employer, and similar real-life situations.

"Nor", proceeded Bilbeau, "have the cultural aspects of life been overlooked, the use of leisure. Sports will receive an additional emphasis—*mens sana in corpore sano*. Community singing and orchestra work will be a feature of our assemblies to an even greater extent in the future, and of course the artistic talents of our students will be developed in the art room.

"The Department of Education has tentatively approved of my—I should say," correcting himself hastily, "*our* plans, the spade work has been completed, and the course will be put into effect immediately after school opening in the fall. In the interim I shall approach each of you personally to inform you of how your work will be affected by the new organization.

"I trust," concluded Mr. Bilbeau, "that this project will meet with your complete approval, and loyal co-operation. Now, are there any questions?"

Miss Willis rose. "Mr. Bilbeau, I am sure we are all impressed by the plan you have just presented and are right behind you. But will this new course enable a student to obtain Matriculation standing?"

"The answer is, yes. We have got around that difficulty

very nicely, I think. Hereafter there will be two kinds of Matriculation: University and Practical."

Angus got up.

John's heart sank. From the look on Angus's face it was obvious that trouble was coming.

"Mr. Bilbeau, do I understand that this course is cut and dried, or will there be an opportunity for the staff to discuss the plan as it affects this school and the welfare of its students, and to make suggestions and revisions?"

Bilbeau gazed steadily at Angus without the flicker of an eyelash, listening attentively to each word. Without standing he replied, a smile on his features.

"Mr. Macdonald, it may interest you to know that I have been two years in the preparation of this plan—in conjunction of course," he added hastily, "with a committee of the Success Club, members of the Board and the Department of Education. We should be delighted of course," and the Bilbeau personality beamed forth with its most winning expression, "to have further help with our plan."

"Does that mean that this staff will be asked to study it carefully and in detail with a view to a thorough discussion at further staff meetings before it is put into effect?"

The staff stirred uneasily. Out of the depths of John's memory the gloomy prediction of old Bill the bush cook sprang suddenly: 'Sooner or later these tough guys take on somethin' one size too large!' John wanted to tell Angus, for God's sake, sit down!

J. C. assumed an air of polite patience.

"Mr. Macdonald," he said, "We are all aware that as a teacher of science you have an enviable reputation. Your recent book has added lustre to our school. In questions of geography" (John mentally corrected the word to geology) "I naturally would come to you. In the matter of school organization and policy I feel that the administration officials and outstanding business men of the city are the experts."

Angus was white with indignation. "Mr. Bilbeau, my personal standing is not pertinent. I should like an answer to a simple question: is the plan closed, or is it open for staff discussion before it goes into effect?"

"I have already stated that we shall welcome your advice, as an expert."

J. C. replied firmly. He paused to survey his staff calmly. "Has anyone any further comments?" he asked gently.

John's heart was racing madly—he was my friend then—he's in the right now—Bilbeau is bullying him—Angus is my friend, I've got to stand by him, he needs me! John rehearsed the words: you're not being fair to Mr. Macdonald, Mr. Bilbeau.

Bilbeau's eyes came to rest on John's face, looked at his open mouth inquiringly. John lowered his eyes, closed his mouth, and rubbed his cheek in a casual manner to hide the blush. Within, he told himself furiously, So this is the way you stand by your friends!

"Then I believe," said Mr. Bilbeau, "that we may now adjourn."

Walking upstairs with Pikestaff John tried to comfort himself. But deep in his soul he knew he had chosen a path; and in the city of success that it led to there weren't any Angus Macdonalds.

School went on; the staff absorbed in setting final examinations, and in drilling their weaker classes feverishly to push as many of them through as possible.

One by one Bilbeau invited them into the office to inform

them of the changes in their work that would be effected by the new plan.

John came away from his interview head over heels with enthusiasm. He had been asked to collaborate with Donald Judd on a Public Speaking course to include dramatics and choral reading, with the practical purpose of developing poise and personality in their students. And he had also been asked to design, in consultation with Angus, a two-year practical science course. He had objected that Angus was better qualified for the task, but Mr. Bilbeau told him that Mr. Macdonald's rare executive abilities were to be directed elsewhere: he would be asked to assume responsibility for all extracurricular activities in the school in addition to his editorship. John was relieved to know that Bilbeau held no new grudge against Angus, and flattered at being asked to design the course.

Donald Judd was quite happy about the project as it affected him. J. C. had asked him to work out a practical art course as well as to work with John on the public speaking.

"Don't get me wrong," said Donald, "all this is simply so much good publicity as far as J. C. is concerned. I'm not plugging the course because I think J. C. is a super-educationist. As a matter of fact a lot of kids are going to be sorry they ever heard of it. But it's the first time I've had a chance to work out the kind of art course I'd like to teach, and it's going to be fun working on the choral reading."

"But don't you think it's a sound idea, giving them these practical subjects instead of dead languages and university mathematics they'll never use?"

"I'll agree that it *sounds* good and let it go at that. Old Parker is out for Number One, as usual. He figures the Conservatives will get in on the next provincial election and wants to make a stir so he'll get picked as candidate. Maybe he even figures on getting the Ministry of Education: these little guys usually have big ideas. And J. C. wants to impress the world with his sound progressive educational leadership. Just where the Success Club fits in I haven't figured out. But as far as little Johnny and Mary are concerned the whole idea is: give them what they want, and to hell with their future!"

"It seems to me you're as hipped on the subject of J. C. as Dot is."

Angus went over John's projected practical science course with him one afternoon in June.

"You can skip the details as far as I am concerned," said Angus. "This is what interests me."

He picked up John's outline and read aloud from it:

"Purpose of the course:

"(a) To acquaint students with general scientific principles so as to understand natural phenomena and the common practical applications of science to popular use.

"(b) To give the students some exercise in the practice of the scientific method."

"Is that *all* you propose to do?" asked Angus gently.

"Did I leave anything out?"

Angus looked tired. "Do you honestly think you can do all this in two or three years?"

John became huffy. "I certainly mean to try."

"So when a student has finished your course he will be

able to understand how a radio, phonograph, electric motor, automobile, and heaven knows how many other gadgets, work?"

"Not the details, but the general principles, certainly."

"And besides that they are going to be able to understand and put into use the scientific method?"

"If I'm any kind of a teacher," said John.

"Well," said Angus, "if you can do that, you don't need any help from me."

"But I have it all worked out here!" protested John. "If you'll just look over the course you'll see how I plan to do it. I know it's ambitious, but I've worked out a new method."

"All right," said Angus. "I'll take your word for it. Tell J. C. it has my approval. Just don't ask me to read it." He got up and left.

John went home, heavy of heart, to tell Mary.

"Well, I'd be mad too," said Mary. "You go and work out the whole thing by yourself and when you're all finished you go to Angus and say, isn't this good?—I did it all by myself."

"No, it's not that, Mary. Angus believes in independence. It's just that he's got such an exalted notion of what science is that he hates the idea of making it popular. And I've always felt that he was never completely sold on me as a science teacher. This has just brought it to a head."

"I still think you should apologize," said Mary.

"For what? What have I done? I asked him for his opinion. But he jumped to conclusions right away and wouldn't even read the course. I hate to say it, but he was really pig-headed about the whole thing."

That night he went over his course again, making corrections, hammering it into final form. He changed the wording of his "purpose" a little so it read more smoothly.

He took it to J. C. in the morning.

"Just leave it with me for a day," said Mr. Bilbeau.

Thursday morning John had a spare. J. C. made one of his rare appearances, holding the new course in his hand.

"Splendid, Mr. Westley, a splendid piece of work. I was showing it to Mr. Parker and Mr. Mullins last night. They were thoroughly impressed. This is exactly the sort of thing we are trying to do."

John's wounded heart began to heal.

Angus's attitude bothered him but he comforted himself with—just wait till I get the course going, he'll see what I'm after. Anyway, I just got him in the wrong mood, I'll show it to him again.

The staff picnic had now become an established tradition.

This year there was an efficient committee in charge. A list was passed around with alternative dates and places. They chose a Monday at Shingle Beach, a beautiful little cove on the south shore just beyond Lover's View where Angus's escarpment disappeared into the lake, neglected by Kirbians for the superior attractions and conveniences of the island beach. The Lakeshore Road swung inland just opposite Lover's View to follow a concession line, so that the beach was quite isolated.

They went on a Thursday afternoon, the Westleys and Hussons driving with the Kleins. Mary brought baby Charles.

Arrived at the beach, the men teachers proceeded to cut driftwood for a fire, the women to unpack the lunches; and the children spread out to play.

The older children retired to the cars and came out in bathing suits. The younger staff members and their wives retired discreetly to the bushes to change, emerging in trunks and swimming costumes.

Seated on the beach after a brief swim—the lake was cold and fairly rough—John and Mary amused themselves watching the others.

"Wouldn't it be refreshing," speculated John, "if we walked into our classes in bathing suits?"

"You'd have your little girls so excited," said Mary "they wouldn't be able to learn a thing."

John scratched the dark hair on his chest complacently.

Dot came up, smartly dressed in blue slacks and shirt trimmed with red buttons, her grey hair tied back in a flame-coloured kerchief.

"Here's the artist," John greeted her as she sat beside them. "Looking them all over, Dot, who wins the beauty contest?"

"Looking the men over," said Dot briskly, "I certainly wouldn't pick Angus."

They laughed. Angus was no beauty in his old-fashioned swimming suit; white top and navy-blue trunks in the style of 1930. His small wiry figure was bony at the knees and elbows; as he picked his way gingerly over the rough shingle he looked stooped and bowlegged: though nothing could spoil the keen, fine head, and alert movements.

"I'd pick Donald," said Mary, looking with approval at his slim graceful figure leading little Susan Judd along the sand at the edge of the water. Frank Jarratt was out in the deep water doing the Australian crawl with consummate, and self-conscious, ease.

J. C. strolled up in immaculate white flannels, looking down at them with an easy smile. He couldn't resist a little dig at Dot.

"We men are gradually getting outdated when it comes to costume," he said, meaning Dot's slacks, but looking appreciatively down past Mary's shoulders. Mary shivered a little.

Angus came up, looking blue from the cold.

"The way you young fellows take to the water!" declared J. C. "Would you like a drop of something to warm you up, Mr. Macdonald? If only I'd brought along something from my cellar," he said regretfully, smiling immediately to make it perfectly clear he was being facetious.

"The water certainly is cold," said John to fill a silence just beginning to be awkward, "but when I was a youngster at home, we used to break the spring ice to get our first swim."

Angus went on to change his clothes. J. C. went back to the group of older people.

Dot was silent, staring out over the lake.

"Let's change," said Mary. "I'm chilly."

Eighteen teachers, their principal, his secretary, ten teachers' wives and the same number of children sat down at a low table improvised from a pile of weathered lumber nearby, gaily commenting on the primitive nature of things.

"I just *love* roughing it!" Miss Pettiker was saying.

"I can just see this bunch in the bush," said John in an aside to Mary, "after a thirty-mile paddle." I'd look pretty well beaten myself, he thought afterwards.

Klein said the grace and they set to.

Fried potatoes and bacon, the usual sandwiches, ice-cream, lemonade, cake, tea and coffee, pies on paper plates, children with sticky fingers, mothers absorbed in keeping them clean and off the table. Some of the older people sat aloof in deck chairs brought for the purpose. The lake breeze was dying, though the sun was still well above the horizon. The breaking of waves mingled with the conversation.

J. C. rose, dusting a crumb from his flannels. The conversation stopped, but the waves went on breaking, seeming louder now.

"Now that the inner man—and woman," he bowed to the ladies present, "has been satisfied, I don't suppose children *ever* are—" all eyes turned to young Charles who had taken advantage of the diversion to grab two large fistfuls of cake. The laughter was general—"Now that most of us have had enough to eat we come to something of a more serious nature. As principal of the school the task is really mine, but in view of his longer acquaintance with the subject I have in mind I am going to ask the head of the science department to say a few words."

Mr. Angus Macdonald got to his feet. His voice was hard to hear, and he seemed hesitant.

"Ladies and gentlemen, we are saying goodbye to one who has been a member of this staff for nearly as long as I have, and that is longer than I care to think of. It is not normally considered good taste to refer to a woman's age in her presence. I do not know of anyone, however, less given to false modesty, or more able to face facts. So I do not hesitate to mention that she is reaching an age at which many of us would begin to look forward to retirement from active life. It is a rare man or woman who at that age dares to become a student again. It is rarer still in teachers of her experience, accustomed as they are to imposing authority and imparting knowledge over many years, to take their seat with the young and begin learning again.

"To some in this town Dorothy Young is an eccentric school teacher who paints incomprehensible pictures. To those of us who are proud to call ourselves her friends she is an unusually intelligent woman, a thoroughly honest person incapable of evading any moral issue, a loyal friend, and, perhaps over everything, a woman of unflinching courage, capable of following her own principles without compromise, without being swayed by popular opinion or prejudice.

"But though our loss is great we have the satisfaction of knowing that Miss Young is at last realizing her life-long ambition—the secret ambition of many teachers—to spend all her time doing what she most enjoys. And though few now enjoy her painting I know that there will come a time when it and she will be so widely known that we shall boast of having known her—when!

"As tangible evidence of our good wishes for your future, Miss Young, we ask you to accept this sketch box and its contents."

Miss Willis appeared out of the background holding a large white parcel suitably beribboned. Dot stood up slowly, accepted it and shook Angus's hand. The staff applauded. She looked down the table either way, then stared out across the lake. Her face was pale, her lips pressed tight, the thin cords of her neck stretched sharply with the lifting of her chin.

"I am not a speech maker. I want to thank Mr. Macdonald for what he said. I know he meant it, but I did not recognize myself in his words. I want to thank all of you for your share in this gift, and the best way I can do that is to use it.

"I have never been strong enough to hide my feelings or opinions: if anyone here has been offended by either I am sorry.

"I suppose it is difficult for some of you to understand what I am doing or why I am doing it. I won't try to explain. I have simply arrived at the point where I could do nothing else. Perhaps only a painter could understand that.

"That's all I can think of. Once again, thank you!"

There was more applause as J. C. rose and Dot sat.

"We are losing," he said, "one who has made a deep impression on all of us. We are glad for her sake, to see her go, and shall watch her artistic career with the personal interest of old friends. We are sorry, for our own sake, to lose her. As your principal and as your friend may I add —Godspeed!"

The final round of applause was broken by a general rising from the table, some to clear up, some to crowd around Dot and inspect the gift which she was unwrapping, others to move off on various missions.

Dot liked her new sketch box.

John joined the baseball game that Frank and Margaret were organizing. The elders gathered along the baseline to watch. Mary and Dot were walking down the beach. Two wisps of cigarette smoke rose from the pair.

Mrs. Starling sniffed the air belligerently, her mean little mouth turned viciously down at the corners. John, walking back from first base, caught out, saw her head turned towards Dot and his wife, happened to overhear her comment to Mrs. Smith. It was only one word.

"Imagine!" said Mrs. Starling.

Dot left West Kirby quietly on the third of July. Angus, Mary, and John saw her off: no one else had been told of her departure.

23

John looked forward keenly to the beginning of his fifth year at W.K.-C.I. Late in June Bilbeau had issued timetables for 1938-39 and there had been radical changes.

A week before school opening the world was informed of the West Kirby Practical Education Project in banner headlines on the front page of the *Twin City News*: even Hitler was forced to an inside page that day. In a special school opening issue the paper presented a complete outline of the plan, and featured James Campbell Bilbeau, recalling his fruitful sojourn in the States, lauding his community spirit, and giving him chief credit as designer of the new project. On the centre page spread the West Kirby staff found its heads grouped around a much larger likeness of Bilbeau, with captions underneath each picture identifying and giving the qualifications of every teacher. There was a special editorial which gave credit where credit was due, and predicted great things for the new order in education.

At school very little was seen of Mr. Bilbeau. Constantly

in demand for luncheon engagements, afternoon teas of women's organizations, and consultations with the Board, he found it increasingly difficult to carry on. It was necessary to ask Mr. Starling to be responsible for discipline, and Angus was now shouldered with guiding all student organizations, besides his work with the *Clarionet*. Miss Jamieson was swamped with work and took out her temper on anyone who came into the office.

"The course," said J. C. Bilbeau, twenty times a day, week after week, "is a twofold training in Perseverence and Personality; a thoroughly practical preparation for life, concerned not with any woolly ideal of teaching the student to weigh the world for himself, but with the concrete problem of getting a job and holding it."

The only disappointing feature that September was the small number registered in the Junior Industrial Course. Instead of the two first year classes expected, there was only one; and half the second year class was composed of academic failures promoted by J. C. on condition that they enter the second year class of the new course. It soon became clear that the first year class, with three or four bright exceptions, was of the same low calibre.

J. C. was not impressed when they told him.

"The success of this course is in your hands," he said. "The Board expects you to make good."

Other things were going wrong in other places.

It was plain now that Hitler was a dangerous gangster, bent on bullying and bluffing all Europe into giving him his way. There was the ghastly week when Englishmen dug air raid ditches in London parks. Then Chamberlain came home from Munich with his umbrella, proclaiming "Peace in our time." John and Mary were too well informed by now of the machinations and history of fascism to enjoy the popular relief. On the edge of war they listened to the news with tense faces six times a day.

Munich.

A tired, frightened man with an umbrella faces the bully of Europe.

An English gentleman wearing a school tie, trained to do business in the traditions of Threadneedle Street, meets a German gentleman of more recent origin wearing a swastika, lusting to do blood business, who gives his word that he wants nothing more than this last concession.

Gentlemen!

In West Kirby there was some talk of mobilization and conscription. But business was picking up.

Mary and John saw eye to eye on conscription, with a difference. Both dreaded it. But to Mary, it was not only the physical threat of death or injury to John that worried her. It was the effect John's absence would have on little Charles.

"A guy would think sometimes," John complained, "that all I existed for was to be a father for Charles."

Mary for once was serious. "John, a child needs a father —it worries me sometimes when I leave you with Charles —you don't seem to have any sense of responsibility for him: and you tie yourself up so much with school work you haven't time to be a father. Sometimes I feel I'm getting a preview of what it would be like if you were in the army."

"But darling, now that they've put in this new course I've got to make good. Don't you see how important it is?"

Mary mended Charles's shirt in silence for a moment.

"John, there are two reasons why I love you: because I know you have the makings of a man, and because sometimes you are just a little boy that needs a mother."

"That's a fine thing to say!" John pretended to feel hurt; but wasn't, perhaps because he had known it for so long. "I have hair on my chest, haven't I?"

Mary went on thoughtfully. "I love you physically, too, of course. But things have changed since Charles came. I have a real baby now, and the baby needs a father. John, I hate the idea of conscription as much as you do, and I'd be proud of you if you openly declared yourself a conscientious objector. Then, if you had to go away I'd be reconciled to it, because your stand would give me the strength to be mother and father to Charles as long as was necessary. I suppose what I'm afraid of is that you'll just take the path of least resistance."

"But, damn it all, Mary. I'm not convinced that all war is wrong, and I'm as brave as the next guy; but if I were conscripted I'd have to fight, and I don't like the idea of killing or being killed, so if I can get out of it I will. If I thought all wars were morally wrong—of course, a capitalistic war is—I'd stand right up and say so."

Mary looked at him with her clear brown eyes. "Would you?" she said quietly.

A surge of resentment sprang up within him. "Mary, let's forget about this damned war—you're always making things so darn complicated—there isn't any war and for all we know never will be. You're just like Angus at the meeting."

Mary looked up quickly from her work. "What meeting?"

"Didn't I tell you about it?" he asked, wishing he had.

She waited. "Well, it was nothing much; only when we had that special staff meeting about the new course last spring Angus kept asking questions that didn't get anywhere except under J. C.'s skin. I'm afraid he'll make trouble for himself."

He told her what he could remember and went on. "It isn't what he said, I suppose in a way he was justified, but Mary, nobody's trying to put anything over on anyone: everybody is behind this new idea. And I told you how Angus criticized my junior science course. Mary, it's not just me or Bilbeau he's bucking, it's the trend of the times. It's progress! He's not practical. He worries about abstract things like academic discussion while we are doing something that really matters." He raced on, seeing Mary about to speak. "It's all very well to theorize, but a school *has* to be run from the top down—if you let all those teachers run things there wouldn't be any efficiency at all."

Mary got up quietly and put her mending away. "I'd better give Charles his supper," was all she said.

John felt a sudden chill of fear. What had she said months ago—if he got like Bilbeau she couldn't go along? Was he getting to be a Bilbeau? But that was before J. C. went south; J. C. had changed—look how nice he had been to Angus. Why couldn't Angus be less critical? The old irritating question. Bilbeau *might* get ugly if he was pushed too far—he was only human after all. I'm *not* sitting on the fence, he protested to himself: I'm actually a sort of bridge between them. He could see himself as a human bridge between two cliffs—strangely, the Bilbeau cliff was black and stark, the Angus cliff green with trees. His hands would be grasping the solid rock, his feet caught in the trees.

He cut off the day-dream with a snort of self-derision, only to find himself wondering a minute later: if I had to, would I let go with my hands or my feet? Instead of an answer to the question the fantasy took another twist. He was clinging to the crest of the steep black cliff, Angus hanging below, desperately clutching one of John's ankles.

John got up impatiently and turned on the radio. A guy's mind is the damnedest thing, he thought irritably.

While homeless, terrified Jews wandered over Europe or huddled along its boundaries, John was getting ready for the Christmas Concert, Angus was slaving over the next issue of the *Clarionet*, Frank Jarratt was leading his team against a rejuvenated K.C.V.S., and Donald was experimenting with his choral reading.

At the last assembly of the fall term, on J. C.'s suggestion, Donald tried an experiment in mass choral reading, using the whole school.

It was a simple little arrangement of "Mary Had a Little Lamb", with a "baa" effect from the first year boys, a groan from the seniors as background for "to *school* one day", and a few other simple sound effects and alternations of carrying voices.

The students loved it, and so did J. C. The older teachers turned up their noses, except Angus, who found it "amusing"; the younger teachers thought it had possibilities. But there and then, for better or for worse, "assembly chorals" were born.

As a further means of fixing the young mind on the goal of practical success Mr. Bilbeau persuaded the Success

Club to delegate two of their best speakers each month to address the school in assembly.

The students loved these speakers, first because they invariably began with a funny story, second because they inevitably spoke longer than their allotted fifteen minutes. Probably J. C. had emphasized the importance of the school schedule sufficiently; but some speakers, remembering their own school days, deliberately lengthened their speeches as a belated act of defiance towards the teachers and as a gesture of good will to these young latter-day martyrs; the others were so overcome by the rapt attention of six hundred young listeners and the spontaneous response to their attempts at humour, that they became intoxicated with success and found the words flowed forth with a freedom never before experienced.

The teachers were in a quandary over the matter. Most of them were still dreaming of success and listened avidly to these men who had achieved it. At the same time their minds were fixed on covering the term's work and with each succeeding phrase beyond the time limit they felt their precious periods slipping away.

In any case John learned the secret of success. It was Smith's formula of hard work, plus the magic word 'personality'. The hard work consisted of sticking to it, concentrating, putting the shoulder to the wheel, ninety-eight per cent perspiration, going the second mile, biting off more than you could chew and chewing it, and so on.

There was, he learned, no such thing as luck. You won success through your own efforts; there were no short-cuts, no easy roads, it was up-hill all the way. One notable, an alderman who owned half the real estate along Central

Avenue, put the whole philosophy of luck in a nutshell by quoting these lines:

> You will find that luck is only pluck
> And trying things over and over;
> Patience and skill, courage and will
> Are the four lucky leaves of the clover.

Of course this was only half the picture.

All the ambition in the world was useless unless you learned to co-operate, to work with the other fellow, to see the other fellow's point of view. You had to sell yourself, one hundred per cent. This selling yourself consisted in getting the other fellow to like you, admire you, want you for his employee, for his regular customer. You must have a sense or humour, be able to take a joke, jolly the other fellow along, listen to his tale of woe, sympathize with him, ask after his wife and family, take flowers to him when he is sick; and John got the further impression that it would probably pay dividends eventually to go the last mile and attend his funeral.

By the end of half a dozen speeches, it began to dawn on him that these men, admirable though they were, lacked one thing. He wanted to call it humility, yet most of them had a kind of "humbleness", even though, unlike Uriah Heep, they knew enough not to drop their aitches. They were nearly all on guard against being thought self-conceited or complacent, and paid lip-service to modesty with such phrases as, unworthy as I am, not that I deserve to be, because I happen to be luckier than the other fellow, or, I don't suppose I'll be able to fool the public much longer. The fact remained that they were successful men, knew it, and valued their success. Their naked message was, "If you're smart and work hard you can be a big success like me."

Listening to one of these big successes one morning John relieved his boredom by putting various members of the staff in his place. It was a revealing experience.

Bilbeau fitted like a glove. No one else.

Angus in that position was grotesque. He imagined a "Y" worker coming to Angus and saying, "Mr. Macdonald, we've all admired the work you have done in geology and your reputation as a teacher. Would you mind speaking to my boys on the subject 'How to succeed in one's life work'?" No, Angus wouldn't blow up. He would just look at the "Y" worker with an expression of pain and say something like this: "Mr. 'Y.' worker, what I have been trying to do for a quarter of a century is to decipher a small fraction of the meaning of the Precambrian formation. I have had no success; in fact I am more confused now than I was twenty-five years ago. The work I have set myself to is science, in which the only success is the creation of new problems. If there is such a thing as success, which I doubt, I don't believe it matters a damn. Tell that to your group."

With Jarratt, of course, success consisted in developing a rugby team that would beat the team from Old Kirby; for Pikestaff and Miss Willis, success was getting all their students through their departmental exams. But theirs was a limited goal: they would never be asked to join the Success Club. For the rest of the staff, some were young teachers who were trying to be successful at teaching. Some who were successful teachers wanted to succeed at something else and were only teachers by necessity. Klein was a successful history teacher, but his consciousness of the questionable motives of society, his desire to change that society, left no room for professional ambition.

Dot Young saw eye to eye with Angus. Art was her Precambrian shield, a vast continent of experience in which she wandered on foot, stumbling over the hard rocks, cutting little paths through the wilderness, from lake to lake. No, she could never be a success, even in New York.

John couldn't make up his mind. Was success the most important thing in life? Did happiness come with success, or from a life like Angus's or Dot's?

Even after he had looked up to see Bilbeau beaming at the speaker on the stage; and across the hall at Angus, thoughtfully regarding a point eighteen feet above the speaker's head, he could not make up his mind.

Charles Westley at twenty months was learning the art of locomotion. Mary found him one day at the head of the wooden stairs behind the apartment pushing clothes pins over the side of the balcony and watching them drop to the concrete sidewalk below.

She told John about it when he came home. "John, we'll just have to move. It isn't safe here any longer for the baby."

"Well," said John, "we might manage it, and save a little too."

They found a brick bungalow with two small bedrooms, a den, a large living room with a bay window and a large basement. The kitchen and bathroom were not exactly "modern", but good enough. The neighbourhood was working-class; they were now on Fifth Street South, instead of North, between First and Second Avenues. They were actually no closer to the school, but the way the streets ran made it a brisk twenty-minute walk, which gave John time to get home for lunch on foot if he hurried. The landlord brightened up considerably when he learned his prospective tenant was a school teacher, agreed to paper the living room—if they bought the paper—and otherwise made himself agreeable after the manner of landlords.

On the first of May they moved in.

Walking to school gave John a new perspective. Klein frequently picked up students on his way, but overawed by the surplus of teachers, they usually said very little.

But now John found himself a single teacher in the company of students going to and from school.

This brought to a head the irritating little matter of smoking.

John was walking home at noon one day with Ken Holden who lived on the same street. Ken pulled out a package of cigarettes and offered him one. John accepted. Five minutes later two second year lads cycled by.

"Naughty! Naughty!" called out one of them, obviously referring to the smoking. John was annoyed.

"Just why is it?" he asked Ken, "that students can't accept a teacher who smokes when most of their fathers have the habit?"

"I don't know," said Ken. "It just seems kinda funny to see a teacher smoking."

"What's funny about it?"

"Oh it's just the idea most teachers have that it's wrong to smoke. You get it in public school, I guess. There's not many teachers smoke, though. And old, I mean *Mr*. Starling, gave Don Lunn five detentions last week—saw him from his car smoking about five feet from the subway corner. Gosh, you'd think smoking was like stealing or something! I guess you're about the only teacher up there that smokes."

"I certainly am not," said John. "Mr. Audubon smokes, Mr. Klein, Mr. Macdonald, Mr. Judd—even Mr. Jarratt takes the odd cigarette."

"No kidding!" said Ken. "Though I knew Mr. Judd did. There's a guy that'd do anything!"

John was itching to hear impressions of his fellow teachers, but resisted the temptation.

In May a staff meeting was held to discuss examinations.

"I wonder how many of you—" and Mr. Bilbeau's little eyes glanced quickly around the table, twinkling with happy reminiscence—"realize that exactly one year ago today you were informed of the sweeping changes to be accomplished in the year that has now passed."

He proceeded. "Progress cannot stand still. There remains much to be done. The present educational structure was closely integrated, and while we have removed new doors, and as it were, forged new paths within, we must replace the old framework with the new."

John found the metaphor confusing, but was filled with pleasurable excitement. Something was coming!

"You are all aware of the somewhat disappointing response on the part of parents and children to our junior industrial course last fall. Registration, frankly, was only half what it should have been. Next year I shall propose the entire elimination of examinations—"

Miss Willis gasped audibly.

J. C. paused inquiringly, smiled sympathetically, and went on: "—the entire elimination of examinations in the junior industrial course only. With regard to this I shall have more to say next September.

"With regard to the more immediate question of promotion in June, I have, with the help of Mr. Starling and Miss Willis, whom I asked to confer with me on the problem, devised a promotion policy which, without in any way lowering examination standards, will encourage our children to remain at school when they might otherwise be too discouraged to continue and attract others who at present find the less academic work of a neighbouring school more attractive. Miss Willis, would you mind reading our summary of the new policy?"

Miss Willis rose, and complied, with dignity.

By this scheme a clear promotion would be earned by those students who passed in every subject. This was to be known as an Honour Promotion. Students with one or two failures and an over-all average of fifty per cent or more were to receive a Pass Promotion. Any students with more than two failures and an over-all average of fifty per cent were to receive a Conditional Promotion. Anyone receiving the latter standing two years in a row would naturally have to repeat his year.

The message was received in silence.

"Could we have that read again?" asked Audubon.

J. C. gave Pikestaff copies of the policy to distribute.

"I propose that we discuss each of these in turn," said J. C. Bilbeau. "Are there any objections to the first type of promotion?"

Angus had objections.

"Mr. Bilbeau, how do you propose to maintain the same high standard, as you put it—"

"Excuse me, Mr. Macdonald," interposed the principal

smoothly, "not as *I* put it, but as Miss Willis, Mr. Starling, and I put it; and I may add the plan has been submitted to, and approved by, the Chairman of the Board."

"The 'you' was plural, Mr. Bilbeau."

"You addressed me personally, I believe." Bilbeau was still smiling, but not easily.

"—as chairman of the meeting," countered Angus quickly, but went on: "How can our high standard of promotion, if we ever had it, be maintained by calling a mere pass an honour promotion, whether the student obtains honours in every subject or in none?"

"I believe," said J. C. with the manner of an elder statesman addressing a novice at a party caucus, "that we were discussing honour promotion, not honour standing." He pronounced the words with careful exactitude.

"I'm afraid the distinction is not clear to me," said Angus.

"Perhaps there are others who feel the same way," said J. C. looking around blandly. "Is there a wish for further discussion?" He went on quickly, but smoothly, "Then I think we may take the first clause as accepted. Mr. Starling, will you read the second clause?"

Angus shrugged his shoulders indifferently, and looked away. The others looked at Mr. Starling.

Mr. Starling read the second clause.

Audubon spoke up. "Does that mean, Mr. Bilbeau, that if a student gets ten per cent in English and five in science but his over-all average is fifty per cent, that we promote him?"

Mr. Bilbeau replied, "We are all agreed, I think, that such a case is most unlikely."

Audubon persisted. "Suppose it did come up?"

"Then of course we should deal with the case on its individual merits. I do not want you to think," he addressed the meeting, "that we are here to impose any rigid system on you. In each doubtful case we shall consider all the factors."

Angus returned to the attack. "Mr. Bilbeau, does not this whole policy boil down to passing every student holus-bolus who has an over-all average of fifty per cent?"

"The hard fact is this," and J. C.'s voice took on a quality of hardness that sent John's pulses racing in the old familiar beat. "If," and he paused ominously, "the school population declines any further it will be necessary to reduce the present staff." The pause that followed these words was even more ominous. Then he went on. "Is there any discussion of the third clause?"

The staff was silent. Angus sat looking stonily out the window. Miss Willis was tapping the table with a pencil. Jarratt leaned forward, biting his underlip more nervously than usual. Audubon's face was eloquent of disapproval. Two or three others were doodling on the paper in front of them. John thought, I ought to say something—but was silent. Judd sat back on his chair, a little smile on the corners of the mouth, his eyes roving from teacher to teacher and seeming to enjoy what they saw.

It was Donald who broke the silence. "Of course," he said, "Mr. Bilbeau's last statement really puts the whole thing in a nutshell very nicely, I think."

No one added a word. Possibly each was asking himself or herself the question: "Would he let *me* go?"

"If there is no further discussion I think we may safely conclude," said J. C., "that the staff accepts this new promotion policy."

Outside Donald was laughing. "As neat a piece of railroad work as I've ever seen," he said.

It was annoying. He already spoke as if the whole affair including the school itself were a huge joke.

"I don't see how you can afford to laugh," said John sulkily. Donald turned towards him smiling, "How much longer do you think you will last?"

"Why?" A coldness seized John's inwards. He attempted to be light about it: "Do you think J. C. has got his eye on me?"

"You mean . . . . ?" Donald laughed. "Lord love a little duck, he certainly has put the fear of God into you. No, I'm not talking about his firing you, I'm referring to your quitting."

"Quitting? A school like this? Are you crazy?"

But Donald only laughed mockingly, leaving in John a vague disquietude.

24

The term was practically over. John came home from presiding at Departmentals feeling depressed. The summer stretched drearily ahead: they had saved enough to see them through without the usual loan from the bank, but the prospect of a year's leave of absence to further his ambitions was infinitely remote. And over all hung the gloom of imminent war. If only they could get away from it all.

Mary met him at the door with that mischievous smile: "I've got . . . ."

"Don't tell me," John interrupted, "you've got another idea. How much will it cost this time?"

"John!" The light went out of her face.

John put his arms around her. Little Charles toddled in and clutched his leg. "I'm sorry. I was feeling sorry for myself and I took it out on you. What's on your mind?"

Mary pushed him away. "You won't like it," she said.

"Ah, come on! Tell me."

"I had a letter from Mom, this morning." She handed it to him.

John read: "How would you and John like to get away for a while this summer? I've been talking it over with Dad and the girls and they're all dying to come up to West Kirby for a visit. We could look after Charles for you and you two could go away by yourselves for a real holiday."

Mary was watching him. "John, you always promised me a canoe trip."

John looked at her, but saw instead a northern lake, the bow of a canoe pointing into the blue distance. He needed the north. "But darling, the money. We weren't going to borrow from the bank this summer!"

"I've got it all figured out," said Mary. "All we need is sixty dollars to cover our return fare to Missanabie. Remember that trip we planned? Look, I found the figures you worked out then—we can do it, John, on next to nothing!"

"What about a canoe?"

"Rent Angus's canoe—freight it up there."

A month later the C.P.R. station, the Hudson's Bay store, the Indian houses of Missanabie were disappearing around the point as John and Mary paddled north through an arm of Dog Lake, under the tracks, and away into the wilderness.

It was a cold grey drizzly day, but they were clothed warmly, had downed a generous breakfast of bacon, eggs, toast and hot coffee, and the swinging rhythm of the paddle sent the blood singing through their bodies. Mary took to the paddle as if she had used one all her life.

They stopped at noon to lunch on canned sausage, bread, jam, and tea. The rain began to get wet.

"Not much of a spot to camp," remarked John, looking around. "But there's no use going on."

They pitched the tent on the only level spot in the vicinity, near a little clump of jack pine, using rocks to anchor the guy ropes where the soil was too shallow for pegs. By the time the tent was ready and the canoe turned over on the rock, big rain drops were hissing in the fire. John rigged up a cook-fly with the tarpaulin while Mary took the tea pail and tin mugs into the tent and made a luxurious divan with the bed roll. They lay on one elbow under the little roof watching it brighten as the rain drops soaked into the canvas.

The hot tea was good, made doubly so by the chill in the air outside.

Mary sighed contentedly: "It's so far away here—from everything."

John felt the years roll away. Somewhere inside of him a knot began to loosen, the very fibres of it dissolving. Somewhere, far away, was a school with a principal called J. C. Bilbeau. Once, long ago, he had taught there. But this, the smell of pine needles and wood smoke, the clean northern air, the solid ground beneath, the wet canvas overhead, and the woman beside him: these were real.

They paddled from dawn till dusk down the long stretches of Lake Missinaibi, lingering a day here and a day there; down the Missinaibi River with its thousands of boulders, its rocks and portages and falls, widening, narrowing, winding, pouring downward, north towards Hudson Bay. They stripped to the waist whenever the sun shone; burned, peeled, browned. They swam naked in the river and lay so on the rocks, soaking in the glare of the northern sun. They caught pickerel and bass, gutted, filleted and fried them. They made bannock over the fire, ate it hot with gobs of canned butter. They portaged over rocks, and deadfall, and fire slash, till the sweat ran from every pore and blinded the eyes, till they were so weary they would fall into bed at night dead tired. They slept under the stars one night, watching the meteorites flash momentarily as the great dome of the celestial sphere slowly circled round. They surprised deer on the portage and moose in the swamp, porcupine, beaver, and the nervous chipmunk. They sat by their fire at night, listening to the wild sad laughter of the loon, the barking of owls, the thrum of the night hawk's diving wings. They slapped at mosquitoes, and deerflies, and dogflies; hunted over their skin for the savage 'no-see-um', heard the roar of frustration outside the mosquito bar at night. And there was the wind: whipping into their faces, holding their canoe back with invisible hands, or filling their sail while they fled silently before it, moaning through the spruce by night, tossing the fantastic emerald pine branches by day.

They had been gone ten days and were camped at Glassy Falls, an easy day's paddle to Mattice and the C.N.R. line. In three days they would be on the train.

John looked up from the rope he had been splicing, at

Mary, peeling potatoes. The tears were dropping on the potatoes; there were dirty smudges under her eyes where she had been brushing them away.

"Mary!" he was beside her in a minute.

"I—I want my baby!" wailed Mary, and laughed tearfully at her own voice.

"We'll leave tomorrow," said John.

At Mattice there was a telegram that set their worries at rest—a night letter from Mom Miller.

KNEW YOU WOULD COME OUT EARLY STOP CHARLES WELL AS CAN BE STOP WE ARE HAVING A LOVELY HOLIDAY DAD IS COMING UP TONIGHT STOP LOTS OF LOVE

MOTHER

There was also a newspaper. They read the news with sinking hearts.

"They can't hold it back any longer," said John, his face set.

"John—all those children in Europe—it's horrible!"

"Well, there's nothing we can do. Maybe there'll be a miracle."

They got into West Kirby on a Sunday. Dad Miller, Sylvia, and Donna were there at the station with Charles. Charles, aged two and a half years now, saw them and shrieked "Da's Mummy!"

Mary rushed to her baby, hugging him tight, tears in her eyes.

John took Charles's chubby little hand and walked him over to the car. Charles inquired whether his parents had brought back any little bears and was plainly disappointed.

At the house Mom Miller had a big dinner ready to put on the table. Clara had gone back to Toronto the previous weekend; but for that, the reunion would have been complete.

"Sure there's going to be war," said Dad Miller to John's question, "but it won't last long. France has the Maginot Line and the best army in Europe. Germany hasn't got the money to finance a long war. And if *we* go in, she hasn't got a chance."

As John watched the work-calloused, knobby fore-finger tamp tobacco into the pipe-bowl, he noticed for the first time that the film of age was beginning to blur Dad Miller's honest blue eyes.

25

WAR! John awoke on the morning of September 1st and rushed to the radio.

Germany had invaded Poland.

Two days later the United Kingdom declared war on Germany.

At school that week there was surprisingly little difference. Nita Collier was worried about her brother doing medical research at Heidelberg, but she was the only one immediately affected. No one on the staff had enlisted. Pikestaff was incredulous when John told him Canada was not at war. "Of course we are," he said. "Britain has declared war on Germany and we are in the British Empire." Miss Willis thought it criminal Canada was not in it. There was talk of the U.S.A. coming in; slurs cast on Lindbergh and isolationism. The general sentiment was British to the core.

The *Twin City News* published an editorial: "Canada's Shame", apologizing to the world for Canada's tardiness.

On the tenth came Canada's declaration.

In a month Poland was conquered and smoking; Warsaw lay in ruins. On the Western Front little happened except the sending out of patrols. Thank God, the Maginot Line would hold the Germans back till Britain was ready.

J. C., following his own advice at the first staff meeting, remained calm in the midst of all this strife; even the war could not shake him from his indefatigable crusade for progressive education. To tell the truth, the war had a stimulating rather than depressing effect on the twin cities. And the war had done what all the concentrated publicity of the previous autumn had failed to do; it flooded the Junior Industrial course with applicants for registration. Of course, it might have been the new promotion policy. It might even have been the newspaper announcement that there would be no formal examinations in the practical course.

J. C. proceeded according to plan.

His first year had been concentrated on internal organization. The school magazine, dramatics, assembly hall exercises, school parties, noon-hour activities, hall supervision, now each had their committees functioning smoothly. The second year had seen the inauguration of the new course; that was now on its feet.

But "practical progress involves the problem of personnel," Bilbeau informed his staff, and to this he now gave his full attention. Happy relationships between parents and teachers, and between teachers and students was necessary to the perfection of the plan.

One obstacle remained in Mr. Bilbeau's way. He was a busy man. Reports of committees on this and that took up too much of his time. He had already delegated responsibility for attendance and discipline to Mr. Starling. At the first staff meeting in the fall he announced that Mr. Macdonald had consented to correlate all extracurricular activities.

John took this as proof that he bore no ill will to Angus, and said as much to the latter.

Angus smiled grimly. "Much more of Mr. Bilbeau's goodwill and I'll have to find some way of eliminating sleep from my programme. As it is I'll have to forget my geology in between holidays."

"If it's too much, why don't you tell J. C.?"

"I suppose it's pride," confessed Angus, "and the way it's put up to me. It's the childish idea of showing my friend Bilbeau I can take everything he loads me up with, and come back for more."

"But Angus, I don't think he's trying to load you up. He told me that you were a first-class executive; and he had to have some help, he's so busy. Just yesterday afternoon, for instance, he didn't get to school till nearly four."

Angus looked at John with a curiously tense expression but said nothing.

At the end of September Bilbeau inaugurated a Parents' Night for the Lower School. Each Lower School pupil was to bring one or both of his parents to a special banquet, and the school incidentally would be open for inspection, with the teachers stationed in their rooms to meet and discuss mutual problems with parents. The project was carefully explained to a staff meeting by J. C. as calculated to make the teachers' work easier by establishing a personal contact between teacher and parent, and received due publicity in the *Twin City News*.

The banquet was held in the gymnasium. Over four hundred children and parents sat down to consume a three-course dinner, served by senior girls and the entire female staff under the indefatigable Miss Willis as chief of operations. After the ice-cream, and tea or coffee, Mr. Starling welcomed the parents, pointing out the desirability of a closer acquaintanceship with the teachers, and invited the parents to inspect the school, meet the staff, and assemble in the auditorium for a brief programme.

The teachers, not having been invited to eat with the parents, ate early at home, or brought their own supper and stayed through from four o'clock.

John went in to help Angus decorate the physics lab with suitably impressive symbols of the sciences. Four Upper School students were nonchalantly setting up experiments to illustrate Archimedes' Principle, osmosis, the laws of transverse vibrations, and Charles's Law. Angus dusted off his pet planetarium and adjusted it for the current month; John began covering the blackboard with brief outlines of the courses of study, and answers to the question, "What is Science?" copied from Angus's neatly typewritten notes.

Before they had finished, a lad came in.

"They're coming!" he said breathlessly.

John hastily shoved the notebook and chalk into Angus's hands and departed. Too late! A mass of parents and chil-

314

dren was moving up the south corridor close on the heels of Mr. Starling. He couldn't face that crowd! He went out the front entrance of the new school, dashed across the frosty ground into the old school and up to his room Donald was attaching a big sign, 'ART ROOM', to his door.

"The thundering herd is on its way!" warned John.

"I can hear them," said Donald, flashing his smile.

John went into his room, glanced around to see if his wall displays of notebook exercises were intact, rushed to his desk which was littered with a week's accumulation of papers, opened the big bottom drawer and shoved every thing into it.

He walked around for a minute, felt awkward, went to his desk and got out his register, pretended to work on it.

A short stout woman stopped inquiringly in the door-way, there were more people behind her. John stood up and smiled his welcome. She came in uncertainly, followed by an even shorter but quite slight man, and a first year student whose name he couldn't remember.

They apparently expected him to speak first.

He turned to the boy and tried the light touch. ·

"So you brought your dad and mother along to find out what a loafer you are?" The lad simpered silently.

"You're Mr. Westley?" asked the man. "I'm Bill's father, and this is his mother." They shook hands.

"Do you know," said John, "I have a wretched memory, I don't remember Bill's surname." Inwardly he was grateful for having learned his first name.

"Andover," said Mr. Andover. "How is my boy getting along? Did you say he was a loafer?"

"Just joking," explained John, wishing he could remember what kind of a student Bill was. "Bill's coming along pretty well, considering. He *could* work harder of course, but he's not bad, not bad."

Mrs. Andover spoke up. My God, thought John, Bill will look exactly like her twenty years from now!

"I want to know why Bill didn't get no marks last week," she said aggressively.

That was a bad guess, thought John. Aloud he said, "Oh, you mean the maths test." Obviously it had been because he didn't know anything, but John didn't want a scene. "Yes, he did slip up there."

"If there's any nonsense," said Mr. Andover, "just let me know and I'll give him a good hiding."

"Oh, Bill's all right," said John, relieved that Bill, and not he, was getting the blame. "You keep him at his homework pretty well, I suppose."

"He don't have none to do, hardly," said Mrs. Andover looking sternly at her son.

"Well," soothed John, "some of the students are smart enough to get their homework done in school, you know." Several parents were lingering in the background. Bill had backed up to a safe distance. "I'll keep my eye on him for you," he said shaking hands again. "It's nice to have met you."

He was on safer ground with the mother that followed, and another couple. He knew their daughters, both of whom were bright pupils. But the next pair made him wince —Fred Peately and his mother. Fred was tall for his age, sulky and restless, obviously a misfit. His mother made excuses for him. "Freddie's health isn't so good," she explained in Freddie's hearing. "Freddie's outgrown himself, and we have to be careful with him. You see when he was three years old he was in the hospital with pneumonia and he's been delicate ever since." Freddie, with his eyes on the ground, didn't look too delicate; John couldn't remember ever marking him absent. He was sympathetic. "Well, Mrs. Peately, we try not to work our students too hard, but you know Fred's marks aren't quite what they should be."

"He gets so much homework, too," said Mrs. Peately, missing the irony.

A little first year girl—she couldn't have been much over four feet tall—came up with an adult version of herself.

"This is my Westley, Mr. Mother!" she introduced them nervously.

The parents were more motley than their children. John was amazed at the variety of them. There were young mothers and old mothers; fathers who were labourers and fathers from the professsions. They were tall and short and medium, dark and grey and blond, some with glasses, some without, some painfully self-conscious, others at their ease, some speaking in monosyllables, some garrulous. Looking at parent and child John again and again had the weird feeling that he was seeing a biography in brief: the same person at fourteen and forty seen simultaneously. And it was depressing.

After it was over John kept thinking, it's horrible: this is what my classes will be like in twenty or thirty years. These young fresh complexions, eager eyes, slim figures, strident voices; all greyed, dulled, pinched or bloated, their voices flat, monotonous, thin or harsh. It was such obvious, dismaying, decadence. Why had it happened? Where had all the life and laughter gone? These were people in the prime of life. Surely life should be richer, fuller, for them! But so many of them had been disappointed—long ago in themselves and now again in their children.

317

And what did most of them want their children to be? University graduates!

Was that all children meant to parents—their second chance? Was that why, when every indication pointed to another future, they insisted on their children taking the paths that they, the parents, now thought they would have chosen for themselves?

He sat down in his chair and scraped with his thumb nail on a hair imprisoned in the varnish. When he finally dug it out the impression left behind marred the varnish even more. He wet his finger, rubbed some dirt into it— as he had fifteen years earlier in the fresh carving of his initials on his high school desk—to make it look old, inconspicuous.

From the assembly hall, far away, came the strains of *"There'll Always be an England."*

Twenty years!

He remembered going home at the end of his last high school term, wishing with all his heart that he could skip the intervening years between youth and manhood, be on his own, be a man.

And now? Was he becoming another disappointed adult? Was he replacing his personal ambitions with hopes for little Charles?

He rose slowly, an old man, weary, crippled like his father with arthritis, and walked stiffly to the door.

Oh, cut the histrionics, he told himself impatiently, striding out across the hall, and down the stairs three at a time.

As a kind of complement to Parents' Night Mr. Bilbeau introduced weekly conferences between members of the staff and any students who felt the urge to carry their troubles to them; to be known as "Problem Clinics". Every Monday at four each teacher would be in his room for fifteen minutes to advise any student in the group assigned to him.

In the first three weeks John had only one patient in his clinic.

As he sat at his desk monotonously filling blank spaces in his register with check marks a young lad came in, with a self-conscious smirk on his face. It was Arthur Selby. John had taught his two elder brothers, both wily lads who got by with a minimum of work and a maximum of personality.

"What's your trouble, Art?"

"Well, it's like this, Mr. Westley. I've got a paper rout"—John suppressed the desire to correct his English —"and I missed two weeks because my kid brother talked me into letting him do it on account of he needed some money to buy a model plane outfit, and some of us boys are organizing a Bantam Hockey League—"

"Isn't it pretty early for hockey?" interrupted John.

"Well, see, we gotta organize and find out if we can raise the dough—I mean money—to finance the uniforms and pads and all that stuff."

"I see." But he didn't. "You want me to help you to figure out a way of raising some money for the league, is that the problem?"

"Well no, not exactly. You see it's like this. If a kid wants to be on a team he has to buy his own outfit, see? And we gotta order the uniforms early."

"Oh," said John.

"Well it's like I said, my brother he took my paper rout. I've got everything saved up except four dollars and I

319

gotta have that by Thursday, and I don't know what I'm going to do."

"Why don't you ask your Dad?"

"Well Dad has missed some work, and I don't like to, see, I'd pay it back—I've got a good paper rout. I could pay it back in two weeks. Maybe I could ask Mom for it, but she's worried on account of Dad and everything."

John looked at him steadily. He was in deadly earnest and returned the look with pleading eyes that held a suggestion of moisture.

My God, I don't want the kid crying on my shoulder, he thought. He stood up, reached into his pocket, pulled out a small roll and counted out four dollar bills.

"I don't know whether I'm doing a wise thing," said John, "but I'll take your word and I'll trust you."

"Gee, thanks a lot, Mr. Westley! You sure got rid of my trouble. I'll pay you back a week from next Monday." Young Art was grinning all over. "It sure is swell of yuh, Mr. Westley," and he was gone in a flash.

The clinic will now close, said John to himself, thoughtfully.

John made no mention of his financial venture to anyone.

Down in the boiler room with Judd, John asked: "How are you getting along with your problem clinics, Donald?"

"Problem clinics!" Donald snorted delicately. "More publicity, more bunk."

"But don't you think it's a good idea?"

"Sure, it's a good idea. J. C. is as full of good ideas as a balloon is full of gas. But what good is an idea if it ignores the facts? Look at you and me, overworked as it is. How many nights do we get home before six o'clock? And these kids: do you think for a minute they are going to tell us what is really on their minds? They may tell you and me a little—we're half human; but look at Jessie Willis, why one look at her face is enough to shut up any kid tight as a clam. Or a poor fish like Pikestaff. And imagine anyone opening up to Starling!" He snorted his disgust.

26

John's soul that winter was torn between a hundred conflicting impulses, doubts, and fears. There was the war and over-hanging threat of conscription. There was the feeling that he and Mary were not as close as they had been. The summer north had restored the old comradeship, but as soon as they came home Charles had come between. Mary had returned late one night in November from her discussion club to find Charles with a croupy cough, snow blowing in the open nursery window, and John sleeping soundly on the chesterfield. She had made cutting remarks about his inadequacy as a father. Later she had repented, but John's sense of inadequacy remained. And Angus no longer dropped in on Sunday nights—school work tied him up now, he told them; though John had felt, ever since their difference over the science course, that Angus was disappointed in him.

John yearned for the simple human relationships of childhood. Angus was too complex a character; John's relationship with Mary too confused by Charles's presence in the home. His mind, awakened to think a little for itself by those walks and talks with Angus, by Mary's humour. and through their social contacts, was bewildered by the war and the conflicting issues at stake; further confused by the uncertainty as to how it would affect him.

In his heart he knew that Angus and Mary and Dot—even Donald Judd—were right about J. C. At least they were partly right. There was a kind of hollowness to Bilbeau, though John told himself his motives were sound. Even if one looked at him in the worst possible light who could say that Bilbeau was wrong? He wanted to get ahead —granted. But who didn't?—except impractical idealists like Angus.

In the classroom John found himself more and more following the Bilbeau pattern. He had tried to make the pupils think for themselves and found when he did that they would rather memorize facts, or just sit and vegetate. In English he began to skimp on the grammar, skim over the serious literature, and linger over what was entertaining. In his public speaking classes he emphasized poise and personality to the neglect of clear thinking and logical presentation. And whenever interest began to lag he stimulated it by rehearsing funny little skits, or employment interviews, or dramatized sales talks.

The university preparation classes gave him little scope for innovations. But Bilbeau's system of mimeographed assignments, which he had explained to John in his first year, was a godsend. All he had to do was distribute the sheets at the beginning of the class, teach for five minutes, and the rest of the period was a cinch. They could even mark their own exercises. In mathematics John had duplicate sheets with solutions. The students exchanged exercises, he distributed the solutions; it was all so simple.

If students had difficulties John would merely refer them to sheet number so and so; and go on marking his register, tidy his desk (he had lately developed a mania for neatness), or work out more assignment sheets for future use.

In practical science John had long since abandoned his impossible ideals. He had worked out a complete set of notes for the year, dictated them, or written them on the blackboard for the students to copy.

But occasionally his interest in science and the urge to exercise his own mind still got the better of him, and occasionally he would go off the deep end with the class into a free-for-all discussion.

In the place of examinations John, like most of the staff, defeated Bilbeau's professed object of relieving the nervous strain on students by instituting bi-weekly tests; although he simply called them "reviews" and sometimes made them oral instead of written. It was a temptation to "cook up" marks where no rigid system of marking was in force, but when John found himself favouring certain students in spite of his sense of fairness, he told himself that after all, a student *should* get credit for personality and willingness to co-operate.

At the end of November the classes that had no exams to write were becoming restless, particularly in science. John thought, what's the use? and threw the discussion wide-open one day.

"What would you like to talk about?"

As usual they wanted to talk about anything rather than science. John would not allow that.

One student put up his hand. "How far are the stars?"

John had already covered the matter and referred the class to their notes on the subject.

One boy, who was a bit of a smart-aleck, raised a hand. "Sir, where is heaven?"

John gravely assured him that heaven came under the heading of religion, not science.

"Isn't it up?" asked one of the girls.

John drew out of them what they *knew* from observation and reading about the areas surrounding the earth.

"It says in the Bible that Jesus ascended into heaven!" a thin girl with black eyes asserted indignantly.

John explained that most people believed heaven was a state and not a place, and managed to steer the discussion into less dangerous channels.

The next day he was called down to the office. Mr. Bilbeau received him gravely, closed the door behind him. John's heart sank. There was something ominous about it all.

"You have been charged," said Bilbeau, his face coldly impersonal, his eyes focussed sharply on John's face, "with asserting in a science class that there is no such place as heaven. I should like a statement in writing from you of exactly what you said and when you said it."

He rose and opened the door. "We shall discuss the matter further when I have read your statement. Please make it out immediately. That is all."

John left the office speechless with resentment. Bilbeau hadn't even let him open his mouth. He had just taken it for granted that John was guilty. So he wanted a statement. Well, he'd get one: a good hot one! What kind of friend was Bilbeau anyway?

The noon bell rang: students streamed out of the classrooms.

Impulsively John headed for the physics laboratory.

A student was arguing with Angus. "Mr. Macdonald, I can't see why it wouldn't be the same in the digestive system of the fish."

Angus was smiling with that warm twinkle in his eye. John felt a sudden nostalgia for the old days. "My boy," he said, "it warms the cockles of my heart to hear you say that. If you can keep that attitude through medical school you'll never make a family physician, but you'll be a good doctor. Now run along and think it out for yourself."

The boy grinned happily, picked up his books and departed.

The friends looked at each other.

John noticed that Angus looked tired, older. Angus saw the trouble in John's face.

"I'm really in a jam," said John, and told him what had happened.

Angus looked worried. "That's one thing you have to be pretty careful about," he said. "The first year I taught here a parent complained that I taught evolution—I was innocent enough to believe everyone took it for granted. Nyes sent the parent scurrying home with a few warm words of advice, and then hauled *me* over the coals. Since then I've been careful to say that evolution is only a theory. But that doesn't solve your problem." He paused thoughtfully, looking at John. "Would you like me to talk to him?" he asked.

John's eyes shone with relief. "I'd be grateful as hell if you would."

"I'll see him right now," said Angus. He put a note-book away in a drawer, got up, and went to the door. His hand on the door-knob, he paused, looking back at John. Even John could see the struggle going on in his mind.

He came slowly back. There was pain in his eyes.

"John," he said, "I don't know how you'll interpret this, but I've changed my mind. This is something you've got to handle yourself."

John's heart sank in dismay. "Why—sure, I guess you're right." He thought, Angus is afraid to face Bilbeau. He can't even face me now, he decided, seeing Angus's averted eyes. Anger and frustration choked him. "That's all right," he said stiffly. "I guess I can handle it myself, anyway," and walked out.

John went slowly home. Going up the front walk he noticed that it was slushy and should have been shovelled. The weather had been mild. Luckily he was wearing rubbers.

Mary was flustered. "Dinner isn't ready," she said, "Charles got in my hair this morning. John, this house is getting so small."

John tried to fight back the words, but they came.

"How would you like to move?" He tried but failed to make it casual, and no smile came.

"John, what's wrong?" there was alarm in her voice as she looked over from the stove.

"Oh, just a bit of a headache," he lied, and sat down at the table. Mary finished getting the meal. "I think I'll shave . . . . I didn't have time this morning."

In the bathroom he looked at his face as he lathered it. His colour was bad.

"What *is* the matter?" asked Mary as they ate.

John finished what was before him. "Flu coming on, I suppose."

"Well you'd better hold off till after the concert. Why don't you take an aspirin?"

When they had finished eating he told her about the interview, but said nothing of Angus. She listened intently, searching his face for the deeper answer.

"After all, you only told the truth," said Mary. "They can't fire you for that."

John pushed back his chair heavily and got up. "Mary, I've got to write out that statement."

John began his statement by outlining the facts as he remembered them and ended it with a final sentence.

I should like to add most emphatically that I never have discussed before, and never intend to discuss again, any religious topic in the classroom.

JOHN WESTLEY

Mary got out the old typewriter—it had belonged to John's father—and made a respectable copy, put it in an envelope, and gave it to John.

Even in this crisis John couldn't help his inevitable reaction to Mary at the typewriter: picturing himself the important executive, dictating.

"Do you know, John," she startled him by saying, as she looked at him anxiously, the gentle arches of her brows straining upward towards two little vertical creases in her forehead, "if it weren't for little Charles I'd say let's get out of this teaching business!"

"Don't worry, darling, I'll be all right," he told her, and kissed her almost with condescension, while the pit of his stomach ached with suspense.

Going back, the statement tucked in his pocket, John found that his resentment of Bilbeau's action had cooled. After all, what had he done that was so unreasonable—merely asked him for a statement. But Angus, who was his friend, had offered to fix the whole thing up, and then changed his mind. It wasn't as if it had nothing to do with Angus either—he was head of the science department, and he had said himself that these things cropped up all the time; there should be a policy worked out.

And it was Angus's idea too, all this free discussion; stimulating the students to think for themselves. Well, if this was the sort of thing that happened, he didn't think much of the idea. If he weathered this crisis from now on he was going to forget about their thinking and stick to accepted facts.

Bilbeau's door was open, but the office was empty. As he stood there indecisively a voice behind made him start. It was J. C.

"Go right in." He preceded J. C. into the office, pulling out the statement as he went.

At his desk J. C. read it impassively; then looked up at John and smiled: a heart-warming smile, a smile of confidence in John that sent his spirits soaring.

"Yes, I think that will do very nicely," he said.

John relaxed.

"You know, John," J. C. was grave again, "it is most unwise to allow any kind of free discussion in the classroom. No matter how innocent the topic may appear to be this sort thing can happen at a moment's notice. That is why," he explained, "in my teaching days, I liked to have everything down in black and white: every assignment, every question, every answer. It's the only way to protect yourself." He leaned forward confidentially. "Even my speeches, every word I say in public, are carefully planned and rehearsed beforehand. A man who wants to get ahead cannot afford to take risks."

"As a matter of fact," John told him, "I'm using your assignment system in several classes now."

Bilbeau beamed. "I am gratified to hear it. One word more about this complaint before you go. I shall give a copy of your statement to the parent who complained and I think we shall hear no more of the matter. I have already made him see the error of his ways and promised him the statement. But, you can see how serious a thing like this might be. I protect my teachers, as long as they co-operate with me. Your record has been a splendid one. For a young teacher you have made a magnificent beginning, and have a promising career in front of you. Do not," he paused solemnly for emphasis, "jeopardize that career by absorbing ideas, let alone expressing them, which are not in accord with those accepted by society."

A guilty fear crept up within John, as he thought of his and Mary's friends.

"Thanks, Mr. Bilbeau," he said gratefully, and left the office.

He went over to the secretary's office and phoned Mary. "Just thought I'd let you know everything is under control," he told her.

At home that evening he gave her the details.

"It certainly looks as if J. C. saved our necks this time," said John.

Mary regarded him steadily for a minute. "John, what would we have done if you had lost your job?"

"Well, if it came to the worst I could always enlist."

"John don't joke about it. It's not funny."

"Well, I didn't lose the job."

"Yes, but you mightn't be so lucky next time."

"Listen, Mary, get this into your thick sweet little head.

329

From now on I'm not expressing *any* opinions in class—I'm just going to be another teacher."

As he led his class in the Lord's Prayer the next morning Bilbeau's words echoed in his ears: "Splendid record . . . . magnificent beginning . . . . promising career." And again came the warning: "Do not jeopardize that career."

That night he dreamed.

In the distance peculiar storm clouds began to gather, there was a weird whistling sound that grew in volume until the whole earth was roaring. He suddenly realized that the black clouds were bearing down on him. A voice said: "This is the dust of dissolution!" My God, my God, thought John, terror pinching his heart between ice-cold strands of thick steel wire, it's the *end of the world!* And woke up.

John tried to sleep again but was filled with disquiet. Why on earth should he have a dream like that? he asked himself. He thought of the hot muffins Mary had made—his mother had always told him that eating food like that at bedtime would give him bad dreams. He tried to remember his mother, but there was only a vague shadow where she should have been. He suddenly remembered the day when his father came into his room where he had been doing homework, trembling with rage and shoving the Winchester .22 repeater into his hand and shouting "Look down that barrel!" He had used it the week before and forgotten to clean it: the barrel was filthy. "I let you use my gun and this is how you treat it! You're not fit to have a gun—you can forget about one of your own for Christmas!" and he had stalked out of the room in heavy silence.

He remembered his mother now, a pale tired face that

seldom smiled. There was another woman he remembered, laughing, gay—she used to tickle him, till he wept with laughter and his sides were sore. With a shock he realized that was his mother too . . . . long before.

But his father would sometimes be very friendly: come up to him, throw a friendly arm around his waist, and say something silly, like: "How's my twelve-year old baby to-day?" As he thought of his father he began to weep, with an ache in his heart for what he might have been and never was. "Dad, dad—what's happened? Why don't you let me love you? Why are you so far away?" The tears trickled down his cheek to the pillow. He wiped them off, turned on his side and tried to go to sleep.

J. C. Bilbeau, M.A. What was he really like? Dot and Angus—Mary—why were they so hostile? He remembered Dot's portrait with a shudder and stirred uneasily. There was nothing sinister about Bilbeau, he tried to tell himself. It had given him a queer feeling, seeing that portrait without eyes. It was as though Bilbeau were nothing but a hollow shell, and yet at the same time it gave you the feeling there was something sinister inside the shell. There were different layers to a person, the one you saw, the one underneath that you sensed, another under that, and under that. It was like the stars and those dark nebulae Angus talked about, one blotting out the other, the other shining through, and space behind . . . . deep space where unseen worlds lay waiting for their turn . . . . coming out into the light—spinning on their planes, their spinning orbits, their orbittings, their planing spins, their great shining axis, getting smaller and smaller in space—or larger—free axe handles, glooming in the night—

John slept again at last.

27

In spite of Judd's popularity there had been a considerable falling off in enthusiasm for assembly chorals that autumn. First year classes always gave a fresh stimulation, but there had been an unusual number of visitors which meant going over the old repertoire with boring frequency for their benefit. J. C. took stock of the situation with Donald and announced a solution.

Early in October it was proclaimed that hereafter the whole assembly would sit by voices for assembly chorals. During the next week Judd and Miles classified every voice in the school as soprano, alto, tenor, or bass. Besides this a special group of forty voices which Donald had trained for the Christmas concert was placed strategically to lead the others and provide special effects.

The first attempt was disappointing. But at the next assembly the results were impressive, even to the students themselves, who weren't in the best position to get the total effect.

As usual they warmed up with two or three old numbers in unison. Then a new poem was flashed on the screen: *Cargoes*, by Masefield. Donald hastened over pronunciations, and read it over once, giving a clue to accent and tempo.

The whole school read it in unison with him, capturing the mood from his face and gestures.

Then they began.

The first verse, *"Quinquireme of Nineveh . . . ."* read by warm alto voices.

The second, *"Stately Spanish galleon . . . ."* by the smooth and mellow basses.

The third, *"Dirty British coaster . . . ."* came in, sharp and harsh, from tenors and sopranos.

"Staccato! Staccato!" marked Donald, interrupting with one of his rare displays of heat.

"DIR-ty Brit-ish COAST-er with a SALT-CAKED SMOKE-STACK! Make it *dirty*, let's *taste* the salt, and *see* the smoke. Now again."

They went through it again, this time gripped by the power of the poetry, Donald's leadership, and the disciplined might of their own voices.

A third time over, with special sound effects from the chorus. A storm of hand-clapping broke out when the last silence died away. J. C. stood for a whole minute before his still figure calmed them.

Walking home with one of the boys that noon John asked him how he liked the new arrangement by voices.

"Not bad!" he said. "Maybe it would pep up our cheering some to do that by voices."

Shortly after the big play of the previous year John and Mary had been sitting over their coffee after supper.

"John," said Mary, "why that introspective look?"

John flushed a little and said, "Oh nothing," then thought better of it. "Do you know what, Mary?"

"What, John?"

"Next year I'm going to put on *Romeo and Juliet* and to hell with the public." He talked quickly to hide the blush that was creeping over his face again. "I've got a marvellous Juliet—she's got *everything*: looks, personality, intelligence—except for her voice, but I can manage

333

that. She tried out last fall for the Christmas play and I'd have used her if I could have found her a good part."

"You mean that Hantz girl?"

"No!" John's voice was full of scorn. "She's not good looking. She can act, but she's got legs like a horse. It's Iris Clark. Don't you remember? I pointed her out to you at the first year party."

"You mean the little dark girl in the red dress?"

"No, she's blonde, platinum blonde, with darkish eyes —I think—and slim!"

"What was she wearing?"

"How should I know what she was wearing? I don't see how you could have missed her."

"Well, John, I can't keep track of all your school amours."

"Oh, don't be silly," he said sulkily. "Anyway, she'd make a marvellous Juliet!"

The more John thought of *Romeo and Juliet* the better he liked the idea. It would need to be streamlined of course and most of the descriptive passages cut; but after all Shakespeare would have done the same with modern stage facilities and audience. And Iris would be a knockout as Juliet. With her he could take the West Kirby public and make them love Shakespeare—well, Iris, anyway. He had played Tybalt in university and remembered the play vividly. The Juliet in that performance had exquisite diction but she couldn't touch Iris for looks.

He found himself out in the hall corridor more frequently, watching the students go by. Unfortunately he didn't teach the fair Iris, but Miss Willis did, every third period. John was supposed to supervise the stairs anyway, so he would stand leaning over the railing that overlooked the stair well watching for that unmistakably blonde head, the flawless poise of the shoulders, as she ascended beneath him, turned at the landing and came up past. He could imagine her dressed in white silk, her blue-grey eyes flashing in the spotlight, her tender mouth shaping the words: *"O Romeo, Romeo! wherefore art thou Romeo?"*

Occasionally he would catch her eyes and a quick little blush would deepen the roses high on her cheeks, and her lips would curve with a subtle sweetness. He knew he was being silly, but he loved it.

The problem of a Romeo began to haunt him; where could he get a Romeo for such a Juliet? He indulged in childish little day dreams of his Romeo being ill at the last moment and of himself stepping in to fill the lover's role. He had never played a male lead—always character parts —and like every character actor dreamed of being the flame around which the female moth would flutter. Or was that the reason? No, he admitted to himself, it's just that she's such a sweet beautiful little kid that I'm half in love with her. And that's ridiculous, he told himself, for a man nearly old enough to be her father.

It might have been his tender relapse into adolescence that led John to begin separating the two chief scenes of his activities, school and home. It was a way of justifying his romantic attachment to the lovely Iris. He could be mentally unfaithful to Mary so much more easily if he could persuade himself that these were two separate worlds.

Or it might have been the war.

At home the radio and newspaper were open doors through which the world's events poured in a restless stream, doors through which one could see lightning against the black clouds and grew vaguely conscious of dark movements of peoples over the horizon. The doors only opened at specific intervals, the stream could be cut off and the mess it made within mopped up: but always there was that pressure on the doors, that could only be relieved by turning the radio dial or opening the newspaper.

Home was a lonely little haven on the great dark ball of the earth, where windows and doors blew unexpectedly open.

But school was a tight little world of its own, it was life in the bright warm interior of a sphere, doors and windows curtained from the cold darkness without by algebra and English literature, and the big dance, or the big game or the big play. Six hundred youngsters with little eye for the great world outside played at living within its walls, creating the illusion for themselves and most of their teachers that this was life itself.

And yet, John protested to himself, this *was* life. Whatever happened outside these walls was only an extension, an elaboration of what was going on within. Here, as there, were the same hopes and fears, clarity and confusion, the same bodies and brains, the same quick or sluggish blood, the same laughter and fears.

All through the fall term John had been looking for a Romeo, and found him at last. Like Elsie Braund, he came from the country, having gone to a continuation school as far as it would take him. He had made the football team with ease and by the middle of the fall term was acknowledged the outstanding athlete of the school. John had noticed him frequently in the corridors and developed a hunch about his dramatic ability. Late in November he appeared in the corridors hobbling about on crutches. John learned he had wrenched his ankle seriously in a rugby game. He invited the lad to come in for a talk after four.

Ronald Smith was hardly the slim youth tradition assigned to the role of Romeo. But there was a certain boldness to his features and bearing; and the usual adolescent awkwardness was missing.

"Have you ever thought of dramatics, just to pass the time?" asked John casually.

"I don't have any trouble passing time," said Ronald. "In fact it's always passing me."

"Well," said John, "every now and then I get a hunch. And I have a strong hunch that you would be good on the stage."

"I was in a church play, once," said Ron, "and I liked it all right."

"Did you ever think of joining the Dramatic Club?"

"No, not particularly. So far it's been all I could do to handle athletics and keep up my school work. But the doctor says I'll have to go easy on this ankle for the rest of the year."

"That's what I gambled on," confessed John. "It must seem a pretty callous way to regard your ankle, but as soon as I saw you hobbling around I decided to play my hunch."

"What's the proposition?" Ron searched his face for the answer.

"The proposition is pretty stiff. Shakespeare!"

"I like Shakespeare!"

"Do you?" John's heart leaped. "Then listen. We've been putting on cheap plays for years—you know, the kind of thing the church clubs put on to make some money, slapstick stuff where the butler trips over the broomstick. Well, I'm sick of it. It's high time we put on something solid."

"So you picked on Shakespeare?"

"That's right. I've discovered a perfect Juliet, and I'm looking for Romeo."

"Me? Romeo?" Ron laughed.

"Listen, I want a Charles Laughton, not a Ronald Colman."

"Well what makes you think I'm Charles Laughton?"

"Just a hunch." John could see that he was making progress. "I tell you what. Right after Christmas I'm trying out Juliet. Will you come in and read Romeo's lines—just read them, no acting?"

"Well . . . ." said Ron hesitantly. Then he grinned, "Say, who *is* Juliet?"

"Iris Clark—in third year. Know her?"

"No," doubtfully. It was obvious he didn't.

John described her briefly.

Ron's frown of concentration vanished into a beatific smile. "Oh is *that* her name," and John knew he had won.

The next day he saw Iris again in the hall. She was taller this year; a little slimmer in the waist. Her complexion was rich and flawless as ever, her silky white hair cut in the current page-boy fashion with a smoothness that was virginal rather than cultivated. But what heightened her charm and set John's pulses racing was the unconscious air of shy expectancy, something quite apart from her reaction to the interview, a sort of innocent looking-forward to the ripeness of womanhood.

John told her of his plans for the annual play, asked her if she were interested in trying out for Juliet. Her blue-grey eyes widened and sparkled with eagerness. John in-

dicated a passage from the play and asked her to read it
from the back of the room.

> *"Thou knowst the mask of night is on my face*
> *Else would a maiden blush . . . . ."*

She read exquisitely, though her voice was weaker than
John had remembered it, the words liquid and golden and
light as air on her lips.

> *"I'll frown and be perverse and say thee nay*
> *So thou wilt woo;"*

John closed his eyes to listen to the magic of the words,
opened them again to see the closer, warmer magic of her
loveliness. My God, he thought, what a Juliet!

Aloud, with what he hoped was an expressionless voice
and face, he said, "now turn to Act IV, scene 3, beginning at 'How if, when I am laid into the tomb'."

She read again.

There was no emotion in her voice—that will come,
thought John—but the words had power in themselves, and
the rise and fall of the rhythm came flawlessly.

> *"Alack, alack! is it not like that I,*
> *So early waking, what with loathsome smells,*
> *And shrieks like mandrakes' torn out of the earth*
> *That living mortals, hearing them, run mad:"*

"That's all," said John. She brought the book up, stood
before him with a little smile.

"Do you think I could do it?"

It was all John could do to stop himself from bursting
out with: 'Do! You were born for it. The lines were written
for you! Shakespeare must have known you were coming
when he wrote them!'

But all he said was, "You're the most promising I've tried out yet. How would you like to read the play during the holidays? I'll lend you this copy . . . . ."

"Oh, we have Shakespeare at home," said Iris.

"Fine!" He rose and followed her to the door, his eyes involuntarily lingering around her waist and shoulders and the lovely silken hair. "There's one thing more," he added, and caught his breath as she turned her head and regarded him inquiringly out of her blue-grey eyes.

"Do all the reading aloud you can. My biggest worry is your voice. See if you can't get it a little lower and stronger. You don't have to worry about diction or tempo or inflection—it's just a little more resonance, and power. But don't worry, we'll look after that in January."

She smiled and was gone.

One day late in the fall, Donald came over to John's room at four-fifteen. John had some detentions—students who had got behind with their note-books.

"Mr. Westley," said Judd, his face a mask of pedagogical correctness, "isn't this the night we were going to see the janitor about stage flats?" He winked solemnly.

John tried to imitate his poker face, but a smirk appeared in spite of his best efforts. He pretended to remember suddenly. . . . . "Oh yes—I'm sorry. Are you going down now?"

He dismissed his class, and the two men descended to the boiler room, finding it deserted. "I have one of the flats here,"—Donald grinned as he pulled out a 'flat' of cigarettes. "From Molly," he said. "Yesterday was my birthday."

John mentioned the examination schedule. Donald had

missed the notice. They agreed that the bulletin board was cluttered up with so many notices that it was next to impossible to pick out the latest one. Donald complained of the accumulation of rules and regulations.

"I wouldn't be surprised to walk into the office one of these mornings and find 'Jimmy' "—his nickname for Miss Jamieson—"had hanged herself with one of those long red tape-worms."

"I know what you mean," said John. "But actually this *is* a good school to teach in. I mean things are a lot easier than they were under Smith."

"Listen, John, Smith was a stinker, there's no doubt about it, but at least he was an honest stinker. He didn't pull wires behind the scenes."

"What do you mean?" asked John.

"I've never mentioned this to anyone before, but it's high time someone heard about it. You know how crazy I am about modern ballet—not what you're thinking, pirouetting around on your toes—but interpretive group dancing, with a chorus that speaks as well as dances—a sort of extension of the choral reading into a kind of rhythmic drama." The words tumbled out in a torrent, as from a pent-up reservoir within.

John was skeptical. "Can boys dance?"

"Boys *can* dance. They could dance better than girls once you proved to them it wasn't sissy. Take the action in a basketball game, formalize it a bit, work out a pattern, put in your cheer leaders—they're *naturals* for dancing—your rooters in the background: the whole thing's *packed* with possibilities." The possibilities shone out of his eyes, repeated in every tense gesture of his lithe body.

"What happened?" asked John.

Donald sat back in his chair, relapsed into his usual calmness.

"Well, I worked out an interpretation of school life, the dance routine, words, choruses. I even sat down and made up the music—something I've never done before. Of course I couldn't orchestrate it, but I have the melodies, and the rhythm. Miles knows enough to work out a simple orchestration. And I went to Marg Brewin. She thought it would be a swell idea—she's nuts about that kind of thing too. Then we went to Angus and he liked it a lot. It was in the bag."

"Where does J. C. come in?"

"I'm coming to that. Marg and I went back to Macdonald with details a week later. He was sorry but he had changed his mind; maybe it wasn't such a good idea. Suppose we couldn't pull it off? I said we'd try it out in a very simple way at first. He asked if we thought it was appropriate for a high school. I said it was a damn sight more appropriate than tap-dancing, and God knows we have enough of that. Then he said he didn't think the boys would take to it, and I told him I'd handle the boys all right. Well, it was one objection after another. I fought tooth and nail for it, and he got more and more stubborn. I asked him what made him think we couldn't handle it? Finally he told us to forget about it: it was just out of the question."

"Still, I don't see . . . ."

"Just as I was going home he came up to me looking worried as hell. Do you know what he told me?"

John had no idea.

"It was Bilbeau who didn't want me to put this thing on. Bilbeau thought I was getting enough publicity. Bilbeau

342

was afraid the rest of the staff would be jealous."

"Well why couldn't he say so himself?"

"Because Macdonald is responsible for extracurricular activities, because his boss didn't have the guts to take the responsibility himself; because J. C. Bilbeau never takes the rap if someone else will take it for him. Pah!"

"Did you see J. C. about it?"

"What would have been the use? He'd have said, Mr. Macdonald has complete charge of extracurricular activities. Don't come to me!"

"But if you told him you knew?"

"Then he'd talk about misunderstanding and Macdonald would get hell for being honest with me. No. He's too smart, John. He can wind any one of us around his little finger."

John said uneasily, "That makes Angus a sort of stooge, doesn't it?"

Donald looked at him sharply. "What else could he do? If Angus had told Bilbeau to do his own dirty work, Bilbeau would have gone straight to the Board regretting to inform them that Mr. Macdonald was not co-operating—don't fool yourself: Bilbeau is out to get Macdonald, and Angus is smart enough to know it."

John protested. "Why that's crazy! Why did J. C. make him editor of the *Clarionet*, and put him in charge of extracurricular work if he held any grudge against him?"

Donald flung out his hands and looked up at the maze of pipes above them. "Listen, my simple trusting little friend," he said gently. "Mr. Bilbeau, as I've told you more than once before, knows exactly what to do when it comes to looking after himself. Angus Macdonald has a reputation and he's popular with the students. Our friend

Bilbeau is too smart to stick his neck out. So he loads him up with extra work. How many science classes have you got this year?"

John, puzzled by this sudden diversion, added them up. "Six," he said.

Judd interrupted. "Do you know what Angus is teaching instead of that senior science?"

"Why I figured J. C. gave him spares to make up for taking on the extracurricular work."

"J. C., my trusting friend, gave Angus five periods a week of first year British history."

John swallowed hard. "But—"

"For a guy that's been around here as long as you have, and a friend of Angus Macdonald into the bargain, you—" he broke off abruptly. "What I can't figure out is why Macdonald didn't leave this hen-house years ago."

"Oh," said John grateful for the change in subject, "Mary's got the theory that Vera, his wife, is a sort of small-town girl and won't leave West Kirby. She *is* pretty well tied to her parents."

"So that's it!" said Donald, as if, thought John, it actually accounted for the situation. Judd stared thoughtfully at his toes. "The poor bastard," he said softly to himself, "they've got him coming and going."

John's resentment was aroused. "What in hell are you talking about?"

Donald butted his cigarette, only half smoked, and got up. "I doubt if you would understand," he said grimly.

The Christmas holidays came and went.

Mary was pregnant again, the baby due early in March, a very lively creature who already struggled so vigorously that Mary frequently had to take pills to get her sleep. In the mornings, the drug left her so drowsy that John had to get his own and Charles's breakfast, and settle his son in the play pen for the morning; Mary usually got up at ten.

John woke on the first morning of the winter term with the kind of warm expectancy he experienced as a child on the morning of a circus or picnic, not remembering what he looked forward to but enjoying the anticipation. Suddenly he did remember, and jumped out of bed. Mary was still asleep, her dark hair tousled over the pillow, her face relaxed. As if to compensate for his errant thoughts he bent over and kissed her. Mary blinked her eyes, got up on one elbow, squinted at the clock in the winter morning darkness. "Did the alarm go off?"

"Not yet, I just felt like getting up. Relax, darling, I'll call you."

Mary looked dazed but was too sleepy to disobey if she had wished to. She sank back into the pillow, snuggled under the eiderdown and went promptly back to sleep.

John shaved with particular care, regarded himself attentively in the mirror. You still look like a kid, he told himself, grinning sheepishly. It suddenly occurred to him that this was the first time in his life he had not resented his youthful appearance.

Outside, the sun was just coming up in the frosty stillness. The trees were strange and beautiful in their delicate fur of hoar frost. The hard snow crunched underfoot. But John was warm.

You silly fool, he thought, she's just a good-looking kid, and *you* happen to be married.

At school he caught himself in the middle of an algebra

class wondering what kind of mother Iris would make if anything happened to Mary. My God, he asked John Westley, what kind of craziness has got into you?

On the way to the lab for 4B physics he would pass 3A —Iris's class. It was a class he didn't teach that year but he knew every girl in it. When the bell finally rang he dismissed the algebra students, picked up his books, and almost pushed the last boy out of the way in his haste. Then he slowed down, fearful of being too early. Down the worn north stairs of the old school, around into the passage toward the gym, along the south corridor . . . . he caught sight of the first 3A girls. Two by two they passed, all of them. No Iris. His heart sank: was she ill?

He was suddenly tired. He looked back to see if somehow he had missed her in passing. His shoulder collided with someone—a girl. Some books spilled on the floor, he stooped to pick them up, a boy helped. He gave the girl her books; the traffic parted to pass around them. There was another girl behind . . . . Iris! Iris, smiling, while he blushed with confusion.

"Oh," he said, then recovered his poise. "How's the Shakespeare coming along?"

"Oh fine, Mr. Westley," she said with a smile that left John feeling uneasy.

A week later J. C. surprised John in the middle of a rehearsal. It was one of those desperate practices when half the cast was missing and the other half didn't know their lines or had forgotten their stage positions. Romeo was refereeing a basketball game in Mr. Jarratt's absence. Mercutio had a detention. Tybalt and Lady Capulet were away.

They were going over the scene where Juliet refuses to marry Paris, with the prompt reading Lady Capulet's lines. Capulet made a wretched task of frothing at the mouth over Juliet's disobedience.

"I'll have to cut those lines some more," said John to J. C. who was standing beside him. J. C. didn't answer. John glanced at him. He was staring abstractedly at Iris, who was doing the only acting on the stage, cowering on a chair, sobbing convulsively. As Capulet walked off stage in much the same manner as he would have walked down a classroom aisle, Juliet raised her head, the hair falling over her face in lovely disorder:

> *"Is there no pity sitting in the clouds*
> *That sees into the bottom of my grief?"*

J. C. stayed on, John inwardly cursing, while wondering at the principal's sudden interest. He felt self-conscious, like a parent in the presence of visitors, itching to correct his children but not wishing to make a scene.

Mr. Bilbeau finally went, remarking to John as he left, with ponderous humour, that he had always wanted to see a great director in action.

Once he was gone John's accumulated tension found vent on his cast.

"For the love of Pete," he shouted, "brighten up! Let's run through that scene again. And USE YOUR VOICES! Iris, your acting's fine, but I *can't* hear you. Myrtle you're not just the prompt, you're an *understudy*. Capulet— WHERE'S CAPULET?" he thundered.

"Right here, sir!" Capulet had been standing beside him.

"Get back on the stage and start that scene again. And this time get mad. Get good and mad. GET MAD!" He shouted with such hearty exaggeration that they all laughed and the air was clear again.

Donald Judd became enthusiastic about the sets and lighting—his stage crew had already built the balcony. John, though he would have been quite happy to produce any play on a bare stage, was delighted with the sets Donald designed. And the two of them talked Starling into renting all the costumes from Malabar's in Toronto, instead of merely two or three for the leading roles as in former years.

It was all building up beautifully.

John's directing had never been so inspired. In the last two or three years he had found himself cutting rehearsals short, finding excuses to postpone them, and only throwing his whole energy into the last three weeks when it began to look as if the play would fizzle.

But this year it was different.

"Will you be home early tonight, John?" Mary would ask. "I'd like to get down town."

John would protest. "I can't Mary. I just can't. I've got to rehearse every night."

"You didn't last year."

"I know, but this is Shakespeare. I've got to put it over. You can't get away with slapstick in a thing like *Romeo and Juliet!*"

The exasperating thing to John was that he was quite aware that it was Iris with the blue-grey eyes that made rehearsals so important and frequent, and he knew that Mary was just as conscious of it as he was. But hang it all, she didn't realize that this was more than a mere infatuation: if it went on developing the way it had there was no saying how serious it might become.

He had told her of his feelings for Iris very lightly at first, pretending to take a detached view of the whole matter.

"It's a curious thing," he would tell her, "how adolescent a teacher can be over a sweet young thing like Iris. I've got all the symptoms of calf love. Of course, I'm nearly old enough to be her father . . . ."

Mary took her cue from him and discussed the affair as if it really were a silly infatuation. She met Iris at a school function and told John she thought "the girl" was really beautiful, that "the girl" would make a marvellous Juliet, that John showed very good taste in discovering "the girl".

The simple little phrase was maddening. John, feeling sulky, tried to make a scene by pretending to make a scene over it. "Darling, I won't have you speaking of the object of my passion as 'the girl'. It's insulting. Kindly remember her name is Iris."

Whatever Mary thought of this juvenile conduct she maintained her attitude of strict neutrality, until John stopped talking about her.

But rehearsals went on.

John's directing technique had always included a good deal of individual coaching. Every second rehearsal he would spend fifteen or twenty minutes with each member of the cast privately. So it was a simple matter to manoeuvre Iris now and then—too often would raise suspicions —into staying behind when the others had gone.

It was her voice, of course, that needed attention most. He knew it was there but it simply wouldn't come out.

After three weeks, she captured the right pitch and her resonance had improved vastly, but he could not get any volume. Her acting and lines were flawless up to a point this side of passion. Her temperament was so even that it was difficult to see how she could ever throw herself into the part with the utter abandonment of great acting. Well, she would never be an Elsie Braund, but he swore he would develop that voice.

Walking home one night it came to him that if he could once make her lose her temper over her voice, if he shouted at her till she shouted back, that would do the trick. But he didn't want to shout at her, how could he shout at Iris?

The weeks went by. The performance drew near. Iris's voice was as quiet as ever. John began to worry.

It happened one night before he realized it.

He was sitting at the back of the assembly hall, gloomily watching. Juliet's line came:

> *"Blister'd be thy tongue—*
> *For such a wish!"*

"I can't hear you!" John shouted from the back.

> *"Blister'd be thy tongue—"*

He cut her off: "I can't hear you."

A third time. Her voice was no louder. He interrupted again. A fourth, a fifth. Juliet flung her arms in despair, was mute.

John thought. My God, now I've done it. She'll walk out on me.

"BLISTERED BE THY TONGUE FOR SUCH A WISH!"

John jumped out of his seat and rushed down the aisle. The cast was laughing. Iris stood there next to tears.

"You did it! You DID it!" cried John. "That's what you should have been doing all the time! That's the voice I've been waiting to hear for six months."

"But that's yelling, it sounds so loud it doesn't go with the lines. I can't do it that way!"

"Listen," said John, "it sounds like yelling to you but at the back of the hall it comes through clear as a bell. If you do it once more we'll go down and raid the cafeteria for ice-cream."

The crisis was past. The only difficulty was, John was so jubilant over his and her success that he loved her more than ever. And she seemed grateful for his persistence with her voice.

Iris was actually abnormal for a girl of fifteen. For one thing she was a first-class student, which in an adolescent of her beauty, was phenomenal. She was apparently unaware of the existence of boys. At least she never walked with them in the halls, or to and from school; and she was very popular with her own sex.

One day after a line rehearsal at noon in John's room she had stayed behind for a moment to explain that she would have to miss the next practice because her aunt was ill. John asked her if that meant missing the school party as well on the following night.

"Oh, I wasn't going, anyway," said Iris, looking down at her feet.

"What's the matter?" he asked. "Haven't you a big sister who will lend you a glamorous dress for the evening?"

"It isn't that," she looked up and John was amazed to see tears standing in her eyes, "you see I don't believe in dancing."

"You mean," he cursed himself for his clumsiness, "you have religious scruples?"

"I just don't think it's right." She turned away to hide the tears.

"Well, don't worry about missing the rehearsal," he called after her. "We'll see you on Friday." And she was gone.

The last week before the play was hectic. The inspector, long overdue, suddenly showed up; and Mary was getting next to no sleep, expecting the new baby at any time.

John got home from his dress rehearsal at eleven on a Wednesday night, did an hour's work, and went to bed. Charles had a cold and woke up fitfully all night whenever his nose blocked. John slept with one eye open, dashing in to quiet Charles to save Mary, who was sleeping that night. In the morning at school there were a dozen details to look after connected with the play as well as teaching; and the inspector was loose in the halls.

At noon Mary went to the hospital, and John stayed home with Charles until a neighbour came in. He had barely arrived at school when a telephone message came to the effect that mother and babe were doing well—it was a girl. They had hoped for a girl and had the name all ready, "Marilyn". John dashed about the school to check last minute details of the play, dashed over to the hospital to see Mary, ate downtown and dashed back to school for the performance.

Iris's new voice, while it brought the final realization of his artistic dreams, awakened a self-confidence in her that tore the web of John's gossamer love life. In the final week of rehearsals his Juliet became aware of boys. It wasn't even Romeo, but a lad in the lighting crew, tall, thin and pimply—Hank Russell. John lay awake for half an hour one night wondering what she could see in Hank.

Romeo and Juliet took the audience by storm. On the second night there was standing room only, and most of that was taken. As one student put it to John, "When I heard you were going to put on *Romeo and Juliet* I thought it would be pure corn! But it was swell!"

Apart from a few little jealous flare-ups when he saw Hank carrying Iris's books home, and the unforgettable moment when the flushed triumphant Juliet came offstage at the end of her first scene and he hugged her in his jubilation, John's infatuation faded into the air of which it was composed.

28

The memorable event of that spring was Donald Judd's resignation.

John first learned of it at the Public Library one Saturday evening in May. He was just entering when he noticed a naval officer coming up the steps and he gave the heavy door a backward push, holding it open for a moment till the man reached it. As he climbed the inside stairs something prompted him to look back again at the officer.

It was Donald Judd.

"For the love of Pete! What are you doing in that outfit?"

Donald grinned handsomely. The uniform of a sub-lieutenant in the R.C.N.V.R. was the perfect costume for him. The curly black hair, dark eyes, and thin bold features, the lithe figure, belonged with the navy blue. The phrase "an officer and a gentleman" popped up in John's mind.

"Didn't you know?" asked Donald. "I'm in the naval reserve—the Royal Canadian Naval Volunteer Reserve, probationary acting-sub-lieutenant." He clicked his heels.

"But why?"

"Join the navy and see the world! *Dulce et decorum est pro patria mori.* Breathes there a man with soul so dead, and greater love hath no man. Also—"

"But why in the—"

"Not so loud," whispered Donald, "we're in the library." They went over to a secluded nook in the stacks.

"When did you join up?" asked John.

"Oh, nearly a month ago down in London. I'll be leaving for an unidentified eastern Canadian port at the end of June."

They talked further but Donald flippantly evaded giving any more information.

John walked home disturbed.

Mary was ironing in the kitchen.

"Guess what?" said John, lighting a cigarette, and sitting on the kitchen table.

"The library was closed and you couldn't get my whodunits" said Mary. She plugged in the ironing cord, remarking, "This iron just doesn't seem to hold its heat tonight."

"No," said John, and told her the news.

"But he can't do that," said Mary. "He has a wife and two small girls!"

"There's no law against enlisting when you have children."

"There ought to be." Mary's eyes sparkled her anger. "I think any man who is selfish enough to do a thing like that has no right to be a father."

"Well, there *is* a war on."

"If they needed him they'd have come for him. For that matter there's a scarcity of teachers, and education *is* slightly important."

"I know, darling. I can't understand it and Donald was evasive when I went into motives. Actually, I wouldn't be surprised if he enlisted to get out of teaching. He never could see eye to eye with J. C., you know."

"Well," said Mary, "that's not so hard to understand. Just the same, don't you get any bright ideas about enlisting. If you did I'd—I'd go home to mother!"

"You'd have to," said John soberly.

Mary gave a little squeal, "The iron!" and ran to pull out the plug.

A week later came the last assembly of the year.

The school knew by this time that Judd was leaving. There were a few preliminary announcements by the student president. Then J. C. rose.

"You all know, I believe, that Mr. Judd has enlisted in His Majesty's Royal Canadian Naval Volunteer Reserve and will be leaving this summer for active duty on the high seas.

"It's hardly necessary to point out the contributions he has made to our school life. Our assembly chorals have become known throughout the province, and beyond. Only last week a letter came to me from the principal of a large

355

school in California making inquiries as to the nature and technique of our choral reading at West Kirby. His art work too has made a deep impression on his students. His invaluable assistance at the annual Christmas concert will be sorely missed.

"I am sure that you, the staff and student body, will join me as principal in wishing him the happy useful life in the navy he has had here and the success in all his undertakings that he so richly deserves. Mr. Judd."

Judd stood and the applause burst upon him overwhelmingly, as he half ascended the platform stairs and gestured for silence. The gesture was greeted with another outburst. Finally the applause died away. Donald stood there, gracefully, smiling his famous smile.

"Well, people," he began. "This is it. I was almost as surprised as you were to find myself in the navy one day. Perhaps I might have backed out, only"—and again he flashed his brilliant smile—"it's a darn sight harder to get out of the navy than it is to get in." Laughter.

"I've been here nearly four years, which is a long time for you, but looking back doesn't seem long to me. We've had a lot of fun together, doing this and that, but now it's over I can't think of much to say . . . . except that, I've had a swell time, and it's been darn nice knowing you!"

Wave after wave of room-rocking sound greeted the end of the speech. A girl sitting in front of John suddenly got up and almost ran out of the assembly hall, overcome with emotion. Another across the aisle was weeping openly.

J. C. rose and stilled the tempest.

"I think," he said, "that the most appropriate way we can express our feelings is to rise and sing the school song."

356

The school rose and sang as it had never been sung before. John thought, would they miss *me* as much as this if I left?

At the staff picnic, which had to be held in the school on account of rain, Donald Judd was to receive his final send-off.

J. C. had asked John to pay the parting tribute. He put in a good deal of time thinking over what he would say. His first reaction to the resignation had been, there goes West Kirby's school spirit. What was there about Donald Judd that made him so popular, that made him get such good results? In preparing his home form reports year after year John had noticed how high the marks had been in Donald's examination results. In art it was to be expected, but in English John had often thought that either he gave marks away or he was an extraordinary teacher. John had run across a few clues to his teaching method: apparently he made up rhymes for all the grammar rules and the youngsters loved memorizing them.

John couldn't help thinking of Dot Young. In a way they had a good deal in common. They were both artists, and though Donald didn't do much painting he was creative. Dot's creative work had been isolated from teaching: a kind of escape. But Donald had put his creative energy to work in the school, in developing the assembly chorals, in teaching voice technique, even in the grammar jingles for his English classes.

There was his attitude too, to the students. Twice in auditorium he had lost his temper. But it had been sharp, clear-cut, and effective: two minutes later he was smiling again, and no antagonism had been created. John had been startled one day to see a senior student slap Donald familiarly on the back. Any other teacher would have bridled with affronted dignity. Donald merely turned to see who it was, smiled with equal familiarity, and behaved as though it happened every day and was the correct social approach of a student to teacher.

Socially, in spite of that first party, the Judds had been a disappointment to the Westleys. Donald and John worked together at school beautifully. But Donald was the type that must always be doing something. In spite of his calm, almost lazy, way of approaching his work, and the apparent ease with which he did anything he put his hand to, it was impossible for him to relax for an evening's conversation. He was a fair pianist, but obviously bored when listening even to the best music. He and Molly played excellent bridge, and the Westleys had never cultivated the game, which in itself was a wide social barrier. Donald painted occasionally: smooth sophisticated landscapes in subtle greys and browns with a good deal of what John considered distortion to emphasize the design. Unlike Dot's painting they seemed to convey no personal feelings: they were like the clothes he wore, a part of his outer costume. When Molly or Mary had a baby the contact was renewed; but never achieved intimacy.

Well, this wasn't preparing a speech. He pulled himself back to the task. What would he say?

Picnic and speech came and went. John didn't do too badly. Nor did Donald, who was presented with a handsome mantel clock, its face within a miniature pilot wheel —"That's what everyone is buying now for the boys in the navy," the jewellery store clerk had told John and Audubon earnestly when they bought it.

The Westleys gave a farewell party to the Judds with a carefully selected group of those teachers and wives who would drink, or at least taste, alcoholic beverages.

The Germans invaded the Low Countries on May the tenth; and in the grim succeeding months Fear stalked openly down Central Avenue, and even looked in the windows of W.K.C.I.

29

Fall came again and with it a new school term. Across the Atlantic the blitz on Britain had begun; but in West Kirby Collegiate things went smoothly on their way. Apart from a replacement for Donald Judd there were no staff changes.

The teacher who replaced Donald was a woman. Men were getting difficult to find. J. C. certainly knew how to pick his teachers, John had thought on first meeting her. Miss Ayres was young, good-looking and competent; she had two years' teaching experience. Her first name was Laura.

Somehow J. C. had discovered one of the few people in the province who knew something about choral reading. But of course she had never attempted to lead a whole assembly. And J. C. expected her to.

"May I come up and see you about it?" she had asked John that first week.

"Sure," said John. "I don't know any more about it than I've seen Judd do, but if it'll help to talk it over I'll be glad to give you some moral support."

She came over to the house later.

"You know," she said, "this school is just a bit terrifying. Especially trying to fill Mr. Judd's shoes."

"How did you come to take this job?" asked John, adding hastily—"not that it's any of my business."

"Oh, I was teaching in a high school just outside of Toronto, waiting for a good job to open up there, and I read the advertisement, applied, and here I am," she smiled, trying to make it brave and bright. "All the Toronto teachers seem to be sitting tight." She went on, sensing sympathy in the Westleys. "You know, what really terrified me was Mr. Bilbeau. He was sweet to me when I interviewed him in Toronto, but when I got up here he just wasn't the same person. Almost the first thing he said to me—and he wasn't smiling—was, 'You know, Miss Ayres, I work my teachers hard, and expect in return the fullest co-operation'."

"He didn't!" Mary's eyes were hard with indignation.

"Oh yes he did." Laura went on. "Of course, after that he was very nice, but honestly, there's something about him that frightens me terribly. And I've been just sick worrying over this assembly choral business."

"Oh well, he won't ask you to jump into that for a while," said John.

"He told me he wouldn't expect anything for a month—time to get my bearings, he put it. Now the month is half gone and I feel more at sea than ever."

"Don't worry," soothed John, "these things are always worst in prospect. I still worry like the devil over my plays and I've been putting them on for—how long have we been here Mary?"

Mary turned lightly to Laura for feminine sympathy, humour twitching her cheeks. "Men," she said in explanation. "We had our fifth wedding anniversary this summer!"

"Then that'll be six years, and if anything I worry more now that I used to."

"But how do you get a crowd like that—big boys and everything—to *listen* to you, let alone do anything?"

"Well, in the first place J. C. will be watching them with that eagle eye. Anyone who doesn't listen will go out on his ear. Secondly, if I were you I'd start with some of Donald's old standbys—ones they know backwards. After you get used to them and know what they can do you can start in working out your own."

"You mean, I should make up the parts?"

"Well, just take something they'll like and figure out who will read what and work out sound effects and so on. Of course *I* should talk: I couldn't do it myself, but it seemed to come easily to Donald."

"But I'd be *lost* doing that," wailed Laura. "I have some books, and the mimeographed sheets we used in the summer course I took, but I wouldn't have the first idea of how to go about inventing choral parts."

They tried to comfort her, to assure her that it would all work out for the best, that the realization would be quite easy compared with the anticipation and so on.

Laura left, only a little comforted.

John shook his head after she had gone. "I'm afraid she's going to be crucified over this thing," he told Mary. "I wonder if I should talk to J. C."

"What would you say?"

"Oh, that it was asking a little too much to push her into this thing so soon. I could suggest that she work with her classes and the Dramatic Club—ease into it the way Donald did originally—give her till Christmas anyway."

"Do you think J. C. would do without his beloved assembly chorals for four months?"

"Well, maybe not. They're pretty important you know —there's really nothing that keeps up the school morale like assembly chorals."

"I should think," said Mary, "that if he wants a goose to lay him golden eggs he would be pretty careful not to kill her before she starts laying."

"Well," decided John, "we'd better let things ride for a while and see what happens."

Early in October came the first assembly choral. Donald had left all his old arrangements behind, with the parts written out, timing indicated—everything but the personality that had put the thing over. The first assembly wasn't too bad: the piece was familiar, the school liked Laura and everybody tried hard. But Laura was obviously nervous, lacking assurance. The next session was noticeably weaker—the students were beginning to lose patience. Laura came to John.

"What'll I do?" she wailed.

"Try something new, just in unison," he suggested.

She tried that. It was better. But there was a quality to her inflections—a too feminine emotional reaction to the lines that rubbed the older boys the wrong way. At the next assembly there were whole rows that were merely mumbling.

J. C. stood up.

362

"This school," he said, "is building up a reputation for choral reading. I am not going to have that reputation spoiled by a dozen boys who don't know enough to co-operate. I should like to remind you that attendance at these assemblies is not essential. If anyone does not care to take part in them I have a number of vacant seats in my office!"

Miss Ayres tried again. The response was slightly better.

So it went through the fall term, Laura getting more discouraged, the school more apathetic, and J. C. more rigidly calm.

With the full impact of the blitz on Britain West Kirby really came alive. Red Cross sewing circles had already swung into action. Panicky aldermen were talking at council meetings in terms of black-outs and air-raid precautions. After all, there were war industries right here in West Kirby! Opinion was sharply divided between optimists who *knew* that Britons never never shall be slaves; and pessimists who were hourly expecting to hear of German invasion fleets invading the shores of North America and sending bombers even as far inland as West Kirby.

A Board meeting decided that W.K.C.I. would play its part. There were things that even a school could do.

A school could raise money: money for War Savings Stamps and Bonds, money for the Red Cross, money to buy food and chocolate bars to go into parcels for the boys in the services. A school was an ideal collecting agency: scrap metal, rubber, rags, paper, magazines. And a school could instruct: science, first aid, the working parts and theory of gasoline engines, aircraft recognition, knots and lashings.

The principal organized.

Angus was instructed to concentrate all extracurricular activities on the war effort.

Green headed the night school.

Jarratt recruited an Air Cadet Corps.

And everyone on the staff had extra work to do.

The main task was to raise money. There were tag days, and concerts, and plays, to organize, rehearse, advertise, promote and produce. There were posters, publicity stunts, seating plans, tickets to sell, records to keep. Scarcely a week passed without some kind of campaign or competition.

Teachers found themselves teaching special war subjects for which they had to prepare themselves with long hours of extra study.

The Christmas parcels were enough to keep half the War Committee busy for six months of the year. Merely to keep up to date the addresses of three hundred former students already in the services was a job in itself.

And J. C. worked in his office, organizing.

To save time, and gasoline, three-quarters of the staff now brought their lunch to school. Mr. Bilbeau brought up the subject at a staff meeting.

"The noon lunch arrangements for the staff are most unsatisfactory," he informed them. "Especially among the men. The women have an electric plate and eat together in the women teachers' room. The men, on the other hand, have no similar plan. As I understand it, some eat alone in their classrooms, two eat in the cafeteria, and three or four in the men teachers' room."

He paused and looked down the table.

"But it's my fault," he said, "I should have organized you."

Something in the silence that followed dissuaded him from correcting this neglect.

Audubon, Klein, Husson, and Pikestaff usually ate their lunches at school. So frequently John would arrive at ten or a quarter after one and find four or five of them in the tail of a discussion.

In the middle of October Klein was ill. No one seemed to know exactly what was wrong, the general diagnosis was, 'some kind of nervous breakdown'. It was a discussion stemming from his condition that John ran into late in the same month.

"The whole trouble is," said Husson, "that we're all so loaded up to the hilt with extracurricular activity, war or otherwise, or both, that we've either got to lay off on the teaching or kill ourselves."

Pikestaff spoke up. "I just wish you had my job with war savings stamps," he said. "I have to make out a statement every week on stamp sales. I sit down on Wednesday nights to write it out, and what happens—somebody hasn't given me their statement. So I phone them up and they're out; or if they're home they can't remember how much their class bought. Every week that happens."

"Why don't you leave them out for that week?" asked John.

"Oh I couldn't do that!" Pikestaff was pained by the thought.

"Suppose he did," the unusually vocal Husson said, "the principal would want to know why they were left out, and someone would be on the carpet."

"Well, why don't we *do* something about it?" asked John.

"That's what we were talking about before you came in —you weren't at the last Teachers' Council meeting, were you?"

"No," said John. In fact he had only been to two meetings of the local teachers' union since coming to West Kirby.

"Well, we talked about this overloading then, and it was decided the teachers in both schools should submit a record of the total time spent by them on school work outside of legal school hours during a school year. I meant to see you about it sooner—the information is supposed to be in this week."

The Teachers' Council collected its figures; met with the School Trustees.

John heard about it from Audubon, who was one of the deputation.

"What's your average overtime per week?" the Trustees had asked.

"Six and a half hours," the teachers had informed them, "but some of the individual cases go as high as thirteen."

"Twenty-seven and a half, plus six and a half, makes exactly thirty-four hours per week." It was Mullins who provided the arithmetic.

"They laughed at us," Audubon told John. "Parker claimed he works ten hours a day, six days a week. Why, if our figures got into the paper the whole town would laugh at us. If we'd been smart we'd have taken each teacher's heaviest week and given them those figures."

"Look at Macdonald," said Audubon. "First thing in the fall he has two solid months straight slugging on the *Clarionet*. On top of that he has to check on every student

366

activity going on in the school. That man is really tough!"

John felt his cheeks flush as Audubon turned to him. "How many hours do you spend on your play the week it goes on?"

John considered: "Well, I figured it on paper as thirty hours but it'd be more like the real truth to say twenty-four hours a day till the darn thing's over. I even dream about it! Seriously I just don't think of anything else the last week."

"There you are," said Audubon. "It's not the work, it's the worry. But how are you going to get figures on worry? Klein was probably only putting in a forty-hour week, but he couldn't take it, and he's no sissy either. No, you've got to work on equivalent hours if you want a fair basis for comparison. Just ask your corner grocer how he'd like to trade jobs with you. He's got war extras too, pasting in ration coupons and so on long after closing hours. But ask him whether he'd rather have a ten-hour day in the store or a five-hour day teaching."

"I wonder what he would say," said Husson.

"I *know* what he'd say. I asked him yesterday. 'You know,' he said, 'my folks wanted me to go through for a teacher. But I'd never have had the patience.'"

"So a teacher doing forty hours a week is working as hard as a bank clerk doing sixty—is that what you're trying to say?" John asked.

"Not working as hard in the physical sense, but he's under more nervous strain."

"Yeah? Try and tell that to the Board," said Audubon.

Poor Laura wrestled on with assembly chorals to no avail. She knew and the whole school knew that it was hopeless. Bilbeau had carefully arranged that visitors would appear only when other assembly features were being conducted.

But early in March things came to a head. John learned of it when J. C. summoned him to the office.

"We are faced with something in the nature of a small crisis." J. C. came directly to the point as soon as John was seated. John noticed that though his skin was as cleanly shaven as ever, there was a certain sagging of the flesh beneath. The nose was sharper, the hair of his shaggy eyebrows no longer seemed aggressive. And the eyes had a slight film around the edge of each iris.

"A week from Tuesday," continued J. C., "we are having a distinguished visitor from Syracuse, New York," he paused, "for the express purpose of hearing an assembly choral."

He paused again. John remained silent, thinking, oh, oh, here's where I come in.

"Miss Ayres has told me she feels no longer capable of conducting our assembly chorals. And, I may add, strictly in confidence, that she has also handed in her resignation to be effective in June. You can see the difficult situation in which I am placed."

"You want—me—to take over the chorals?" John asked with the cold certainty that the answer would be yes.

J. C. was transformed.

"Mr. Westley, I should like to say this. I have always had the highest regard for your ability and your willingness to co-operate. That you should volunteer for this task does not surprise me, but I feel bound to say it is highly gratifying and confirms my opinion of your character. I have arranged for three assemblies before next Tuesday. If necessary we may have four."

"If I can't make the grade in three tries, I won't make it in thirty," said John. "But I hope Mr. Bilbeau, you'll not expect me to duplicate Judd's success. I don't even know if I can do any better than Miss Ayres, though I think her chief handicap has been simply as a woman succeeding a man."

"Mr. Westley, since you have volunteered to do this, I'll expect your best efforts. I am confident you will succeed." He rose and shook hands with John; the grip was firm, but the flesh was soft.

John opened his mouth to protest, but J. C. was already smoothly ushering him out with, "Could you have two pieces ready for tomorrow morning?" and he was outside before he knew it.

Not until he was back in his room did he realize what had happened, and sat down full of dismay.

What was he going to say to Laura? What was he going to tell Mary?

He saw Mary first.

Mary was indignant.

"Well, you can just call him up on the phone right now and tell him you won't do it."

John buried his head in his hands. "I can't Mary. I can't. You know what he'll do."

"He won't like it naturally, but he can't fire you. Did he say he would?"

"No, but Mary, you don't understand. I don't know how he did it but in half a minute he had me twisted around into a position where I felt it was up to me to make good on this, or else. After all, there's a good chance a teacher will be dropped from the staff this June."

"But there's Laura. She's going."

"That's another thing," John clutched at the straw. "If I refuse then he'll put the pressure on Laura to carry on, and you know what a state she's in already."

"Isn't there someone else that can do it?"

"Who? Jessie Willis—she's poison to the kids—anything they do for her is out of fear. Green? He's a pompous ass the kids haven't any respect for. Angus? No voice. Can you see Klein handling it, or Audubon, or Doug Husson, or Pikestaff, or Jarratt or *any* of them? No. Whether we like it or not I'm the only one that has a chance and God knows I'm no Donald Judd. I can forget myself directing a play but up on the stage in front of that crowd I'll be as nervous as a cat."

He got up, looked out the window, came back, got up again. "Damn it! Oh damn it! Why did this have to happen to me!"

Young Charles came in the back door.

"Hi!" he called.

Mary ran out. "Don't track that mud on my floors."

Marilyn began to wail, having wakened from her afternoon sleep.

"Even a guy's family won't let him alone," muttered John, going in to pull up Marilyn's blind and forget his own troubles in hers.

That night he and Mary went over to the public library. It was Mary who saved the situation with *Edom o' Gordon*.

370

"Oh John," she showed him the poem. "This is just what you're looking for."

"A ballad. Donald used a lot of ballads, but not this one. I know it, too. Mary, you've struck oil!"

They were home by nine and excitedly worked out the parts.

"Keep it simple!" Mary kept saying whenever John thought of an extra effect.

Twelve hours later John found himself sitting on the stage alone with J. C.

J. C. rose.

How is he going to pull *this* off, wondered John, wishing he could get rid of the dry sensation in his throat, the ache in his bowels.

"A week from next Tuesday," J. C. announced, "a distinguished educationist whom I had the privilege of meeting four years ago in Syracuse, New York, is to be our guest on this platform. He has heard of our assembly chorals and is coming to West Kirby for the express purpose of hearing you." There was a subtle accent on the pronoun 'you'.

"Unfortunately," he went on, "Miss Ayres is ill." John started—yes, her place *was* vacant, "and it is doubtful whether she will be back by then. However, Mr. Westley has volunteered to fill her place in the interim. I am sure you will give him full support. Mr. Westley."

John stood up, came forward. There was a heart-warming round of applause.

"I'm afraid . . . ." his voice was husky, he cleared his throat and tried again. "I'm afraid I'm a pretty poor substitute for Miss Ayres but we'll do the best we can. We only have two more sessions after this one to get ready, and we want to be good—good enough to show these New Yorkers a thing or two." They laughed.

The assembly ended with a round of applause. John watched the students march out, and felt as if he had come out of a steam bath.

"I think," J. C. told John, beaming, "that Mr. Judd could return and get a pointer or two from you on assembly chorals."

"We haven't got round to the actual choral arrangement yet," John reminded him, feeling the insidious gratification of the flattery.

"I think you'll find you have very little difficulty." John went back to his room elated that this first hurdle was behind him, wondering how he would get over the others.

He passed Starling in the hall. "That was good work, Mr. Westley!"

"Thanks," said John. Maybe he could be as good as Donald.

The distinguished educationist sat on the platform in the assembly hall of West Kirby Collegiate Institute, and was properly impressed by the school's performance, which, if it failed to reach the Judd standard, was at least passable. The visitor himself was not very impressive, a dry little man with spectacles. But the magic of the name New York, had the power to inform him with the vast sophistication of the great city. West Kirby Collegiate was determined to show New York a thing or two, and felt that it succeeded.

John was in the embarrassing position of a tyro who is

assumed to be an experienced professional. J. C. smoothly interpreted his protests of unworthiness as delightful evidence of a profound modesty that made it impossible for him to see his own virtues. And even if the demonstration had failed the principal's supreme showmanship would have sent the American visitor away with the impression that he had seen and heard tremendous things.

Laura Ayres returned the next day and John went to see her immediately at four o'clock. He waited till she dismissed a half dozen students lingering in the classroom.

"Listen Laura, I feel like a heel taking over this assembly business; and I'm three-quarters sorry that it went across. The truth is I just didn't have the guts to talk back to J. C."

Laura smiled. "I know," she said. "It doesn't matter anyway. Did Mr. Bilbeau tell you I was fired?"

"Fired!" John gasped. "He said you had resigned—he certainly didn't tell me you were fired."

"Would that man have the courage to fire anyone in so many words?" she asked. "No, he's right. I'm resigning. He wanted to be fair to me, he said. He didn't want me to leave the school with a blemish on my record, so I could resign in June."

"A blemish! My God. You sweat and worry and do your damnedest to make the thing go and he has the—the gall to call that a blemish. Are you *sure* he said that?"

Laura smiled faintly. "My hearing is pretty good."

John looked at her bewildered. It didn't sound like J. C. —there was no need to fire anyone. Registration *was* down, and there had been talk of letting a teacher go; but Laura wasn't a weak teacher.

He said, "If it's true, you ought to go to the Teachers'

Council. I've a good mind to let the staff know about this. It's—it's a cowardly trick." But already within him the sudden anger was dying out.

"I'd rather you didn't say anything," said Laura. "You see, I have my pride. I'm glad you and Mary will know the truth, but it wouldn't do me much good to have it get around that I was fired, would it?"

John drummed his fingers futilely on the desk at which he was sitting, feeling relieved at the same time that Laura was going. It would be darned embarrassing carrying on the chorals with her still around.

"But damn it all," he said, with not quite enough conviction in his voice, "something ought to be done about it."

John went home in a quandary. Should he tell Mary? He might as well, she would get it out of him anyway. The trouble was he would have to admit to Mary that J. C. was a little like her picture of him. Oh damn it, why did things have to get so complicated? Why did Donald have to enlist?

Mary listened with a troubled face, but clear eyes.

"John, I'm almost glad this happened—you've always clung so hard to your ideal of Bilbeau that you frightened me. Maybe he isn't as hollow as I think he is; but, darling, at least you know now that he's not perfect."

John looked at her pleadingly: "Mary, I honestly don't want to have anything more to do with this choral reading. What am I going to do?"

"Let's talk it over with Angus," Mary suggested.

John was troubled. "Mary. I've hardly seen Angus since this business started. If you want the truth I'm ashamed of myself . . . . besides, Laura asked me not to say anything."

374

"Darling, which is more important, Laura, or *us*? Anyway you don't have to tell him the truth about her resignation. I'll give him a call."

"Mary, I don't think you'd better."

"Why not?"

"He couldn't help."

"Well he certainly could give us some good solid advice. John, if you don't do something now you're just going to be putty in Bilbeau's hands. John, it's important! It's not just you. It's you and me."

John said bitterly, "A fat lot of help Angus would be."

"John, why do you talk like that? Angus is our friend."

"The kind of friend that offers to help and then lets you down."

"What are you talking about?" she asked.

John told her about his going to Angus when he had been up on the carpet for saying heaven was a state, not a place.

"Oh John, if you'd only told me then! It's so obvious. How could you have been so blind? Do you think if Angus were afraid of Bilbeau he would speak his mind in staff meetings the way you say he does? And don't you realize how much Angus loves you?"

"Loves!" John was bewildered.

"Yes, loves you!" Mary's eyes were flashing now. "Why do you think he took such a shine to you from the first? Because you were so intelligent? Or because he took a shine to me? Oh John, I could cry sometimes, you're so blind to how other people feel about things. You are his son all over again, the one he lost just as he was beginning to grow up. You mean more to Angus than anyone else in the world!"

John opened his mouth, closed it and swallowed. He stared at Mary with a tight feeling about this eyes.

"He was going to Bilbeau and stick up for you—be your daddy, protect you. And then, like a real father he stopped himself in time. If he did this for you, you would lose a battle you had to fight for yourself. He knows just as well as I do that you're a baby at heart, that you won't grow up till you *face* the situations you find yourself in. And you thought he was a coward!"

"Wait a minute, Mary." John's face was pale, his voice choked. "You called me a baby. Maybe I am. Maybe I'm not. But when a man's own wife—" he could go no further, he got up abruptly and went out into the bedroom where he flung himself on the bed, buried his head in his arms. Tears of self-pity welled up in his eyes. My own wife, he kept repeating to himself, blinking his eyes to make another tear come.

There were quick footsteps outside. He felt the sudden warmth of Mary's cheek beside his own, smelled her hair. heard her voice as she encircled his head with her arm and said, "Oh John, darling, I'm sorry, I'm sorry. I've hurt you, I love you so much!"

"So much!" She breathed the words again as John turned and clung to her like a frightened child.

At school Klein was back again, thinner, not so hearty-looking. Audubon was still grumbling about the red-tape. More and more at staff meetings he saw eye to eye with Angus, questioning the necessity of this and that new regulation, asking embarrassing questions. Now and then Husson too would come out with a surprisingly sharp remark for such a mild fellow.

As his success with assembly chorals grew John's indignation over Laura Ayres's experience faded out completely. Only on the rare occasions when Mary referred to it could he rouse himself to a show of his former disillusionment with Bilbeau. Actually, what could Bilbeau do? He had to get rid of a teacher—she was the most recently hired, and she had been hired for that express job. As for Angus's substitution of himself for his dead son! When you looked at it in the cold light of day, the idea was fantastic. Mary's imagination.

They had finally decided that John would look around for another job. When the advertisements came out in May they would look them over and he would apply for the likeliest.

"It would be nice," Mary had said wistfully, "if you could get a Toronto job, or some place close: it's so far away from the family up here."

Audubon was making a mistake talking the way he did about Bilbeau. John felt uneasy in his presence. It was the Judd business all over again. But Donald had laughed at Bilbeau. Audubon took him seriously, or rather his method of handling school routine and organization.

Bilbeau rarely visited the classrooms any more. But he did come in during one of John's spare periods, early in April.

He was looking very spruce and tailored in his light grey suit with a wine-red tie. John thought again how out of place he looked in a school.

J. C. sat down affably in a chair John pulled up for him. "This is my visiting day," he explained cheerfully. Then his face clouded, "I don't suppose anyone realizes how busy a principal must be. I often wish I could get around more often for personal chats with my staff, but the pressure of business—" he raised his eyebrows and turned his head slowly from side to side. "I've repeatedly asked for more office help—Miss Jamieson is flooded with work—but, the taxpayers, there are always the taxpayers. Sometimes when I have spoken to twenty or thirty organizations in the course of a week on the importance of education and the work you and I are doing here, and see the apathy, I get discouraged."

John looked sympathetic.

J. C. brightened visibly, throwing off the weight of his cares with an effort. "But I didn't come here to unburden my load on your shoulders. How is your work coming along?"

John told him as well as he could.

"And your family?"

His family was well.

"A great pity Mrs. Westley is not interested in Sunday School work—a great pity. Now Mrs. Macdonald—as devoted to her Sunday School as her husband is to the work here. You know, John, sometimes down in my office, when the work piles up, or problems confront me that seem too much for any mere human to tackle, I stop working, lean back in my chair, and think of my staff. You have no idea what a feeling of strength it gives a principal to know that he has the loyal co-operation of a devoted staff. Miss Willis, a splendid woman! And Mr. Klein—it was a great blow to us, his illness last fall. Strange how appearances differ: Mr. Klein, so robust, breaks down, and Mr. Macdonald who works as hard as any man on the staff, or harder—"

J. C. laid a peculiar stress on the word "harder"—"takes it all in his stride."

"I remember," said John, smiling reminiscently, "Mr. Judd used to think Mr. Macdonald was overworked."

"Mr. Judd—have you heard from him lately?"

"Oh no," said John, "the only letter we ever had from him was a card from Halifax last summer."

"I suppose it's not quite conventional to talk about the members of my staff, but there actually isn't one whom I wouldn't do everything I could to keep. Miss Ayres, of course, is going; but then she is to be married. And there's nothing any of us can do about that kind of situation!" He laughed with that peculiar rasping sound on each intake of breath.

John was inwardly relieved to hear of the marriage.

"Even a man like Mr. Audubon. A great man to argue, Mr. Audubon. But I like spirit in my staff—where would we be without Mr. Macdonald's splendid critical abilities? You know, John, a principal has a pretty shrewd idea of what is going on in his own school. Mr. Audubon's grumbling, for instance," he smiled tolerantly.

"Oh he doesn't grumble much," said John, "and it's just the way he's made. Some people on the staff, Husson, for instance, keep it all to themselves. You wouldn't know what they were thinking except that they have to let go now and then. But with Mr. Audubon it's just a habit that doesn't mean anything."

Mr. Bilbeau's eyes lit up, and he smiled slowly.

John thought, he really is an understanding kind of guy. I couldn't say things like that to an ordinary principal. Why, I suppose, he thought to himself, with the vaguest suggestion of uneasiness, there are some principals who would use confidences like these against their teachers.

When the advertisements for teaching positions came out in May, Mary scanned them eagerly, John trying to show the same enthusiasm. There were two Toronto schools asking for an experienced science specialist. John wrote applications to both principals outlining his training qualifications and dramatic work. He purposely refrained from mentioning assembly chorals. Within the week he had favourable replies saying they would be pleased to interview him.

John went in to tell J. C. After all, they would get in touch with him for references.

"It's really Mary's idea: I'm actually very happy here," explained John. "Mary's parents are getting old, and she doesn't like to be so far away from them."

"She's the only child, I presume," said J. C.

"No, she has three sisters, but she's the oldest, and she's never been really happy away from her folks. Of course," he added, "I may not find anything I like."

J. C. apart from the one little thrust, took it very nicely. "Naturally, family needs come first. I can't say I wish you success—we need you here, we *want* you, John." John felt a sudden regret that he was making the move. "You will let me know how you get along, of course."

John's Toronto interviews were pleasant but unproductive. As he explained afterward to Mary he had 'played hard to get', and they had taken him at his word. The salary, too, was a consideration that took the enthusiasm out of his interviews: he learned that extra salary allowance was made for only two years' teaching experience. To teach in Toronto he would have to take a $275 drop, with moving expenses and increased cost of living on top of that.

He had no further word from either principal; John learned later through a friend that one of them had remarked to a mutual acquaintance, "Westley didn't seem to want the position very badly."

And that was the simple truth.

30

The staff picnic that June was held over on the island. Audubon caustically remarked that it was the right place to have it, since the island was now Bilbeau's. John had heard rumours of recent real estate developments in the vicinity of Angus's place, and that Bilbeau had been building a house on the island; but knowing Angus's passion for privacy he guessed that any discussion of the matter with him would be unpleasant. Besides, although their relations at school were friendly enough, the old intimacy was gone, and they merely talked school when they found themselves together.

Miss Willis offered to pick up the Westleys sharp at four; and right on the dot her car drew up in front of the Westley residence. John and Charles brought out the picnic things, and Mary came out carrying the little bundle that was Marilyn. It was Miss Willis's first view of Marilyn, and the way her hatchet-face melted into something quite human was a sight to remember.

Settled in the car and on their way it was only a matter of minutes before they were purring smoothly over the bridge. It was one of those humid days when the water lies flat and listless, the sun shines heavily, and a rose-grey haze creeps up from the horizon to dull the blue of the sky. John turned down his window to get a breath of air until Miss Willis, solicitous for Marilyn, said firmly to John, "I think we had better have that window closed. It makes quite a draft in the rear seat."

As they left the bridge they turned left up Crescent Drive instead of right toward the island park. On Mountain Crescent John said, "This is a blind street isn't it?"

Miss Willis looked at him in surprise. "Why, no," she said. "This goes right through now to Lakeview Boulevard —that's the new street they're building. Why Mr. Bilbeau's new house is right around the curve."

"Oh no!" Mary had leaned forward from the rear seat, looking ahead between John and Miss Willis. What had been a dirt road, petering out just opposite Angus's place, was paved now and swept smoothly around to the right to disappear behind the trees. Workmen were busy on a new sidewalk. Angus's garage had disappeared and an ugly gash had been cut into the slope going up to his house. Just beyond the red roof of the Macdonald house was a freshly painted green roof-peak.

As they swung around there was a fresh shock for them. The hog-back ridge where Mary had stood with John and Angus on her first day in West Kirby was half blasted away, the remainder standing stark and raw above the road. In the place of jack pine, birch and the old tangle of brush stood telephone poles. The little gully was filled with gravel from the road grade: sun and lake glared through nakedly.

"There's Mr. Bilbeau's new house," Miss Willis pointed

to a new brick building an easy stone's throw north of Angus's place, "isn't it nice?"

"Oh John., it's cruel!" said Mary.

Miss Willis looked back sharply at her.

"She means the way they've messed up Angus's private corner of the island," John explained. "I remember when you could look up this way from the lake and it looked just as it must have looked to the Indians before Columbus."

"And fit for nothing but Indians, too, if you ask me," Miss Willis snorted. "Why Mr. Macdonald ever chose a place like that to build a house, away from everyone else —" her profile was rigid with disapproval. "Of course his frame house will have to be torn down before long: I understand they are putting through building regulations that specify nothing but brick buildings in this section."

"But they can't make him tear down the house he's living in. That's ridiculous!" Mary's voice was angry. John looked back quickly and hardly knew her profile—the warm curve of her lips bitten white and tense, angry tears trembling in her eyes.

"No, they can't do that," said Miss Willis sharply. "But when people find that the value of their land is being impaired by its neighbourhood to an old frame house, on land that is still clutttered up with bush and rock—" she broke off suggestively.

Mary said nothing more for the rest of the trip.

John was due for another surprise when the picnic supper was over and the children were dismissed from the open-air table to play on the swings and slides.

Laura was presented with an end-table as a combined

farewell and wedding gift from the staff. She made a pleasant speech, spoke of her happy associations with West Kirby, added a few more conventional comments before sitting down.

Then, at a nod from Bilbeau, Klein stood up.

"It will come as a shock to some of you," he said slowly, "as it came to me, to learn that we are losing a younger member of our male staff who has, in a quiet unassuming sort of way, won the respect, and I think I may say, affection of a good many of us."

John's heart unaccountably began to beat faster, as though he knew the name Klein was coming to would be his own.

"He is leaving us, like Mr. Judd a year ago, to serve his country. Mr. Judd chose the sea. Mr. Husson has chosen the air."

There was a sudden stir along the table, quick curious glances towards the Hussons. Husson was pale, his little mouth compressed.

"We shall miss Mr. Husson," Klein paused as though he had suddenly lost his breath. John realized that he was moved. "Men like him, who say little and think much, who quietly and conscientiously perform the sometimes tedious tasks of a teacher with no thought of any reward except the consciousness of a job well done, are all too rare in our profession.

"In token of our—affection, we ask him and his wife to accept this parting gift."

Green came forward with a bulky round parcel wrapped in tissue paper. Husson took it in unsteady hands, swallowing, clutching the parcel as though it contained some inner virtue that would restore his self-control.

"Open it!" said someone.

It was a table lamp. Husson looked at it again.

"Thank you for the table lamp. We needed one." He took a deep breath.

"It is difficult to say what a person should say, on an occasion such as this." For a moment he looked as though he would faint.

"I have been thinking a lot about—teaching, as a job, these past months. So much has been said that anything I add is likely to be trite—or tripe.

"But I won't have many chances to talk to teachers about teaching in the future. Maybe you'll overlook it if I put in my nickel's worth now.

"People look down on teachers." John thought, it's true.

"When these same people went to school they were taught to look up to their teachers, to respect them. It seems to me that *that* kind of respect is just a polite word for fear. Real respect comes from inside a person as a reaction to qualities in another that we recognize not by what he says, but by what he is and does. And so when these people grow up they react to the first artificial respect, and replace it with a real contempt.

"We ask a boy to address us as 'Sir'. Why? To teach him manners. But do we teach him real manners or just a poor surface imitation? For real manners don't come from fear of what others will think of us if we are rude; real manners come from a desire to look at things from another person's point of view. To teach him to say 'Sir' does not touch the problem. It does worse, it tends to hide the real problem.

"That, I have begun to think, is the chief weakness of teachers. We are problem dodgers. Perhaps I am dodging a problem now by leaving this school and joining the air force. We are faced with the most difficult and important problem that mankind has to face: how to teach the next generation to think for itself. And we are not encouraged to face the problem. We are given a specified dose of facts to cram into our classes in a specified time. We are surrounded with a hundred chores which have little or nothing to do with our real job. We are faced with youngsters who don't want to think and parents who all want their children to get university degrees whether it will make them happier or not.

"But I don't think that is our real problem. Our real problem is ourselves. We live in fear so we rule by fear.

"When I first succeeded in rousing fear in a student I was proud of myself. I have learned since then to put fear into a class of thirty by standing perfectly still and raising one eyebrow. But when I realize how fear has stunted my own life, when I look around and see how it has stunted the lives of others, and when I read in the papers of thousands of naked corpses stacked for burial in a pit outside a European concentration camp, I am ashamed—and afraid of what fear can do.

"Fear is not the way to rule. It's a vicious way to rule. We've *got* to find a better one. Maybe it's love—I don't know.

"I suppose you might call this a sermon, and I know I'm not qualified to preach one. But if there's anything in what I've said, it comes out of what I've learned by experience.

"Mrs. Husson and I will miss a lot of you. And we're going to miss the lake.

"Thanks again—for the table lamp—and thanks from Mrs. Husson too."

Mr. Bilbeau closed the meeting with a few appropriate remarks, his face grave, impassive—and perhaps a little tired.

Driving home again Miss Willis commented, "That was the queerest speech I ever heard in my life. What was he driving at?"

Mary said, "It's nice to hear someone tell the truth for a change."

John was silent. Within him a cold finger was touching his heart. He felt sick, trying to forget a casual chat he once had had in his classroom with Mr. Bilbeau one spare period.

Early in July the Westleys had a letter from Mary's sister, Sylvia. During the previous winter she had married a young doctor in the Medical Corps. He had gone overseas in June leaving the car with Sylvia. How would they like her to drive up to West Kirby and bring them down to Toronto for a visit? Dad Miller was head over heels in work, Clara had a war job, and little Donna had entered nursing. There was no chance of the family coming up to West Kirby.

So the Westleys went away for the summer.

In Toronto one morning, Charles was excited to find a different kind of prepared cereal on the breakfast table. On the box was a picture of Niagara Falls. When Dad Miller explained to him that the Falls were real and could actually be seen he was all for jumping on his tricycle and going there.

John explained that it was nearly a hundred miles away. So Sylvia suggested they borrow her car and drive down for the day. The Westleys jumped at the idea.

An hour later Marilyn was in her play pen, her schedule for the day pinned up over the kitchen sink, Sylvia and Mom Miller having promised to observe it faithfully. Charles was dressed in his best, a picnic lunch was ready, and away they went.

Mary was in high spirits. She had changed her hair-do that week, bunching it up on top of her head in the new style. John had discovered a fascinating spot to kiss her; the nape of her neck, where a few wisps of fine hair always escaped the upward sweep of the comb, giving a more delicately feminine air to the head that made him feel he was kissing a strange woman.

John at the wheel drove carefully—he had scarcely touched a wheel since their summer at Wasaga Beach. Mary laughed.

"John, you're driving like an old school teacher."

He drove on carefully, ignoring her banter, till they reached the end of Bloor Street and the open highway.

Down went the throttle and away went the Westleys.

The car was new, the tank was full of gas, the sun shone cheerfully behind, and the smooth highway rolled out before them. The indicator crawled steadily up: fifty, fifty-five, sixty, as the tires whined shrilly on the pavement and the windshield ripped through the air.

Sixty-two—"All right," said Mary. "I take it all back—there's a speed limit, you know."

John glimpsed a motorcycle behind and slowed quickly to a staid forty miles an hour. The motorcycle roared past —just a boy and a girl out for the day, dusty, goggled and helmeted, the girl behind grinning briefly into the car as they went by.

The heat shimmered over the hot pavement ahead. Along

the surface of the rises John noticed again the slivers of silver that had always puzzled him. Reflections? Refractions? Maybe diffraction. He thought with a sudden pang of Angus. Angus would have had a theory and they would have argued about it, Angus ruthlessly adding up examples and instances, explaining exceptions with inescapable logic, till the theory was proved to the hilt. Oh well, West Kirby lay a hundred miles away to the north-west. To heck with the school!

They stopped at Clappison's Corners for a milk-shake, went through the blistering summer heat of Hamilton without a pause, and swung east into the Niagara fruit belt, heading for the Falls.

"What's a fruit belt?" asked Charles.

"A fruit belt?" repeated Mary. "Well, it's made of braided apple and pear peel, studded with big purple grapes."

Charles's eyes widened with amazement, then he smiled. "Aw, you're just makin' that up."

"Making, not makin'", corrected John, and explained gravely what a fruit belt was.

"I like Mummy's fruit belt better," Charles decided, and Mary gave him a squeeze.

One by one the orchard-bordered miles moved up to meet them and fell away behind.

Charles wanted to know where all the water was going to, and looked at it earnestly when John told him that very likely some of that water had come out of their tap at home in West Kirby, describing the journey it took from the Westley drain to the brink of the Falls.

"I don't think I recognize any of it." said little Charles

seriously. He was puzzled when they laughed; then deciding he had said something clever, laughed too.

They ate their lunch in the park, John talking learnedly of the Niagara escarpment with its cap of hard dolomite that kept the Falls vertical. Charles couldn't understand how the Falls were moving backward when they were so obviously going forward.

In the afternoon they drove along the gorge through Queenston and over through St. Catharines down to Port Dalhousie. John dutifully described to Charles the events of the War of 1812-14 as well as he could remember them: Laura Secord driving her cow before her through the American lines to warn the British, Brock dying gallantly on Queenston Heights. Mary flippantly explained that the Americans had tried to climb the monument at Queenston but Brock had got up first and pushed them all off until one of them bet him ten dollars he was afraid to jump off. Brock won the bet but was in no condition to collect.

John was not amused. "Mary, what do you want to mix him up like that for?"

Charles was frowning with concentrated thought. "Daddy, where were the Canadians when the British was fightin' the Murricans?"

Mary doubled up over John's attempt to explain that the Canadians were really British then because Canada wasn't a country; but that now Canadians were really Canadians they were still British. By the time he had finished Charles's mind was elsewhere.

Crossing the canal that morning there had been no ships in the locks. John proposed that they drive up through Merritton, Thorold, and Welland to Port Colborne, and maybe they would see the locks in action. At Welland a boat was going through and Charles's eyes snapped with excitement when he saw the bridge lift before his eyes.

"It's folding up all by itself!" he exclaimed unbelievingly.

At Port Colborne John looked at his road map. "Let's go back by Number Three, see, it joins up with Six at Hagersville."

Charles was suddenly sleepy: they wedged him in the back seat and soon he had dropped off into slumber.

"How's the gas?" asked Mary. "We ought to fill up the tank before we get back; it's the least we can do for the use of the car."

They were approaching a small village with a gas station. John slowed down. There was no pop-stand so they drove on, watching for the combination.

Out in the country again they were just passing a lonely gas station when Mary gave a little squeal of surprise.

"John, stop the car, and go back."

"What for? It's nothing but a one-pump station."

Mary insisted, and John complied, grumblingly.

It was an old blacksmith shop with one gasoline pump and a freshly painted sign. Mary pointed to it.

It read GEO. BILBEAU, PROP.

"John," Mary was excited, "do you think it might be a relation? Just get a couple of gallons, I'd like to talk to George."

Instead of George a big middle-aged woman came out. She filled the tank with the ease of long practice.

"Is Mr. Bilbeau around?" asked Mary. John nudged her to forget about it, but she ignored him.

"No, he ain't here today. Gone in to town with the truck, should be back soon."

"You don't happen to know if there are any other Bilbeaus living near here, do you?"

"No. Used to be a family down by the lake at—" she named a village neither of them had heard of. "The old man was a dentist—George's uncle—had a son taught school for a while there."

"What was his name?"

John listened, interested in spite of himself.

"'Curly', we called him. I went to school with him for a couple of years. I don't know what his real name was —the kids used to call him 'Curly' on account of his nice curly hair. He had a lot of it. But he was a kind of a spoiled kid—" she broke off suspiciously. "Was you related?"

"Oh no," said Mary, "we knew a Bilbeau up north, and it's such an unusual name."

John said, "We'd better get going, Mary." The way women poke their noses into things, he thought.

"What was the father's name?" asked Mary.

"Doctor—let me think—I remember just the way his shingle looked. He had his office in a old house right next to the post office—'J. G. Bilbeau, Dentist'—that's the way it read. He died away back before Curly got his entrance, I remember the funeral. People liked old Dr. Bilbeau—he sure could fix teeth. But he used to drink a lot—I guess he was a kinda bum in a way, though he sure could fix teeth. Curly was a mean kid. His maw spoiled him, I guess, and his sisters too. Never did a real day's work in his life."

John paid her for the gas and got back in the car; put his foot on the clutch and reached for the gear shift. But Mrs. Bilbeau craved company. She rested her arms on the window-sill and put her head in the open window, one oil-smudged finger transferring the smudge to the side of her nose as she rubbed it, and pushed away a wisp of hair.

"Never figured out where they got the money to put him through Normal. His Ma sure must of scraped some. George and me moved out to a farm near here after we got married, but we used to see them once in a while. Only, Curly was pretty stuck up once he got to teaching."

"What did he look like?" asked Mary.

"Quite a good size—medium-like for weight—I'd say. But I never seen much of him after we growed up. It was a mean trick he played on his sisters, though."

John put the gear shift back into neutral, released the clutch. He nudged Mary again.

"The old lady died—left him maybe a thousand dollars, and he was supposed to share up. Not Curly. The oldest girl was going out with a young fellow called Bill Oakes— his family had a farm out our way—and he told her the old lady wouldn't have stood for it, so she didn't get a cent. I don't know how he talked his way out of giving the other sister hers, but anyways he walked out one summer with the whole caboodle and he ain't been seen around since. Some say he's holdin' down a big job in the States."

John impatiently raced the motor and said, "That's very interesting, but I don't think there's any connection with the Bilbeau we know."

Mrs. George Bilbeau could take a hint. "I guess likely he wouldn't own up to knowin' Curly if he was a relative," she said, and smiled her farewell as the car crept forward.

Out on the highway Mary was still excited. "John, J. C. and 'Curly' are one and the same person—I know it!"

"Nuts!" said John. "In the first place it's a most unlikely coincidence, in the second place J. C. is bald as an egg."

"He didn't have to be bald then. And didn't J. C. come from somewhere along the Lake Erie shore? John, it all fits in so perfectly."

John answered Mary irritably. "The way you let your imagination run away with you!" he scoffed.

Mary said thoughtfully, "The only thing that makes me wonder about it is that it all fits so perfectly—almost too perfectly."

John drove on in resentful silence trying to forget the story of 'Curly', the mean kid who taught school in the village for a while and then ran off to the States with his sisters' share of the money.

An ancient Ford truck came down the road. As it passed, John started, almost called out. He could have sworn he had seen the broad snub nose and sour face of Bert Willoughby, the school engineer. But Bert, he knew, was a training sergeant now at Camp Borden. This man had looked more like a farmer.

Just a coincidence.

He felt better.

That's what the whole business was. Pure coincidence.

31

The Westleys were back in West Kirby three weeks before school opened. Everyone seemed out of town, even the Rushes, who had taken their holidays in August this year. John weeded the garden, worked lethargically on a new set of lesson assignments, slept a lot. Occasionally he and Mary would take in a show or go over by trolley to the island beach and laze in the sun, though it embarrassed John to see his female students so scantily clad, and the beach seemed always crowded with them.

Elsie Braund surprised them by coming over one evening. Elsie's dramatic talents lay in fallow; her life was confused. On leaving school at the end of the fifth year she had gone back to the farm to help out. Her father's back had been crushed by a falling tree, fracturing two vertebrae, and he had been in a cast for six months. When he was able to take over completely again Elsie went to Normal School in London, but at Christmas time gave it up. She hated the very idea of teaching. So she clerked in a store for three months, then came back to West Kirby. Now she was working days in the packaging room of the mill at Old Kirby, taking typing and shorthand at night school, living with her aunt.

In spite of having lost some weight, she was no better looking than she had been. Only when she forgot herself, describing some incident that involved her emotionally, did John catch a glimpse of the vivid personality of her hands and gestures that had so impressed him earlier. Her dramatic experience had given her poise, which remained even in her frequent moods of depression; but there was little charm.

A week before school opened Angus came back to town and dropped in on a Sunday evening. He had been in Ottawa again, but where formerly he had gone into detail about the nature of his work he merely dismissed it with a shrug as routine. No, it was not really research, he replied to John's probing, and left it at that.

There had always been a nervous tension to Angus's

movements, but it never had been so obvious as now. It seemed impossible for him to relax. He had begun smoking cigarettes lately, rolling his own; taking the finely shredded tobacco out of a worn leather pouch, laying it deftly along a fold of paper, rolling paper and tobacco together with quick nervous fingers, putting his tongue to the gummed edge and producing a miraculously smooth, round cigarette. As he made the cigarette he gave a little dissertation on the kinds and quality of different cigarette papers—which kind was preferred by the experienced bushman and why; but it was plain his mind was not on what he was saying.

He wore his glasses habitually now, where once he had spurned them as unnecessary, having claimed that his summers up north compensated for the eyestrain of teaching. He had, too, a favourite theory of eye exercises: eye trouble was nearly always the result of a habitual focusing distance; if you varied the distance, no eye trouble. But now, when he took his glasses off, the eyes had that weak look one saw in others who wore glasses constantly. The eyes shifted constantly from place to place with an almost haunted look, as if they betrayed an inner spirit constantly seeking rest and never finding it. Only when they rested on Mary was there a second's relaxation, and a ghost of the old twinkle.

Not that Angus's humour was gone. But it was sharper, more cynical, lacking the easy tolerance that had once taken the sting out of his sharpest thrusts.

His hair, once almost black, had greyed since John first knew him, especially in this past year. The skin of his face seemed thinner, taut around the mouth and eyes—revealing more clearly the neat skull, suggesting age along the jaw line and under the ears.

Apart from a few post cards promising longer messages, and her annual Christmas cards, neither Angus nor the Westleys had received a real letter from Dot Young. She was in New York taking classes at the Students' Art League, doing etchings and lithographs on the side for a living. She didn't like New York but she wanted desperately to learn how to paint. One postcard complained that she was completely at sea in her painting, another that there were as many little people among the artists she had met as there were in West Kirby.

"How old is Dot's mother?" Mary wondered.

"Nearly ninety—so Dot may have another thirty years to go."

"We've met her mother," said Mary, "and we've often wondered that Dot should leave her when she's so old."

"You didn't know that she never got along particularly well with her mother?"

"No," said John. "Though we were surprised she wasn't down at the station the night Dot left."

"Dot's leaving was no particular hardship for Mrs. Young," Angus told them. "She has her boon companion, Miss Keyworth, some fifteen years younger. Miss Keyworth has been living with them ever since I can remember, and the few glimpses I've had gave me the impression there was never much love lost between Dot and the other two."

"Do you think she'll ever come back?" asked Mary.

"Each spring when the willows are red in the swamp I get the feeling she might turn up," said Angus. "But Dot has always been unpredictable."

The conversation ended, as it always did in those days, with a discussion of the war. Angus was as sardonic as ever when the topic came up.

"The Atlantic Charter," he said bitterly. "Freedom for all. It reminds me of that American campaign slogan back in the early thirties, 'Two chickens in every pot.' The four freedoms on paper. Well," he conceded, "I suppose it's something to have them down in black and white. The trouble is that some of our statesmen think we still live back in the eighteenth century when the idea of the rights of man meant something.

"It means something to the enslaved people of Europe," said John.

Angus looked wearily over at him. "Who isn't a slave? I suppose," he said, almost as if arguing with himself, "a man is free when he is surrounded by his native culture, and a slave when an alien culture takes its place. What you would call him when there is no culture—" he broke off apologetically and smiled something like his old smile.

Marilyn was eating her meals in the high chair now but had developed the habit of poking. When John, who sat next to her, tried to put a spoonful of food in her mouth she would resolutely shut it, but the minute he gave up and turned to his own meal she would smile gleefully and let out squeals of triumph and defiance. At first everyone laughed, it was such a cunning thing in a baby; until finally the habit was firmly fixed. On one occasion she was two hours over a dish of Pablum.

Mary and John tried all the tricks they knew. John would pretend the spoon was an aeroplane and make it z-z-z-z through the air to dive into her upturned open mouth.

When she realized this was a trick they would try diverting her attention. "Look at the birdie!" they would call, and while she was looking, with her little lower lip hanging down, John would pop another spoonful in. Then she discovered this was a trick too, and each time it happened would howl with disappointment. So they would put her in the next room to eat by herself, until she ended that by picking up spoonfuls of Pablum and throwing them generously in all directions.

Spankings and bribes were of no avail. They tried meagre helpings and special combinations. Each trick worked for a while and then had to be abandoned. "If this keeps up," John complained, "I'm going to have to give up teaching."

Back at school there was the usual scurrying around to get the season's activities under way, made all the busier by the extra activities of war, and the increased registration in the Lower School. Both Laura Ayres and Husson were replaced, and the timetable, designed for four first year classes, had to be revamped to look after the needs of five. Audubon complained that his timetable had been ruined, pointing out to John that although he was head of the department he had no Upper School Latin.

John laughed it off. His own timetable was almost ideal: six spares a week, no English, and full control over the public speaking course which he had shared originally with Judd, and during the last year with Laura. The new art teacher, who had some experience with dramatics, would, Bilbeau explained, work under him in that department. So in a sense he could say he was head of two departments, even though they weren't recognized as such officially.

During the summer a little idea of someone's had been put into effect: up the centre of all the stairs ran a series of wooden strips, three inches high, firmly screwed to each lift. These were painted a bright orange, and students were instructed to keep to the right of them hereafter when going up and down stairs.

The idea worked admirably in the new building, but in the old there was trouble. The stairs were narrower, the stairways darker. In the first week of school three first year students had falls, having tripped on the lifts. J. C. warned the school of the hazard in assembly, and for a time there were only minor stumbles.

But in October a senior girl fell down a whole flight of stairs, cracked her head on the radiator on the landing, and was rushed to the hospital.

A special staff meeting was called by the principal at which he appointed three teachers to stand at the foot, landing, and head, respectively, of the south stairs in the old building. "The idea is sound enough," Mr. Bilbeau declared. "Unfortunately, there are always a few thoughtless students who ignore regulations and bring trouble on themselves."

Klein asked whether it wouldn't have been much simpler in the first place merely to have painted the strip. Mr. Bilbeau thought not: he firmly believed the wooden obstacle much more effective in preventing students from crossing over.

Miss Willis mentioned the worn condition of the stairs in the old school. "I have gone into the matter," said Mr. Bilbeau, "and the cost of replacing them for these war years, when we are straining every nerve to win the victory, was prohibitive."

Unreasonably, students kept falling. Bilbeau explained in auditorium that it couldn't possibly happen unless students disobeyed regulations and crossed over to the wrong side.

Then Miss Collier fell downstairs. She was in bed for a week with six stitches in her scalp and a bad dose of shock.

The staff was indignant. It was bad enough when students fell downstairs; but that a teacher should be victimized put the thing in a totally different light. Even John felt that J. C. ought to do something.

At the next regular staff meeting Klein, who taught downstairs in the old building, brought up the subject.

"Mr. Bilbeau," said Klein in his even casual voice, "a number of us who teach in the old building have been wondering whether something cannot be done about the markers on the stairs."

Bilbeau looked up belligerently. "I do not believe the topic is on the agenda for this meeting."

"It should be," said Klein bluntly, but without raising his voice. "After all a member of the staff fell on those stairs only last week."

"The regulations cover the matter adequately, I believe," said Bilbeau. "Now in the matter of—"

Klein's voice came through again, in the same tempo and the same key. "I think, Mr. Bilbeau, we should have an answer to the question."

Mr. Bilbeau took a deep breath; then smiled. "I agree with you Mr. Klein, would someone make a motion to that effect?"

Audubon moved, Klein seconded, that the Board be requested to take immediate action in removing the markers from the stairs of the old building.

"Is there any discussion?" asked the principal.

John felt he should say something. "I think," he said, "if the Board member who thought of the markers in the first place would teach in the old building for a couple of days he'd be the first to have them removed."

There were a few quickly suppressed smiles and quick glances at the principal. Bilbeau was calm as ice. A cold shiver ran down John's spine. My God, he thought, it must really have been J. C.'s idea!

"You have heard the motion. All in favour?"

John thought, I've put my foot in it now. I might as well go through with it, and raised his hand slowly. Klein, Angus, and Audubon raised theirs. No one else. John glanced uneasily at Bilbeau.

"Apparently," said J. C. without asking for a show of hands opposing the motion, "a majority of the staff has complete confidence in my policy on the matter. One final word on the question of the stairs. I have already requested the Board to have the strips in question removed. Having done so I feel that we are amply protected in the matter."

Angus protested: "But Mr. Bilbeau, the students themselves—"

"Mr. Macdonald, there are a number of important items on the agenda. If you have anything further to discuss perhaps you could spare a few minutes with me after the meeting." He picked up a sheet from the table and looked calmly at it. "In regard to the menace of gum-chewing—" he proceeded with the agenda as planned.

That fall little Charles Westley entered kindergarten. To Mary's distress he was rather shy about it all. When she took him in the morning he clung to her sobbing bitterly

402

and saying, "Don't let me stay here, Mummy, I'm going to be late." It took all her tact to solve the situation and at the first opportunity she told John about it indignantly. Thereafter meals were sharp on time, and Marilyn now ate her food with tolerable promptness.

But the kindergarten teacher at Queen Mary School was an exceptionally gifted woman, and Charles soon settled down to a happy new life.

When John began going to school again Marilyn's eating habits took a turn for the worse. At noon, particularly, they had trouble with her. Formerly John had made a practice of leaving for school before one o'clock, but now he found himself so absorbed in getting Marilyn to eat that before he knew it it was five or ten past one. Jumping up, he would throw himself into his coat and out the door with a hasty peck at Mary and go striding down the street, buttoning his coat as he went.

Mary found it amusing and began calling him Dagwood.

It was not so amusing for John one afternoon two or three weeks after the staff meeting at which he had spoken out of turn. For the third time that week he had reached school after one-fifteen, which strictly speaking, was the designated hour for teachers to be back in the afternoon. John dashed into the front door of the old building, up the steps, and almost knocked down Mr. Bilbeau who was standing with arms folded at the top.

"Excuse me!" exclaimed John, in confusion, and went hurriedly on.

"Mr. Westley." Bilbeau's voice from behind. John stopped and turned. Mr. Bilbeau came up. "I wonder if you would come into the office at four o'clock?" John's heart sank. Something was wrong. J. C.'s voice was cold.

"Yes, Mr. Bilbeau," and John went on up to his room. At four Bilbeau was waiting for him.

"Close that door please." John shut it after him.

"Now will you sit down." John sat.

"I have called you in, Mr. Westley,"—Mr. Westley thought bitterly, you'd think he had never called me John,—"on the matter of punctuality. Have you any good reason to offer for your habitual lateness?"

John stammered: "I—I haven't been late so often. And besides, I'm not the only one."

"Perhaps not," admitted J. C., "but does that make your offence any the less?"

John was silent.

"How," asked Mr. Bilbeau, "can I expect students to be punctual when they see teachers arriving at all hours?"

John nibbled painfully at his lower lip, his eyes fixed on a mole which he noticed for the first time in Mr. Bilbeau's shaggy right—no it was his left—eyebrow. He felt sick with humiliation. Mr. Bilbeau's cold blue eyes bored into John's as he paused for his words to sink in.

"There is another matter I should like to discuss with you, Mr. Westley."

John's eyes dilated in new alarm. What else was there? But he knew.

"I should like to know now, once and for all, where you stand."

John said weakly, "I don't understand—"

"Mr. Westley, until recently I had regarded you as one of the most loyal members of my staff. There are certain persons, who, for reasons known best to themselves, seem to harbour a personal animosity towards their principal. One of those members has been replaced"—John thought of

404

Husson at the staff picnic saying 'Fear is a vicious way to rule'—"others may find themselves in an insecure position."

"But Mr. Bilbeau, I have always backed you up—I've even—"

"Nevertheless," said Bilbeau coldly, "the fact remains that by the act of listening you have encouraged some of these persons in acts of disloyalty. You have revealed your own discontent by applying for a position in another school —in spite of the Board's generosity to you when I was acting principal, and at a recent staff meeting you openly associated yourself with those who question my judgment.

"Mr. Westley, I repeat, where do you stand?"

"Mr. Bilbeau, I tried to tell you," said John earnestly. "I've often stuck up for you when some of the others criticized your policies."

Bilbeau waited.

"Well, as far as applying for another job is concerned, I didn't really want to. It was my—" he broke off. No, he couldn't blame it on Mary. "Anyway, if I had really put my heart into it I could have landed one of those jobs."

Bilbeau kept his silence.

"And the meeting—I honestly didn't know it was your idea—those strips on the stairs, I mean; and then it was too late."

"Mr. Westley, I should like to give you a further word of warning. There is one member of the staff with whom, as everyone knows, you have been exceedingly thick. For that person I have the greatest admiration as you know. and in spite of his unfortunate attitude to me I have given him perhaps more than his share of prominence in the school organization. If you know me, John, you know that

I go out of my way to be fair." Just when the change had taken place John didn't quite know, but a great weight was lifted from his heart when he heard his first name again. "I shall continue to be absolutely just, no matter what my personal feelings may be. The school organization needs the person to whom I am referring, needs his great abilities. But," and here Mr. Bilbeau thrust out his belligerent under-lip, "this unfortunate attitude of his is spreading. I am well aware of what goes on within this school—and by your very association with him you encourage—"

"Oh," broke in John, "I see very little of him now. You see we quarreled over the practical science course—" Bilbeau was watching him intently—"and it's never been the same since. Mr. Mac—"

"We are mentioning no names," interrupted the principal sharply.

"Well, we aren't real friends any more," John concluded.

"For his sake, I regret very much to hear that. But you are wise, John, very wise. Let me warn you: it is very, very easy for a man to manoeuvre himself into a false position. I confess that I have misunderstood your actions and your motives. You understand, John, that I have done this for your own good, and the good of the school we serve. After all, education is a bigger thing than any one of us. It is a great privilege to be a teacher, and a great responsibility. Now that we understand each other perfectly I shall expect even greater co-operation from you in the future than you have shown in the past. I promise you the little matter of lateness will not come up again."

He rose and went to the door with his subordinate. In parting he laid a friendly hand on John's shoulder, the sun of his smile beamed full and clear from a cloudless sky, as he added: "But try to be punctual, John, try to be punctual."

As John passed Angus's room, his erstwhile friend standing in the doorway gave him a friendly nod. John averted his eyes, pretending not to have noticed, a deep blush hanging heavily on his face. Within him a little voice said mockingly, "Hi, Judas!"

John clutched the windpipe of the little voice and savagely tore it apart.

There was one way John could show J. C. that he was loyal, without troubling his own conscience: he firmly resolved never to be late again.

So much so, that leaving on time came to be an obsession. As the hour drew near the tension grew greater. If Mary's morning work had delayed dinner, John would make semi-sarcastic remarks: "Let me help you, dear," or "Let's just have a bowl of soup, and eat tonight."

Marilyn's poking at meals became, if anything, worse. At one o'clock John would blow up: "There, you've made Daddy late again!" he would shout at her, and leave the house in a turmoil, with Charles, whom he had taught to champion his little sister, pounding his father's buttocks in a rage, Marilyn howling, and Mary saying heatedly, "It's a pity you have to take out your feelings on Marilyn!"

Even Charles was becoming difficult at meal time. He would get into a panic in the middle of a meal and gulp his food. "What's the matter with you, Charles?"—"I'm going to be late," Charles would say, with fear in his eyes. "Late for what?" Mary would ask, and he would repeat fearfully, "Late like Daddy!"

Mary stood it as long as she could. At last when the situation began to repeat itself at the supper table she reached the end of her patience.

One evening after putting the children in bed she came into the living room where John was reading the paper, and said quietly, "John, let's have this thing out."

"What thing?" said John irritably, hiding behind the paper.

"John."

He lowered the paper and looked across at her. She was sitting on the one armless chair in the room, tensely.

"Well?" he said, having resolved to say nothing about the interview with J. C.

"You know what's on my mind, John."

"Well, is it my fault if Marilyn pokes with her meals?" he asked bitterly.

"That's not quite the point, is it John?"

"So what is?" John thrust out his underlip, and quickly pulled it in again. Why had he made that gesture?

"This mania of yours for getting to school on time. You didn't used to make a scene over a few minutes' delay."

"Marilyn didn't used to poke either."

"Marilyn's behaviour is beside the point. She's a baby, you're her father."

John thought desperately, if I don't stop her she'll probe it out of me.

"I thought you told me once I was a baby," he said harshly.

Mary looked at him, pain in her eyes.

Resentment burned in John. He thought to himself, take it easy, and ignored his own advice. "Okeh!" he said, "what are you going to do about it?" and hated himself for the words.

Mary said, "John, there's nothing I can do about it. You're the only one now who can save us." Her lips trembled slightly, and John thought with grim satisfaction, you can be the first to cry this time.

Aloud he said, "Mary, I don't think you're very considerate of me. If you knew the strain I was under at school —teaching isn't just sitting with your feet up on the desk asking kids questions, you know."

"Isn't it?" asked Mary, dully. "Let's forget I said anything," and she walked out of the room.

John put down his paper to follow her, but changed his mind. After all, she said he was a baby—he'd show her who was the stronger of the two! He picked up his paper again and stared at the editorials without reading. He forced himself to glance over the captions. "Japanese War Scare a Hoax", he read. Impatiently he turned to the second last page and buried himself in the comics.

32

On John's first day of the new school year Bilbeau had taken him aside and reminded him of his promise to take a regular Sunday School class at All Saints. John had no memory of such a promise, but a glance at J. C. was enough to engage his consent. After all he couldn't afford to antagonize his own principal.

Mary was furious. "Haven't you got a mind of your own?" she asked. "Or did you really want to teach six days a week?"

"Of course I don't want to, but he practically forced me into it—it's all very well for you to talk, but the way he put it up to me I hadn't any choice."

"What kind of a man is he?" asked Mary. "It has nothing to do with your job. What business is it of his?"

"Well, it's only an hour, after all, and it's in a good cause."

"John, it's one more thing between us. We've got to stop building this wall. John—it's getting so we can just see each other over the top as it is."

John was sulky. "Mary, why do you always have to dramatize things?" He suddenly had an idea. "Listen, why don't you come along too? They need teachers—J. C. asked me why you didn't teach Sunday School one time—"

"So he could add me to his harem of admiring female teachers? No, thank you."

"But Vera teaches there, maybe we could talk Angus—"

Mary broke into her old laugh, mingled with a little of her new bitterness. "Angus!" She laughed again.

"Darling, *you* may be an honest pragmatist who can teach things he doesn't really believe because of the good it will do, but I'm not. I've got to stand on my principles or I've nothing left to stand on. And I will *not* be a hypocrite. I don't believe in the virgin birth, and I think the miracles are myths, or examples of skilful psychotherapy. And I wouldn't last two lessons in Bilbeau's Sunday School. Jesus was at loggerheads with the religious institutions of his time, and when he went to church they threw him out. I don't believe Jesus was God, but I do believe he was a

Man, and if we had only had a few real men in the world today the mess we are in would have been impossible. You run along to Sunday School if you have to, but don't ask me to go with you."

At Sunday School it was as if the Lord had rewarded John for his virtue. Teaching in the class next to his was a girl he had never seen before, a girl who quickened his pulse the minute she looked up and smiled as John reached his class. He tried to smile back, and sat down in confusion.

Thereafter he stole glances in her direction whenever he could.

She wasn't really good-looking, except that the colour of her skin was full and rich, her brown hair soft and abundant. Her face was wide, her figure almost plump, but a yielding, feminine kind of plumpness. She's like an apple, John thought, the luscious kind of apple that makes you want to bite, deep into the core, the minute you see it on the shelf.

Her name, he learned, was Lillian.

Thereafter Sunday School became the highlight of John's week. Polishing his shoes John would hum little snatches of music, to Mary's amusement.

"John," she said one Sunday, "who's the good-looking Sunday School teacher?" He blushed crimson over his shining black shoes, thanking his stars she hadn't asked him at the dinner table.

Early in October it was the custom of the Sunday School teachers to have a hike and a wiener roast. To fill the male vacuum those who felt so inclined could invite their boy friends. The few older women stayed away: by common consent it was a young people's affair.

"Didn't they invite me, too?" asked Mary when he told

her of the outing. John fought back the blush and said as casually as he could that only the girls were asking boys. He was the only married man apart from a couple of old fossils who ran the boys' Bible classes; he supposed they hadn't thought of it. He went on to explain further, but Mary just laughed.

"Don't worry sweetheart, my feelings aren't hurt." As he was leaving she added, smiling in that uncannily understanding way she had, "John, darling, have a good time. Remember," she added mischievously, "you're only young once!"

As he stood waiting for the bus he thought gratefully, my little woman is so darned understanding! He would have told her about Lillian only she would have laughed at him.

Yes, Lillian was there.

The party met at the church and took the bus out to the King Street corner. They would walk out to McAdams Falls, roast their wieners there and drive back: Mr. Bilbeau, Mr. Springett, the Rector, two wardens and a vestry man would drive out and get them at eleven. And also prevent any questionable gossip.

John found himself sitting beside the one creature he despised, Miss Hyacinth, a big dumpy girl whose only right to the name was maintained by a generous application of cheap perfume. Lillian was three seats ahead, with another girl, the friend that always tagged along. John's heart leaped with anticipation: she had no boy friend.

Assembled at the corner, there must have been over thirty in the crowd. Harry was there. John resented his presence, wondering how he had horned in on a teachers' party. Harry immediately took charge of proceedings, swinging his flashlight demonstratively, though it was not yet dark, and making well-worn witticisms about the moon. John moved up to where Lillian stood smiling beside her friend. She was dressed, daringly for such a party, in slacks, and a bright red jacket.

It was a crisp autumn night that invited brisk walking. The party moved down the road in twos and threes, Harry vociferously leading the way, occasionally rending the air with "Are you happy?" to which a few more boisterous spirits responded "Yeah!" Harry hit on the brilliant variation "Are you yappy?" which brought on a variety of yaps, howls, shrill whistles, and any other sound that would destroy the dark silence around them.

"It's a perfect night for a wiener roast," John said to Lillian, heartily cursing the tactlessness of the other girl. Why couldn't she have brought her own boy friend?

Lillian's laugh was as soft as her throat. "I just love a night like this!" she answered, looking at him sideways with a glance that made John's knees tremble.

As they talked John was plotting desperately as to ways and means of getting rid of Lillian's companion, who seemed determined to cling to her friend. As they neared the Falls he became more and more furious with her—there was simply nothing he could do.

It was Lillian who turned the trick. Stopping suddenly she said in a startled voice, "I've lost my purse."

"You didn't bring it with you," said her friend positively.

"Not the big one—I had a little change purse in this

pocket," and she touched a little pocket over her breast. "It was stupid of me—I'm always losing things out of it. Usually I pin it up."

The three of them stopped on the road. It was quite dark now. The moon was up, but behind the trees. In the distance they could hear the thresh of water falling by the old mill, and the voices of those ahead.

A couple came up suddenly, and quickly disengaged themselves. Lillian explained her loss to them. "I had it only a moment ago." The five began to retrace their steps slowly, straining their eyes in the darkness for the lost purse.

John felt a soft little hand in his own. "Quick, this way," breathed a voice, and she led him through a hole in the fence, across a little pasture, her hand warm in his. In the blackness of the woods they stopped and listened.

The friend's voice was calling "Lillian". Lillian stood close to John, still holding his hand and laughing softly. "They must have gone ahead," called another voice and faded into the night.

John took Lillian in his arms and kissed her soft mouth hungrily. "You're beautiful!" She melted into his embrace, warm and yielding, for a whole exquisite minute as he kissed her again. Then she tensed and pushed him away. "Not now," she whispered, "there's a short cut through here," and she took his hand, leading him along as if she knew the way blindfolded.

In a few breathless moments they were almost at the Falls. Through the trees they could see flashlights circling in the blackness, and hear the voices of the party. At the edge of the trees she turned to him for another clinging embrace. Her nose was cool and soft against John's burning cheek; her parted lips seemed almost to dissolve as he pressed his to her teeth. She drew away. He tried to pull her back, but she was gone, laughing, out to the road.

Someone caught her in the beam of a flashlight as she walked ahead. John dodged behind a bush and waited until the voices had disappeared. Out on the road he almost bumped into Lillian's friend. "Where's Lillian?" he asked her, congratulating himself on his quick wit.

Lillian's friend attached herself to him for the rest of the evening: Lillian laughing and munching her wieners on the other side of the fire, where Harry regaled them with snatches of mouth-organ harmony in between bites. Only half the couples seemed to be in the firelight.

Looking up from toasting a wiener he noticed Lillian had disappeared. The first chance he had John went up the path looking for her. The moon was higher, its cold light filtering through the path. John almost tripped over a couple sitting in the shadows and hastily withdrew. But already he had recognized their voices: Lillian's low laugh and the raucous adolescent voice of Harry.

John rode back in the Reverend Mr. Springett's car, crushed under the weight of a giggling Miss Hyacinth—one of the church wardens failed to show up and they were packed eight and nine in a car. But John's knees were not as numb as his self-esteem. Just a common little bitch, he kept telling himself, the subtle scent of her hair, the softness of her lips, the feel of that little warm hand, fading out before the stinging memory of those two laughs in the darkness.

Mary was reading in bed when he got home, wearing the silk nightgown he had given her two weeks before on her birthday.

As he turned out the light and got in beside her she asked him with a smile in her voice, "Did you brush your teeth tonight, darling?"

His only answer was to draw her savagely to him.

By this time John's reading choir was in as great demand as it had been in Donald Judd's time. John never felt at ease with his choir; his direction was awkward, and it took him three rehearsals to Donald's one to achieve comparable results. He lacked, too, Donald's power of invention. At first he had felt that his work was only a clumsy echo of Donald's. But memories were short, and it was the novelty that appealed to the public. John was beginning to share the general opinion that his work was just as good as Judd's had ever been.

Of late he had been losing interest in dramatics—assembly chorals and his choral group brought quicker results with less effort. And they gave him a new confidence in public. Formerly his public speaking had been hesitant and nervous. But when the Y.M.C.A. invited him to speak to a young business men's group on choral reading he found himself at ease. That had really been a smooth talk he had given. "Choral reading relates literature to life", he had said. Even Bilbeau couldn't have improved on that!

Frequent requests came in from city organizations which Bilbeau, to spare his star performer, usually turned down. But one request could not be ignored. The combined service clubs of the twin cities decided to raise war funds by organizing a super-concert, to run for one week at the Bijou

Theatre in Old Kirby. K.C.V.S. possessed a boy 'cellist of exceptional promise. W.K.C.I. had its choral reading group. Each was to provide a number: all other performers were 'names' from outside the city, real 'artists'. Tickets were to range from fifty cents to five dollars: the proceeds to be applied to the purchase of a bomber for the R.C.A.F. to be named after the twin cities.

The concert was billed for the week beginning November the twenty-third.

But even as he worked and worried over the concert a flush would come over his cheeks at the memory of those laughs.

On Sunday morning, the twenty-second, John woke up at three, a sharp pain in his stomach, his head reeling with nausea. By eight o'clock he had vomited five times. Then he slept till noon. There was still some pain but after he had a glass of milk, it disappeared.

Mary wanted to call a doctor.

"I'll be all right," said John, "it's just a bilious attack, maybe stomach flu."

He ate a little soup at noon. By nightfall he was back to normal.

Monday morning it happened all over again. Mary wanted him to stay in bed.

"But darling I can't—we're having our last rehearsal at noon—I've got to go."

That week was a nightmare. Each night John pulled himself together and went to the Bijou, somehow dragging himself through the performance. Each morning the nausea attacked him.

Finally on Wednesday afternoon at five Mary called in the doctor and John submitted to an examination.

"It's just overwork and nervous fatigue," he diagnosed. "But if you don't take it easy you're going to have real trouble."

After the concert Thursday night Angus, Mary, and Vera came backstage.

"It really was smooth tonight," said Mary.

Vera was enthusiastic. "Mr. Judd never did half as well with his choral group."

But Angus drew him aside. "Listen, John," he said, "you'd better take tomorrow off and have a good rest."

John said lightly—"Oh, I'm all right. I saw the doctor yesterday." He felt annoyed with Angus's manner—fussing around like an old hen.

"What did the doctor say?"

"Oh, he said I wasn't pregnant. He told me to come back in a week and he'd have another look at me."

Angus looked sharply at him without smiling, "You've had nausea?"

"Sure, every morning this week."

"You should have an x-ray," declared Angus.

The cold hand of fear clutched at John's heart. "You think it might be appendicitis?"

"I'm not a doctor," Angus reminded him, "but in your place I'd insist on an x-ray."

"That's what I told him," said Mary coming up, "but he's so stubborn."

On Saturday morning the attack was quite mild; Sunday morning at last he had complete respite. He spent the day in bed, reading, listening to the radio; Mary shooed the youngsters outdoors in the morning and Charles off to Sunday School in the afternoon. Except for a slight pain in his stomach John felt better than he had for weeks.

"You see," he told Mary, "all this fuss was over nothing at all. Tomorrow I'll be back to normal."

On the morrow he had the worst attack yet. Mary was white with worry. He needed no persuasion to stay in bed. The doctor told him to remain there, put him on a milk diet.

The next morning he went to the hospital and was fed a barium meal. "If you can call *that* feeding," John told Mary afterwards. On Wednesday he was x-rayed.

That afternoon the doctor came in, bringing the x-ray plate with him. "You're a very lucky man," he told John. "You have a stomach ulcer the size of a pin-head. A few more weeks and your condition would have been serious. As it is, we can clear it up, and you will be none the worse for it—*if* you are sensible."

John spent a month in hospital; the first three weeks on a diet of cream and milk and a small glass three times daily of a horrible thick white concoction that tasted like chalk and seemed to cling to the walls of his gullet without ever really being swallowed.

On the third day a huge bouquet of flowers arrived with a card from his home classroom group. The Dramatic Club sent him, much to his surprise, and more to his taste, two copies of *Esquire*. There were cards too from individual students, some of whom dropped in to see him on their way home from school. John took these attentions gratefully— he had not realized that they liked him enough to take a little trouble with a gift or a visit. When more magazines came from the staff he smiled: only two weeks ago he had paid fifty cents into the teachers' fund for such emergencies. Routine!

He slept a good deal by day, and consequently often lay awake for hours at night.

It was the first time in years he had time to think. And he had time to think about everything. His mind went back to his early school days and returned to his present school days: the change from pupil into teacher. How many years had he been going to school—thirty years? The thirty was a shock. Half his life was gone. What had he done with it, what would he do with what was left? No, he would never be another Geikie or Agassiz, that ambition was dead. He would go on teaching all his life. Well, he had a wife and two beautiful children. The old discontent with teaching was gone. Suppose he *had* become a geologist, what would he be doing now? Probably stuck in an assay office working on interminable assays at the whim of any prospector who came to record his claim. Or working for a mining syndicate trying to doctor up his reports to make attractive bait for prospective shareholders. And there wouldn't be any two-month holidays in the summer.

West Kirby was a good place to live. Eventually they would build a home on the island, facing the lake, somewhere along the new Lakeview Boulevard. When Angus retired, John Westley would be science head, and younger teachers would come along to relieve him of his dramatics. The war would end, and things would be normal again.

More often than he wished he found himself thinking about Angus. His mind would linger over their moments of companionship: the survey . . . . that first afternoon in Angus's study . . . . looking over the lake with Angus and Mary . . . . the snowshoe tramps . . . . Mary's fantastic idea that John was a sort of substitute for Angus's dead son. He could see in a way how plausible it would seem to

Mary: her mind jumped to conclusions and then picked the facts that filled her conclusions. And that silly idea of hers that he was a child and her love for him was more of a mother's love—why did she insist on Angus being his father? Did Mary really love Angus? Not consciously of course, she was too loyal for that. No, he decided. In his heart John knew that Mary would go on loving her husband even if he murdered his best friend. She could say what she liked about not being able to respect him as a father for their children, but as a lover—he smiled. Then he thought of Lillian, smiling again, but sourly. He *had* made a fool of himself. Was that the kind of thing that happened to Angus—not the unfaithfulness of course—but meeting a pretty face like that with nothing behind it? Oh nuts! Just another of Mary's fancies. After all Vera should have been the perfect wife: it was Angus who was queer, with his highbrow ideas, and his old-fashioned idealism. It came to him as a shock that Angus was more genuinely religious than anyone he know; even his cynicism and next-to-atheism were the result of his impractical ideals. The trouble with Angus was he set too high a standard; after all, people were human.

Angus came in several times, with Mary, or Vera, or both. But even when Mary came with him the old comradeship was gone. Once, Mary tried to bridge the gap: "Angus, when John is home again why not revive the Sunday evening habit? It used to be so much fun."

There was embarrassment in Angus's eyes as he looked away. "I'd like to," he said, "but somehow what little leisure I had has disappeared."

"You can't work *all* the time!" protested Mary.

Angus looked across the bed at Mary with a sudden

curiously belligerent smile. "You're wrong," was all he answered.

The one time he came by himself it had been awkward. Angus was quite unlike himself, making light nervous conversation that shifted constantly from one topic to another —in the same way that his eyes had been behaving lately. He looked harassed, the skin folds about his eyes were tight with fatigue, and the eyes were too bright: occasionally John could see the whites all the way around his pupils. John happened to mention J. C. during the conversation and after that Angus's efforts at light chatter fell flat. After the second long silence he rose to go; only staying a minute to refer again to a worn volume of Geikie's *Great Ice Age* he had left with John on a previous visit. John had mentioned dipping into it.

"Sometimes I envy you, John. My idea of happiness right now is lying in bed with nothing to do but read Geikie. He's one of the English classics—" a spark of his old enthusiasm lit up his face"—the only other book I'd put beside it is *Arabia Deserta*. I must bring that over—you'd enjoy it."

He left, John thinking as he went, poor old Angus. He's a nice guy; but just a bit of a fogey. What was the point of working himself to death the way he did? At this rate he would crack up before he was sixty. His mind jumped ahead to the day when first year students would whisper to each other, "That's Mr. Westley, head of the science department."

After twenty days John ate his first egg since the milk diet started. "I could kiss the hen that laid it!" he told the nurse who brought his tray.

Charles came along with Mary two or three times in the

afternoon and every time he seemed to have grown a couple of inches. Mary told John what a manly little fellow he had become since John had gone to the hospital—the unaccountable sulky spells were gone completely. "You'd almost think he was an adult the way he understands," said Mary, proudly. "After all, he'll be six in May," John remarked, as though it were an answer. Little Marilyn came once, staring up at the high bed with bulging eyes. She cried when John pulled her up beside him on the bed. "She's been 'making strange' with people ever since you came here," Mary told him.

The most flattering feature of John's hospital sojourn was the frequency of J. C.'s visits.

John counted them up at the end of his last week: he had come seven times. Apart from Angus, only Audubon had dropped in once for about fifteen minutes. That quarter of an hour was long enough. Audubon still had the impression, from that voting at the staff meeting about the stair business, that John was on his side. "Hurry up and get well," he said, "We need you on the home front. Now that Husson is gone there are few enough of us in the opposition." John smiled feebly. He lacked the courage to disillusion Audubon, or even to warn him.

But J. C.'s visits were really pleasant. J. C. had the bedside manner to perfection: he was such an ideal sickroom visitor that one would swear he had taken a series of lectures and practical demonstrations on the art. There was just the right amount of hearty cheer, just the right touch of unobtrusive sympathy; and always he brought some light reading along and casually dropped a compliment or two that warmed John's heart.

He dropped in once in the middle of the afternoon.

"I'm playing hookey," he confided playfully, his eyes twinkling.

"You know, John," he confided on another visit, "the secret of being a good executive is finding other people to do your work for you. Of course," he added hastily, "my weakness is that the moment I have delegated all my responsibilities, I sit down and worry over inventing new ones. A good principal is like a great artist: never satisfied —never satisfied." He sighed heavily. "Even on my way to and from the school I am thinking constantly of ways and means of increasing efficiency. You have no idea how much help my American research has been. Of course, I made extensive notes—most extensive—I carried a notebook wherever I went. You'll hardly credit this of course, but it took an entire week for Miss Jamieson to type them out after my return."

On another occasion he became even more confidential. "This is not general knowledge of course but just between you and me and this bed-post—" he chuckled heartily over the humour—"I am writing a book."

John made it clear that he was impressed, and Bilbeau went on.

"A book on education. Not a book on pedagogy—" he broke off: "Have you ever read Carlyle's *How to Win Friends and Influence People?*"

John didn't venture to correct him—after all it was only a slip of the tongue. He said he had read a review once.

"A great man, Carlyle. I want to do in the field of education what he has accomplished in philosophy. I first conceived the idea years ago and have been building up my ideas ever since. Occasionally, when Miss Jamieson has an idle minute I dictate a chapter. But it is difficult to find

424

time for all one's projects," he sighed, and touched his forehead delicately; then raised his chin and smiled—exactly like those pictures of Roosevelt, John thought again.

John learned a good deal from Bilbeau's confidential chats. It was Grossart who was really behind the new practical course at W.K.C.I. Bilbeau admired Grossart tremendously. "We have a good deal in common," he confessed. "We are both self-made men. Of course, Mr. Grossart did not have the advantages of formal education, but he's a brilliant graduate of the school of hard knocks, a brilliant graduate. And a far-seeing man." Grossart's philosophy, according to J. C., was basic. He wanted everyone to be happy. To be happy a man must be contented with his work. And to be contented with his work he must be trained in practical habits of thrift, industry, and punctuality, must learn to think for himself—"along the right lines, that goes without saying", added Bilbeau—and have the right respect for those in authority.

"If our plans work out," declared Bilbeau enthusiastically, "I envisage the day when industries by the score will be attracted to West Kirby—Mr. Grossart aims at producing a community where labour is happy and contented, taxes are low, and power is plentiful. The students of today are the workers of tomorrow. That is where your responsibilities and mine lie. That," he said impressively, "is our part in building the greater Kirby of tomorrow."

The only visit of J. C.'s which John did not enjoy was one that coincided with Mary's, late one afternoon—usually she came in the evening. J. C. went out of his way to be gracious, but Mary made polite conversation so obviously that John protested after the principal left.

"I hate his guts," was Mary's single frank comment.

33

John's homecoming three days before Christmas had been in the nature of a triumphal return. Mary had dressed up Charles in an absurd costume: Indian headdress, ribbons hanging like clerical stoles about his neck and down from each shoulder, a belt in which had been stuck—it was Charles's own idea—a pop bottle, two toy guns, and a long dirty stick to which he was particularly attached. On his feet were his dad's great galoshes. In his hand he held a long scroll of paper which he gravely handed to John as he came up on the veranda from the taxi. Marilyn was sleeping at the time.

The writing was Charles's, the words were Mary's:

To the Most High Head of the Household:
We thy most humble and dutiful servants and subjects do most heartily and joyfully welcome you back to this, thy exalted mansion

—and more nonsense to the same effect.

John felt a sudden wave of emotion as he hugged Mary, and picked up Charles, who squirmed to be let down, protesting, "I'm no baby: I go to school!"

Marilyn looked a little doubtful when she awoke, rosy from sleep, but on being reassured that it was her own daddy, held out her chubby arms and dutifully gave the stranger a kiss.

It was good to be home.

But home had its routine, John or no John. It was not long before Mary was asking him to do little jobs.

"John, my hands are covered with flour; could you get Marilyn and take off her snowsuit?"

426

Or he would hear a wail from the nursery. "Oh John, come here! Look what Marilyn has done again. I'll just have to wash everything."

At first he could come cheerfully; then he would protest, "Just a minute Mary, I'm right in the middle of marking a question."

There were discipline problems, too. Marilyn responded to Mary's directions beautifully, but John, with leisure on his hands, spoiled her till she would lie screaming and kicking on the floor when it was time for her afternoon sleep. Charles was more and more demanding, and when John dismissed him with "Can't you see I'm reading the paper?" he would go and sulk, sometimes deliberately wrecking Marilyn's toys, or pulling out the contents of all the drawers when sent to his room.

Finally it reached the point where Mary said in exasperation, "John, I wish you would go back to school. There just seems to be twice as much work with you around to help me."

Then John would sulk.

A few times following John's return Mary would lay her head on his breast and snuggle up to him saying, "Oh John, it's so good to have a man around again. I used to worry so about everything when you were in the hospital." But lately when the children were tucked in bed and they sat down to relax, they would begin to argue about the children.

"Mary, they must have more discipline," John would say. "Children are like little animals; they need a good scare once in a while."

Mary would protest vehemently. "John, you don't understand children—they want love and security—not violence."

John would illustrate his point from school experience and the argument would go on till Mary would succumb from sheer nervous exhaustion.

The Westleys celebrated Christmas with especial thankfulness, even though John was allowed only to taste the turkey. It had not been a disappointment when the doctor informed him that a little mild marking of examination papers would do him no harm. By the end of the holidays he had most of them done, with Mary's help.

Mr. Bilbeau called up the Saturday before school reopened. How was John? That was fine. He was to stay away as long as he felt like staying—have a real rest. But could he give him an approximate date? John consulted his physician. "Another week," he said, "if all goes well."

Back at school John developed new habits.

"No extra work!" the doctor had decreed, and John was delighted to pass the dictum on to Bilbeau.

"Take your time, and get well," J. C. had told him.

So he left school at four instead of five-thirty or six. There was a good deal of catching up to do in his school work, and he developed the habit of spending whole evenings at his desk. When Mary objected, he said bitterly, "We only squabble anyway when we spend the evenings together." It was so true she had nothing to say.

When the inspector came just after his return to school, John pulled his best lessons out of his sleeve. He made a point, too, of having a confidential chat—a tip that J. C. had given him in hospital. "Inspectors are human, John, they like to feel important. Ask their advice, take your problems to them, make them feel that you take your job, and theirs, seriously." So John had spent hours carefully planning what he would say to the inspector.

He had his reward. After the inspector's departure J. C. called him in. "You made an excellent impression, John, excellent. The inspector remarked on your work particularly at the Board meeting."

A person could learn a lot from J. C. In discipline, for instance. The substitute teacher who had taken John's place had been a woman who knew her work but couldn't control her students. John used his own well-tried technique to restore discipline, but a few individuals still gave him trouble.

He sat down one night and asked himself, how would J. C. deal with one of those kids? It occurred to him that if he recalled his own sessions on the carpet with J. C., they might throw some light on Bilbeau's technique. One by one he set down his own immediate problems and what he thought would be J. C.'s solution.

He had three kinds of problems: the student who did not respond to normal treatment, the student who got away with things behind his back, and the student who was developing into a menace.

John's interviews with students after four had never been very satisfactory. Now he realized what was wrong. He had made the mistake of giving the student a metaphorical kick in the pants *or* a plate of ice-cream. He had never thought of combining the two. J. C. did it every time. First, he scared the living daylights out of you by jumping on you unexpectedly; then he laid on oil until he had you sobbing on his shoulder.

John tried it. It worked.

But it worked best when he could get the goods on a student without his even knowing John suspected anything. If John kept his eyes open, he found he could catch him at something and note down on the sly exactly what he was doing. For a week or two he would add to the list. Then one day he would quietly ask the victim to drop in after four and suddenly confront him with his crimes. It was all John could do at first to keep his face straight, seeing the ludicrous effect of his bolt from the blue.

But there were some students who were just too slippery to catch with anything. John learned that vague accusations like "your unfortunate attitude", were just as effective as concrete incidents, if he made his manner grave enough: if he created an atmosphere of uncertainty. Actually, the vaguer the accusation the better. And some students were natural gossips: you could learn a lot by cultivating them, and having a friendly little chat now and then.

It was the sort of approach of course that Mary wouldn't understand; he never confided in her over these discoveries. But she hadn't the same problems to face. And after all, what decided the rightness or wrongness of anything? Wasn't it the results? The results were good. John's discipline had never been so perfect. And by now all his lessons were on paper: assignments for the whole year for every subject he taught. John would look over the neatly indexed piles in his cupboard shelves with justifiable pride. He had even begun working on a permanent system of science exams, one hundred standardized questions, a common mark for each, so that all he needed to do to set an examination was to juggle the numbers in a box, pick out ten numbers at random, and copy out the corresponding questions. At first he had worked each year at revising his courses. But gradually he came to the conclusion that the first draft was as good as any; and besides revising the course meant changing his assignment system and that was a nuisance.

The war went on. Pearl Harbour had come and gone while John was in the hospital. At last the Americans were in. So what? Conscription came and John found his fears of being drafted were groundless: they had not yet begun taking even the married men in their twenties, and it was becoming plain that teachers were most useful teaching. It took a war to bring the value of the teaching profession home to the public.

For nearly three years men had been fighting in Europe; for nearly three years, graduates and former students of W.K.C.I. had been moving out over the face of the earth ever further from the little school world that had once been all they knew. Hong Kong, India, the islands of Great Britain and Ireland, Iceland, North Africa, were no longer vague shapes on dusty school maps; now they were alive, inhabited by people, under the shadow of the grim reality of war. Students of W.K.C.I. had already died far from the island beach where they had once gone swimming on Saturdays. More would go and more would die.

Occasionally Miss Pettiker, who handled a vast correspondence with students overseas would read a letter in assembly.

DEAR MISS PETTIKER:

Received your most welcome parcel only two weeks late. It sure was good to hear from the old school and you can bet those chocolate bars didn't last very long.

431

Perc Evans is here with me. He's the only West Kirby boy in this outfit and we often get together to talk over old times.

Is Mr. Klein still holding forth with 'what's news today is history tomorrow'? (laughter) *And how about good old Mr. Macdonald, does he still get names mixed up the way he used to?* (more laughter) *We sure miss the old times out here. We never knew it then, but believe me we know now that those days were the happiest we ever had.*

Well, I guess that's all I have to say. Thanks again, and we'll be looking forward to hearing from you again.

> *Yours sincerely,*
> Roy Ritchie

Miss Pettiker paused and blushed. "I really should explain," she said in her timid voice which somehow everyone could hear, "that I changed a name in this letter. Instead of good old—Mr. Macdonald—" she glanced appealingly at Mr. Starling who sat beside her on the platform, while the school listened for what was to follow—— "I *should* have read 'Good old Mac'." The assembly laughed again. Necks craned to get a look at Mr. Macdonald.

Angus was so plainly embarrassed that the laughter broke out again.

But there was proof too that war was not simply an overseas holiday jaunt for the boys. One by one the reports came in. "Wounded . . . . Missing . . . . Killed in action." It was strange thinking of a boy whose head you had once banged with a book, bleeding to death beside his Bren gun on the other side of the ocean.

Early in March, Mary, relaxing over the paper in the interval between putting Marilyn to bed and washing the dishes, gave a quick exclamation:

432

"John! Listen to this!"

John looked up from the comic section of his newspaper. "Someone's baby fall out of a window again?" he asked callously.

"No! The death notices!" She read: "'*Young*—after a brief illness, at the Kirby General Hospital, Sophia Beatrice, widow of the late George Henley Young, in her ninety-first year. Resting at the Frank H. Bobier Funeral Home, 452 Second Street North, where a private funeral will be held on Thursday, March 19th, at 2.30 p.m. Interment in Spruceland Cemetery.'"

"So what?" John scarcely heard.

"So Dot will be coming home, that's all!"

"Uh?" John dropped his paper.

"Just her mother's death notice—if you'd only listen! John, I'm sure this was Dot's mother."

"It could be I suppose," said John indifferently. But inwardly he felt something close to panic. He didn't want Dot back.

Mary phoned the Macdonalds. Vera answered. Yes, she had read the notice, yes, it was Dot's mother, no doubt about that, no, they hadn't heard from Dot.

Twenty-four hours later Dot was sitting with them in their living room, scanning them almost as eagerly as they her.

Four years.

Dot was greyer but seemed no older.

"You've lost weight," she told John, "but you still haven't grown up." John flushed, but tried to pass it off lightly. He hadn't realized how impossible a person she was.

Mary mentioned Dot's mother.

"Oh," Dot shrugged her shoulders, "she was old and tired, and disappointed in her only daughter. I don't suppose she minded going so much." She gave them the details of her mother's death and her quick trip back from New York.

"We've missed you," said Mary. "There's so much catching up to do."

"There will be lots of time. I'm staying on after the funeral."

They gasped.

"What are you going to do?"

"I don't know—yet. But I might go back to teaching."

"Teaching!" the Westleys spoke together. "Not at W.C.K.I.!" exclaimed John.

"Well, hardly," she smiled dryly. "No, but there may be an opening in Old Kirby at the Vocational School."

"But why go back?"

Dot shrugged her shoulders. "Say it's good for my soul. Or maybe I'm just rationalizing and its because teaching's in my blood."

"But you're . . . ." John hesitated.

". . . . too old? Not with the teaching shortage—and I only plan to teach two or three years. I have enough saved to keep me going for a year or so; but I don't want to dip into that; and two years of teaching would give me a nice little nest egg for a backlog." She laughed, "There's a mixed metaphor!"

"But your painting!" protested Mary.

Dot laughed. "You make my painting sound important. I suppose it is, to me, and I'll go on painting week-ends.

Actually I should get in more painting now than I did in New York."

She explained that for the last three years she had become so involved in print-making that she had almost forgotten what an oil brush looked like. She had bought a press, and ran off etchings not only for herself but for half a dozen fellow artists. The dealers took everything she made and came back for more.

Dot had been shrewder than they had given her credit for. She had not withdrawn her pension fund, and she now planned to teach until she qualified for her pension, which would enable her to paint what she pleased, where she pleased, and when she pleased for the rest of her life. New York had been stimulating, but she hated the constant tension of city life. The quiet Kirbys were enough for her.

"Quiet!" John's irritation found vent. "How can you use that adjective to describe the most thriving and progressive community in Kirby County? Why, we're expanding in every direction. Even the island is building up!"

Dot looked at John as though she couldn't believe her ears.

"You won't like that much better than Angus does," said Mary. "The wilderness you used to paint back of Angus's place is pretty well gone. Mountain Crescent goes bang through the middle of it to join up with Lakeview Boulevard. And J. C. has built a new house just a stone's throw from the Macdonald home."

"No." Dot's disappointment was even keener than they had expected. "Angus would find that hard to take."

"Well," said John, "he can't expect to be a hermit all his life."

"No," agreed Dot, looking at John strangely. He flushed under her direct gaze. Damn it, he thought, she hasn't got any manners at all.

"How is Angus?" asked Dot. "I talked with him over the phone and he sounded ill."

"Ill?" Mary was alarmed, then smiled. "Oh, he must have had one of those headaches of his." She explained that Angus had driven her over to the hospital one Saturday to see John and seemed so depressed that she dragged the confession out of him. For the last year and a half he had been subject to sudden splitting headaches that left him feeling wretched. "He was so depressed on the way out," Mary told them, "that I was terribly worried, but coming home he was so much better I forgot about it."

"How has he been getting along with Mr. Bilbeau?" Dot asked.

"Oh fine!" John flushed again. "Well, they aren't exactly friends, but J. C. has made Angus head of extracurricular work, and he took over the *Clarionet*—of course, you were here when that happened."

"I remember the compliment," said Dot dryly. "The idea was that anyone who could write a book on geology shouldn't be wasting his time on anything so trivial—he should be editing a school magazine. I suppose Angus loves his new duties."

"Well, he's making a darn good job of them," said John, more hotly than was necessary.

"And how is our practical progressive education coming along?"

John almost lost his temper. "It's doing pretty darn well, if you ask me," said John hotly. He recovered his self-control, and smiled. "I get excited when anyone criticizes it," said John apologetically.

Dot turned to Mary who looked flushed too.

"When is the happy event?" she asked.

Mary smiled gratefully. "Sometime around the end of June," she said. "If it's another girl we're going to name it after you."

Dot laughed. "Godmother Young. That will be something new for me."

Angus arrived. It was good to see how his face lit up when he and Dot met. He was on his way to pick up Vera and could only stay a moment.

When he had gone and they were sitting again in the living room, Dot asked bluntly, "Just what has happened to Angus?"

Mary and John didn't know of anything.

"I was shocked," said Dot. "Terribly shocked. He looks twenty years older, he's almost lost his sense of humour, and he has a hurt look as if he didn't know what had happened to him, or why."

Mary said, "He *has* aged. I think he's terribly overworked at school." She looked at John for confirmation.

"It isn't just overwork," said Dot thoughtfully. "No, it's got something to do with his pride. How do you and he get along now?" she asked John abruptly.

"Oh fine!" said John. "Only we don't see as much of Angus as we used to—we've both been so busy I guess— you've no idea of how the war—"

"The war is a wonderful alibi for a lot of things," interrupted Dot. She was about to say more, then glancing at Mary, changed her mind and the subject.

Dot was on the occasional staff now, in Old Kirby. There was talk of the art teacher of Kirby Vocational leaving and Dot was toying with the idea of applying. But her immediate concern was the weather.

"Every spring in New York I would go half out of my mind," she told John and Mary, "thinking of the colour up here: the luscious yellow ochres of last year's grass and the grey-purple rocks up here, with patches of old blue snow lying in the hollows—and the cool red of young willows in the swamp. I can't wait till the snow begins to go."

As Mary's confinement approached, Dot came over more and more frequently. She saw little of John, absorbed in marking papers; but frequently took Charles out for walks. Charles took to her immediately and loved to go sketching with her.

Occasionally he would bring home something recognizable, a drawing of a flower or a figure. But more often he would arrive home tired but happy with a big sheet of paper splashed over with meaningless daubs and streaks of colour.

"What's that?" John would ask, only half amused.

"It's not anything," explained Charles. "It's a d'sign, like Dot makes," he added.

"Aunty Dot," corrected John.

Charles pouted. "She lets me call her Dot, and so does Mummy."

Dot was standing in the doorway, ironical amusement in her eyes.

Later John questioned the value of Charles's excursions into abstract painting.

"Do you think he'll ever make an artist?" John asked skeptically.

"All children are artists," declared Dot, "until it's bullied out of them by ignorant adults."

A subtle but definite antagonism had developed between John and Dot which both of them strove against, though John felt he had cause enough for complaint.

He blamed Dot for the wall that had grown up between him and Mary. The wall was there: there was no longer any room for doubt about that. Of course Mary's pregnancy didn't help matters at all; as the weather became warmer and Mary's weight increased, her irritability grew with it—although, John had to acknowledge, when Dot was around, her sense of humour seemed to be as quaint and fanciful as it had ever been. Charles and little Marilyn could hardly wait for bedtime when Dot was over for supper. She and Mary would tell what Charles called a screwball story between them.

"Once upon a time," Mary would begin, "there lived a little fountain pen—but not an ordinary little fountain pen. This little fountain pen was made of green sugar and for eyes it had two big pumpkins—"

"So they cut up the pumpkins and everyone had pumpkin pie that night for supper," Dot continued.

Mary would pretend to cry. " 'Oh my poor eyes!' cried the little fountain pen, and she cried so hard that the green sugar melted into a lovely green alley, that rolled along the sidewalk till it came to a big lake. And do you know what happened then?"

"No," the children would say breathlessly.

"That big green alley opened its big green mouth and swallowed the big green lake right down!"

"Nuts!" said Charles, "it wouldn't be that big."

John, busy in the bathroom next door would call out. "Don't say 'Nuts'." And the screwball story would go on.

There were other questionable expressions Charles was using: "Damn!" for instance.

"Dot says that when she's painting and makes a mistake," Charles pleaded.

"Just ignore him, he'll get over it," said Mary, but John insisted on a spanking.

Charles had been going to Sunday School, partly because his playmates went and he wanted to, partly because it had given the Westleys at least an hour's peace on Sundays. John had given up his class at All Saints since his hospital session but as Easter approached Charles was all keyed up to go to church.

"Why don't you take him on Easter Sunday, John?" asked Mary teasingly. "I would, only I'm not quite decent the way I am."

"Maybe I will," said John slowly.

Charles had wanted to go to St. John's, where he went to Sunday School, but John insisted on All Saints. "There's a big coloured window there," he explained to Charles, "and Mr. Bilbeau, the principal, takes up the collection."

That did the trick, Charles had been very much impressed with J. C. at the staff picnic the previous year. "He called me Mr. Westley Junor," he often recalled proudly.

So on Easter Sunday father and son took the bus and went rolling merrily to church.

John felt happier than he had been for weeks. He put his arm around little Charles and hugged him affectionately.

"Are you glad you're going to church with Daddy?" he asked.

As they walked up the sidewalk, climbed to the basement roof that would some day be the floor of the largest church in Kirby County, John scanned the crowd in an exquisite confusion of fear and hope. He knew most of the youngsters and not a few of the adults.

"There must be thousands and millions and hundreds of people that know you," said Charles proudly.

Charles was awed by the Grossart window; and Mr. Bilbeau, standing at the back to give out prayer books, patted his head, shook his hand gravely and said, "So this is Mr. Westley Junior."

They found a pew in the crowded church. John eagerly scanned the faces around them and over in the two transepts, but saw nothing he was looking for.

The service began. The choir came sweeping past in melodious procession, singing *Christ the Lord is risen today* in unison.

"Are they angels?" asked Charles anxiously, a little frightened by his nearness to heaven.

John smiled tolerantly, amused by the idea that the huge woman with the powerful alto just passing them might be an angel. Then he gripped the pew ahead of him hard, almost dropping his hymn book.

Lillian!

He caught only a glimpse of those soft lips he had crushed to his, parted for the "ah" of "Hallelujah!" and

441

the soft white throat disappearing into the virginal white-
ness of the surplice.

You damn fool, he told himself, even while he thought,
I *knew* she would be here, somewhere. He felt suddenly
weak with desire for that warm soft body pressed to his.

The feeling passed. As she stood in the front row, half
facing John, he recovered his balance. There she was. So
what! He tried to concentrate on the words of the hymn.
Would she look his way? During the prayers and responses
he tried in vain to keep his eyes away. Suddenly she smiled
under her hand, and turned back. The tenors were kneel-
ing in the row behind. One of the tenors was saying something to her with a smug grin—it was Harry! She smiled
again, turned quickly back, but her shoulders were shaking
with mirth at something he said.

That was enough. John grimly closed his eyes and concentrated.

*Almighty and most merciful Father, we have erred and
strayed from Thy ways like lost sheep . . . .*

"Like lost sheep." The words echoed through his mind
The only ballet he had ever seen suddenly flashed before
him: Paris and a chorus of sheep—shapely little sheep on
their hands and knees around the beautiful Greek, rocking
their little woolly bottoms. He pushed the scene away
fiercely, replacing it with the picture in the Sunday School
he had gone to in his childhood, a big paper picture "Jesus
the Good Shepherd", with a little lamb in His arms. Nostalgia flooded John's soul till his eyes moistened. He began
to pray:

Dear God—our Father, which art in heaven—God knows
I need a father, he thought—a real father, not like mine.

442

That day when she died he didn't even look at me or touch me—he just said, Your mother is gone.

Dear God, I'm alone.

Even Mary—Mary doesn't understand me. I'm not a child, I don't need a mother now.

The smell of her hair! Was I crazy, getting mixed up with a mere kid, a cheap little kid that wants to be kissed?

Dear God, I'm a fool. I'm a literal goddamned fool. thought John. How can I break that wall down? There is a wall, but what can I do? Who's building the wall? The word building made him think of J. C. Bilbeau, Bilbeau, Bilbeau, kept boiling through his brain. It's not Bilbeau— I can't face Bilbeau—anyway there's nothing wrong with Bilbeau. He's a success, and I'm not—that's what bothers Mary. If I'm a success she'll have to admit I'm a man. They don't make kids head of a science department. Maybe she hates him because he's a success, because he shows me up.

Oh God, help me to be a success!

He rose from his knees with the congregation. Lillian recognized him from her choir stall and smiled. John smiled back absently, absorbed in his inner struggle.

What was Success?

John was muddled, confused. Life was so terribly complicated. Suppose he did break with Bilbeau. There was Husson, and don't forget Laura Ayres, and Elsie Braund, and he would get Audubon one of these days. He was fair to Angus, though—he wasn't trying to get Angus. Whatever the others said against him, he was fair.

Mr. Springett preached a long sermon. Charles went sound asleep nestling against John's side.

Poor little kid. He needed a father too.

The recessional hymn at last. The angels floated past holding their hymn books, singing hallelujahs to the Lord. Automatically, John watched for Lillian. She came, passed, and was gone. John saw her, smiled to her smile, and all the while he was telling himself hopelessly: even if Bilbeau were my worst enemy I couldn't do anything about it.

After that, when Charles would beg to see the big window again, John would say, "Maybe some Sunday next month."

He never went to All Saints again.

Mary's confinement came three days after school officially closed—another girl with dark hair: the lightest in weight of the three. They called her Dorothy.

The Westleys had found again that their undertakings were a little beyond their monthly income that spring, and summer was coming with its absence of pay cheques in July and August.

"We're not going to borrow," said Mary firmly.

"But there's a baby coming any time now," John had protested.

"Well, you have a good strong back."

"All right," said John, "We're not going to borrow. I'll get me a job this summer. I wonder if Hicks at the lumber yard could fix me up."

Hicks had an office job for him but John turned it down.

"I want to work outside," he insisted.

A week after little Dot was born, John rose at 6:30, breakfasted, took his lunch pail and strode manfully to work—building houses at seventy-five cents an hour.

It was the most satisfying summer he had spent outside of his months on the geological survey.

"The trouble with teaching," he explained to the carpen
ter he was helping, "is that you can't see what you accom-
plish. Now on a job like this when you go home at night
you can *see* what you've done."

Dot had come to stay with them while Mary was in the
hospital. Lately she and John had got along much better
together.

"It's not only being able to see what you do," he told her
as he finished wolfing down a hot dinner, still in his overalls. "It's so damned satisfying using your hands and your
back and your legs—and you have to use your brains too.
You feel so much more like a human being, building
houses."

But Charles put the whole thing in a nutshell, boasting
to his young friends:

"My Daddy works now."

35

At school
in the fall of '42, teachers of the staff, reinvigorated by
two months' respite from their duties, were arguing ener-
getically over two quite unrelated topics. One was the
Canadian landing at Dieppe; the other was the latest Bilbeau innovation. The tragedy of Dieppe—or heroic epi-
sode, whichever way they looked at it—was part of the
past. And though Mr. Bilbeau's new gadget was in the
school for all to see, yet it was still a thing of the future.

It was completely installed except for the control switch.
Mr. Bilbeau explained it all at the first staff meeting. It

appeared that the apparatus was in full working order except for this one switch. And the switch was actually ready, except that one irritating little part was missing. That had been ordered and should have been here already but for the war. John could see that Mr. Bilbeau's patience, great as it was, was sorely tried.

The name was as complex as the gadget. It was known as the Brunwald Improved Public Address and Intercommunication System. There were other schools in the province that had telephones in every classroom, there were some that had public address systems; there were even a few that had the combination. But West Kirby was the only school in the province, perhaps the only one north of the border, that had a Brunwald Improved Public Address and Intercommunication System. That much at least was clear.

Mr. Bilbeau explained at some length how busy he was and how the intercom would make unnecessary the typing of notices and the student messenger service; and that announcements could be made at a moment's notice, to every class simultaneously. Educational phonograph records and radio programmes could be piped into any room or any group of rooms.

It sounded like a good idea. Even Audubon could find no fault, though Miss Willis feared the students might play with the phone in an empty room.

But Mr. Bilbeau had already thought of that.

"Hereafter," he announced, "every room not in use will be locked. Mr. Hubble has instructions to lock any unoccupied room on sight."

Angus asked, grinning in a way that Mr. Bilbeau must have found intensely irritating, "Did you instruct Mr. Hubble to look before he locks?" The staff laughed.

Mr. Bilbeau allowed only one side of his face to smile.

"Measures have been taken," he said, "to prevent anyone from being locked in an empty room."

John found it rather comforting to have the speaker in his room, even though it didn't work. It made the school more like a business organization; it gave him a feeling of importance. It was strange how a little gadget on the wall could do that even when one couldn't use it.

The staff met again at the end of September to discuss scholarships. Due no doubt to the disturbing influence of the war there had been a regrettable decline in the number obtained. Mr. Bilbeau pointed out that even in Mr. Macdonald's department there had been a sharp falling off. John looked up uneasily; two Upper School classes in science were his now. Angus suggested there had been a relaxation in marking standards through the influence of the promotion scheme in the practical course. J. C. smoothly suggested that Angus head a committee to go into the whole question of scholarships.

Angus looked out the window then turned back to the meeting wearily. "Mr. Bilbeau," he said, "do you not feel that in view of the fact that I am now editing the *Clarionet* and organizing the coming election campaign, to mention a few of my current duties, that the work might be done more efficiently by someone else?"

"Mr. Macdonald, we are all aware of the heavy load you are carrying. Of course if you feel that this assignment will prove to be the straw that broke the camel's back—" he paused, delicately, sympathetically.

Angus flushed. He does look tired, thought John. The whole staff watched him. There was a curious suspense in the air, as if some issue hung on Angus's reaction. "Mr Bilbeau," he said, his lips tense, his diction precise, and a quality in his voice that impressed John in spite of his prejudice against it, "the camel is a remarkable animal." A sudden flash of humour illumined his face.

The eyes turned to Bilbeau. He had turned white; his underlip protruded. "Are you suggesting that you are the camel?" he said cuttingly.

"The suggestion was yours I believe, Mr. Bilbeau," said Angus, the light gone from his eyes, his voice weary again.

Bilbeau opened his mouth to speak then changed his mind. "Very well," he said, "I take it that you will head the committee. And I believe the timetable adjustments could be made to allow time for the committee to function without impairing its efficiency."

John was depressed by the incident. Why must Angus go on bucking J. C.? The only person he hurt was himself. Angus's health was certainly suffering. Angus *was* a kind of camel, he reflected, a camel who took pride in carrying a load too great for the normal back, the pride of a man with a persecution complex or a martyr complex or something like that, that said to Bilbeau, lay on all you like, you can't break me!

Of course there wasn't any persecution—it was the war: teachers were scarce, the school was understaffed, and anyway, as J. C. had said, Macdonald had so much ability it was inevitable that he should be asked to carry a heavy load.

The intercom was still not operating but Mr. Bilbeau had something further up his sleeve.

He pulled it out one morning in assembly.

Seated beside him on the platform was a former student. John had never taught him although he remembered him having been around during his first year at West Kirby. J. C. introduced him as Douglas Sharp, one of his most brilliant English students in the days before he assumed the principalship, already today one of West Kirby's most promising young business executives, and—what was more immediately significant—president of the W.K.C.I. Alumni Association. The vice-president of the W.K.C.I.A.A., a fairly good-looking young woman, was seated on the platform beside him; so were Mr. Macdonald, as head of student activities, and the former student president of the school.

John had never been so conscious of the contrast between J. C. and Angus. J. C.'s bulk and fleshy neck, his air of supreme well-being, of belonging where he sat, made Angus's slight, spare figure look unsubstantial, and not quite convincing. As Angus turned his head sharply now and then with a quick nervous movement, his neck looked almost scrawny. And when he faced the audience his glasses reflected the light so that his face looked blank. But nothing could conceal or contradict that quick nervous intelligence. And John had to admit that there was something about J. C.'s expression and movements that gave the opposite impression. That was nonsense of course. Angus was undoubtedly intelligent; but J. C. was no fool.

Mr. Douglas Sharp rose and told a funny story which established the correct atmosphere of interest. He came representing the Alumni of his old Alma Mater, W.K.C.I. He lingered briefly but touchingly on the happy days of his own schooling, on the great debt he owed his teachers; then came to the point.

The Alumni, in collaboration with the principal and

after consulting Mr. Macdonald and the student executive, had drawn up a plan for student government.

Doug went into details. School elections were to be conducted along adult lines. There were to be two parties, Liberals and Conservatives; there would be election speeches, election campaigns and polling booths. They had even considered the possibility of a student parliament with official government and opposition—a suggestion of Mr. Macdonald's—but on considering the time it would subtract from more vital school work the idea had been abandoned as impractical. In any case a fundamental grounding in democratic government would be obtained through student participation in an election campaign. Doug became most enthusiastic over the possibilities. Student elections as he recalled them had been dull affairs. Now there would be real advertising campaigns: posters, sandwich boards, skits in auditorium—why he could think of publicity stunts that would clinch the election for the student who put them over, and have the whole school splitting their sides with laughter.

Of course students were not adults; and since the student executive would represent the school, care would need to be exercised in choosing candidates. Mr. Bilbeau had been consulted in the matter and they all felt that suitable safeguards had been developed to be announced in detail later.

Mr. Sharp sat down to appropriate applause, while Bilbeau beamed. Election day was announced for the second Monday of October and the assembly was dismissed.

The first week in October was full of excitement. Preparations for the school election were under way. Equally momentous, the missing part had arrived: The P.A. and intercom system was working!

John and his class got the shock of their lives one day. They were working at their desks in silence when a kind of low ringing hum came from the wall. They stopped working; looked at each other and the wall.

A voice came out of the wall: clear, with a metallic resonance that raised the baritone to a higher key—the voice of Bilbeau.

"YOUR ATTENTION PLEASE. This is your principal, J. C. Bilbeau speaking. The public address and intercommunication system is now in full working order. From time to time announcements will be made over this system. Teachers are asked to see that there is complete silence and attention during such announcements."

There was a pause. Suddenly the voice said: "Mr. Westley!"

John started, looked at the gadget on the wall in nervous surprise. The class began to giggle. He checked them with a stern glance, looked over at the wall as though expecting to see Bilbeau's bald head and shaggy brows protrude through the little screen. "Mr. Westley, I wish to test your speaker. Will you let me hear your voice?"

John walked hesitantly over toward the wall. The class roared with laughter. He turned savagely towards them, but the Voice anticipated him. "Will you kindly control your class, Mr. Westley?" The silence was instantaneous. There was a weird quality to this new machine. A feeling of awe filled the room; it was like being projected into the Buck Rogers world of the twenty-fifth century. "Mr. Westley, are you there?"

John gulped and answered, "Yes, Mr. Bilbeau."

"Thank you, Mr. Westley, that is all."

The speaker went dead; the hum disappeared. Everything was normal again.

Except for one thing. The Voice was there in the wall. At any time, with no warning save that electric humming sound, it might resonate metallically through the room:

"YOUR ATTENTION PLEASE."

In the men teachers' room at four Audubon was looking flushed.

"What's on your mind today?" asked John.

Audubon's eyes snapped behind the thick glasses. "It's a damned spy system!"

"What's a spy system?" John thought, I knew he'd find a flaw in it.

"This P.A. and intercom system!" flashed Audubon. "Do you know what I've just learned?"

Pikestaff and Klein came in together, and stopped to listen. "When that humming sound is on Bilbeau can talk to us. But when the thing's dead, Bilbeau can hear everything that goes on in every room of the school!"

They turned to Klein for confirmation.

Klein nodded. "He can if he wants to. There's a switch for every classroom, the assembly hall, cafeteria and gym. If Mr. Bilbeau wants to talk he turns the switch one way, if he wants to listen he turns it the other. He can leave it in neutral, too, of course."

Pikestaff said, "He was talking to me today and I answered him from right across the room."

"That whole business has got to come out," declared Audubon.

"We'll get used to it," said Klein. "There was nearly a strike over the intercom when they installed one in the war plant in Old Kirby" he told them, "till they got the foreman over and explained the time and running around it saved."

"Bilbeau had better start explaining to the kids right now," said Audubon ominously. "Just wait till they catch on. They're starting to ask questions already."

But interest in the intercom waned: elections were in the air. By dividing each class arbitrarily in halves the membership in the two political parties was decided. Klein was all for adding a third party, the C.C.F., but Bilbeau pointed out caustically that if one were to confuse the issue with all the minority parties it would disrupt school unity. Would Mr. Klein include the French classes as a political element and disturb the issues with racial and religious questions? Klein retorted that it might be a good training in Canadian citizenship. Whereupon Miss Willis reminded Mr. Klein that West Kirby was in Ontario, which had no French problem. Klein got red and bullish: but J. C. calmed the storm before it had a chance to become serious.

So the parties were organized and their candidates elected.

The only office for which there were no candidates was that of student president. Most of the staff felt that the office involved too much responsibility to be thrown open to free election. The Alumni plan provided that the student president should be chosen *in camera* by a committee presided over by Mr. Bilbeau, and composed of two Alumni representatives, two teachers, and the former student president and vice-president. A girl president was naturally out of the question. Women might wear overalls and do war work, but that was a war emergency. West Kirby had its opinions about a woman's place and duty in society.

Nomination Day came a week before the election. The school gathered tensely in assembly. Cheer after cheer went up as one by one the candidates of each party were named, stood up and announced the office they were running for.

The week went by in a furore of excitement. The art department went crazy making posters and to these were added professional showcards paid for by the wealthier candidates. One girl whose father was a printer distributed handbills on which were printed the words:

> The whole school pants
> For Mary Hantz.
> Better be chary,
> And for a good secretary
> Vote for Mary!

The Dramatic Club put on skits and stage displays at a special daily series of election assemblies that had the teachers grumbling over shortened teaching periods.

One Upper School boy went about the halls covered with a huge polar bear rug, grinning jaws and all, followed by a little first year lad bearing the sign:

> Come forth, come forth
> And vote for North—
> Conservative candidate for Upper School rep.

As a final feature of the pre-election week Mr. Parker was to introduce the new student president at a special assembly.

On the platform with him sat the principal, Angus, and such former members of the student council as were still attending school. The principal spoke, the former student president spoke. Mr. Parker rose, made his speech and reached the announcement. The school leaned forward, ready to burst with suspense.

"Cecil Grey."

There was a brief silence of shock and dismay. Someone in the hall gasped audibly. A teacher started the applause and the school automatically took it up with obvious distaste. John noticed students looking at each other, amazement, disgust, or plain bewilderment on their faces.

John thought, my God, not Cecil, anyone but Cecil! He remembered teaching the lad in first year, one of the smallest boys in the class, and such a perfect little prig that it was all John could do, and sometimes more than he could manage, to treat him normally.

The new president, with no apparent awareness of his unpopularity, ascended the platform, said the right things, smoothly. He even told the conventional funny story and got a laugh from first year students, till they suddenly realized their seniors did not approve. There was no demonstration other than one barely audible "Hear! hear!" from the back of the hall when Cecil made the usual remarks about being unworthy of the responsibility thrust upon him.

But there was tension in the air as the school dismissed that night.

Monday morning, the second Monday in October—Election Day dawned clear and bright, John went to school.

Before nine o'clock he noticed that very few students went into Miss Willis's room, the polling booth in the old school; though a fairly large number of students were moving aimlessly in the hall. Going down to the office he noticed the same thing elsewhere. Coming back, he went in to cast his own vote, and discovered only three names checked off the voting lists.

"Voting's a bit slow," he remarked to the girl in charge.

"Most of us vote at noon," she told him.

On his return at one-fifteen it was obvious something was wrong.

"Revolution!" said Audubon exultantly when they met in the hall. "Nobody's voting, and I can't say I blame them."

"What's the matter?" asked John, pretending ignorance, but smiling.

"Did you ever see such a lousy nominee for president?"

At a quarter to two John was in the midst of a fourth year physics class when the warning hum came over the intercom, as everyone now called it.

"Your attention please."

The class that had been restless, was now electrically quiet.

"All fourth and fifth year classes are asked to come to the assembly hall at once."

On the way John wondered how Bilbeau would deal with the insurgents.

In the assembly hall there was no Bilbeau to be seen. As the classes filled in the seats at the front of the auditorium Angus came forward and half ascended the platform steps.

The banging of seats and shifting of feet subsided.

Angus looked uncomfortable, his voice oddly hesitant.

"Mr. Bilbeau has asked me, as the person responsible for student activities, to discuss with you the present situation. We of the teaching staff cannot of course ignore what

456

has happened. It is bad for the school, and may achieve the opposite of what you hope for. It seems to me that what you have done is a bit childish. But the only way to solve this problem is for all of us to get our opinions off our chest in a reasonable way and then get together on a solution. Are we agreed to that?"

There was some clapping but the air was still tense.

"Well, let's hear what you have to say." He paused uncertainly as if wanting to sit down, but unwilling to take a platform chair.

As he waited chairs creaked uneasily. Here and there someone coughed discreetly. Then, slowly, "Chick" Hubbart stood up, a thin figure with straight black hair brushed straight back, but continually falling over one ear or the other. John remembered how, when he taught him in first year, he could scarcely keep himself from picking up the falling strands. He had taken an instinctive dislike to the lad then, but somehow found himself admiring him now.

Chick could hardly speak for nervousness at first, but his voice cleared. "Mr. Macdonald, we didn't vote because nobody wants—I mean, we don't think the right president was picked." He paused as if to add more, but merely said, —"And that's a fact!"

Again applause; but the tension had not broken.

"It seems to me," said Angus, "that the student body is too level-headed to take radical action over the appointment of one student to a job for one year." He looked out over the group decisively. "I have heard rumours that something else has been worrying you."

John was puzzled. What else was there? A boy whispered in the row behind him: "Why doesn't someone tell him about the intercom?"

Angus said stubbornly. "We're going to get to the bottom of this thing if we stay here all day." He hesitated. "I have heard that there are misgivings about the new intercommunication system. Am I right?"

"YES!" The school spoke with one voice. A storm of applause burst out.

Chick Hubbart rose again.

"I've stuck out my neck already" he said—cheers and laughter interrupted him—"so I guess I might as well stick it out all the way." There was a sudden hush. Chick braced himself to say it. "Nobody wants to talk because they're scared he's listening to us right now!"

Pandemonium broke loose, cheers interspersed with boos.

John thought, if he's listening now his ears will be burning.

Angus went up on the platform and pleaded for silence. Gradually the noise subsided.

"If," said Angus, his eyes flashing, "the principal had listened he would have heard a sorry exhibition of rowdyism. If you are going to behave like an irresponsible mob there's nothing anyone can do for you." He sat down, disapproval strong on his face, his chin lifted aggressively.

A murmur of conversation filled the hall, concentrating around Chick Hubbart. At last another student rose, a girl.

"What do you think we should do, Mr. Macdonald?"

"I think you will find," said Angus, "that the intercommunication system is here to stay. If you feel the system might be abused you should express your feelings in an orderly reasonable way. If you try to get tough, you will only learn that those in authority can be tougher. As far as the student officers are concerned the same thing applies.

458

The obvious thing is to nominate a committee to interview the principal."

There was more private discussion.

Finally, the group nominated five students—three boys and two girls; who, it was agreed, would go with Angus and talk the whole thing over with Mr. Bilbeau.

"If I promise to see this thing through with you, how many will vote at four?"

Every hand in the hall went up, and the crisis was past.

"Mr. Macdonald." Chick Hubbart was on his feet again. Everyone listened. "I think we all know that if you are on our side we can't lose."

The applause burst out again and lasted a full minute. Angus reddened and turned his head as if wanting to escape. When the applause died down he ended the meeting with the words: "To say that I am on your side suggests a fight. I am on the side of reason. I think the principal is a reasonable man and will listen to you. Now go back to your classes and leave the matter with your committee and me."

At four the school flocked to the polls.

Two days later the news went round: Chick Hubbart had been expelled! The school was indignant—and helpless.

The boiler room was locked now, but occasionally John would stop to talk shop in the men teachers' room. It was Audubon who told him about Chick's expulsion.

"Nobody knows exactly what happened, except Angus Macdonald and the members of that committee. All I could find out was that they had a big surprise waiting for them —Bilbeau had two members of the Board there. I can't understand Macdonald—I'd have sworn that he would stick up for the kids. Anyway the next morning Chick was expelled, and the other four kids are going around without opening their faces to anyone. And when I asked Macdonald about it directly, he just gave me a sour look and changed the subject. I can't figure Macdonald out." He put his little finger in one ear and vibrated the whole hand vigorously as he half sat half leaned on the table.

"I guess they had to be pretty drastic," said John, "or the kids would have got out of hand. Anyway Angus certainly did the right thing."

Audubon looked at him speculatively. "I can't figure you out either, sometimes." He got up and walked out.

John was fairly happy at the way things had turned out. Angus had backed down when he was up against J. C. and the Board: that was plain. So after all John Westley wasn't the only one who was afraid of Bilbeau. It was the first time he had consciously used the word "afraid". He remembered that day in church with Charles; how can I break that wall down? he had wondered then. And he knew how, but he knew it was hopeless. He was afraid! John dismissed the notion with an uneasy tension and relaxing of his fingers.

John had seen very little of Klein since the days when they drove to school together. So he was surprised when he came into his room one day at four-thirty just as he was leaving for home. It was evident that something was on his mind.

"I'll drive you home," he said. "I happen to be going out your way."

John was duly grateful, and puzzled.

They drove out Lakeshore Boulevard in silence. As they waited for a truck to pass, Klein asked, "Have you talked to your friend Mr. Macdonald lately?"

"Angus? Why no." He remembered the assembly hall meeting nearly a month ago with sudden uneasiness.

"I was talking to him at noon today," said Klein.

John waited. They turned off Central Avenue before Klein spoke again: he was a careful driver.

"Did you know he had resigned?"

The question struck John like a great jet of cold water.

"Resigned!"

"That's right." Klein's profile was grim as he watched the street.

"But why?"

"He came over for a talk last night. I asked him if you knew how things stood, and he said you had problems of your own and he preferred not to talk to you. But you're his friend—I thought the thing over, and decided you and Mary ought to know."

They turned down John's street. The snow was piled high on either side: two ruts were worn deep into the icy snow. They stopped in the middle of the road in front of John's house.

"Will you come in for a minute?" asked John hesitantly.

"No, I'm driving over to the hospital—a youngster from my Bible class just had his appendix out." He glanced back to see if any traffic was coming, and seeing none continued his story. "Macdonald told me that he and the student committee never got a chance to present their case. Parker made a little tirade against agitators, identified young Hubbart as the ringleader and expelled him permanently from the school. Then he told the other four that if they didn't keep their mouths shut they would follow."

John felt sick. "Didn't—" he swallowed hard—"didn't Angus say anything?"

"Macdonald said plenty when the youngsters were gone —everything a good many of us have been thinking for quite a while. Then he resigned."

"Did they accept?"

"They asked him to think it over, but he said he had promised to help the youngsters put their case; and he was forced to resign because he couldn't keep his promise. He's writing the letter tonight."

"What about the Teachers' Council?"

Klein was bitter. "All the teachers with any guts have left the school: Judd, Husson. Of course there's Audubon," Klein hesitated a second "—and you. But Jarratt and all the others would jump into Bilbeau's wagon as soon as the first shot was fired. Anyway Macdonald won't hear of going to the Council. He says he believes in handling his own problems."

John went into the house hoping Mary was in the kitchen. But she had seen the car.

"Wasn't that Klein?" she asked.

"Yes," said John, "we were talking about the war—the same old stuff."

"The war is like the weather now," said Mary and went back to feed the baby. As John watched little Dot sucking in greedy absorption at her mother's full, blue-veined breast he thought, wretchedly, aren't babies lucky little devils?

No, he couldn't tell Mary.

At school he avoided Angus now more than ever. Angus came in to see him once about a detail of the Christmas concert, and John had hinted timidly, "You look worried about things, Angus." But Angus, to his relief, had passed it off with an evasion. John told Klein that Angus wouldn't talk to him and asked to be kept informed. Through Klein he learned that Angus had sent in his resignation, to take place as soon as a substitute could be found for him. The Board had answered his letter agreeing to release him but setting no date for it. No advertisements had yet appeared in the papers and it was getting close to Christmas.

"Obviously they're stalling," thought Klein, "until everybody cools off. It would be embarrassing to have Macdonald leave at Christmas."

John thought, I would be science head then. But the thought was gravel in his mouth. And a great fear filled him. If Mary should ever find out there would be hell to pay. The fear was strongest every time Dot came over. Suppose she heard about it!

School routine slipped evenly along. The *Clarionet* came out—another competent job. Three hundred dollars were cleared to buy Christmas parcels for the boys overseas. Bilbeau made a special ceremony of the student editor handing over the proceeds to the student treasurer. Angus sat on the stage—his first platform appearance since the student insurrection.

Mr. Bilbeau made a few appropriate remarks, and ended by saying, "Before I ask the student editor to produce the cheque I am going to ask my friend Mr. Macdonald in his double capacity as editorial adviser to the *Clarionet*, and director of student activities, to say a few words."

Angus got up.

From somewhere back in the auditorium there were low boos. Angus paled, gripped the chair beside him agonizingly. "We're all happy," he said in a thin strained voice, "to have played our part in producing the money that will en-

463

able us to send parcels to our boys. My one hope is that every boy now on Miss Pettiker's list will live to get his parcel and to return when this long war is over." His voice as he finished was almost a whisper. The school sat still as though the smell of death were in the air.

John had been dreaming a lot of late: nightmares that brought him suddenly wide awake with a hideous fear hammering at his heart. They were all variations of the same old theme: the play that should have been ready and wasn't rehearsed, the steep road that got steeper, the enemies pursuing him, driving him into desperate straits. But a new theme was added: he would meet a stranger with peculiar eyes—sometimes it was an acquaintance, who would talk to him casually at first and then suddenly produce a gun and mercilessly empty a volley of slugs into his belly, or put a friendly hand on his shoulder, then noiselessly stab his windpipe with a hidden knife. John died three times in a week, each time waking in the cold certainty that it was all over forever. And sometimes a figure like his father's would stand watching silently in the distance.

36

Christmas came and went, but Angus stayed. Somehow the story had got around that he had sent in his resignation. But surely the Board's refusal to release him from his post was proof enough that J. C. was not following any vindictive spirit of revenge or indulging in any persecution. And that Angus should stay on when he had every legal right to leave at Christmas revealed a weakness John had always felt was there. He sometimes had the urge to talk it over with Mary, to see how she would interpret things, but in his heart he knew what she would say. Angus was staying on because he was too conscientious to leave his students with a mere occasional teacher as a substitute. And besides she would have added, what kind of a job is he going to get at his age in war time? He would have to leave West Kirby, and Vera would refuse point blank to go; there would be an impossible situation all round. And Angus had a deep pride that had been hurt again and again. Mary would talk that way about Angus. But what would she say to John when she learned the facts? A chill would grip John's bowels. He could hear her cold voice: "You call yourself a friend of Angus's!"

Angus was cracking. The boos in assembly had done what nothing else could. As long as his popularity with the students endured nothing could touch him, worn though his strength might be from overwork. But now they thought he was a stooge.

Sometimes when he passed Angus in the halls a quick stab of mingled guilt and pity would pierce him. Angus no longer looked at people. He would often pass another teacher in the hall without speaking, without even seeing him—like Smith that year when Bilbeau was away. Once John passed the physics lab during school hours and saw Angus through the glass door window, in a rage; gesticulating, banging his pointer on the desk.

There was a general feeling of discontent among the staff and students; but no one did anything. There was not only a Voice in the wall of each room: there was also an Ear.

Bilbeau clamped down even more tightly on keys and gave instructions for the teachers to keep traffic moving in the halls. Room keys were to be turned in to the office at four o'clock Friday and picked up again Monday morning. The school doors must close every night at a quarter after five. Jarratt and Margaret Brewin objected that their team practices could not end so soon, but Bilbeau was adamant. Fred Hubble was instructed to see that everyone was out at the specified hour. Fred, who formerly had left shortly after five, leaving the last teacher in the school to check the doors, now lingered overtime while the youngsters had their showers and got dressed.

"It's fine for me," said Frank. "I get home at a quarter to six instead of half-past. But Hubble has to stay on an extra half hour: we can't get the kids out before five-thirty."

Relations between Hubble and Jarratt became strained. J. C. never stayed late enough to check, and finally Jarratt's boys were staying till nearly six. Hubble was disgusted.

"I don't give a damn *who* locks the school," he said. But John discovered he was coming back after supper to check on the doors.

There was no more slipping down to the boiler room for a smoke after four or in the noon hour: the boiler room door was locked. And no more visits to the cafeteria for a bottle of pop: the cafeteria was locked. There was a requisition form to fill in for special keys for the use of special rooms, made out in duplicate, signed by the teacher, the janitor, and J. C. Bilbeau, principal.

"First thing you know," said Audubon, "we'll have to pay a deposit on our keys."

"Why shouldn't every teacher on the staff have a master

key?" said Miles. "If we're responsible enough to teach, can't we be trusted with a key?"

"Why not take it up with the Board?" John suggested.

"There's a little rule in the Board Blue Book," Audubon explained, "to the effect that teachers shall take any complaints they may have to the principal of the school."

At home, things were moving smoothly. Mary was so tired when the youngsters were finally tucked in for the night that she relaxed with a book or a magazine and left John to his own devices. They still argued about the children, but whenever the tension grew dangerous Mary would simply walk out of the room and find some work to do. And John no longer chatted about school affairs.

The wall was slowly building higher.

When they went out or friends came over they reverted to their old selves and relationships on the surface. Only Dot's visits revealed the change between them. John would take the opposite point of view from Dot whatever subject came up and Mary would side with her, till Dot would take a middle position to keep the peace. Usually, however, she came over in the afternoon when John was out.

Dot had spent Christmas with them and had given them one of her recent sketches for a present. At first John couldn't make head or tail of it. Was it upside down? Then he recognized the lake shore, painted from above at an almost vertical angle. There was the rock, in crimsons, umber and ultramarine; and the water, blue-green, deepening beneath the rocks almost to black, writhing on the surface under a kind of lashing stroke, and swirling around the edges of the rocks with vivid wet splashes of cerulean blue. Through it all was a boldness, a strength and honesty that made John's heart sink in self-condemnation.

"I like it," he said, without conviction.

Mary was thrilled. "It's so vivid—and honest! And there's so much of—of everything we love in it."

"You'll have to call it 'West Kirby Plum Pudding'," Dot commented dryly.

Later they had quarrelled about the picture. John had wanted to move it into the hall. The suggestion brought out all Mary's pent-up frustration. "What's the matter?" she asked fiercely. "Is it too honest for you?" John had closed his mouth tightly and worn the look of pained silence which he knew irritated her more than anything else he could do. She got up, took the picture off the wall, got a hammer, and hung the painting in the hall. Later John had replaced it. And Mary, watching him, had smiled and left it there.

One Friday, in March, John left school briskly at four; free for once from extracurricular duties. Spring was in the air. His spirits rose as he reached the Lakeshore Road and looked out over the long familiar vista of the bridge, the bay, the island, and the lake out to the north. The snow-blanketed island lay bathed in golden sunlight: even the bare trees took on a dusky amber against the hazy blue beyond, and patches of bare rock showing here and there on the southern slopes were edged with garnet. Sky-blue spaces of melted snow lay here and there over the old grey ice of the bay. Far out on the lake stretched the intense blue of unfrozen water. John took great lungs full of the sweet air, trying to throw off completely the depression he had been under all day.

Spring is coming, he told himself reassuringly. We'll all feel better when we can get out of doors again.

Coming into the stillness of the house he shouted exuberantly, "Oh, Mary!"

There was no answer.

She must be out at the back he thought, feeling slightly irritated. He went through the hall into the kitchen on his way out.

In the kitchen he stopped dead.

Mary was there, sitting at the table, staring stonily at the wall beside him.

"Mary!"

She looked at him listlessly.

"What's wrong? Is there bad news from home?" He thought, Mary's family—someone has died!

Mary opened her mouth as though to speak, and closed it again.

"Mary!" He went to her, awkwardly put his hand around her shoulders. "Did you—" how could he put it? "Did your mother . . . .?"

"No, it's nothing," she spoke at last, as listlessly as she looked.

"For God's sake tell me. It can't be nothing. Are you sick?" He thought wildly of all the calamities that could overtake them. The children! No, she wouldn't call that nothing.

She smiled wanly. "I suppose I'll learn to get used to it."

His heart beat wildly. "Get used to what?"

Mary looked up at him, apathy and suffering in her eyes.

"You," she said simply and without emotion.

John felt as though there were no blood left in his body.

"John, you can't hide things any longer. I know about Angus. You remember Angus Macdonald, the man who used to be our friend?"

John said "Oh," and could say nothing more as shame proclaimed itself redly on his face.

Mary said nothing either.

"Mary, what was the point of telling you? There was nothing I could do. After all Angus got himself into the mess."

"Did he?" It was not a question.

"Sure he did. I heard him myself. He promised the kids he would stick up for them which he had no right to do in the first place and then he let them down."

"And what did you do?"

"Mary I didn't know anything about it till Klein told me, and then, well, it was too late."

"I think you're right, John."

John looked at her bewildered. Her eyes expressed anything but approval.

"It was too late."

Charles burst in from school and talking was at an end. John went heavily into the living room, picked up a magazine and tried to read but could not even focus his eyes on the printing.

Mary ate no supper though she kept up a brave pretence of cheerfulness before the children. To John the macaroni and cheese tasted like stale porridge and lay like uncooked dough on his stomach.

After the children were stowed away for the night Mary said, "Let's have this thing out." They sat down at the kitchen table, on opposite sides.

"John," said Mary, "I've thought about this all afternoon, ever since Dot—"

"Dot!" said John. "I thought so," he added bitterly. "Ever since Dot came back she's been pouring poison—"

"Please!" Mary said. "Dot has never, even this afternoon, said a word about you behind your back. She isn't made that way."

"Oh no," said John sarcastically. "Dot's perfect."

"Let's not be kids. This is too serious to get emotional over."

"Oh sure! Let's control our emotions. The only people who control their emotions are people who haven't got any. What do you care how I feel? What attempt have you made to understand me and the hell I've been going through at school?"

"Hell?" The question occurred to John even as Mary voiced it. The word had risen to his lips from some unknown buried part of himself.

"Yes, hell!" he said. "Do you think I could watch Angus cracking day after day, week after week—watch him, unable to lift a finger to help—and not be going through hell?"

Mary looked at John as though her eyes would reach down through all the muddy water in his soul to see if there was anything pure and wholesome left.

"It's the truth, Mary, the truth!" he said desperately.

Mary's face was old with pain.

"Is it the truth, John? Maybe it is your kind of truth. Maybe your honesty and my kind are two different things. Sometimes I think everyone lives alone—terribly alone. But I must tell you my truth, and I have lain awake more nights than I care to think about trying to straighten things out in my mind."

John watched her as a guilty prisoner looks up at the face of his judge.

"When I married you John, perhaps I expected too much —perhaps I fooled myself. I said to myself, I'm walking into this with my eyes open. My husband is just a kid at heart but he is fine and honest and when the children come he will grow up and be a man. When I came to West Kirby and met Angus I told myself I couldn't lose: here was a man who loved you as his own son, a man who was everything you might turn out to be, and I thought of the way you had worshipped him and would inevitably follow his pattern.

"But I didn't figure on Bilbeau. Maybe that's why I instinctively hated and feared him from the first—yes, I was *afraid* of him John. I could laugh at his hollowness, but I was afraid of what he could do to us.

"Maybe it sounds as though I'm trying to justify myself —to find an excuse for my own failure as a wife. But, oh John, I have tried with all my heart and soul to beat this thing—and there was no one to help. My husband was a child who had to have a big benevolent father to hide behind, even to spank him when he was bad. And his weakness was so great that the more I tried to separate him from this creature the more desperately he clung to him. John, if only I had pretended to like him; if only I could have hidden my hate and waited till you were ready for the truth. But I *can't* pretend, John, that's my weakness!"

John said, "It's not a very flattering way for a wife to talk about her husband."

"John, there's no place for flattery between husband and

wife; there's no room for pretence or deceit. John, our souls must be as naked to each other as our bodies. It doesn't matter how pitiful the nakedness is; at least it's genuine. Cardboard rocks look nice and solid on a stage set but you can't build a house out of cardboard and expect to live in it all your life. Oh John, we were so close once!"

Mary was suddenly on the verge of tears. John half got up to go around to her. But she raised her head and stopped him with her eyes. He sat down again.

"What are we going to do?" he asked, thinking, if I could use words like Mary I could make her see my side.

"There's only one thing left for me to do," said Mary. John thought, it's coming, I can't stop it. She's going to divorce me!

"I'm going away."

"We can't get a divorce," said John, "it would—"

There was scorn in her eyes now.

"Who said anything about divorce? I'm going home with the children—you can tell everyone I've gone for a visit."

"How long?" asked John, his heart like a stone.

"I don't know," said Mary. "That depends on you."

John thought bitterly, she's throwing it all on my shoulders. Well, let her.

"John I've only one thing left to say. I love you. God only knows why I still love you, but—" there was a catch in her voice,—"I do. Even now. But I love our children too. I will not" she said with sudden swift female passion, "bring them up with a husband who is not a man. And John, I know as truly as I know my own name that until you face up to J. C. Bilbeau man to man, until you cut the strings that tie you to him and to your childhood, by your own decision, without any help from me or anyone else, until

473

then you'll be a child. John, darling, I would give one of my own babies to save you, but I can't. No one can save you but yourself."

"You want to save me, so you leave me, is that it?"

"That's it," said Mary simply. "John, I'm gambling my happiness, and yours, and our children's, on this last move. If I'm wrong, God help us."

She got up slowly and went to the bedroom, without looking at him again.

John sat where she had left him. Let her go. She would come back. She would see where she had made her mistake, and then she would be sorry. And then he would show her what terrible damage had been wrought by that imagination of hers; that created fantasies out of nothing, cancers that had eaten into the core of their happiness and destroyed it for ever. She would be sorry then, when it was too late.

He slept on the chesterfield, in his clothes, only loosening his collar and belt, and taking off his shoes.

All day Saturday Mary washed, and ironed, and packed. On Sunday morning she finished packing, dressed the children in their best clothes, opened two tins of soup for a light lunch. By common consent she and John acted as though it was going to be just a routine visit.

Mary's firm resolve almost broke on the rock of Charles's schooling. John had made the most of it.

"What are you going to do? Send him to school in Toronto? And how are you going to explain it to him, then?"

Mary faltered for a moment, then looked up. "John, if Charles asks about us he is going to learn the truth."

"You mean you are going to prejudice him against me."

"No," said Mary. "I am going to tell him that you have a big fight on your hands and that we are in the way until the fight is over. I am going to tell him that I think his dad will win."

John said nothing more.

At two Dot drove up in her car and took them to the station. John checked the bags and carried little Dot on the train. To all appearances Mary seemed unaffected. John thought sullenly, she told me she couldn't pretend.

Charles noticed the gloom on his face. "Don't worry, daddy, you can come next time."

Wife and husband kissed each other briefly in the coach, the conductor called "All aboard", and John got off.

Dot stood on the platform just under the window where the children were waving excitedly, Marilyn's nose a flat white button on the glass. John joined her, did his best to smile, as the train slowly gathered speed, and shrank away, hooting dismally down the tracks.

He told Dot he would walk home.

"That's silly," she said in a matter of fact voice. They got into the car and drove away.

"Would you like to come in?" John asked as they stopped at his door. He felt afraid of being alone.

"No, not now," she said with decision.

He went inside, closed the door, and stood irresolutely in the hall. Silence crept around from room to room. John was alone.

At school no one seemed to think it out of the way that Mary and the children had gone home for a visit.

At home John wandered disconsolately about, pitying himself as he made his own meals; turning on the radio, reading magazine articles, sleeping when there was nothing else to do.

On Tuesday noon his heart leaped to find a letter from Mary inside the door. He tore it open, his fingers trembling. Just a few words.

Darling, it's harder than I thought, but I must. I'm not telling Mother and Dad for a while.

Darling, if it should happen, just call me and I'll come. I want to, so much.

It would be so much easier, if I didn't love you.

MARY

37

A week passed. March went out with a wild storm on the lake that broke up the ice in the bay and along the shore. Spring was on its way.

School routine went on. John went on teaching school automatically, bought cans of soup and half-pounds of sausages, loaves of bread, and quarts of milk; and a pound of butter when the half-pound Mary had left was gone. His mind was without spirit and blank; if he thought at all it was to ask himself what he should get at the store on the way home, or what classes he would teach in the morning.

As a bitter gesture he sent the March pay cheque to Mary, deliberately running himself short. He put the cheque alone in the envelope, but could not resist heavily underlining the "John" of his endorsing signature. There was no reply from Mary, not even a receipt. Well, the cheque would be a receipt.

The second Sunday came. The house was like an empty shell—a roof and walls, ceilings and floors, with a furnace in the basement to keep the air warm. But there was no other warmth.

On the second Tuesday John came back from school at noon, certain there would be a letter from Mary. A white envelope lay inside the door. He snatched it up—the Hydro bill.

Back at school before one o'clock he found Audubon, Klein and Miles talking excitedly. They looked at him strangely when he came in.

"What's going on?" asked John lightly.

They showed him an advertisement in the Toronto *Globe and Mail*. The Board was advertising for a science specialist, duties to commence on the first day of the spring term.

"Looks like you'll be the new science head," commented Audubon dryly.

John stammered, his face red, "Has Angus—did the Board—"

"Why don't you go and ask him?" said Klein.

John went out abruptly. You'd think it was my fault the way they looked at me, he protested to himself bitterly.

John had a spare. He was just settling down to his register when the intercom came alive. "Mr. Westley, will you come down?" John sat there, frozen to his chair. "Mr. Westley, are you there, will you kindly answer?"

What that thing needs is eyes, thought John, as he answered, "I'll be right down, Mr. Bilbeau."

Mr. Bilbeau received John gravely, closed the outside and inside office doors; motioned him to a seat. John felt his heart hammering. What was he afraid of? His heart hammered harder.

"Mr. Westley," said Bilbeau formally, "I called you

down to inform you that you are now officially head of the Science Department."

John scarcely heard. He was waiting for something else.

"I might add," added Bilbeau, "that the Board has decided that hereafter heads of departments will receive an additional fifty dollars per annum in view of the greater responsibilities entailed in the position."

John was still waiting.

"You have been aware, no doubt, that the present department head has been found remiss in his duties. I need not mention the part he played in the student insurrection of last fall.

"I am revealing to you, in confidence, as a former friend, that there is now a much more serious charge against him."

John looked up. Bilbeau's face had never looked so heavy: heavy with flesh, and heavy with disapproval.

"You have long known of Mr. Macdonald's atheism."

"Well, yes," said John, "but what's the—"

"Of course. The fact has been common knowledge for a good many years. As a former intimate friend you have, no doubt, heard him state his beliefs."

"Well he never said that he was—"

"Mr. Westley, he has never denied the charge in your presence? Think carefully; if we can find one instance in his favour we shall be only too glad to protect Mr. Macdonald."

"Well, I had an argument with him once that I remember. I said that you needed God to explain the way the universe is planned, and he claimed there wasn't any plan: just chaos."

"Exactly."

There was such a note of triumph in Bilbeau's voice that

John looked up and said earnestly, "Mr. Bilbeau I never said he was an atheist, you won't use what I've said—" he looked at the principal anxiously.

Bilbeau rose. "Of course not John," he said benevolently, "Mr. Macdonald has already resigned. The matter is closed.

"I am extremely pleased," he added as he showed John out, "that you have had the wisdom to avoid Mr. Macdonald as I suggested. This final revelation has come to me as a great shock—a great shock. That such an outstanding man in his field, whom so many had come to respect as a teacher and scholar, should betray his responsibilities to the Board and the parents is a sad commentary on the weaknesses of humanity—a sad commentary."

John went back to his room weak with fear and self-reproach. What had he done? Why had he said that about Angus? Why was he so pitifully ineffectual in Bilbeau's hands?

As he climbed the stairs to his room he noticed that the orange strip of paint dividing right from left was wearing off. The screw holes where the wooden strips had been still showed.

The bell rang and classes started moving as he reached his room. Automatically he got out the assignment sheets for first year algebra. As he did he thought, after Easter I won't have any first year classes.

After four he sat in his empty room waiting for the dramatic club executive to assemble, his door left open for them.

He heard it shut, and looked up.

Angus!

John rose.

Angus looked haggard, ill.

"Can I see you alone, John, for a few minutes?"

"Sure," said John, "the dramatic executive is coming in for a meeting, but they won't get here for another ten minutes."

He looked at Angus anxiously. What did he want?

"Can you postpone the meeting?" Angus still stood there, holding the door as if he feared pursuit.

"Not very well—" John hesitated. "Well," he said, "I suppose I could put a notice on the door."

"Lock it, too," said Angus, and walked across the room to the window, looking out and nervously fidgeting with the window blind cord.

By the time John had put the notice on the door and locked it—a slight smile on his face as he humoured Angus's request—Angus was sitting at a desk in the corner of the room which could not be seen through the door from the corridor. John crossed the room to pull the blind halfway, even with the others, then came over and sat self-consciously at his desk.

"What's on your mind, Angus?" He was thinking, once he was head and I was junior: now, in a way, it's opposite.

Augus rubbed his forehead wearily, then pulled himself together and said, directly, with some of his old keenness:

"I think you know what's on my mind." He paused as though he found his next words difficult to say. "John, once you came to me when you were in a jam, and I failed you. I thought then that it would be better—but that's beside the present point. I knew that it might separate us permanently, and I value the few friends I have. I haven't any right to ask favours of you. But now the only thing I have left is at stake—my reputation. Bilbeau has seen to it that every-thing else has been eliminated." His mouth was twisted bitterly. "Now I'm charged with teaching atheism."

"Teaching atheism!" John repeated the words stupidly.

"Evolution and atheism are the same thing, didn't you know that? Bilbeau has been waiting a long time for his chance, and now he's got it. A parent has complained that I taught evolution—and therefore atheism—to his child. The parent came to Bilbeau, Bilbeau sent him to Parker. Yesterday when I got home from school I found this waiting for me."

He pulled out a letter. John read it.

DEAR SIR:

You have been charged, by the parents of one of the children you teach in West Kirby Collegiate Institute, with disseminating atheism in your science classes. In the Board files there is a record of a similar case, and your reputation in West Kirby as a non-religious man is well established.

Kindly report to this office at five o'clock tomorrow prepared to answer this charge.

It was signed by Parker.

John thought desperately, what could he do? Bilbeau had said the case was closed. But it wasn't. Would J. C. use John's statement? If he hesitated any longer Angus would suspect the worst.

"I can't believe it," said John. "Anyway, why are they bringing it up—haven't they accepted your resignation?"

"No," said Angus. "But I told them by letter last week that since no attempt had been made to replace me I would not feel obliged to return after Easter."

"But Angus, if J. C. wanted you out of the school your resignation would have been accepted long ago."

"You underestimate the man," said Angus. "I might have landed a better job. Mr. Bilbeau can be very thorough. He didn't want me to go till he had finished what he's been after these last five years. If this charge is not disposed of I am through as a teacher. It would follow me all over the province!"

John managed a gruesome kind of smile. He thought, Bilbeau isn't like that; after all he promised not to use what I said.

"Listen Angus, they can't touch you."

"Don't fool yourself. John, you were in the same kind of spot a few years ago, and Bilbeau protected you. Why shouldn't he deal the same way with me? You know the vicious way the student committee was dealt with after I promised them a fair hearing. And you know, better than anyone else on the staff, that my views on teaching and atheism are incompatible with this charge." He looked away for a moment, then turned his eyes, dark and intense, full on John. "I know there are enough decent members on the Board to force Bilbeau and Parker to drop the whole thing once they learn the facts. But my word is not enough." Unconsciously his eyes widened, revealing the whites, as he forced the next words out. "John, I'm swallowing my pride to ask you simply—when I go down to see Bilbeau and Parker tonight can I count on you to back me to the limit?"

He held out his hand impulsively. John took it. He'll know, if I don't take it firmly, thought John, and tightened his clasp.

Angus smiled. His haggard face lit up with courage.

"Together," he said, "We'll fight it through," and left.

John came back from the unlocked door, crumpled into a chair and cried like a baby.

At the corner grocery on the way home there was only one other customer. The delivery boy, who lived only three doors down the street from the Westley house, waited on John. He leaned forward confidentially and whispered, "We have some beans in the back room. Mr. Westley. I'm taking a can home, and I saved one for you." He dived into the storage room without waiting for John's reply and reappeared triumphantly with the beans. "It sure is hard to get them now. How soon's Mrs. Westley and the kids comin' home?"

John mumbled that he expected them in a week or so and carried his groceries home.

In the kitchen he hunted high and low for the can-opener. It was nowhere to be found. Stubbornly he made up his mind to find it. Perhaps he had carried it into the living room—sometimes when drying the dishes he would go in to change the radio programme carrying towel and dishes with him. He felt in behind the cushions of the chesterfield, got down and looked under all the furniture. No can-opener. There was a lump under the carpet. Triumphantly he lifted up the corner. It was one of Charles's alleys. He dropped the carpet as if it had burned him, leaving the alley where it was.

Back again in the kitchen the search became a mania. Finally, he spread newspapers on the floor and dumped the garbage out on them. In a pile of moulding potato peelings he found it, a little rusty but as good as ever.

Somehow he felt better for finding the can-opener, and when finally he sat down before a plate of hot beans, a big glass of milk, and plenty of bread and butter, he ate a good meal.

As he ate he read the evening paper. The war still crowded off the local news. Well things were looking better now. The German lines were crumpling back in Russia. He turned to the inside page to which most local news had been relegated. A headline caught his eye.

'W.K.C.I. Principal Named Twin City Superintendent.'

'At a recent meeting of the Board of Education . . . .' he read avidly, perspiration on his forehead, scarcely noticing the eulogies of Bilbeau the outstanding educationist, looking for one name.

When he finished he drew a deep breath. There was no mention of Angus's resignation, or the charge against him. Maybe it would blow over. What had Bilbeau said to him once? "You'll find when these little storms come up the best thing to do is lie low and say nothing till they blow over. They usually do," he had added with that supreme—and fatuous—air of confidence. An unaccountable burning hate for Bilbeau suddenly sprang up within him. It was half an hour before he had reasoned himself back to neutrality.

What had happened when Angus saw Parker and Bilbeau at five? He thrust the question away, and when it refused to stay put he turned on the radio to drown it out in music. He was grateful for the raucous jungle rhythm that blared out. Normally he pretended to despise swing music. Mary liked it sometimes and other times, illogically, turned it off. "I like jazz when it's honest," she had said once. How could you tell when music was honest?

He switched programmes. A news analysis came on. He listened for a moment.

War.

He switched the radio off.

In the sudden silence he heard feet on the veranda steps. For a moment the crazy fear came to him that he had dreamed of. THEY had come to get him.

Whoever it was knocked.

The same inexplicable fear gripped him again. He threw it off; but turned on the veranda light switch and stood back a little from the door as he opened it.

It was Angus.

John couldn't find his voice.

Angus said, "John," and swayed a little as though he were drunk.

"Come in," said John.

"No," Angus's face was distorted. The harsh light from above threw into horrible relief the intense struggle between mind and emotion visible on his face. The features came under control. "I came to ask one question," said Angus, his voice like ice. "I talked with the Board Chairman and Principal. They told me that a former intimate friend—" his voice wavered, "a former intimate friend had stated positively that he had heard me express atheistic views." Again he wavered, again controlled himself.

John waited, rigid with guilt, knowing what would come.

"Were you the friend?"

He stood there immovable, a great weight on his heart, steel locks on his tongue.

Angus looked at him for a moment, without reproach, then turned and walked swiftly to his car. John heard the engine start; saw the lights go on, the car drive down the street and turn the corner, heading south.

A little breeze blew in the door past John. He felt the cool air on his forehead as if it were the forehead of someone else. Slowly, he shut the door.

38

John went back to the living room and sat down.

He could neither think nor feel.

As time passed he became conscious of an overpowering drowsiness, as though he had taken a sleeping tablet. He moved over to the chesterfield, stretched out, and fell asleep.

One hand was his hand; but whose was the other?

It was a contest of wills: John felt the other hand tighten inexorably forcing his wrist back. Desperately he tried to overcome the other's superior strength. He knew that behind him lay an abyss—he hadn't seen it, but it was there.

The other hand was really a neck. If only he could use his full strength he could dig his thumb deep and cut off the circulation to the head. Or the other hand—if only he could use both hands he could grasp the windpipe and stop him from breathing. But the other hand was clinging to the edge of a rock—if he were to let go . . . .

He was afraid. Not just an ordinary kind of terror. It was the hideous fear of some inhuman quality that came from another existence outside his own, with different dimensions. He could see the dark nebulae swarming together behind in a thousand varying shapes, each shape powerfully significant, but he couldn't read the symbols. Each nebula reached in and pulled out a shred of his heart, but the shreds were elastic, they kept twanging back with a sharp cutting recoil. It was not ordinary torture.

His wrist was practically shattered. He could hear the little bones cracking one by one, could feel the cartilage tearing. The nerves of his arm throbbed.

"Mary!"

He woke with a start. Who had said that? It must have been himself. His wrist still hurt—his right wrist. He must have had his hand doubled up under him as he slept. The wrist throbbed.

He was wide awake—he had not needed even to rub his eyes. He stared at the wrist, compared it with the other. It was definitely swollen. He went out to the kitchen, turned on the cold water tap, put the wrist under the stream of water. Better alternate it with hot, he decided. He stood there for ten minutes, putting his wrist under either tap by turns.

That felt better. He looked at the clock. It was only ten. Tomorrow was Saturday, he could sleep in.

His wrist began to throb again—he could think of nothing but his wrist. Better try some liniment. He went to the medicine cabinet. A bottle of iodine caught his eye, with a skull and cross bones printed in red on the label. "Poison." He found the liniment and a roll of bandages; soaked the bandage with liniment, wrapped it around his wrist. He could feel the skin burning. There, that was better.

He went through the old routine—radio, magazine, book, newspaper—but could not interest himself in listening or reading. He found an old deck of cards: played solitaire. It was awkward with his wrist—it hurt to move his fingers.

Usually when it wouldn't come out he would cheat a little until he turned up an ace or king that kept things moving. But tonight something stopped him. He would painfully reshuffle the cards and patiently go through it again.

An hour passed. The cards still wouldn't come out. He was tired now. Time to go to bed.

He brushed his teeth with his left hand. It was difficult undressing. Every now and then he would turn his wrist the wrong way and stabs of pain would shoot up his arm. Finally he climbed into bed.

He was used to sleeping alone now. In a way it was nice because he could stretch his legs freely in all directions. He closed his eyes.

It was no use.

The wrist was throbbing painfully: he couldn't sleep. He should see a doctor—if it wasn't better in the morning he would.

He got up, went into the kitchen, ate some bread and jam, with a glass of milk. As he ate, he thought, I've got to keep my emotions under control. No point in having more stomach ulcers. The main thing is not to think about things; if you keep your mind a blank for the first few days it all passes over. It takes time to digest things.

He went back to his solitaire. Jack, ten—where's the red nine? Here's one. The two on the three, the two of clubs on the ace . . . .

The telephone rang.

John looked up at it, startled, then over at the clock.

It was nearly two o'clock.

Mary!

His heart bursting with relief he jumped to the phone. She couldn't take any more. She was coming back.

"Hello?"

John's heart sank.

It was Vera's voice, anxious, apologetic.

"Is Angus there?"

Angus? An unaccountable dread seized John. It doesn't happen in real life, he told himself.

"He went out in the car early in the evening. He didn't answer when I asked him where he was going. I'm worried sick. He never stays out as late as this!" Vera's voice was almost hysterical.

Maybe Angus had engine trouble.

"Why doesn't he phone?"

John couldn't imagine. He couldn't tell her Angus had been to see him.

"John, do you think I should call the police?"

The police. No!

"Why not wait till the morning and see if he turns up?" John suggested. "Angus can look after himself."

"I've been so worried about him," said Vera. "He doesn't sleep. He doesn't eat. Do you think he might have had an accident?"

Finally she hung up. John put up his receiver, drenched with sweat. He felt cold. His wrist throbbed violently. There was a tight knot in his stomach. He went to the bathroom and vomited.

He couldn't hold them back any longer. They came rushing through his mind: pictures of Angus. Angus. Angus.

Angus standing on the veranda, swaying a little . . . . Angus shaking his hand and smiling . . . . "Together" he had said . . . . Angus on the survey, sitting at the fire with the black swamp spruce standing straight and silent all around, playing on a mouth organ the same tune John's mother used to play on the piano—*Song of the Isles.* "I think you'll like it here," he had said that first day. Angus, looking over John's new course, disapproval on his face; Angus's keen critical head at staff meetings, talking back to Bilbeau.

Where was Angus now?

Driving out on the highway, miles away, thinking of the friend who had betrayed him?

Worrying, not watching the road? Crashing into a ditch?

His eyes weak from lack of sleep, blinded by the glare of a passing transport? Crashing headlong into the truck?

John leaned forward as he sat, pressing his hands against his face as if to squeeze out the thoughts that swarmed through his brain. His wrist ached. His head ached.

It wasn't his fault. He had only done what anyone else would have done. Mary, I wanted to help him; Mary, if you had only stayed!

Mary.

He would call Mary. Mary would understand. When he needed her—really needed her, she had always come through.

Mary, Mary! I'm in terrible trouble. I need you Mary. Come home Mary.

He went to the phone.

"Long distance please."

"Long distance." That lilt in the operator's voice would disappear when she heard him tell Mary.

He gave the number, listened, his heart beating wildly as the Toronto operator dialed the number. The Miller phone a hundred miles southeast of West Kirby began to ring.

It rang once.

"Darling if it should happen, just call me and I'll come."

The phone rang again in the Miller home.

"No one can save you but yourself."

He hung up.

Mary would be coming downstairs now, full of hope. She would hear no more rings. She would know he had called. Of course it might have been a wrong number. But Mary would know. And she would know he had hung up.

Mary, it hasn't happened yet.

He thought of Bilbeau the wall-builder. Surely all the people in West Kirby couldn't be wrong. Not all the people. Angus had laughed at him, at first, and Mary too. And Donald Judd. A bag of wind . . . . a front with no behind . . . . a masher . . . . He thought of the Niagara trip . . . . Geo. Bilbeau, Prop. . . . . Curly was a kind of a mean kid . . . . went to the States . . . . Personality versus pedagogy . . . . practical progress . . . . after all the build-up this guy had better be good . . . . Chick Hubbart expelled . . . . did you know that Angus had resigned? . . . .

Now Angus lay out on the highway somewhere, calling out a name—"David . . . . my son!"

Well, it wasn't John's fault.

He went over and over the events of the day—and days that were past. He thought of Mary and little Marilyn poking at her meals, taking Charles to church, the tiny red face of baby Dot.

Those had been happy days, the first two years in West Kirby—evenings and afternoons with Angus, out on the lake, in his little study, along the shore.

491

After a time John, lying on his bed, fell into a kind of torpor. His head ached, his wrist throbbed—a curious hum rang through his brain like the hum of the intercom. The Voice! "Mr. Westley, will you come down?" He had the curious sensation of being a point in the centre of expanding space, a space that throbbed as it stretched out past the borders of the brain. John was a point somewhere within a great lump of clay that was shaped into hands and feet and head, legs, arms, and body.

What had happened to Angus?

The question suddenly rose up inside of him overwhelmingly. He must *know*.

He dressed with trembling hands, put on an old windbreaker, his shapeless bush hat, heavy boots.

The lake shore.   Somewhere along the lake shore.

A little after five he stole out on the veranda, quietly closed the door, tiptoed down to the sidewalk and swung briskly down the street.

At the corner he turned south.

39

As John's feet struck the loose gravel of the south shore beach the stars were growing faint in the sky. A wind was blowing gently in from the lake. To the northwest long cirrus streamers reached into the zenith, grey-purple against the cold grey sky. Beyond, there were no stars; a great bank of solid cloud lay over the lake.

The suspense was less unbearable now.

It was not that he worried any the less about Angus. But he was doing something. The dread of what he would find still grew upon him but at least he was not sitting in the house waiting for that phone to ring. He wasn't running away. He was going towards the truth, not hiding from it. The pain was no longer the terrible fear of the coward, it was the pain of self-imposed punishment.

If he had been guilty of murder, at least he was going now to face the final scene and confirmation of his crime.

The snow was all gone. Even the ice lingered only behind bushes and boulders where the sun never shone. The air was almost like summer, warm even in the dawn.

> Red in the night, shepherd's delight;
> Red in the morning, shepherd's warning.

John recalled the old couplet as the sun rose in the east, dull red in the humid air, charging the purple cirrus wisps with warmth, casting rosy purples over the clouds to the west. The sky above was luminous and deep, as though the air were a transparent solid, like dusky glass.

Gentle waves lapped along the shore.

John walked closer to the water where the gravel was finer and he could walk faster.

Far to the south he could see a misty little headland thrusting out into the lake beyond the undulating line of the beaches. His heart beat faster and he quickened his pace. It must be another three miles yet.

The shore was low here, low enough for the rising sun to cast its warm colour over the sand and gravel, giving the earth a curiously orange hue against the cold grey of the water and the clouds beyond. The wind shifted southward, increasing to a brisk steady breeze.

Irrelevant details obtruded themselves as John strode on: a little heap of feathers and bone where a predatory hawk had made its kill, a piece of green glass protruding sharply from the smooth sand, the jagged line of flotsam and jetsam higher along the beach. A dead minnow, half in, half out of the water, moved gently in the overflow and undertow of the little breakers.

He was still half a mile from the headland when he noticed two little dots moving along its crest. John almost stopped, then went on slowly. As he approached he made out two men looking out over the lake. He stopped to watch. Finally they disappeared.

John remembered the first day Angus had shown him the little cliff. He remembered the lecture on the West Kirby escarpment. Angus's speculations on its cause and course beneath the lake.

They had stood on the cliff together looking down.

Angus had told him: "The remarkable thing is the depth here." He had tossed a stone into the water. As John watched the ripples widen over the slow swell from the lake he had said, "That stone will sink nearly two hundred feet before it hits bottom."

John had said jokingly, "Not a bad place to end it all!"

"The very best," Angus told him. "There's a curious undercurrent here that makes swimming difficult. The same current that keeps filling up the west channel."

The beach narrowed and disappeared. John climbed up the bank, then followed it as it sloped up the escarpment.

At the top he looked around. There was a path back through the trees: people often came here for a look at the lake—Lover's View they called the spot. On impulse he followed the path.

He stopped suddenly close to the highway. There were voices. Through the last trees he saw a motorcycle, and a provincial policeman talking to someone else. He moved cautiously closer, his heart pounding.

It was Angus's car, unhurt, parked just off the highway. As he looked the car began to move—a second policeman at the steering wheel. All John could make out was a word that sounded like boats. The first policeman got on his machine, kicked the starter, and thundered away towards town, Angus's car following more soberly.

John turned, followed the path back to the edge of the cliff; stood looking down into the grey water. It moved uneasily, as if knowing what it contained.

John felt nothing.

"Water, just water," Angus had said that once.

And the wild northwest wind had swept in over the gusty lake under a deep blue sky patched with white clouds, so that Mary had flung her arms out and sung, "I love you! I love you! I love you!" to the elements.

A deep pain gnawed into the core of his body, leaving as quickly as it came.

John wondered dully why no tears came. He felt no sorrow for Angus or for himself. The hard grim impact of tragedy, a tragedy outside of himself, a tragedy that somehow fitted this great theatre of air and earth and water, stunned him beyond any physical expression of pain or fear.

Alone. Mary had said he must face himself alone.

What was he?

A child she had said. A child who must run to a stronger parent whenever there were problems to be faced.

It was true.

Underneath he had known all along that Bilbeau was hollow; that Mary and Angus were right and he was wrong. But somehow he hadn't been able to face the fact.

Why?

Because he wanted to like and be liked by Bilbeau. Wanted it out of all proportion to its value. That first time he had seen Bilbeau, it had been like finding a rock to lean against—he had needed a rock; something solid, enduring, that nothing could move.

Mary had lacked it, and Angus. They had been human, weak. But Bilbeau—how he had wanted Bilbeau to be solid!

And now?

John suddenly groaned aloud.

How he had fooled himself.

Fooled himself into believing he could be a Bilbeau; that to be a Bilbeau was the way to success.

Fooled himself because he lacked the courage to face the fool he had become.

He found himself sitting on a stump. He got up and began to walk home.

Far down the shore a wisp of smoke was rising. John watched it as he walked.

In half an hour he recognized a little steam tug, like the one that had taken him out fishing with Grossart. It came to shore down by the island. A black dot moved away from it. The tug moved out again, and came on, parallel to the shore.

John wondered why it was so close to shore.

Suddenly, he knew.

The tug was getting near now. It was pulling a second boat. There were five or six men on it looking in towards the shore.

Boats. With grappling hooks.

In sudden panic he slipped behind a bush, and watched the tug go past; while the last, little, unconsciously nourished hope died.

Angus had not been found in the car.

It must have been ten o'clock as he approached the place where the first boat was slowly moving along the shore near the west channel, slowly moving, and turning again. There were a few figures on the beach watching.

Almost close enough to be recognized, John paused. Nearby, wooden steps from a summer cottage descended the bank. He climbed them, walked along till he came to some trees.

Another hour passed.

The tug came back, chugging slowly, dangerously close to shore. It was dragging, too.

They figured on the shore current. It varied in speed Angus had once told him, from half a mile an hour to a full mile. Angus had known why and where it varied.

The tug went by, turned, came back, and disappeared towards the little escarpment.

John suddenly felt an electric taste in the roof of his mouth, at the back. The boat had stopped. Two men were leaning over the stern, pulling at something. A figure down the beach suddenly came running to join the group standing tensely opposite the boat. One of the men reached down into the water. The other leaned further over the back of the boat. The first one turned, and motioned his head to the man at the oars. The boat headed in, slowly. Something dragged at the stern.

Eager hands tugged at the bow as the boat touched the beach. One of the crew jumped into the water, bent over.

lifted—straining. Another helped from the boat. The little crowd gathered around.

A deadly sickness crept through every vein in John's body. He panted like a dog.

He knew now.

Inside the door of his own house he paused, trembling with fear and fatigue.

Slowly he faced the hall mirror—and turned away from his reflection, sick with loathing.

As he moved into the kitchen and sat wretchedly at the table he thought, after all, it's really Bilbeau's fault.

John turned on himself, furiously. Was that the kind of coward he had become?

He felt suddenly exhausted, heavy with fatigue. He had been up all night. He must have walked fourteen miles that morning. He went into the bedroom, lay down on the bed with his shoes on, closed his eyes.

As he began to sink into sleep fear struck him sharply awake. I mustn't, I can't, he told himself. I've got to fight it out, here and now. If I don't see it through I'm lost.

And Mary's lost too!

He stood up and went to the window.

The memory came to him of all the patience and understanding, the sweet crazy humour of Mary in the old days. He had killed that too.

How much had she suffered?

My God, he thought—remembering his face in the mirror—she saw it happening to me every day, every week, every month, she saw it happening and tried to stop it and couldn't.

He remembered how she had looked after little Marilyn

was born: white, listless, shadows in her face. She had borne three children in pain, and all that pain must have been as nothing to this.

With slow resolution he went to the bottom drawer of the bedroom chest and opened it. One shirt left, the last of the four Mary had ironed that Saturday night. He had used the others, then sent them out to the laundry as he needed fresh ones, keeping this last: somehow he hadn't wanted to wear it. He laid it on the bed, went to the bathroom to wash and shave, came back and dressed himself carefully. His wrist was getting better now. It must be close to one o'clock he told himself, and smiled grimly. The timing would be perfect.

Groomed and dressed he went into the hall. A few drops of rain had blown on to the window panes of the front door. He put on his hat and light overcoat. He had changed his shoes. They needed shining, but not badly.

Out on the veranda he changed his mind and came in again. No, Mr. Westley, he told himself, I don't trust you. He went to the phone and called a taxi.

They drew up in front of a new house with a green roof. John went slowly up the steps and clapped the brass knocker.

The door opened.

"Is Mr. Bilbeau in?"

"Oh, Mr. Westley! Yes, he's just finishing his lunch. Come in."

John entered a spacious front hall, gave up his hat and coat, and was ushered into the living room.

Long minutes passed. Someone was moving about upstairs; downstairs all was silent.

John got up, his heart thumping, and moved to the hall door. He walked down the hall into a dining room. A door handle clicked to the left. John walked to the door and knocked boldly. Steps sounded inside. The door opened.

Bilbeau stood there, looking miserable, attempting his hearty manner.

"Why, John! Mrs. Bilbeau told me you were waiting. I was just on the point of coming to ask you in. I've had a slight digestive upset—oh, nothing serious—but I was wondering whether we couldn't postpone this—"

"No, Mr. Bilbeau!" said John, his voice thin and high. "It can't wait," and he went in.

Bilbeau sat down heavily at his nice new desk. Rows of nice new books lined the bookshelves behind him. He reached for his glasses and put them on. John had never noticed his glasses before, but these were pince-nez with a black ribbon attached to one side. Mr. Bilbeau hastily tucked the loose end of the ribbon into a vest pocket, and looked across at John, in a very distinguished sort of way.

"Sit down, Mr. Westley."

John ignored the request. He had reached the point where he wanted to break out of the room and run away; away from Bilbeau, and West Kirby, and that sodden lump of clay he had seen them drag ashore.

"You're not feeling well, John." The voice was full of gentle sympathy, but the eyes were nicely calculating.

"No, Mr. Bilbeau, I'm sick. I'm physically sick and mentally sick and—and morally sick like you."

He sat down, lacking the strength to stand any longer.

Bilbeau went white. "You must be sick to say a thing like that."

"No, Mr. Bilbeau, you're wrong. I couldn't have said

that if there hadn't been a little health in me somewhere. But that's not the point—" he paused, trying desperately to think of what he really wanted to say.

"Mr. Bilbeau, I didn't come here for a fight. And I didn't come to make accusations. I thought I did, but now I don't."

"Well," said Bilbeau with heavy irony, "what did you come for?"

"I think," John said, "that I came here to find out if you were an honest man."

Bilbeau looked at him between narrowed eyelids.

"Just what do you mean by a statement like that."

"Mr. Bilbeau, I believe you broke a promise to me. I made a promise to a man who is dead now. I broke that, and I've been through hell since. I think what I want to know now, more than anything else, is how *you* feel."

Bilbeau's eyes suddenly dropped to the desk. When he looked up there was pain in them. "John," he said, "you are naturally overwrought by the death of your friend. It's a great loss to all of us—a great loss. All the more regrettable in view of the recent misunderstanding. I may add that the whole thing was cleared up at a meeting yesterday afternoon; naturally, you had no way of knowing."

A great wave of anger swept through John. He would rise and thrust the lie in the man's teeth. But the anger cleared his brain. He stifled the impulse. "Do you mind telling me just what happened," John said, almost in a whisper.

Bilbeau hesitated for only a second. "The parent confessed that the recent head of the science department had mentioned evolution only as a theory. I fear that in her religious enthusiasm his daughter misinterpreted the whole incident. I confess," he added, "that the whole affair has given me cause for deep concern. In a way I feel partly responsible for last night's sad tragedy."

John stared at him unbelievingly.

"How?" he asked. He had forgotten that he was talking to his principal.

"Because the strain of that experience might have been still weighing on his mind as he moved among the rocks, engaged to the end in the scientific research so close to his heart."

"What in hell's name are you talking about?" asked John.

"My boy, I know you have been through a good deal, but please try to restrain yourself."

He continued, with wounded dignity: "Mr. Macdonald's body was found near the west channel where it had been washed by the lake current nearly eight miles from the point where the accident occurred. His car was found on the highway opposite the place which is known, I believe, as Lover's View. His wife last saw him at seven o'clock. Obviously he had a particular theory or investigation in mind, went out to examine the cliff, was over-tired, and— the tragic sequel."

"Do you honestly believe that, Mr. Bilbeau?"

Mr. Bilbeau looked surprised.

"Why, certainly, John."

John stood up. So did the principal.

Bilbeau began, "I'm glad, John, that you came to me and—"

John Westley cut Mr. J. C. Bilbeau in the middle of his speech.

"Mr. Bilbeau, I have something left to say."

502

The principal elevated his shaggy eyebrows, took off his spectacles, laid them on the desk, and listened politely.

"I've taught under you I don't know how many years. Some teachers I know—and one I knew—saw through you at once. I didn't. I never saw you for what you are until today."

"One minute, Mr. Westley. I take it this is a resignation. Kindly—"

"You could not accept the honest criticisms of a man more competent and intelligent than yourself, so you persecuted him till he had nothing left to live for."

Bilbeau was white and speechless.

"You could not meet him in an open fight so you used every unscrupulous trick you could think of to break him."

Bilbeau was choking with rage, or fear.

"Your resignation—"

"I came here fully prepared to give it to you. I am sick at the thought of living in the same city with you; but I am sicker of living with myself—the self my weakness and yours created. I am not resigning and you are going to keep me on. Because Mr. Bilbeau, there is one thing you did not know. I talked to Angus Macdonald last night at nine o'clock."

"Mr. Bilbeau, I am not staying on to save my own precious hide. I haven't much use for my hide right now. I am staying in West Kirby to carry on the best I can where Angus Macdonald left off. He was a man who fought falsehood and pretence without fear. He was my—" John choked with emotion and turned to go.

"Mr. Westley!"

He turned back. Bilbeau was a pitiful sight. His big cheeks were flabby with fat and fear. His little eyes were staring. He tried to smile the old Bilbeau smile and succeeded only in a leer uncannily reminiscent of Dot's memory portrait. He fumbled for his glasses.

"You did not know, John, that I have just been appointed superintendent of the twin city schools. The principalship will be vacant. Your name has come up—"

John left him there, still mumbling.

Outside it had begun to rain. The unfinished boulevards of the new street already were a sea of mud. John strode swiftly along the temporary board walk towards Mountain Crescent, walked beneath the wall of rock that had been the hog-back past the Macdonald home, fighting the urge to go up and stand once more in the study that would now always be empty.

The rain poured down. Let it come, thought John, exultantly, at least *it's* clean!

There was one thing left to do.

He reached into an inner pocket to touch gently a worn piece of folded paper. No need to take it out: every word was inked white in the darkness of his mind—he could see the pen-strokes in each letter of her name—the final despairing plunge in the tail of the Y, the hope in the hair-thin upward lift where the pen had lifted from the paper.

"Darling, if it should happen—"

"It's happened, Mary. It will tear your heart when you know how it happened. I'm even weaker than you thought I was, and you'll have to know that, and know that it cost Angus his life."

The rain came down in torrents, spattering up from the sidewalk in a fine mist, soaking into the grass, running in rivulets down the gutters, blackening the fertile earth of the little city gardens. A bus drove up and stopped just as he reached the corner. John smiled and a sharp ache filled his breast as he thought, Mary would have said that the bus knew what he was going to do and came along to help.

"You forgot to drop in a ticket, Mac," the bus driver told him. John came forward with the ticket, and returned to his seat again vaguely conscious of smiling faces.

"I'm not a child any more, Mary, and I've done what we both knew I had to do."

A sudden flood of fear came roaring down on him. *Had* he really changed, wouldn't he slip back, down again in the annihilation he thought he had escaped?

And then came the answer, from within, a solid certainty, that rose like a rock of salvation out of the flood.

There is Angus now.

Angus alive had been betrayed, abandoned: Angus dead was John's new strength and courage. John looked out into the rain with steady eyes, the future clear before him. "Together" Angus had said. A sharp pain seared his lungs and heart. No, Angus wasn't dead. He would go on fighting through John Westley—and Audubon, and Klein. No, there was no fear left: a new strength rested in him, deep and permanent.

The tires sang on the wet pavement. John was speaking to Mary. Mary? This is John, yes, it's John. Come home, Mary! He could feel his voice choking on the imaginary words. He could hear her answering at the other end: John. John, I'm so glad. I'll borrow Dad's car and drive up. I'll leave now. Just five hours, darling.

The bus somehow had reached his corner and stopped. Automatically John got out. It was still raining—a good earth-soaking downpour. There was no wind.

He could see the shabby old family car straining along the highway a hundred miles away—Mary, for God's sake drive more carefully; you have three children, and you have a husband now. He began to run as though the car had already turned the other corner and were racing to meet him. His feet were soaked, water poured in a spout from his hat-brim, and sprinkled across his flapping coat.

Mary!

He dashed up the porch steps, through the unlocked door, and into the kitchen.

Breathless he picked up the telephone receiver, heard the metallic professional voice ask him for a number.

John paused a moment to catch his breath before he said, with the crisp diction of a teacher:

"Long distance, please."

AUTHOR'S NOTE

There is no such place in Canada as West Kirby. There is no John Westley, no Angus Macdonald, no J. C. Bilbeau.

If I have been so fortunate as to make the reader believe otherwise, it is because there are hundreds of West Kirbys in Canada, thousands of John Westleys and J. C. Bilbeaus, and, I sincerely believe, many Angus Macdonalds.

The Bilbeau of this book is more than a dramatic device, because the Bilbeaus of this world are very real—and the more dangerous because they are often amusing.

THE NEW CANADIAN LIBRARY